TAKE M~~O~~

Fiona was born in a youth hostel in Yorkshire. She started working on teen magazine *Jackie* at age 17, then went on to join *Just Seventeen* and *More!* where she invented the infamous 'Position of the Fortnight'. Fiona now lives in Scotland with her husband Jimmy, their three children and a wayward rescue collie cross called Jack.

For more info, visit www.fionagibson.c~~o~~
follow Fiona on Twitter @fionagibson.

FIONA GIBSON

Take Mum Out

AVON

A division of HarperCollins*Publishers*
77–85 Fulham Palace Road,
London W6 8JB

www.harpercollins.co.uk

A Paperback Original 2014

First published in Great Britain by
HarperCollins*Publishers* 2014

Copyright © Fiona Gibson 2014

Fiona Gibson asserts the moral right to
be identified as the author of this work

A catalogue record for this book is
available from the British Library

ISBN-13: 978-1-84756-365-1

Set in Sabon LT Std by Palimpsest Book Production Limited,
Falkirk, Stirlingshire

Printed and bound in Great Britain by Clays Ltd, St Ives plc

MIX
Paper from
responsible sources
FSC™ C007454

Huge thanks as ever to Caroline Sheldon, my wonderful agent, and to Sammia Hamer at Avon for being the best editor a writer could hope for. Thanks also to my lovely, morale-boosting friends: Jen, Kath, Cathy, Liam, Wendy R, Wendy V, Michelle and Marie O'Rary, and to Chris and Sue at Atkinson Pryce. Jennifer McCarey shook off my doldrums when I was holed up in a Glasgow hotel, finishing this book. I'm also lucky to belong to a fantastic writing group: thank you Tania, Vicki, Amanda, Sam, Pauline, Hilary and Xenia. We chat, we drink wine – occasionally, we even get around to doing some writing. Finally, much love to my husband Jimmy, and to Sam, Dex and Erin who I can barely refer to as our children anymore (and who bear no resemblance to the teenagers in this book).

For Gavin, for setting me up on a very
significant blind date
('I don't think he'll fancy you though')

Chapter One

Inspection day

'So you're setting up a meringue business,' Erica says as I show her into my kitchen.

'That's right,' I reply. 'I've been testing different recipes and I'm all ready to go – as soon as I have official permission, of course.' I'm aware of this thing I do – of putting on an oddly posh, grown-up voice when I'm in the company of an Official Person. In her navy blue trouser suit, with her shiny auburn hair swinging around her pointy chin, Erica falls into this category. She is an inspector from the council's environmental health department. Her job is to ensure that I don't poison the public – i.e. that my fridge isn't seething with listeria or my cooking quarters populated by mangy cats. They aren't, of course, but still, Erica's very presence is making me nervous. It's like when you're being followed by a police car while driving. *Is something broken on my car?* you start wondering. *Could the wine I guzzled two nights ago still be swilling around in my bloodstream?*

'I love meringues,' Erica enthuses, peering into my fridge which I've scrubbed so thoroughly even its light

1

seems to shine more brightly. 'It's the texture, isn't it? The crunchiness on the outside, the gooey bit in the middle . . .'

'That's right,' I agree. 'I imagine it's impossible to feel depressed when you're biting into a meringue.'

She laughs politely and marks a few boxes on the form attached to her clipboard. I try to sneak a look, but can't read it. Anyway, I must stop feeling so paranoid. I spent the whole of yesterday preparing for her visit, and so far it seems to be going well. Erica caresses my cooker hob and ticks another box on her form. 'D'you have a name for your business?' she asks.

'Yes, I'm calling it Sugar Mummy.'

'Oh, that's cute. That definitely has a ring to it. I assume you have children then?'

'Yes, two sons.'

'*Sons*,' Erica repeats with a slight shudder. 'Oh, I take my hat off to you. I don't know how people cope with boys.'

'Really?' I say, acting surprised. In fact, I have encountered this anti-boy attitude on numerous occasions since Logan and Fergus were tiny; a fierce aversion to young males, as if they are not miniature humans but incontinent pitbulls, prone to violence and likely to pee wherever the mood takes them (as opposed to little girls who'll quietly colour in and groom their teddies for weeks on end).

'Well, *I* couldn't,' Erica asserts. 'My sister has three and her place is a wreck. She used to collect Danish glassware and of course that's all been trashed.'

'Oh dear,' I say, wanting to add, *Why didn't she put it away in a cupboard?* However, it's crucial to keep Erica on my side. I'm itching to get my business started, and need to convince her that Logan and Fergus won't be constantly charging into my 'professional' kitchen, bringing in live bugs to show me or using my mixer to blend potions of rotting leaves and soil.

'Well, they're thirteen and sixteen,' I tell her, 'so we're past that crazy stage now.'

'Oh, *teenage* boys,' she goes on with a dry laugh, 'and their terrible bedrooms. *Eugh*. That horrible dank duvet smell . . .'

'They're actually incredibly helpful around the flat,' I fib, trying to quash the defensive edge to my voice.

'Really?' Erica widens her eyes. 'Handy with the Mr Sheen, then?'

'Yes, very.' Actually, they back away from it as if it's pepper spray, and neither seem capable of operating the Hoover without choking it. Plus there *is* an underlying smell around here, which I've tried to obliterate by burning the sandalwood and ginger oil my friend Ingrid gave me, with the promise that it would 'uplift the senses'. On this rain-lashed November afternoon, both boys are off school with streaming colds, and the flat is tainted with the whiff of the unwell.

'D'you have any children yourself?' I ask pleasantly as she peers into the oven.

'Just the one, a little girl.'

Ah, that figures.

'I was terrified she was going to be a boy,' Erica adds, straightening up. 'In fact, I paid to have an extra scan to determine the sex as early as possible.'

'Really?' I have no idea how to respond to this.

'If it was a boy,' she goes on, 'I wanted to be prepared.' What could she possibly mean? Line up an adoptive mother for him? Just as I'm about to say they're not that bad really – I mean, look at me, I'm healthy and happy and alive (well, *alive*) – Fergus, my youngest, yells, 'Mum!' and stomps along the hallway towards us.

'I'm still with the lady,' I call back. 'Won't be long now.'

'*Mum.* Can't get this stupid thing to work at all.' He marches into the kitchen, wavy caramel hair askew, clad in just a pair of baggy grey boxers. He is clutching a small silver gadget which he thrusts into my face.

'Fergus,' I say, 'you might want to go and put your dressing gown on, love.'

'Nah, I was really boiling up, like my whole body was soaking. And the tubes at the back of my nose are totally bunged up with phlegm . . .'

Erica pretends to study our spice rack. 'I'm a bit busy right now,' I say briskly, trying to transmit the message: *Please leave this kitchen immediately.* Curiously, Ingrid's sandalwood oil appears to be failing on the mood-lifting front. Fergus sneezes without covering his mouth, and something actually shoots out, causing Erica to shrink back in alarm. Christ, he's probably infected her now. 'It's stopped working,' he says, stabbing at the gadget's buttons. 'It's gone weird.'

'What did you expect for two pound fifty?' Logan asks, wandering into the kitchen bare-chested in a pair of particularly unfetching tracksuit bottoms, bringing with him the powerful meaty pong of unwashed underarms. Neither of my boys have acknowledged our visitor.

'Er . . . what's gone weird?' Erica asks Fergus politely.

'My translator,' he mutters, scowling at the gadget's tiny screen.

'Oh, what's that for?'

'For *translating*,' he replies, rolling his coffee-brown eyes as if to say, *Who is this bloody fool?*

4

'He likes buying old gadgets from charity shops and trying to get them to work,' I explain.

'That's, um, resourceful,' Erica says unconvincingly as Logan blows his nose on a square of kitchen roll.

'Anyway, boys,' I say firmly, 'could you leave us for a minute please? This is important. Remember I told you—'

'It has translations for thirty six thousand words,' Fergus cuts in, 'in seven languages.'

'Wow, that's impressive,' Erica says, checking her watch.

'Tell it to say something,' he demands.

Our visitor's jaw tightens. 'Er – hello, how are you?'

Fergus prods a few buttons. *Ich bin diabetika*, it chirps robotically. *He touched my breast—*

'It said it's diabetic,' Fergus starts.

'And someone touched its breast,' Logan chuckles, twanging the elasticated waistband of his trackies.

'Yes, we heard that.' My posh voice has disappeared and now I, too, am sweating as I try to figure out how I might remove my sons from the kitchen without shouting or manhandling them in front of Erica.

'It doesn't have any,' Fergus sniggers.

'Have you been groping it?' Logan ribs him. ''Cause it wouldn't say that unless there was a reason—'

'What are you on about?' Fergus retorts.

'You must've assaulted it,' his brother exclaims as the darn thing starts up again: *Ich bin diabetika. He touched my breast. Ich bin—*

'Fergus,' I bark, '*please* put that thing away. We don't need it right now . . .'

Logan rubs his upper lip where the faintest moustache is beginning to sprout. 'We'll never need it. It's obsolete. What's the point of a piece of crap like that when there's Google Translate?'

'Logan!' I try to shoo him away with a fierce glare.

'Well,' Erica says dryly, 'I suppose it has a certain retro appeal.'

'What does *non posso mangiare che* mean?' Fergus asks, mouth-breathing over the screen.

'I've no idea,' I mutter. 'I don't speak Italian.'

Erica clears her throat. 'It means "I can't eat that."'

'Great line for a meringue company,' Logan snorts. 'Maybe that should be your slogan, Mum.'

'You can't speak German either,' Fergus reminds me, 'or Polish or Dutch . . .' No, because, clearly, I am an imbecile. *There are many cockroaches in my hotel room*, the translator bleats. *I require police assistance immediately. Help! Help! Where is the nearest unisex hair salon? Ich bin diabetika—*

'Type in "goodbye",' I snap. 'Type in, "It's been very nice to meet you, Erica, but now I am going to leave you both to get on with important things."'

I have been raped! the machine squawks, at which Logan honks with laughter.

'Excuse me a second.' Grabbing Fergus by his clammy hand, I march him out of the kitchen and into the living room where I hiss, 'Stay here until she's gone, okay? I'm trying to create a good impression and you're *really* not helping.'

He fixes me with a challenging stare. 'It'll be useful on holiday if I can fix it.'

'You're going to the Highlands with Dad, remember? As far as I'm aware, they speak the same language as us.'

'I don't mean for Easter,' he calls after me as I leave the room. 'I mean our *summer* holiday. Are we going anywhere this year?'

'Haven't decided yet.'

'We never go abroad,' he bleats. He's right – but how far does he think we'll get on the bit of fluff I have left in my purse at the end of each month?

By the time I'm back in the kitchen, Logan has returned to his bedroom and Erica is clutching her brown leather briefcase in readiness for leaving. Meanwhile, I'm wondering if it would really be so terrible if the translator suffered an unfortunate accident, such as tumbling from our second-floor window and being run over by a car.

'Well, Alice,' Erica says coolly, 'I'm pleased to tell you that your premises have passed.'

It takes me a moment to process this. 'You mean everything's okay?'

She nods. 'Yes, you're ready to go.'

'Oh, that's great! Thank you.'

Her clear blue eyes skim the room, settling momentarily on the scrunched-up piece of kitchen roll which Logan deposited on the table. Then, just as she makes for the door, another small object catches her eye. She frowns, and I follow her gaze towards the cooker – or, more precisely, to the small, turd-like object that's poking out from under it.

It's a bit of old sausage. Time seems to freeze as we stare at it. *It hasn't been there long*, I want to explain. Or I could joke about cutting it open to date it, the way you can count the rings in a tree. But instinct tells me that Erica wouldn't find that amusing so, mustering a brazen smile, I saunter towards it and send it scooting under the cooker with a sharp kick. Our eyes meet and she smirks. 'Well, good luck with your meringues,' she says. 'I think it's a great idea for a business. And I do hope your son manages to get his translator fixed.'

Chapter Two

Four months later

It's a cool, breezy afternoon as I leave Middlebank Primary where I work as the school secretary. Having texted the boys, who'll head straight home from their nearby secondary school, I take a short detour via Betsy's, a smart, airy cafe housed on the ground floor of a converted chapel. In recent years, there's been an explosion of quaint tea shops here in Edinburgh. While there is no shortage of cupcake suppliers, meringues appear to have novelty appeal, which has proved good for business. Betsy's is owned by an eager young couple who look like they're barely out of college.

'Just wondered how it's been going this week,' I tell Jenny, who offers me tea in a gilt-edged china cup.

'Really well,' she says, 'especially the tiny ones – the meringue kisses.'

'People seem to prefer them with coffee,' I tell her.

'We'll take more next week,' she adds. 'What d'you think, Max?'

Her boyfriend turns from the coffee machine and grins. 'Oh, sure. If Alice can handle it.'

Jenny laughs. 'We were just saying we don't know how you manage to fit it all in. With your job and family, I mean . . .'

'Oh, it keeps me sane, actually,' I reply truthfully.

'Well, you're obviously doing something right,' Jenny says with a broad smile. 'They're the new cupcakes, right?'

Max nods. 'Far superior in my opinion. All that thick, cloying icing . . .' I leave the cafe filled with optimism and pride. While meringues have always been a personal favourite of mine, maybe I've hit on a gap in the market here.

My mobile rings; it's Ingrid. 'So what happened?' she asks eagerly, referring to her party on Saturday night.

'We're meant to be going for dinner next Friday,' I tell her.

'I knew it! I saw you two, huddled together in the kitchen . . .'

I laugh. 'We weren't huddled, we were *talking*.'

'Talking intently,' she remarks.

'Well . . . it was just chit-chat really, but he seemed interesting . . .' It's true: while I don't think either of us was bowled over, I could see no reason not to see him again. After all, my dating activity is roughly on a par with a solar eclipse these days.

'Well, he seemed hugely keen,' Ingrid goes on as I march up the hill at a brisk pace. 'Every time you wandered off to talk to someone else, he was prowling about looking for you. I hope you're going to give him a chance.'

I inhale deeply. 'I don't know, Ing. It's just been a hell of a long time, you know?'

'All the more reason then.'

9

'And there's the boys,' I add. 'You know what it's like.' She doesn't really; happily married to Sean for a decade now, and with a charming daughter who plays no less than *three* musical instruments, Ingrid is more sorted than anyone else I know. There's the matter of being unable, inexplicably, to conceive another baby after Saskia, but following a failed IVF cycle they are trying again, and Ingrid is always keen to stress that another child would merely be the icing on the cake.

'That doesn't mean you can't date,' she says firmly. 'It's not as if they have to meet every person you have a drink with. You're hardly going to haul him home after dinner, going, "Hey boys, meet your new Uncle Anthony . . ."'

'Christ, no,' I exclaim.

'And it's been, what – over a year since that finance guy? The one who wanted to inspect your bank statements?'

'And told me off for not having an ISA,' I add with a grin. 'Yeah, more like eighteen months actually.'

'Well, they're not all like that. I've only met Anthony a couple of times but he seems lovely. Handsome, didn't you think? In that groomed, takes-care-of-himself sort of way. Not gone to seed. Has a personal trainer, Sean reckons, and he's brilliant at golf . . .'

Golf! Checked trousers, diamond-patterned sweaters . . . no, no, I mustn't think that way. I replay last Saturday night, when I was leaving Ingrid's party: *It's been lovely talking to you,* Anthony had said, fixing me with intense grey eyes, like wet slate. *I don't suppose you'd like to come to dinner sometime? There's a friendly little local place I know . . . how are you fixed on Friday night?* A proper date-night, then. All we'd talked about was who we knew at the party, how long we'd been living in Edinburgh and a few sketchy background details about our lives. I hadn't exactly experienced an urge to kiss him, or to glimpse that nicely honed body naked – but maybe ISA-man killed my ability to fancy anyone at all. And surely, any normally functioning woman would find a tall, smiley, smartly dressed man like Anthony attractive? Which is why I agreed to meet him for dinner – because I was bloody flattered to be asked.

'I have a good feeling about this,' Ingrid adds, 'and I know you're excited really.'

'Am I?' I say, laughing.

'Yes, you're *panting*.'

'Ingrid, I'm marching up a hill . . .'

'Well,' she sniggers, 'I can't wait to hear about it. I mean, eighteen months. Christ. It's time you were back out there.'

'Back out there? Sounds like a sign in an NCP car park . . .'

'Oh, stop it,' she says, mock-scolding. 'Promise you'll go and not make up some crappy excuse about the boys being ill or whatever. I know what you're like, Alice Sweet.'

She does, too, in the way that a friend of twenty years – since our second year at college – is aware of the difference between a mere reluctance to date, and full-blown terror at the very prospect. Which is, admittedly, the situation right now. Plus, with a track record like mine, I have to ask myself, is it worth it, really? Getting 'out there', I mean? It's not just ISA-Man, and his perpetual nagging about share acquisition. It's the whole, sorry dating debacle since I split with Tom, the boys' father. A handful of encounters scattered over six years

11

of single parenthood – each one making me question why I was in some gloomy, sticky tabled bar, or having sex with someone who might well have been simultaneously calculating the net profit on his investments. Frankly, I'd rather have been cosied up on the sofa with Logan and Fergus, munching crisps and sniggering over something daft on TV.

'So you *promise* not to back out,' Ingrid says firmly.

'Promise,' I say.

A small pause. 'It'll be great. I'm not sure what he does exactly but he seems like a really driven, thrusting guy.' We both bark with laughter as I finish the call, trying to convince myself that Ingrid is absolutely right.

*

On Friday, as I pull on my new dress – sapphire-blue linen, grabbed from some sale rail one lunchtime – my thoughts fast-forward to tomorrow when the date will be over and I'll be happily regaling Ingrid, plus our other college friends Kirsty and Viv, with the details. It's a pleasant spring evening, the kind that coaxes dog-walkers and couples out to our gently sloping park, with its wide open sky and a glimmer of the Firth of Forth beyond. Hell, is it really eighteen months since I last slept with someone, let alone had a date? In contrast, Tom had found himself a wife less than a year after we split (he and I had never got around to tying the knot). He is married to the fragrant Patsy, founder of a children's sleepwear company called Dandelion. They live in a vicarage in Cumbria surrounded by rolling fields and cattle, and have an adorable golden-haired daughter, Jessica, who regularly models for the Dandelion catalogue. We're not talking Hello Kitty nighties or

SpongeBob pyjamas; the only embellishment allowed on Patsy's top-quality garments is a tiny embroidered dandelion clock.

Tom's contact with our sons is sporadic and largely dependent on his 'work commitments'. We're talking a weekend down at the vicarage now and again, although he is whisking the boys away to the Highlands during the Easter holidays, which they seem to be regarding as a rare treat (no complaints about it 'not being abroad' where their dad's concerned). 'Patsy said I can model the teen boys' range,' Fergus told me recently, startling me with his enthusiasm. So, while he's reluctant to be seen walking down the street with me these days, he'd be perfectly happy to risk being spotted by his friends in a checked seersucker ensemble in a bloody catalogue. Of course, Logan and Fergus have no idea that, for much of our relationship, Daddy modelled the same three pairs of limp, not exactly box-fresh underpants in rotation, until they literally shredded in the washing machine. Nor are they aware that he spent virtually all of our thirteen-year relationship in a fug of Southern Comfort and beer. (Granted, Tom was never a horrible or, God forbid, violent drunk. He'd just go all floppy and canine, pawing at me and trying to lick my face.)

All that limpid puppy stuff had been okay-ish pre-kids, when we'd been students in a house share together. It was still bearable – just – when I gave birth to Logan, perhaps because, as a twenty-three-year-old new mum, I was so freaked out that I couldn't fully register anything else that was going on around me. We muddled on for years because I still loved Tom, despite his unsavoury pants and habit of penning poems along the lines of: *Lovely Alice/I don't need a palace/with you at my side* . . . Until the day arrived when the boys were seven and ten and I realised that, unless we split, I'd spend the rest of my life coming home from work to have Tom glance up from the sofa and ask, 'Do we have any milk?'

You see, back then, Tom didn't go out to work. He wasn't a partner in Dandelion, giving talks on the virtues of organic brushed cotton and formaldehyde-free dyes. In his early thirties, and with both Fergus and Logan at school full-time, he was still trying to figure out 'what it is I really want to do'.

As I am, an hour later, as I pause outside the restaurant which Anthony has booked for our date tonight. It is housed in a creamy sandstone crescent, sandwiched between solicitors' offices, a small, white sign the size of a postcard offering the only hint of its existence. It is called, simply, 'chard' (lower case 'c'), which I know vaguely to be some kind of leafy vegetable, although I can't say I've eaten it. However, it's clear that Anthony wasn't being completely honest when he described the restaurant as a 'friendly little local place'. Unless this is the kind of establishment he frequents all the time; a possibility which causes my hands to become instantly tacky with sweat.

I inhale deeply, wondering if the boys are okay at home, and reminding myself that of course they are – Logan is old enough to leave school, have-sex-God-forbid, get married and even buy a scratch card without parental consent. And I've left them with a stack of cash, takeaway pizza menus and permission to order whatever they like.

Christ, I could murder a Four Seasons right now . . .

I push open the heavy glass door and step in. There he is, smiling broadly at a table in the centre of the

14

sparsely populated room. I fix on a smile and am greeted with a kiss on the cheek.

'Hope you like this place,' Anthony says, sweeping out an arm in appreciation of the grandeur of the building. 'It's a favourite of mine.'

Or maybe the thin crust with pine nuts and spinach, which never fails to disgust Logan: 'Like, why would anyone want a pizza with salad all over it?'

'It's lovely,' I say, taking a seat.

'I thought we'd have the tasting menu,' he announces. 'It's the only way to fully appreciate what they do here.'

Those slate eyes sparkle. I swallow hard and glance down at my menu.

'That sounds great.' *Be positive*, I remind myself as the waiter appears and Anthony orders. Ingrid was right, I absolutely should be here, because this is what grown-up single women do. And it's time to move on, to be proactive and seize the moment, after six years of crap dates and sex which has been at best, a mild diversion and, at worst, made me seriously consider celibacy as a more satisfying option.

'So you mentioned you're a teacher,' Anthony says, his confident tone snapping me back to the present.

'I'm actually a school secretary,' I remind him, having imparted this fascinating information at the party.

'Oh, I see.' His eyes fix on mine.

'It fits in with the boys' school hours,' I continue, tugging down the hem of my shift dress, 'which I really needed when they were younger and their dad and I had broken up.'

He nods, and I notice that his teeth aren't just white – they are verging on *blue*-white, and quite disconcerting.

15

The lighting in Ingrid's kitchen clearly hadn't illuminated them to full effect.

'And I've set up a business from home,' I go on, sensing his gaze flickering across the restaurant, 'making meringues for local cafes, delis and special events . . .'

Anthony tastes the wine that's being offered and nods approvingly. 'That sounds like a fun little sideline.' Why this riles me, I'm not sure. He's right, it *is* a little sideline. While I love it, and it's boosted our finances, I am hardly heading for global domination of the meringue market.

'You mentioned at the party that you have your own business,' I remark, 'but I'm not quite sure what it is.'

'Ah, well,' he says grandly, 'we're all about offering a complete bespoke service and taking care of the whole client. It's about complete personal attention every step of the way.'

I study him, assessing the angular jaw, the intense little eyes and neatly cropped dark hair. While he is certainly handsome, and more than likely employs a personal trainer, there's something disconcertingly plasticky about him. He looks sort of *moulded*, as if there could be a secret join up the back of his head, like Barbie's boyfriend Ken.

'Erm, okay,' I say, 'but I still don't know what you do.'

'Oh,' he wrinkles his pore-free nose, 'we're a clinic.'

'Are you a doctor?' I ask, taking a big swig of wine.

'No, we deal in aesthetic procedures.'

Ah – that explains the glowing teeth. 'You mean Botox and all that?'

He emits a patronising laugh. 'Yes, but there's a *bit* more to it than that. Our ethos is to assess every client individually so, with the very latest techniques, we can

16

work in synergy with her own, unique beauty and the natural contours of her face . . .'

To stop myself from choking, I take another gulp from my glass. Hell, I'll be smashed at this rate. Better slow down and have some water, the way the magazines always tell you to. At long last our first course arrives; at least I think it counts as a course. It's an 'amuse-bouche', consisting of a sticky beige blob served on a ceramic spoon with a dribble of green liquid around it, like bile.

'This looks delicious,' I fib, wondering what possessed Anthony to ask me out in the first place when he is clearly not remotely interested in anything about my life – and also why he played down the restaurant's poshness when it's turned out to have a bloody Michelin star. Is he showing off, trying to impress me by dropping in words like 'bespoke'? And what's with the six courses? I told the boys I wouldn't be too long, but troughing our way through this lot will take *weeks*. I'm more annoyed with myself, really, for allowing Anthony to decide what I must eat. Tonight may call for an emergency measure, like feigning illness or a faint . . .

'. . . These days,' he says, a little fleck of spit flying out of his mouth, 'it's about women making the most of what they have. For instance, you wouldn't think twice about buying a new dress on a whim, would you?'

'Er, I'm not a huge shopper actually . . .'

'Yet, for a similar level of investment,' he goes on, 'instead of buying a cheap piece of cloth' – his gaze drops briefly to my blue shift – 'a woman can regain her youthful bloom, which has a *far* greater impact on her confidence.'

I swallow down the bile sauce from my spoon. *I* know. I could go to the loo, climb out of the window and run

17

all the way home. Rude, yes, but then so is mocking my fashion choice . . . although, I have to admit, I wish I was wearing something else. The dress is a little tight around the hips when I'm sitting down, and keeps riding up, *and* my shoes are pinching like hell. I overdid it, I realise now. I'd forgotten that, rather than lending me an elegant air, teetering heels have the effect of making me feel like a big, hairy trucker with a secret penchant for cramming his vast size tens into his girlfriend's stilettos. It's all wrong – my outfit, the restaurant, the man (who has started on about 'boosting a woman's confidence' again as if, without his poky needles, any female should be terrified of leaving the house).

'The thing is,' I cut in, 'you said it's all about working with natural contours . . .'

'Mmm-hmm.' More food has arrived. As Anthony nibbles the end of an asparagus stalk, I picture Logan and Fergus chomping happily on a side order of garlic bread.

'I mean,' I continue, 'I don't have a problem with that, if that's how people want to spend their money. But it's not *completely* natural, is it? Natural is leaving everything as it is. Natural is bunging on a bit of mascara and lip gloss and hoping for the best.'

'Yes, well . . . that's an option I suppose,' he says scathingly, as if I'd confided that I'm partial to smearing my face with lard.

'So,' I continue, 'what would you recommend I should have done to *my* face?'

'Oh, I don't want to get into that, Alice . . .'

I force a smile as plates are whisked away and replaced with others. Every course is tiny; I feel as if I have stumbled into the dining room of a doll's house.

18

'Go on,' I say. 'I'm just interested to know what could be done. I'd like your . . . *expert appraisal*.' This might be entertaining, I decide, curiosity having superseded my initial nervousness. Actually, there is no reason to feel anxious sitting here. It's a one-off, an 'experience', certainly, and at least I can report back to Ingrid that I didn't chicken out.

'Okaaaay,' Anthony says plummily, 'you really want me to tell you?'

'Yes,' I say firmly.

'Hmm. Well, I'd say around here' – his fingers dart close to my eyes – 'we're talking a little Botox to soften the crow's feet, plus dermal fillers here' – I flinch as his spongy fingertips prod my cheeks – 'and more fillers here, here and here, to plump up those marionette lines.'

'What are marionette lines?' I frown, wishing I hadn't started this.

'These crevices,' he says, sweeping a thumb and middle finger from my nose to mouth corners. 'In fact, the whole jawline,' Anthony continues while I take another fortifying swig of wine, 'can be lifted with the careful use of fillers, creating a youthful springiness. We call it the non-surgical facelift.' Now the twerp has reached across the table and cupped my chin in his clammy hand, as if trying to guess the weight of my head. 'And those forehead lines could be lightly Botoxed for a smoother appearance with no loss of movement.'

'That's not true,' I retort, leaning back to maximise the distance between my clearly ravaged visage and his gropey hands. 'You *can't* say that. We've all seen celebs with their weird, frozen foreheads, unable to form normal expressions.'

He shakes his head. 'That never happens when it's expertly done.'

'But it *does*,' I argue. 'We're talking Hollywood A-list – the wealthiest, most photographed women in the world. Surely they go to the best people. I mean, they're hardly resorting to some shoddy little clinic with a seventy per cent off Groupon deal.'

Anthony makes a little snorting noise. 'If it's properly done, it's merely enhancing. It's the way forward, trust me.'

'Okay,' I laugh involuntarily, 'so how much would all of this cost, just out of interest? All the procedures you've mentioned, I mean?'

'Well, we look upon it as an investment . . .' I know what this means: *a fuck of a lot of money*. Anthony pops a raw-looking pink thing, tied up with what looks like green raffia, into his mouth.

'I'm sure you do,' I say, 'but how much are we talking exactly?'

'Ahh . . . at our top-tier service, we'd probably be looking at around four thousand pounds.'

'Four grand,' I exclaim, a little too loudly, 'for a new face?'

'Not new,' he declares. 'We never say new. We say you'll still be you – but *better*.'

I swallow hard, trying to dislodge a seaweedy strand that's lodged itself in my throat. To my horror, I am starting to feel rather wobbly and emotional. It hasn't helped that the waiter has been diving over to refill my glass every time I've taken a sip. It's not just the booze, though. It's the realisation that I clearly have the face of a withered crone who needs extensive reconstructive work. Why has no one told me this before?

'You might also benefit from microdermabrasion,' Anthony adds, flicking a crumb from his pale-blue striped shirt.

I blink at him. 'What's that?'

'It's when we use a little spiky roller to stimulate your skin, accelerating the replenishment of collagen deep within the dermal layers.'

Jesus Christ. 'Excuse me, Anthony,' I say, getting up, 'I just need to nip to the loo.' I march to the Ladies, conscious of my dress clinging to my hips in unflattering folds.

In the swankiest facilities known to womankind, with Jo Malone hand creams lined up on a glass shelf, I stare at my reflection in the mirror. God, that slimy man. Obviously, he doesn't want to get to know me at all. He just wants to give me a good going-over with his spiky roller. Still fixed on my reflection, I widen my eyes to try to stretch out the crow's feet, and open my mouth as far as it'll go, like one of those scary bottom-feeding fish, in an attempt to iron out those damn marionette lines. Then, placing a flattened hand on each of my cheeks, I push back my entire face – the free facelift effect – which does improve things somewhat, even if I look a little like a rabbit in a sidecar . . .

'Oh!' A smart, reedy woman in clicky heels has trotted into the loos.

'Ha,' I guffaw, whipping my hands away and rubbing ineffectually at my cheeks in the hope that she'll think I'm applying moisturiser. She purses her lips at me before disappearing into a cubicle.

Grow up, I tell my reflection silently. *Just be nice and polite and get through this without getting too pissed and making a complete twit of yourself. Surely there can only be another couple more courses to go.*

I rejoin my date at our table. Anthony beams at me, and I'm transfixed by his dazzling dental work and

21

unmoving forehead as he says, 'I'd imagine it's tough as a single mum, Alice. But for you, covering all the treatments we talked about tonight, I'd be happy to draw up a special payment plan.'

Chapter Three

On the damp pavement outside the restaurant, Anthony is looking decidedly crestfallen.

'But it's only just gone ten,' he protests. 'I didn't imagine you'd have to rush off so soon. Thought we might pop back to mine for a nightcap . . .'

'I don't like leaving my boys too late,' I say quickly. 'I'd really better get back.' It's a cool, drizzly Edinburgh night, and the fishiness of the amuse-bouche has somehow clung to the inside of my mouth, having obliterated all the other taste sensations. I have also, for the first time tonight, happened to notice Anthony's curious footwear. I'm not one of those women who's obsessed with checking out men's shoes because, they are, after all, only water-resistant coverings for feet. For instance, before she married Sean, Ingrid only ever dated men who favoured black or dark-brown brogues, which seemed crazily picky to me. 'If you look down and see grey slip-ons,' she once advised, 'start running very fast.'

And on this damp pavement I have glimpsed not just any old slip-ons, but basket-weave ones, in tan or possibly mustard, with a little strap across the front and a flash of gold buckle. I have nothing against basket weave – for *baskets*. But for shoes? And he had the nerve to criticise my choice of attire?

'Don't you have a babysitter?' Anthony wants to know.

Oh God. Having insisted on paying the bill, he'd clearly anticipated that there would at least be a snog in return. Or perhaps he expected that, having been treated to the tasting menu, I'd feel obliged to hot-foot it to his boudoir to remove my 'cheap bit of cloth'.

'No, well – it's a bit tricky,' I explain. 'Logan's sixteen and he'd die if I suggested booking a sitter. I mean, most of the ones we know are in his school year so I could hardly ask them to come over and look after him.'

His eyes glaze briefly, as they did when I mentioned being a school secretary. 'Well, that's a real shame.'

'So I really should get back . . .'

'Right.' He blinks at me, studying my face. I'm convinced now that every time he looks at me, he's planning how to fix me up, like an over-zealous decorator about to be let loose on a clapped-out house.

'It's been a lovely evening,' I add, 'and thanks so much for dinner.'

'My pleasure. We must do it again some time.'

Just how does a woman wriggle out of arranging a second date in these modern times?

'I, er . . . I've got a lot on over the next few weeks,' I explain.

'Hmmm. Busy lady, are you?'

'Er . . . yes, especially with the meringue thing taking off these past few weeks . . .' *I'll be busy whipping up egg whites into the small hours, you see, with no room in my life for a weasly man who's starting to look more*

24

and more doll-like. Not Ken, I decide. More Action Man with his angular jaw and painted-on hair.

'Meringues.' Anthony rolls the word around his mouth. 'I'd love to try them. I'd imagine they're quite delicious.'

'Um . . . yes.' I check my watch unnecessarily. 'Well, they sell them in Peckcry's – you know the coffee shop in Hanover Street? And Betsy's next to St Martin's Church. Anyway, thanks again—'

'Can I walk you home?'

'Oh, no – you live miles away in completely the opposite direction.'

'Let's get you a cab then.' He goes for my arm, clutching it as if, without his support, I might topple over. However, although I felt mildly pissed in the restaurant, the cool drizzle on my face has miraculously restored me to one-hundred-per-cent sobriety.

'Anthony,' I say firmly, 'I only live twenty minutes away. I'd actually like to walk.' I smile again, and this is when I make my crucial mistake. As I stretch up to give him a polite kiss on his waxy cheek, my brief, bird-like peck is somehow misinterpreted to mean that I desire him very much, and next thing I know, he's got my face in his hands and has jammed his wet lips on mine as he goes in for the full-on, tongue-jabbing snog.

'What are you doing?' I exclaim, springing away from him.

'Oh, come on, Alice. You're a saucy minx – I can tell . . .'

I stare at him, speechless.

'You older women,' Anthony adds in a throaty growl, 'I know what you're like. You know your onions . . .'

'I know my *onions*?' I bark. 'How old d'you think I am?'

He shrugs. 'Thirty-seven?'

'Thirty-nine actually.' I omit to mention that my fortieth is a mere month away. 'How about you?'

He smirks. 'You might be surprised to learn that I'm actually forty-five.' And he's calling *me* an older woman? 'My last girlfriend was twenty-eight,' he adds, 'but I've finished with younger girls now. Their bodies are great but they can be so vacuous. It's refreshing to spend time with someone who's genuinely interested in what one has to say.'

'I'm sorry, I really have to go,' I say, cheeks blazing as I turn on my stupid heels and march away.

Mercifully, Anthony doesn't protest or try to follow me. I walk briskly, overcome by the terrible realisation that, for a 'woman of my age', this is probably as good as it gets. God, if that's a typical example of dating today, then it's something I'll avoid from now on. Ugh . . . the creep, with his foot-baskets and darting tongue, like a lizard trying to catch flies. My bouche is *not* amused. I walk faster and faster until, by the time I'm almost home, I have virtually broken into an ungainly trot. I take a quick left turn, hurrying past the grand, detached Victorian houses, then alongside the terrace of tenement flats. Although this is a fairly smart area, with an arthouse cinema and coffee shops galore, our block is rather shabby. I am beyond seething as I head in through the main entrance and clatter upstairs to my second-floor flat.

'I'm home,' I announce jovially, trying to sound as if I've had a perfectly enjoyable night out. In the darkened living room, Logan and Fergus continue to stare at the blaring TV. On the coffee table in front of them lies the detritus of a boys' night in – greasy pizza boxes, milkshake cartons and a few stray socks. 'Everything okay?' I ask, tearing off one shoe, followed by the other.

'Yuh,' Logan replies, picking up his red and white stripy carton and taking a big slurp. In the absence of any further response, I commence a slightly deranged conversation with myself: '"Hi, Mum, did you have a nice time?" "Yes thank you, it was lovely . . ."' In the kitchen now, I click on the kettle. '"Actually,"' I continue under my breath, '"it was pretty shitty. But maybe I misread the signs, or I'm so out of touch with dating that, if a man has paid for the six-course tasting menu, he at least expects to ram his disgusting fat tongue down your throat . . ."'

'Huh?' Fergus is standing in the doorway, clutching the pizza boxes to his chest.

'Nothing,' I mutter, peering into the fridge so he can't see my blazing face.

'You were talking to yourself,' he sniggers. 'That's the first sign of madness, Mum.'

'Yes, you're probably right,' I reply.

He smirks as I straighten up and pour too much milk into my mug. 'What was that about a fat tongue?'

'Nothing, take no notice of me, I was just babbling on.'

'Who were you out with tonight?' he asks.

'Just someone I met at Ingrid's party last weekend.'

He arches a brow. 'Was it a man?'

Clutching my tea, I lower myself on to a kitchen chair. 'Yes, sweetheart, but I won't be seeing him again.'

Fergus cracks a grin, extracts a packet of Jammie Dodgers from the cupboard and rips it open. 'Good. What d'you need a boyfriend for anyway? You're a *mum*.'

Chapter Four

His words are still ringing in my head when I wake up early next morning. While he may only be thirteen, and unable to tolerate virtually the entire vegetable food group, Fergus is absolutely right. I don't need a boyfriend. I've managed perfectly well – well, I've *managed* – being by myself all these years, and have now reached the conclusion that any single men around my age are so baggage-laden they can barely face leaving the house, or are looking for girlfriends born in the early nineties or, as in Anthony's case, are so clearly wrong for me that I shouldn't have gone in the first place.

You only went because you were flattered, I remind myself, examining a tea towel which appears to have been used to stem the flow of ink from a leaking biro. In other words, I was momentarily grateful for a glimmer of male attention, which is no way to go about things. Also, that vile, slimy kiss – I can't get it out of my mind. Is that how it happens these days? In agreeing to a date, was I sending the message, 'I'm desperately starved of affection so, yes, of course I'll welcome your fat, probing tongue into my mouth? In fact, you needn't have bothered with the tasting menu. Half a cider would have done the trick . . .'

I worry, too, that it's not just about Anthony, and that the real issue is I have become sex phobic. In fact, I suspect that the mere act of removing my underwear in front of any adult male would trigger a panic attack. It sounds ridiculous and it's not because I've had terrible experiences in the past. Even when our relationship was in tatters, getting it together with Tom was always pretty good – but now, doing it with anyone seems wholly alarming and unnecessary. It's like when you pass your driving test and think, this is amazing – I can finally do what all those other grown-up people have been doing all along. It's incredibly exciting and liberating. Then months – *years* – pass by before you find yourself behind the wheel again, and when you're suddenly thrown into the situation, it's bloody terrifying. Only with driving, you can at least book a course of refresher lessons . . .

Anyway, as Fergus so succinctly pointed out, I have no need of a man in my life. I have two big, gangly, gorgeous sons. We have a decent, three-bedroomed flat. (I'll gloss over the fact that Logan describes it, inaccurately, as 'poky, like our car – why is everything so *mini* around here?') And yes, I do have a Mini – the car, that is, a bright-red model which I like very much. I also have a job I enjoy, at least some of the time (the kids are mostly fantastic, the insurmountable paperwork less so) and there's my 'little sideline', which I absolutely love. So what do I need a boyfriend for really? I'm starting to wonder if meringues really do fulfil all my womanly needs.

For one thing, they are so pleasingly uncomplicated,

requiring just two main ingredients: egg whites, beaten to a cloud-like froth, and caster sugar, whisked in until satiny smooth. Follow the correct method and a meringue will never flop disappointingly. There are no nasty surprises, like discovering a portrait of an ex-lover tattooed on the pale curve of a buttock (as glimpsed during an ill-advised one-night stand several years ago), or being informed that four grand's worth of work might just about salvage my face. Yet they're far from tedious, as the possibilities for flavourings are virtually infinite. As kitchen inspector Erica observed, the perfect specimen is satisfyingly crisp on the outside, and gooey within – where would I find a man to beat that?

To obliterate lingering thoughts of Anthony's tongue plunging towards my tonsils, I busy myself by gathering up the jotters which Fergus has left scattered across the kitchen table, and remove the two bulging schoolbags which have been dumped in the middle of the floor. As it's Saturday, the boys are having their customary lie-in. Perhaps I should be demanding that they get up and do something useful, but I actually cherish these peaceful weekend mornings when there's no one to moan about my choice of radio station.

I set out my ingredients and start cracking eggs, separating whites from yolks. Humming along to some faintly familiar chart music, I whip up a batch of basic mixture to divide into three bowls, one for each new flavour I'm trying out: strawberries, pistachio and rose water, and little gravelly shards of buttery salted caramel. Kirsty, Ingrid and Viv are coming over later for a taste-in. That's what we call our regular gatherings, suggesting that my friends come over not just to chat and drink wine – or, in Ingrid's case, supposedly fertility-boosting raspberry leaf tea – but to 'help'. I remind Logan of this whenever he declares that I am 'always' having them over, as if, at my advanced age, there is something a little unseemly about being in the company of other human beings, purely for fun. Presumably I should interact only with colleagues, tradespeople and Tesco employees.

At around eleven, Fergus is the first to emerge from his boudoir. 'God, I need food,' he groans, jabbing a finger into the strawberry mixture and licking it.

'Hey, hands out of there,' I exclaim.

He pokes at the caramel bowl.

'Stop sticking your fingers into everything!'

'Why? I'm starving. I'm about to keel over, Mum, and you just don't care . . .' He sniggers and makes for the pistachio bowl but I manage to swipe him away.

'Uncooked meringue mixture isn't proper breakfast food. If you can wait two minutes I'll make you some eggs.'

'Not too runny,' he warns.

'No, sweetheart,' I reply, feigning subservience, 'I'll try to do them properly this time.'

'You doing scrambles, Mum?' Logan has emerged now, rubbing his bleary, pillow-creased face.

'Yes, love.'

'Can I *not* have mine rubberised like his?'

'Of course! I'll do both differently, according to your precise wishes.' With a smirk, I grab my piping bag and start to pipe out strawberry kisses on a paper-lined tray, frowning as Logan starts jabbing his fingers into the mixture. '*Please* stop sticking your fingers into my bowls,' I bark.

'Whoa.' He backs away, turning to Fergus. 'You'd think I'd spat in it.' They both chortle as I swap the two trays of cooked meringues in the oven for the freshly-piped batch.

'So,' I say, now turning my attention to their eggs, 'what are you two up to today?'

'I'm going to fix my translator,' Fergus says confidently.

'How about you, Logan? Is Blake coming over?'

He sighs loudly, clearly overwhelmed by my relentless questioning. 'I'm going out.'

'Where to? Who with?'

'Just *out*, Mum, with *people*.' No further information supplied.

'Logan,' I say, stirring their eggs on the hob, 'you'll have to be a bit more specific than that. I need to know where you are, hon.'

'Why?'

'Because I'm your mum, dearest.'

'Yeah, and I'm sixteen, I'm an *adult*—' He stops short as my mobile starts trilling; I don't recognise the number but take the call anyway.

'Hi, Alice?' comes the strident male voice. 'It's me.'

'Sorry?'

'It's *me* – Anthony from last night. Don't say you've forgotten already.' He chuckles disconcertingly.

'Oh, er . . . right.' I shudder. It takes years, and probably living under one roof, before you're allowed to announce yourself as 'me'.

'Thought you might like to come and see a movie later,' he goes on.

'You mean today?'

'Well, yes, if you're not doing anything. I've checked out the Filmhouse . . .'

God, that's a little presumptuous. Maybe he interpreted

32

me leaping away from his suckering lips as a sign of being unable to manage my yearning for him – like when you nudge away a chocolate cake in case you lose all control and end up devouring the lot. Or maybe he's just eager to give me a good going-over with his roller.

'Sorry, I can't today,' I reply, wondering what possessed me to add 'today' – *ever* is what I should have said.

'Ah, yes, busy with your meringues, I'd imagine,' he says with a snigger.

The boys are shooting me curious looks. 'Actually, yes, I'm making a batch right now. Sorry, better go. Can't leave the uncooked mixture sitting around too long . . .'

'Oh, what'll happen?' he asks leeringly. 'Will it *lose its stiffness*?'

'What?' Something sour rises in my throat; sixteen hours later, that amuse-bouche is still fermenting away in my gut.

'Or are we talking more the texture of *soft peaks*?' Anthony enquires.

'Yes, sort of,' I say tersely.

'I'd like to see you brandishing your whisk,' he growls. 'I imagine it'd be handy for a little light beating . . .'

'Logan, keep an eye on those eggs in the pan,' I order him, striding through to the living room so as to distance myself from the boys' flapping ears.

'They're rubberised,' Logan shouts after me. 'These are, like, *teeth-bouncing* eggs.'

'What *are* you talking about?' I hiss into the phone.

'I mean,' Anthony drawls, 'a little tap on the bottom would be pleasing.'

I peer at a small muddy smear on the white wall and wonder, briefly, how it got there. 'You mean with my whisk?'

'Mmmm, yes . . .'

The small pause is filled by the sound of his rhythmic breathing.

'You have a thing for kitchen utensils,' I say flatly. He whispers something I don't catch. 'Speak up, I can't hear you.'

'I said,' Anthony whispers, 'I've been a *very* naughty boy . . .'

'Oh, for Christ's sake,' I splutter, 'you're not a boy, you're a forty-five-year-old man, and I hate to tell you but I use an electric mixer. D'you honestly think I could whisk up twenty-four egg whites with a hand whisk? I'd get repetitive strain injury or tennis elbow—'

'Yes, but I just thought—'

'*Goodbye*, Anthony.' Having ended the call, I return to the kitchen, trying to emit an aura of serenity as I grab my mug of milky coffee and take a big gulp.

'Anthony?' Logan repeats with a smirk.

'Was that Fat-Tongue Man?' Fergus sniggers.

'Who's Fat-Tongue Man?' Logan enquires.

'No one you know,' I say quickly, serving up the eggs, even though no one seems especially interested in eating them.

'Who's got a fat tongue?' he persists.

'*No one*, Logan. It was just something stupid I said without thinking.'

'Anthony's the man she went out with last night,' Fergus announces, 'and he tried to kiss her. That's why she's on about tongues. He tried to stick it in her mouth—'

'For God's sake,' I cut in, 'of course he didn't. I barely know him . . .'

'He snogged her,' Fergus adds with a shudder, 'and now he's calling her *at home*.' I dump the egg pan in the sink and blink at my sons. Now, although I still have no plans

34

to see Anthony again – and can't believe I found him pleasant company as we snacked on Ingrid's canapés – I do take exception to the suggestion that no man should phone me 'at home'.

'Where else would anyone call me?' I ask mildly.

'Dunno.' Fergus shrugs.

'I mean, I assume it's okay for me to take private calls here,' I add, aware that I'm verging towards overreacting now, 'seeing as I pay the bill *and* the mortgage on our flat in which our phone resides.'

'Yeah, all right, Mum,' he says, shoving aside his substandard breakfast and swaggering out of the kitchen, closely tailed by his big brother.

'Why does she do that?' Logan's voice rings out from the hall.

'Dunno.'

'Clemmie doesn't. She never talks to Blake like that.'

'Nah, I know,' Fergus agrees.

'She respects him,' Logan observes, then the TV goes on in the living room, cranked up to its customary old person's volume, so I can overhear no more.

I stand there, heart hammering in my chest, as a TV advert for fence preserver blasts through the flat. Only when it has returned to a relatively normal speed can I concentrate on the matter in hand. I resume piping meringues, wondering why any interaction between me and an adult male is viewed as tawdry, whereas their father is regarded as the height of respectability. Having put the last batch to bake, I clear up the kitchen, and find the boys still lolling on the sofa.

'You know Dad's coming to get you at lunchtime tomorrow,' I remind them, 'so you really should start packing today.'

35

No response. They are watching a programme about the building of an eco-house, a dazzling wedge of glass clinging to a hillside in a remote part of Wales.

'Look at that,' Logan murmurs. 'Imagine living somewhere like that.'

'Yes, imagine,' I say distractedly, surveying the scattering of shoes, batteries and backless remote controls on the carpet.

Fergus turns to me. 'It's an eco-house, Mum. It's hardly got any carbon footprint.'

'Amazing,' I agree.

'We should be more eco-friendly,' he goes on.

'In what way?'

'Well, like, our oven's always on, isn't it?'

'Not always,' I correct him, 'but quite a lot, yes, when I'm baking, obviously . . .'

'It's on so much, Mum! Think of what it's doing to the planet.'

I take a moment to digest this. 'Meringues take a long time to bake, Fergus. There's not much I can do about that.'

He scowls, as if I might be making this up, and enjoy consuming vast quantities of electricity just for the hell of it. 'Couldn't you make something different? Something that cooks quicker?'

I burst out laughing. 'What d'you have in mind?'

'I dunno, *you're* the baker.' With that, he turns his attention back to the TV where the presenter is extolling the virtues of a composting toilet.

'Oh, and just so you know,' I add, my voice drifting like tumbleweed, 'the girls are coming over later to test flavours.'

Logan throws me a bemused look. 'The girls,' he sniggers.

36

'Okay,' I say, my voice rising a little, '*the women* are coming over. Is that better?'

Fergus chuckles. 'That sounds as if you don't actually like them very much.'

'So when are they coming?' Logan wants to know.

'About seven-ish.'

'Ugh, all that talking and laughing . . .'

'I know – hideous,' I snigger, catching Fergus's eye who grins in return. 'We shouldn't be allowed to congregate en masse.'

But thank God we do, I think, leaving him to ogle the eco-house while Logan gets up and heads out, to meet his *people*.

*

'I never realised Anthony was like that,' Ingrid exclaims later as I set down plates of freshly baked meringues on the kitchen table. 'What a complete creep. I feel so responsible. If I'd known, I'd have warned you off.'

'It's not your fault,' I assure her as Kirsty and Viv munch on my confections, equally dismayed by the outcome of my date. 'You didn't exactly throw us together and force me to go out with him. I thought he was nice, actually. A proper grown-up . . .'

I'm aware that I have this *grown-up-in-a-good-way* thing, probably as a reaction against all those years spent with Tom. I don't mean grown-up as in, 'Every Saturday will be spent trundling around Homebase until I drop down dead.' More, 'It's okay – I can fix things and throw a meal together, and I'll never expect you to remember my relatives' birthdays.' An in-this-together sort of feeling . . . like we're equals. If I occasionally yearn for anything, it's that.

'I guess there was no way of knowing he likes being smacked with utensils,' sniggers Kirsty.

'Well, *I* thought he looked creepy,' declares Viv, smoothing back her neat auburn crop. 'I tried to communicate that to you every time I came into the kitchen.'

'No, you didn't,' I tease her. 'Whenever you glanced over you gave me an indulgent smile, as if to say, "Ah, that's nice, Alice enjoying some adult male company for a change."'

'No, I didn't. God, you'd have no end of male company if you wanted it, if you *put out some signals*. You'd be fighting them off with sticks . . .'

We all laugh, and I quickly shush them as Fergus scampers in to grab a bottle of Lucozade from the fridge and barks a speedy hello before disappearing again.

'Does he know about your date?' Kirsty murmurs.

'Yep. Heard me muttering to myself about Anthony plunging his tongue down my throat . . .'

Viv splutters. 'That's the kind of conversation you have with yourself?'

A strawberry meringue dissolves in my mouth. 'Sadly, yeah. I probably traumatised my poor boy . . .'

'Bet he'd love you to meet someone, though,' Kirsty suggests.

'You really think so?' I laugh dryly. 'He interrogated me after Anthony called today. God knows how things would be if I dared to bring a man back to the flat. I'd have to smuggle him in, covered in a blanket, like a criminal being ushered into a police van. And then we'd lie in bed, as silent as lambs in case Fergus – his bedroom is next to mine, remember – got wind of some action and set off his translator to spite me: "*I have been raped!*"'

38

Everyone howls with laughter. Seriously, though, is it any wonder I find the very thought of sex rather anxiety-making?

I glance at Viv who, perhaps in an attempt to inspire me, has switched the topic to her current dalliance with some whippersnapper she pounced on in a bar. Although the four of us are close in age, Viv has by far the whizziest life these days. As studio manager at a textile design company, she easily passes for a decade younger with her Mia-Farrow-esque crop, which she carries off beautifully with her large brown eyes, pronounced cheekbones and the rosy complexion of the child-free. Viv married young, at twenty-one; the ring had barely been slipped on her finger when her husband started to micromanage the way she dressed (no hemlines above knee-length) and even her make-up (i.e. none). So jealous was he, she used to joke that he'd probably implanted some kind of tracking device in her while she slept – then he caused an almighty scene when she was chatting to some man at a party, and it stopped being remotely funny. Sick of being 'under surveillance' as she put it, Viv packed her belongings into two battered old cases and walked out. There's been a dizzying amount of flings since, though nothing remotely approaching serious.

'You need to cast the net wide,' she instructs me now, smoking a cigarette at the open kitchen window. 'Find yourself a younger man. Everyone's doing it these days.'

'You mean *you* are,' I snigger. 'Anyway, how young is too young, d'you think? I mean, what are the rules?'

She takes a drag of her cig. 'Half your age plus seven is perfectly fine.'

'And how did you work that out?'

She grins and drains her wine glass, refilling it to the

brim from the bottle. Viv drinks fast, with seemingly no ill effects next morning; but then, my hangovers were child's play before I had kids.

'Well,' she explains, extinguishing her cigarette under the running tap and dropping it into the bin, 'that way you avoid people crowing that you're *twice* his age. And think of the energy levels, Alice. Younger guys don't need much sleep, and when they do it's at the proper time – you know, at night, and not when you're watching a movie together.' My mind flashes back to Tom sleeping, seemingly for days on end, like a hibernating dormouse in his duvet nest on the sofa. 'Although, I have to say, it's not all good,' Viv goes on, cheeks already flushed from the wine.

'Sounds pretty good to me,' Kirsty says ruefully. I know she and her husband Dan have been having problems lately; their three children are home educated, and he appears to have reneged on his part of the deal, which was to teach them science and maths. As Kirsty has pointed out, home educating is a cinch when you're sitting in a peaceful office, ten miles from home.

'I mean, look at the state of my face,' Viv laments. 'I'm so sleep deprived, I can't tell you.' She jabs at the faintest hint of under-eye baggage.

'That's normal,' Kirsty retorts. 'I've had mine for so long, they're permanently etched on my face.'

Ingrid leans forward. 'You know the best treatment for those? Pile ointment. Alice, d'you have any old tubes kicking around?'

'Thanks a lot,' I scoff. 'When you think of my bathroom cabinet, you're not picturing a beautiful pot of Crème de la Mer. You're thinking a mangled tube of Anusol.'

'Well,' she says with a smile, 'you have had that . . . *problem* over the years, haven't you?'

'Not for ages,' I insist, heading to the bathroom anyway and returning with the requested tube.

'Great. Dab it on,' she instructs Viv.

'What are you doing?' Fergus, who's returned to the kitchen for further supplies, stares at us from the doorway.

'Emergency beauty treatment,' Viv explains, patting an eye-bag with a finger and waggling the tube. 'This, Fergus, is your mum's bum cream but as you can see, it has other uses. It *multitasks*.'

She is slurring a little, and he regards her with horror before backing out of the kitchen.

'Thank your lucky stars you're not a woman, Ferg!' she cackles after him. 'Our lives are so fucking complicated.'

'Viv,' I scold her, only half joking, 'you've traumatised my poor boy. He's thirteen. He doesn't need to know alternative uses for haemorrhoid ointment.'

'It's good for him,' Viv insists, 'to learn about the quirks of womankind. You cosset those boys, keeping them all wrapped up in cotton wool . . .' Christ, what *is* she on about? 'Anyway,' she adds, 'never mind that. Who are we going to fix you up with after that disaster last night?'

'No one.' I crunch a rose-scented meringue.

'Come on, there must be *someone* . . .'

'What about Derek?' teases Ingrid, flicking back expensively blonded hair.

I splutter with laughter. Derek is the janitor and sole male employee at my school, where Ingrid's daughter Saskia is a pupil.

'He's lovely but he's also pushing sixty, I'd imagine. I don't want a boyfriend who's twenty years older, thanks all the same.'

'You don't want a younger one either,' Viv teases.

'God, she's choosy,' Ingrid snorts as Logan barges in. He glances around, transmitting a silent message – *Christ, pissed middle-aged women* – even though Viv's knocked back most of the wine so far, and is already grabbing another bottle from the fridge.

'How are you, Logan?' Kirsty asks pleasantly, causing his expression to soften. He likes her the best, approving of her earth-mummy credentials (although, when I jokingly asked if he'd like to be home educated, he shrieked, '*God* no!').

'Good thanks, Kirsty,' he says gallantly, helping himself to a Tunnock's teacake from the cupboard.

'Not having any of these meringues?' Viv asks.

'Nah, maybe later.'

'Poor boy's all meringued out,' Ingrid chuckles, sipping her tea as Logan beats a hasty retreat from the kitchen.

'What a handsome boy,' Kirsty declares.

'Like his dad,' I chuckle, and it's true; however useless Tom may have been, he also happened to be one of the most striking men I'd ever met, if you go for that whole intense, brown-eyed brooding thing, which he – and now Logan – possess in spades. Plus, Tom is hanging on to his looks remarkably well. Due to a lack of stress or exertion, probably.

'Anyway,' Ingrid says, 'I still feel bad about Anthony and his whisk thing.'

'Oh, I don't care about that,' I declare, refilling Kirsty's empty glass. 'It did make me think, though, that I'm not going to bother going on random dates any more.'

Ingrid catches my eye. 'And by random dates, you mean . . .'

I shrug. 'Just some man who happens to ask me out.'

'Why not?' Viv asks, aghast.

'Because . . .' I shrug. 'I'm not even sure I want to meet anyone. I mean, I *like* being able to please myself and not be answerable to anyone. And I kept thinking, when I was in that restaurant with Anthony with all the silly, tiny food, why am I doing this? I'd have had a nicer time at home with the boys.'

Kirsty gives me a concerned look. 'That's because you knew virtually nothing about him, apart from that he plays golf.'

'We should vet the next man you go out with,' Viv suggests.

'I *am* thirty-nine,' I remind them. 'I can usually weed out the weirdos and whisk-pervs.'

'I'd never have imagined a whisk could be considered erotic,' Kirsty muses. 'What d'you think he'd have made of your piping bag?'

We all snigger, then Viv adds, turning serious, 'All I mean is, we could find suitable dates for you. If each of us picked someone – really carefully, I mean, putting lots of thought into it – then you'd have three really lovely, eligible men to choose from.'

I frown. 'But surely, if you knew someone that appealing who you thought might be interested, then you'd have told me about him already.'

'No, we wouldn't,' Ingrid declares, 'because you've got this whole thing going on of, *I am perfectly all right by myself, thank-you-very-much.*'

'You can even build flatpack furniture,' Kirsty observes.

'Well, yes – if you take it step by step it usually turns out all right.'

'You've been single far too long,' Ingrid observes. 'Flatpack's no fun unless there's a load of swearing and someone storms out in a furious temper.'

I nibble a salted-caramel meringue; good, but the caramel shards should be ground finer so as not to stick to the teeth.

'Okay, so you reckon I need someone to say, "Stand back, fragile maiden, allow me to fly into a complete rage while building this bookshelf for you."'

Viv shakes her head. 'No, you just need some *fun*.'

'You mean I'm a miserable trout?'

'No!' everyone cries.

I laugh, appreciating their concern, but eager to swerve the conversation away from my sorry love life.

'So what d'you think of these flavours?' I ask, indicating the shattered remains of the meringues on the plate. 'Can we put them in order of favourites?' Everyone starts debating, and I scribble down comments and suggestions.

'Our flavours sort of match us,' Viv observes when everyone has nominated their favourite. She's right; I'd have guessed she'd nominate pistachio and rose water, the on-trend flavour combination in confectionary circles. I expected Kirsty, fresh-faced with her tumble of light brown curls, to go for strawberries, while Ingrid – all languid beauty with her refined features and salon-fresh waves – is definitely a salted caramel girl (sorry – *woman*).

'Shows how different we are,' Kirsty agrees.

'And how we'd all pick a very different sort of man for you,' Viv adds with a grin.

There's a burst of laughter from the TV in the living room. 'I'm just not keen on the idea of being set up, you know?' I venture. 'It feels too . . . forced.'

'But almost everyone's set up at our age,' Ingrid points out. 'How else d'you think it happens, apart from online dating, which you won't even consider?'

'I just don't want to turn it into a project,' I say, feeling ever-so-slightly bossed around now. 'Anyway, if you did all pick someone, what if none of them were right? I'm not being negative here, but it's pretty likely, isn't it? I mean, three isn't that many.'

'We're thinking quality over quantity,' Viv explains.

I nod, considering this. 'But then, if it didn't work out, I'd feel bad because each of you had put so much thought and effort into it.'

Kirsty shrugs. 'It wouldn't matter a bit. You could reject them all if you liked. It's just a bit of fun.'

'For you lot, maybe,' I snigger, topping up my glass.

'Oh, come on,' Viv says, 'just give it a try. I mean, who knows you better than us?'

'We've known you for twenty years,' Kirsty points out.

'That's sixty years' combined experience of Alice Sweet,' Ingrid says with a throaty laugh.

I crunch a pink-flecked meringue. Kirsty is right; the combination of heady strawberries, and the chewy sweetness of the meringue, are a perfect match. 'Okay,' I say, 'I'll give it a try.'

'Brilliant,' Ingrid exclaims.

'We'll start thinking of candidates,' Viv announces as everyone starts babbling excitedly. 'My God! You might even love them all . . .'

I laugh, buoyed up by the wine and being with the

women I love most. 'Okay,' I say, 'but let's hope they're not too appalled when they meet me.'

'They'll think you're gorgeous,' Viv declares, shaking her head. 'God, Alice, what's wrong with you? Have some *belief* in yourself.'

Chapter Five

'Now, Alice, I've been thinking about your weight,' my mother announces as the boys and I arrive on her doorstep next morning. It's a thing with Mum – my appearance, I mean. Considering her fierce intelligence – until her recent retirement she was a university professor of Medieval Studies – she places an awful lot of emphasis on how people look. It's probably why I'm wearing my favourite skirt and top, plus a cardi I absolutely love; cashmere, in a beautiful deep-raspberry shade, bought for my last birthday by Ingrid.

'Have you, Mum? I'm kind of fine with the way I am,' I say as the three of us follow her into her ancient, low-slung cottage. It stands alone, as if sulking, in the treeless landscape of the North Lanarkshire moorlands and seems to sag in the middle, as if someone has sat on it.

'Well,' she goes on, smoothing back her pewter-flecked hair which she wears in a long, low ponytail, 'I just thought you might be interested in this diet I cut out for you. You know, if you wanted to lose a few pounds.'

Logan suppresses a snigger as we blink in the gloom of her kitchen.

'What sort of diet is it?' I ask pleasantly. *The one where you exist on some terrible, fart-making soup? Or staple your mouth shut and eat nothing at all?*

'Oh, I've got it here somewhere . . .' She frowns and starts flicking through mountains of ratty old paperwork on the gnarled oak table. We've been here for less than five minutes and already I can sense a vein throbbing violently in my forehead. It's my fault; I should have spent the forty-minute drive mentally revving myself up into the sparkling game-show hostess persona that's required on these occasions, instead of berating the boys for moaning about visiting Grandma. 'It's my *Sunday*,' Logan kept lamenting, as if he'd been slaving away at the coalface all week. 'I was gonna do stuff.'

'I don't mind going,' Fergus conceded, 'but we're not staying long, are we? Like, we're not gonna be there *all day*?'

And now it's too late. I'm gritting my teeth in defensiveness, while trying to reassure myself that being a size twelve is actually fine, at my age – at any age, in fact. We're hardly talking morbidly obese. But then, I have never matched up to Mum's expectations of what a daughter should be. She couldn't understand why I never gleaned the clutch of A grades that had come so easily to her; the fact that I enjoyed drawing, baking and simply *playing* as a child left her utterly baffled. I don't blame her especially – she's just made that way – and, thankfully, she's a little warmer to her grandsons.

As Logan and Fergus install themselves on the scuffed leather sofa beneath the kitchen window, Mum continues her search for a snippet of paper which will save me from a gastric bypass operation. Newspapers are piled up on wonky wooden chairs, and bookshelves are crammed with formidable tomes, all dusty and sticky with kitchen grease in which *evr'thing is spellte lyke this*. Finding her library oddly fascinating, Fergus selects one from a shelf.

'What does this mean, Grandma?' he asks, proceeding to read in a grand, theatrical voice: '"Tehee, quod she and clapte the window to!"'

'Hang on a minute, love,' she says distractedly.

'I think it means he's telling her to shut the window,' I venture.

'But why?'

'Um, maybe it's draughty . . .'

'Yeah, but what's the "tehee" bit about?' Fergus wants to know.

I glance at Mum in the hope that she'll stop excavating the paperwork and answer him. 'I think she's laughing at someone,' I say, bobbing down to help her gather up a heap of yellowing journals which have slid off the table in a dusty heap.

Fergus frowns. 'Is it meant to be funny?'

'What's that, Fergus?' my mother asks.

'Mum was just translating something Medieval for us,' Logan says with a smirk.

'Was she?' Mum chuckles. 'Good luck with that, Alice. It's not like you to take an interest in my library.' I form a rictus grin. Mum is of the impression that I can barely manage to read anything more taxing than *Grazia*, which these days isn't too far from the truth.

Having dumped the book on the table, Fergus pulls something from his jeans pocket. 'Look, Grandma – I've got a translator.'

'That's nice,' she says. 'I'm glad you're taking an interest in language, Fergus.'

'Yes,' I say quickly, 'but it doesn't speak Medieval. In fact it doesn't make much sense at all. Please put it away, darling.' *Before it starts squawking about rape* . . .

'Ah – here it is, I knew I'd kept it safe for you.' Mum brandishes a scrap of paper as if it's a treasure hunt clue and presses it into my hand.

'Thank you, Mum.'

'Let me know how you get on . . .'

'Of course I will.' *If I'm not too sodding fat to stagger to the telephone* . . .

'Anyway,' she says, visibly relieved now, 'I thought I'd do burgers for lunch, okay, boys? That's what you like best, isn't it?'

'Yeah, that's great, Grandma,' Fergus says dutifully. I drop my gaze to the diet. In fact, it isn't newfangled; rather, it appears to have been snipped out of a Medieval copy of *Woman's Own*.

Breakfast: half banana, black tea/coffee.
Lunch: One spoon cottage cheese, 4 Tuc biscuits.
Dinner: Tinned hot dog sausage (NO BREAD), unlimited green beans.

As Mum clatters around, managing to locate a frying pan in a jam-packed cupboard, I scrunch up the diet into a tight ball in my fist. I know I'm being churlish but I can't help it.

'I hear your father's taking a holiday soon,' Mum is telling me now. 'An Easter holiday, like one a year isn't good enough for him.' She extracts a clear plastic carton of burgers from the fridge.

'Really? I hadn't heard. Where are they going?'

'Penzance!' she exclaims, in a voice more suited to 'the Maldives'.

'Well,' I say carefully, 'maybe you should have a holiday too. A change of scene might be good for you.'

She frowns, assessing my apparently ballooning figure. 'Who would I go with?'

'Mum, you have plenty of friends. I'm sure Penny or Joan would love to go away with you.'

'Oh, I don't know,' she says crossly.

A small silence descends as she lights the gas ring with a dented silver wand and sloshes yellow oil from a large unlabelled bottle into the pan.

'When are we going home?' Fergus mouths at me.

'Never,' I hiss, prompting him to mime a throat-cutting motion.

'Please, Mum,' he mouths back.

I shake my head and whisper, *'You will die here.'*

Mum turns back to us from the cooker. 'I'm afraid I'm not doing chips, boys. Can't be doing with all that fat.'

'That's fine, Grandma,' Logan mutters.

'Oh, I brought you these,' I say in an overly perky voice, lifting the tin of meringues from my bag and removing the lid. 'I've been testing new flavours. You can give me your verdict if you like.'

'That's kind of you,' she says, wincing as if I might have expelled them out of my bottom.

'I thought you might like the chocolate ones. I made them specially.'

She forces a tight smile. 'So, as I was saying, it's all right for your father and his fancy woman to swan off here, there and everywhere at the drop of a hat . . .'

51

'Uh-huh,' I murmur, unwilling to be drawn into a character assassination of Dad right now. Okay, he left Mum for another woman – Brenda McPhail who, with her reedy ex-husband, ran a dump of a pub on the moors called The Last Gasp (we are not talking gastro-pub, although they do stock a fine range of pork scratchings). Understandably, Mum was horrified; she'd had not an inkling that anything had been going on. In his holey sweaters and faded jumbo cords, Dad – an academic like Mum – hardly seemed capable of sparking a scandal among the sparse community in this blasted landscape. But eight months ago, he and Brenda hotfooted it to Devon, where they now keep chickens and goats. Although he's rarely in touch, I can't bring myself to hate him for it. After decades of Mum pointing out his failings, perhaps Brenda made him realise he didn't have to live out the rest of his years feeling like a colossal disappointment after all.

Mum slices open four rolls on the cluttered worktop. 'Can I help you with anything?' I ask, conscious of hovering ineffectually.

'No, it's fine.'

A tense silence descends, and I glance at my boys, both of whom are slumped on the sofa as if awaiting an unpleasant medical procedure. At times like this, I'd give anything for a sibling to share some of this. As it is, I feel guilty if we don't visit, and guilty when we do – for dragging my boys here and because, in truth, I'd dearly love to be somewhere else too. In fact, coming here is *more* guilt-making than staying at home.

Plus, I'm annoyed with myself for not having the gumption to say, *Please stop badmouthing the boys' granddad in front of them. It's really not what we came here for.*

'Logan's exams are coming up,' I remark, sensing myself ageing rapidly, like a speeded-up film of the life-cycle of a rose. By the time we leave, I'll be entirely withered.

'I'm sure you'll do well,' Mum remarks. 'You've always been a very bright boy.'

'Thanks, Grandma,' Logan mumbles.

'You'll be studying hard in the holidays, I'd imagine?'

'Well, um, Dad's taking us to the Highlands . . .'

'But you'll take all your books with you—'

'Of course I will,' he says quickly, flushing a little. I see a flicker of tension in his jaw, and am seized by an urge to hug him and say I'm so sorry it's always like this, and I wish you had a storybook granny with an endless supply of cuddles and cakes and, actually, she *does* care about you. She just wants you and your brother to have successful lives, perhaps to compensate for me not having risen to the dizzy heights of academia . . . I start extracting plates from the cupboard and cutlery from the drawer, wondering if it would be so terrible to stop off to buy cigarettes on the way home, plus strong drink like vodka or gin.

'How are *you* getting along at school, Fergus?' Mum asks.

'Great,' he says brightly. 'It's loads better than primary school . . .'

'Why's that?'

''Cause we're allowed to go up the street and get chips.'

She throws him a disappointed look, then turns to rip the cellophane lid off the carton of burgers, allowing a pungent odour to escape. Dear God, they *stink*. She's planning to poison us all with rotten beef. Adopting the

53

nonchalant air of someone planning to shoplift, I stroll around the kitchen table, bending to stroke Brian, her malevolent ginger tom, who hisses sharply from behind the propped-up ironing board. Working my way towards the cooker now, I casually peer into the pan where the slimy burgers have landed with feeble sizzle.

'Um . . . are you sure they're okay, Mum?' I venture.

'Of course they are. Why wouldn't they be?'

'Er, don't you think they look a bit . . . peaky?' What is *wrong* with me, an almost-forty-year-old woman, terrified of crossing my mother?

'They're fine,' she declares as the remainder of our weekend flashes before me: of the boys puking copiously during the car journey home, culminating in twenty-four hours spent in bed. *I* can handle her cooking – I'll stuff my burger in my shoe or something, as a sort of grease-soaked insole – but my boys won't know unless I alert them. 'I tried that diet myself,' Mum informs me.

'Did you? Well, you look great. Very trim.' It's true: she could spear someone's eye out with those collarbones. Her moss-green scoop-necked sweater and dog-tooth-checked trousers are probably a size eight. Defeated now, I perch on the edge of the table and survey my poor sons who are about to ingest a swarm of seething bacteria. I'm their mother, for crying out loud; I can't allow that to happen.

'*Don't-eat-the-burgers,*' I mouth as Mum turns back to the stove.

'Eh?' Fergus says loudly.

'The meat's off. It'll *kill you.*'

'What?' Logan barks as Mum heads for the fridge to rummage for her pre-war ketchup.

'*Don't eat the meat!*' I mouth again, more forcefully this time.

'Mum, what are you on about?' Fergus asks.

I make a petrified face, indicating the pan on the hob, then poke two fingers into my mouth to mime vomiting. Logan bursts out laughing and Fergus stares at me uncomprehendingly.

'She's gone mental,' he whispers to his big brother. 'This is it   she's finally flipped.'

Mum turns back to us, setting down the sauce bottle, then goes in search of the generic lime cordial that I suspect only sees daylight during our visits. While she checks several crammed cupboards, I glance around wildly, wondering how to alert my boys to their imminent fate. If only we had some kind of secret family code, like a series of coughs, or knew semaphore or Morse . . .

Pretending to study a newspaper from the pile, I squint at the fiendishly difficult, completed crossword. While Mum continues her search for the cordial, I snatch a pencil from an overstuffed jam jar on a shelf and quickly scribble in the margin: *BURGERS BAD DO NOT EAT!!!*

Logan frowns at my scrawling. 'Shit,' he breathes.

'What'll I do?' Fergus whispers, dark eyes wide. This is the tricky bit. We can't eat them, obviously, but nor am I keen on incurring Mum's wrath. Would it be possible for us to somehow dispose of our burgers, perhaps by throwing them out of the window, if she happens to leave the table? Could I send her off on a fake errand – to find us a different kind of sauce, or a selection of fine pickles? No, she doesn't exactly run around fetching things for people, and anyway, the small kitchen windows are all painted shut. Could we feed the burgers to Brian? I slide my gaze over to where he is eyeing us from his ironing board hidey-hole. No – that wouldn't be fair.

Even if he did manage to guzzle them, they might poison or even kill him, and I'd never forgive myself for that. We all take our seats at the table as Mum slides the burgers into four rolls.

'There's one spare,' she announces. 'Who wants the extra?'

'No thanks,' the boys blurt out.

'Aren't you having one, Mum?' I ask as she brings a small plate of crackers, and a slice of the industrial dyed orange cheese she allows herself as a treat, to the table.

'Oh, I can't be doing with all that rich food in the middle of the day.'

'Um, I'm not that hungry either, Grandma,' Logan says meekly. Poor boy, usually so full of swagger. In less than an hour he's been reduced to a husk.

'Come on, a growing lad like you needs to eat.' She cuts a tiny triangle the size of a Trivial Pursuit piece from her cheese, and pops it into her mouth.

Fergus clears his throat. 'I've been thinking of becoming vegetarian. Or even vegan and, you know, just eating plants.'

Mum laughs dryly. 'Whatever for?'

'Because I don't think such a big proportion of the earth should be used for cows to graze on.'

'Well, you can be vegan at home,' Mum says, prompting him to throw me a stricken expression which says: *HELP*. As both boys nibble at the edges of their rolls, I pick up mine and give it a discreet sniff. It smells oddly sweet, and I picture Erica-the-Inspector's face if she were to examine it.

'Well, tuck in,' Mum prompts us.

I pause, feeling her curranty eyes fixed upon me across the table, and aware of the boys throwing me panicky looks. I've always known what to do in a crisis; I've managed to eradicate verrucas, threadworms *and* nits, and didn't even freak out when Fergus plucked King Nit from his head and made me watch it writhing on his history jotter. Yet now, when they depend on me to be quick-witted, I am useless. What kind of mother sits back while her children ingest rancid flesh? Then a small miracle happens. Having emerged from behind the ironing board, Brian prowls towards us across the kitchen. He gives each of us a sly look, then stops on the murky Aztec-patterned rug where his entire body appears to spasm. While I've never been one to derive pleasure from seeing an animal in distress, his actions – causing Mum to leap up and hurry towards him – give me just enough time to snatch all three of our burgers from their buns and ram them into the small side pockets of my cashmere cardigan.

'Is he okay, Mum?' I ask as Brian vomits and the boys convulse with silent mirth.

'He's been doing this a lot lately,' she mutters, wiping up the small pool of puke with the cloth from the sink. 'He's been on a cheaper brand of food since your father left and it's not agreeing with him.'

'Yes, I can see that.'

'I can't afford his trout pâté any more,' she adds.

I take a big bite of roll, hoping that any beef residue is minimal. 'That's a real pity.'

'Poor Brian,' Fergus adds for effect. 'Maybe he should see a vet, Grandma.'

'As if I can afford that,' she exclaims, rinsing out the cloth at the sink while I give my cardi pockets a tentative pat. Grease is already seeping through the fine raspberry knit. I could grumble about this, and point out that it's the *only cashmere garment I've ever owned* – but its ruination is a small price to pay for my boys' wellbeing.

As I finish my bare roll, my mobile rings. 'Excuse me a sec, Mum,' I say quickly, marching to the back door and letting myself out into the scrubby back garden.

'You okay to talk for a minute?' Kirsty asks.

'Yes, but I'm at Mum's . . .' I fill her in on the rank burger incident, knowing that Kirsty, who hasn't eaten 'anything with a face' for twenty-five years, will be sufficiently appalled.

'And your lovely cardi's ruined?' she laments. 'That's awful. Ugh. Anyway, this'll cheer you up. I think I've found a man for you . . .'

'Who is he?' I glance at the row of industrial beige knickers wafting gently on Mum's washing line.

'His name's Stephen and he's our new dentist . . .'

'A dentist,' I repeat.

She laughs. 'Keep an open mind. He's brilliant with the kids – they actually look forward to going now. And I ran into him again at a birthday do Hamish was invited to. You know how most dads tend to hide away in corners at kids' parties?'

'Tom never went to any,' I say with a snort. 'It's a miracle he actually showed up to Logan and Fergus's.'

'Well, Stephen was great,' she declares, 'getting stuck in with the games, being the wolf in What's the Time, Mr Wolf? and helping the kids to build a fire at the bottom of the garden. He had them all toasting marshmallows . . .'

'Wow,' I breathe, unable to decide whether this is a hugely attractive quality, or smacks of over-zealous and eager to please. Perhaps I'm just not used to party-fabulous dads.

'His daughter Molly's around eight,' Kirsty goes on.

58

'She's in Hamish's class. He's a single dad, has been for years as far as I can make out . . .'

'And you're sure he wants to meet someone?'

'Oh yes. We got chatting and I told him all about you. What else? Um, he's tall, slim, fairish hair, greenish eyes . . . he's just *nice*, you know? Good-looking but not intimidatingly so.' She pauses. 'I did warn him that you're a pusher of meringues and he seemed fine with that.'

I laugh, my spirits rising as I fish the burgers from my pockets and fling them one by one, like miniature frisbees, over the drystone wall.

'Okay,' I say, 'but can we leave it until the boys are away on their jaunt with Tom? I feel bad, expecting Logan to look after Fergus all the time.'

'Yes, like, about once a month,' she says, not unkindly.

I bite my lip. 'It'll just be simpler that way.' This isn't entirely true; after amuse-bouche night, I need time to rev myself back up into a dating frame of mind.

By the time I'm back inside, Mum has produced a collection of illustrations showing Scotland in the Middle Ages. The scene – of the boys dutifully studying the creased, fly-speckled pictures that she's spread out on the table to show them – twists my heart.

'That's amazing, Gran,' Logan says gamely.

'Yeah, they're really cool,' Fergus adds, stifling a yawn.

She turns to him and smiles. 'Before you go, let me have a look at that translator of yours.' He hands it to her and, while she takes the thing to pieces and prods at its innards, I select a leather-bound book from a shelf and flip it open at a random page:

With hym ther was his sone, a yong squier
A lovyere and a lusty bacheler . . .

A lusty bachelor! Could a child-friendly dentist fit into

this category? We all wait patiently as Mum fiddles about with the gadget's innards, then finally puts it back together. 'There,' she says, handing it to Fergus.

'Is it fixed?' he gasps.

'Yes, just needed resetting. Go on, ask it a question.'

He turns to me, perhaps fearful of what it might say.

'Er . . . "Where is the station?"' I ask nervously. He taps some buttons. *Où est la gare?* it chirps.

'Wow, Grandma.' Fergus grins. 'That's amazing. You're so clever.'

'It really wasn't difficult,' she blusters, as if unaccustomed to praise. We say our goodbyes then, all heading outside where I give her a hug; it's like trying to cuddle an icicle. She is a little more receptive to Logan and Fergus's hugs, and doesn't appear to notice their eagerness to jump into the car.

Before I climb in, perhaps in an attempt to spark a glimmer of warmth between us, I add, 'Oh, I meant to tell you, Mum – that was Kirsty who called earlier. She's setting me up on a blind date.'

'Really?' Mum fixes me with small pale grey eyes. 'Who with?'

'Some dentist guy.'

'A *dentist*,' she repeats, clearly impressed. 'Ooh, you'll be glad I gave you that diet then.' So what's she implying now? That I have fat *teeth*?

Chapter Six

'That was *so* embarrassing,' Logan declares as we pull away. 'Never put me in a situation like that again, Mum. Can't believe you did that to me.'

Like *I* flaunted the use-by date on those burgers!

'Listen,' I say, 'I stopped you being poisoned, all right? I might've even saved your life. *And* I ruined my best cardi.'

'That's disgusting,' Fergus crows from the back seat, 'putting cooked food in your pockets. You'd go mad if we did that.'

Jesus Christ. We reach the main road and I speed up, the cigarette and gin scenario becoming more appealing by the minute.

'There wasn't an awful lot of choice, Fergus. Anyway, I think you had the right idea. Next time we go, I'll tell her we've gone vegetarian . . .'

'You mean we're going *again*?' Logan whines.

'Well, at some point, yes. I mean, that wasn't the last time you'll ever see Grandma.'

'No, I know that,' he says gruffly.

'And she loves our visits,' I add. 'Being around such vibrant young people brings sunshine and sparkle into her life.'

Fergus cackles with laughter, and the fuggy weight of the day starts to lift as we head along the main Edinburgh-bound road.

'What would she give us,' Fergus muses, 'if we pretended to be veggie?'

'God knows. A tin of potatoes, maybe.'

'You can't get tinned potatoes,' he retorts.

'Oh yes you can. You've been spoilt, that's your problem . . .'

He barks with laughter. 'Well, they sound better than stinky old meat . . .'

'Maybe,' Logan muses, 'she'd be better in an old people's home.'

I cast him a sharp look. 'Grandma doesn't need to go into a home. There's absolutely nothing wrong with her. She's as strong as an ox, you know – managed to erect that fence at the front all by herself . . .'

At the term 'erect', both boys dissolve into cackles. 'They're actually not that bad,' Logan adds.

'What aren't?'

'Old folks' homes. Blake's granddad's in one.'

'Yes, I know, love . . .'

'They're allowed to sit around and watch telly all day and at Christmas they get a Santa.'

I splutter with laughter. 'Oh, Grandma would love that. She's only sixty-six and a world authority on *Beowulf*. She doesn't need a patronising old bloke asking what she wants for Christmas.'

'What's *Beowulf* about?' Fergus asks from the back.

'Er . . . I think there's a monster in it.'

'Yeah, but what happens?'

'A bit like Little Red Riding Hood, is it, Mum?' Logan enquires.

I throw him a quick sideways look. Smartarse. Bet *he* doesn't know about *Beowulf* either. The two of them just enjoy exposing me as a fluff-brain, capable only of whisking up eggs and manning a school office – which is actually bloody complicated, what with the endless paperwork and the diplomatic handling of tricky parents.

'Talking of which,' I say with a smile, 'how's the revision going, Logan? It's, what, three weeks till your first exam?'

'It's going fine,' he says between his teeth.

'Are you sure? Can I help at all?'

He snorts.

'Seriously, love. I wish you'd let me. I could be a *useful resource.*'

'I don't think so, Mum.'

'I'm *starving,*' Fergus reminds me. 'I only had a bare roll . . .'

'. . . With a greasy stain on it,' Logan adds. 'That was a nice touch.'

'I know,' I reply, 'and I plan to fix that as soon as I can.' Shutting my ears to further grumbling, I turn off the main road and follow the narrow country lane towards the nearest village. 'Isn't it lovely around here?' I muse.

''S'all right,' Logan says.

'I mean, the countryside. It's so pretty and peaceful . . .'

'Don't see the point of it really,' Logan says. 'Anyway, where are we going?'

I pull up in front of a small parade of shops where there also happens to be a chip shop. 'Here.'

The mood lifts considerably as, installed in a booth, we tuck into steaming platefuls of fish and chips. As we chat and giggle, eking out the pleasure of our unscheduled stop, it strikes me how lovely these unplanned events can be. You can feel as if you're losing your children as they grow up, shunning your attempts to help with revision and regarding you as if you're a particularly troublesome boil. Then there are occasions like this when, completely unexpectedly, you're drawn back into being a family again. It no longer seems to matter that my own mother thinks I'm a fat dimwit or that my sole date this year recommended four grand's worth of facial enhancements. Right now, it's just me and my boys all happy and stuffed with delicious fish and chips.

The day improves even further as we set off back to Edinburgh and pass a farm where some pigs are copulating, at which the boys shriek with laughter. It's moments like this, I always think, that a parent should cherish.

*

My mobile starts trilling as I let us into the flat.

'I've found someone!' Viv shrieks. 'Am I first? Bet I'm first . . .'

'You mean for our *thing*?' I hiss.

'Yes! Bet the others haven't found anyone yet . . .'

'Well, Kirsty called when I was at Mum's . . .' I turn towards Logan and Fergus who are regarding me with rapt interest. 'It's all right, boys, thank you. I'm just having a private conversation with Viv.'

'A *private conversation*,' Logan repeats mockingly as they slope off to their respective bedrooms. 'Bet that's thrilling.'

'Yes, we're discussing the best way to fold tea towels,' I call after him. 'God,' I mutter to Viv. 'I'll never be able to bring a man back here with those two policing me. I'll have to wait until Fergus leaves for uni.'

'How long away is that again?' she asks.

Heading for the relative privacy of the kitchen, I pull off my jacket which retains its fuggy smell from Mum's house, mingling with the vinegary tang of the chippie. 'Only five years. Half a decade. I'll be forty-four by then.'

'Isn't Tom taking the boys away soon?'

'Yes – on Thursday, when they break up. But I'm not planning to bring anyone back and jump on them the minute they're gone, Viv.'

'No,' she giggles, 'you'd better at least wait until his car's gone round the corner.'

'Camper van actually. He's hired some amazing, top-of-the-range model . . .'

'He's moved up in the world, hasn't he, from that leaky two-man Argos tent?'

'Yes, but he married well, remember . . .'

'There you go then,' she says triumphantly. 'You'll have an empty flat. Perfect opportunity.'

'For what?' I ask, laughing. 'I'm not planning to rush in, Viv.'

'Why not?'

Because it's too sodding traumatic, that's why. Because – if truth be known – I can barely remember which bits go where.

'I just want to take things slowly,' I say feebly.

'Hmm. So, who's Kirsty found for you? One of her beardy single-dad mates?'

'She didn't mention a beard,' I say with a smile, 'but, yes, he is a dad . . .'

65

'. . . Wears tie-dyed trousers, reeks of hummus . . .'

'Actually, he's a dentist.'

'Ugh. Not very sexy, is it?'

'What,' I say, 'being a dentist? I don't see why not.'

'Oh, you know,' Viv goes on. 'Cavities, plaque, poking about with other people's rotting molars . . .'

I shrug off my cardi, lay it on the kitchen table and frown at the greasy patches which have seeped through the pockets. There's a small lump in one of them; it's the Tuc biscuit diet, scrunched into a tight little ball.

'It was you who said I should keep an open mind,' I remind her.

'Well,' she says, 'I've a feeling mine'll be much more your type.'

'Not that this is a competition,' I tease.

'Of course it's not. God. It's all about *you*, not just cheap entertainment for us.'

I smirk and flick on the kettle.

'In fact, we've all had a chat,' Viv continues, 'and we decided that, no matter how much you like the first one, or the second, you still have to go out with all three of them just to be sure.'

'To give you all a fair chance of winning,' I remark with a grin.

'Yeah. No! Oh, you know what I mean. We feel it's important to follow the whole process right through to its conclusion.'

'Okay, so who d'you have in mind?'

Viv hangs off for a moment, in order to pique my interest. I picture her pacing around her small art-filled flat, drawing on a Marlboro Light. 'Okay – his name's Giles.'

'Sounds posh.'

'Well, he's not. At least, not especially. He's a new guy at work – cute, really fun, dark nicely cut hair and the most stunning blue eyes . . .'

'Wow,' I exclaim. 'And you're sure he's single?'

'Yes, absolutely.'

'And you said he's new . . .'

'Yeah.' Curiously, she has become a little reticent.

'Is he a designer?' I ask, faintly intrigued by the idea of someone who could give me tips on transforming our 'space'.

'Um . . . not exactly.'

I slosh boiling water into my mug – one hand-painted by Viv, incidentally, all cerise and gold swirls, almost too pretty to drink from. 'Is he in the accountants department?'

'Nooo . . .'

I blow out a big gust of air. 'Viv, listen, you know I don't care about job titles or how much someone earns. It really doesn't matter.'

'Yes, I know that,' she says.

'But you're actually being really cagey, which is a bit weird. I mean, if you like him and think we'd get along, that's fine – I don't care if he's the maintenance man . . .'

'He's the intern,' she interrupts.

'The intern?' I repeat. 'I can't meet the *intern*, Viv. God.'

'Why not? You just said you don't care about job titles.'

I'm laughing so much now, Fergus pokes his head around the kitchen door to see what's funny. 'I don't,' I say, grinning and waving him away. 'It's not that. It's about *age*.'

'But he's gorgeous,' she insists. 'He has amazing bone structure and great teeth . . .'

67

'Yes, well, milk teeth usually are.'

'Oh, for God's sake, he's not *that* young. Just meet him, have a drink, go to a movie or something . . .'

I pick up Mum's diet from the table and ping it in the vague direction of the bin. It bounces off it and lands on the floor which is currently littered with enormous, boat-like trainers and a smattering of orangey dust which I presume to be crushed Doritos.

'I'm not sure a movie's ideal for a first date,' I say, 'and I'm not really up for watching *American Pie* or the latest Pixar . . .'

'Alice, he's not a teenager. He's worked for years, done this and that – taught English, travelled, hung out in Ibiza for a while . . . he's a really interesting person.'

'I'm sure he is,' I reply, as a collection of gap year jewellery – leather thongs, yin yang symbols and the like – shimmers in my mind. God, I haven't even been to Ibiza; the whole clubbing thing passed me by. In my younger days I was happier installed in a pub with my mates and a load of crisps and beer.

'And he's always wanted to work in design,' she continues, 'so when his grandma died and he inherited some money, he decided to apply for an internship. He was so impressive at the interview, very *passionate* . . .'

'Were you orgasming at this point?' I enquire.

Viv snorts. 'I was a bit distracted, I have to admit. Anyway, it's a career change for him.'

'A change from what? Sitting on beaches and taking shitloads of drugs?'

'Stop that. He's serious about this. Hopefully he'll be taken on properly after a few months.'

I push back my dishevelled dark hair, detecting a faint chip-shop smell, and nibble a finger of Kit Kat that someone has left on the table. 'So how old *is* he?' I ask.

'Er . . . twenty-nine.'

'That's ten years younger than me, Viv. I'd feel like his auntie or something. Like he'd expect me to suggest a game of whist.'

'Don't be ridiculous. You're still *young*. Anyway, no one cares about age any more. Remember that half-your-age-plus-seven rule?'

I perform a swift calculation, rounding myself up to forty to avoid pesky fractions: 'Twenty-seven.'

'There you go then. He's comfortably within range . . .'

'Viv,' I say thoughtfully, 'why don't you ask him out? He sounds far more your type . . .'

'Because we work together,' she says in an overly patient voice. 'It'd be so awkward, especially with me technically being his boss.'

'Oh, of course. So have you mentioned me yet?'

'I might have casually said something,' she teases.

'But we only hatched this plan yesterday and you haven't been at work . . .'

'We had to finish off an advertising shoot this morning and he offered to help,' she says. 'He's very dedicated.'

'And, er . . . he's up for meeting me, is he? I mean . . . he knows I have two sons, and that one of them will be old enough to drive a car this time next year?'

'Yes, well, I didn't go into detail, but he knows you're a *bit* older and he was perfectly fine with that.'

I sip my tea. 'Listen, he's not one of those, "I love older women" types, is he? The kind who fantasised about his friend's mum or his well-preserved biology teacher . . .'

Viv honks with laughter.

'I'm not up for any of that creepy, "Oooh, you mature ladies, you know your onions" kind of crap,' I add firmly.

She laughs some more. 'I promise you, Giles will not be interested in your onions. He's not that kind of boy – I mean *man*.'

'Only just,' I chuckle.

'Well . . . yeah. So can I give him your number?'

'Sure,' I say, feeling suddenly, horribly conscious of my age, and spotting a whacking great frown line when I glimpse my reflection in the chrome kettle. Which, I fear, doesn't bode terribly well for the actual date.

Chapter Seven

To clear a backlog of filing I've done an extra hour at school, so the boys are home before me on this blustery Monday afternoon. I can hear jovial chatter, dominated by my neighbour Clemmie's booming tones, as I hurry upstairs to the flat. She is Logan's best mate Blake's mum, and often pops round to monitor the sorry state of my life. (Clemmie runs her own events management company and her husband Richard is something in property – he basically owns pretty much all of Scotland, as far as I can make out.)

'Hope you don't mind me dropping by,' she says with a red-lipped grin as Blake sips on a Coke and Stanley, her Cairn terrier, snuffles around my kitchen. Flaunting health and safety regulations, but never mind that.

'Of course not,' I say, noticing Logan's previously perky expression deflating, as if I have brought in something terrible stuck to my shoe. Why is it perfectly acceptable – *enjoyable*, even – to chat pleasantly with his best mate's mum, but not the woman who birthed him? (And whose body has – to be frank – never fully recovered. Apart from the obvious sagging of boobs, we are also talking a knackered old pelvic floor, plus outbreaks of piles – glamorous, I know – from time to time.) Fergus, meanwhile, is too busy chomping on a biscuit to pay much attention to anyone.

'D'you take milk, Clemmie?' Logan asks, in the process of making her a cup of tea. This is astounding. He has never made me a hot beverage; I've never been sure if he's capable of operating the kettle, to be honest. I have to clamp my mouth shut to stop myself from saying, *And thank you for my much-needed cup of tea, Logan.* Instead, I watch mutely as he shoves my raspberry cardi up to the end of the table – I'd laid it out to inspect the burger stain damage – and places the cup in front of her. 'Biscuit?' he asks, maturely.

'Yes please,' she replies. 'What do you have?'

'Only Rich Teas,' I cut in, at which Clemmie's enthusiasm wilts.

'Ah, I'll just leave it.' She pats an ample hip. 'Meant to be fasting today but I suppose, if you have some of your lovely meringues, I wouldn't say no . . .' She runs a tongue over her lips. 'I mean, they must be about ninety per cent air . . .'

'Here you go,' I say, offering her the tin with a smile.

'Thanks, darling. Yum. Anyway, the boys were just telling me about their visit to their grandma's . . .'

'Oh, yes. A bit trying as usual.'

'And I hear you had to intervene over lunch . . .' She laughs, causing her spectacular breasts to jiggle like crème caramels.

I take the seat beside her. 'Well, there was a bit of an incident with the Medieval burgers . . .'

'So I heard. Gosh, she's *such* a one-off.'

72

I chuckle uncomfortably, torn between my shameful feelings of irritation towards Mum, and a bizarre sense of loyalty.

'Anyway,' Clemmie goes on, indicating the small stack of magazines on the table, 'I've finished with these and thought they might give you a few ideas.'

'Great, thanks.' I eye the uppermost title: *Stylish Living*.

'But I'm really here to ask a favour,' she goes on, adjusting her plunging neckline. 'It's a bit of a rush, I'm afraid. You know I've been working on the Morgan relaunch . . .'

'Yes, you mentioned that.' The Morgan is a sprawling Edinburgh Hotel. For years, it looked rather decrepit – all faded tartan carpets with a depressed-looking bagpiper droning away under the wonky awning outside – but it has recently undergone a major overhaul, for which Clemmie is masterminding the launch party.

'Well, it occurred to me yesterday that it would be cute to have party bags,' she says, 'just like at a children's party – only ours would contain something people would actually want to eat. And I thought, Alice's meringues! The client thinks it's a fantastic idea.'

'Sounds great,' I say. 'So what were you thinking of?'

'Those cute little ones you do in cellophane bags.'

'Meringue kisses . . .'

'Yes, those. They're *delicious*. I was thinking five flavours in each bag, and I'll need three hundred bags . . . could you do that by Wednesday morning?'

I frown, figuring out the logistics. 'This Wednesday? Like, the day after tomorrow?'

'That's right. I know it's a rush . . .' She smooths the front of her rose-pattered wrap dress – Clemmie is never knowingly underdressed – while I perform a quick calculation: thirty meringues per tray, six trays per bake. That's, um . . . eight bakes in total at an hour each . . . Christ, it's doable – just.

'That's fine,' I say, wishing Mum could have witnessed how speedily I worked that out.

'What would you charge for that?' Clemmie asks.

'Er . . . well, a bag of five kisses usually sells at around three pounds but that's retail, of course. I normally do them for one pound fifty . . .'

'Four hundred and fifty quid for three hundred bags,' chips in Blake.

'God, that's loads, Mum,' Logan says, appearing to warm to me a little. 'You could get me an iPad.'

I laugh dryly, momentarily distracted as Stanley starts sniffing at my cardigan sleeve, which happens to be dangling down from the table.

'That's not enough,' Clemmie retorts. 'The consortium that owns the Morgan has more cash than you can imagine. What they're spending on the party alone would make your hair curl. You need to charge more – how about six hundred pounds?'

'Wow,' I gasp. 'For *meringues*? Are you sure?'

'That sounds good,' Logan barks greedily.

He's right, though. This order alone could make the difference to us having a summer holiday this year – perhaps the last one with the three of us all together.

'Absolutely,' Clemmie says as Stanley starts barking fretfully. 'Shush, Stan. Stop that. Anyway,' she goes on, 'let's talk flavours, shall we?'

'Sure. How about rose water, orange water, that sort of thing?'

'Hmm, flower waters . . . sounds lovely. In fact a whole spring-like, blossomy feel would be great . . .'

'Violet is pretty,' I suggest, 'and a primrosey shade would look . . .' I stop abruptly as my cardi, which until now had been lying as still as you'd expect an item of knitwear to be, starts jerking to our left along the table. It's moving faster now – so quickly, in fact, that Clemmie and I can only gawp as Stanley, who must have snatched a dangling sleeve, sets about savaging it on the floor.

'Stanley, no!' I shriek, leaping from my seat while Clemmie, who's gushing apologies amidst hysterical laughter from the three boys, tries to yank it from her dog's jaws.

'Stanley, *drop*,' she commands.

'He's eating your best cardi, Mum,' Logan says cheerfully.

'Yes, I can see that . . .'

'He's chewing it to bits!'

'I don't want to rip it any more by pulling it,' Clemmie cries. 'God, Alice, I feel terrible.'

'Drop, Stan. DROP!' Fergus commands.

'Oh, he won't,' Blake says loftily. 'Tug of war's his favourite game, this is *fun* to him . . .'

Clemmie is pulling at it now, using her considerable strength to stretch my cashmere treasure about four feet long. Letting it drop, she bobs down to her knees and expertly prises open Stanley's jaws.

'There. Naughty dog. Honestly, he's never done anything like that before.' She picks up my cardi and examines it. 'He's actually bitten off both of the pockets. Where did you buy it? I'll replace it as soon as I can . . .'

'It's years old,' I say quickly, 'and I hid Mum's burgers in the pockets and hadn't got around to washing it—'

'God, Alice, your *life*,' Clemmie splutters. 'Are you sure I can't buy you a new one?'

75

'No, don't be silly.'

Planting a hand on a hip, Clemmie throws Stanley an exasperated look. 'Well, if you're sure. Anyway, I'm so glad you can do those meringues for me. I'll leave the final flavour choices up to you. And you must come over for lunch in the Easter holidays.'

'Thanks, I'd love to,' I say.

'You can see what we've been doing to the house.'

'Oh yes, Blake mentioned he's getting a new bedroom . . .'

'It's an *annexe*, Mum,' Logan corrects me, 'with enough space for a full-sized pool table.'

'An annexe?' I repeat. 'You mean an extension?'

'Yeah! It's got a little kitchen and everything, with a mini fridge and an oven . . .'

'An oven?' I repeat with a laugh. 'What are you planning to do, Blake? Make Victoria sponges?'

'Nah, just, like, pasta and stuff,' he says with a shrug.

Clemmie smiles. 'It's not an extension, darling. It's just the loft conversion we started in the autumn. It's taken forever to get it right, and cost a small fortune, but we felt it was time Blake had his own space. And the idea of the kitchen is it's a trial run for fully independent living. I don't want him living on takeaways when he leaves home, not with their salt content.' Yes, but couldn't he learn to cook in the family kitchen?

Blake smirks and looks down at his feet.

'He's having the *whole upper floor*, Mum,' Logan adds. 'It's like a flat, all to himself.'

'Sounds great,' I say.

Summoning the now obedient Stanley to heel, Clemmie turns to her son. 'You coming home for dinner, darling?'

'In a bit,' he replies.

'He's welcome to stay and eat with us,' I say, at which Blake looks genuinely delighted.

'Thanks, you're a darling.' Clemmie flashes a bright smile before clip-clopping down the stone stairs, with Stanley at her side and a cloud of freesia fragrance in her wake.

Alone now in the kitchen, I drop my ravaged cardigan into the bin.

*

Blake Carter-Jones is the boy who has everything. My eyes watered when Clemmie let slip how much she shells out for his clothing allowance, *and* he's never dragged halfway across Scotland to his grandma's to be presented with rotting beef. However, he does seem to be extremely fond of our place, despite his palatial abode at the end of our street, which is pleasing. He also shames my own, slothful offspring by loading the dishwasher after dinner *and* wiping the table while I get cracking with the meringues.

By the time the third batch is in the oven, the flat is engulfed in a sweet-smelling blur. In need of a breather, I run myself a bath. Generously, Fergus had left one millimetre of the L'Occitane Relaxing Bath Oil Ingrid gave me (Ingrid is incredibly generous on the posh present front), so I squirt in the pathetic remaining drops. Why does Fergus use it anyway? A thirteen-year-old boy doesn't need essence of geranium and tea tree, not when his entire *life* is relaxed.

Into the bath I sink, with a large glass of wine carefully placed in the little porcelain indent, meant for soap. If I were doing this properly there should be scented candles flickering in here too, but I've brought in one of Clemmie's *Stylish Living* magazines and need decent light because, actually, I could do with reading glasses. (Shall I mention this to the intern on our date? Should I also inform him that Abba were at number one with 'Waterloo' when I was born?) Luckily, our bathroom is so bright, you could perform surgery in here. On the downside, it's hardly flattering to one's naked form, cruelly illuminating every dimple and vein.

Inhaling the sugary aroma drifting in through the gap under the door, I start to flip through the mag. Here we go: an impossibly beautiful living room with pale-grey walls – a shade which would look cell-like if I were to use it, but which in this instance is the height of tastefulness. There's a darker grey sofa, scattered with cushions in fuchsia and lime, and an elegant wooden seventies-style coffee table on which sits a small stack of jewel-coloured silk notebooks.

Who lives like this? Even Clemmie's place, with its five bedrooms and two lounges – the annexe – looks a bit scruffy around the edges sometimes, despite her gargantuan efforts to keep it tidy (not to mention a cleaner three times a week). Now, I know homes magazines have stylists to make everything beautiful, but *still*. I'd thought a glimpse of perfection might offer some welcome respite, seeing as I'll be up baking until at least two a.m., but instead it's drawing my attention to the almighty clutter of the boys' Clearasil washes and scrubs and lotions which are crammed on to the single shelf, plus, I notice now, a small white cloth with a brown smear on it tucked behind the loo. I'm not a high maintenance woman, and I like to think my tolerance levels are pretty high. But from where I'm lying – in this rapidly cooling bath – it would appear that someone has nabbed my Liz Earle Hot Cloth muslin square and wiped their arse on it. Dear God – they're *teenagers*, shouldn't the wanton destruction of my possessions have stopped by now? Maybe Erica had a point all those months ago when she looked alarmed by the concept of parenting boys. But they're not all like that, smashing Danish glassware and using their mother's sole face cloth because they're too bloody lazy to reach for the cupboard where the loo roll is kept. Look at Blake, wiping down kitchen surfaces. Where have I gone wrong?

I glare back at the magazine, in which no less than ten pages are devoted to the stunning country home. Naturally, the garden is just the right side of wild, with cornflowers and poppies running rampant all over the place. 'We designed our haphazard planting scheme to say, "Chill out and kick back on the lawn with us",' the caption reads. I glance at our bathroom windowsill where Fergus's beleaguered cactus sits in its red plastic pot. We don't *design* a planting scheme, we win it at the school tombola (along with a bottle of Lulu perfume which had actually gone off), and if it's saying anything, it's, 'For Christ's sake, dust me.'

I flick my gaze back to the mag. 'Patsy grows fresh herbs to add zing to spontaneous suppers with friends', it goes on. Well, good for Patsy. My own children are primed to reject suspect greenery; they can detect the snipping of parsley even from a different room. My heart slumps even further as I study my unpainted toenails poking out of the water. *Spontaneous suppers.* How long is it since I had one of those? Or a spontaneous anything, come to that? As I work school hours, five days a week, I tend to resort to that deeply unsexy thing of Planning

Ahead. As a tactic, it works, in that the three of us generally wind up with something edible on the table at dinnertime. At least, Blake seems to enjoy my offerings. But I can't deny it's slightly joyless, knowing you'll be eating lasagne in five days' time.

I also batch-cook. How terribly . . . loin-stirring. I must remember to tell Giles-the-intern about my sessions with a steaming vat of bolognaise when we meet. That'll get him all revved up – at least, if he nurtures secret dinner-lady fantasies.

In another photo, pastel-coloured bunting is strewn across the perfect garden, and a little blonde girl in a white dress is playing with a syrup-coloured spaniel. Bet *he* doesn't devour his owner's knitwear. 'It's a gorgeous spring afternoon', reads the text, 'as Patsy Lomax, founder of sleepwear company Dandelion . . .'

PATSY LOMAX??? It can't be. But it is – it's my ex Tom's wife Patsy who grows herbs for spontaneous suppers, and the little girl in the garden is their daughter, Jessica. That's their rose-strewn home, and their silk-covered notebooks artfully arranged on the coffee table. I flip through more pages, studying each photo in forensic detail, until I reach the final page of the never-ending extravaganza and here he is – Tom, no less, who'd happily inhabit the same ratty Smiths T-shirt for three days running when we were together, and would use our car keys to pick out dirt from between his toes while we were watching TV. Tom, who could barely operate a can opener without severing an artery, is now depicted wearing a chunky cableknit sweater, plus jeans and suspiciously pristine wellies, clutching an armful of veggies: curly kale, purple sprouting broccoli and some particularly knobbly-looking carrots.

'Tom's kitchen garden evolves with the seasons' runs the caption beneath.

I explode with laughter and sling the magazine on to the bathroom floor. Tom, cultivating legumes, when he used to refer to salad as 'women's food' and had never knowingly ingested a tomato. Still sniggering, I clamber out of the bath and wrap myself in a large towel with all the softness of a gravel driveway, then snatch a bit of loo roll to give the cactus a cursory wipe. Maybe it'll start *evolving* now. Perhaps vivid pink flowers will burst forth, like the tombola lady promised. Then I brush out my hair and pull on pyjamas and a dressing gown in readiness for baking the fifth meringue batch of the evening.

As I emerge from the bathroom, Blake is lacing up his trainers in the hallway (this boy even removes his footwear on entering someone's house) while Logan fixes me with a stare.

'Why can't we extend our place?' he enquires.

'Because it's a flat,' I reply pleasantly.

'Is there *nothing* we could do?'

I blink at my son, aware of Blake straightening up and smirking at us. 'Well,' I reply, 'I suppose we could build a kind of sticky-out construction that pokes out over the street, like a giant shelf, and you could live on that.'

Grunting with mirth, Blake remarks, 'You're lucky, Logan. At least your mum's not always on at you like mine is. She's not obsessed with the house being perfect . . .'

'Thank you, Blake,' I say, wondering whether to take this as a compliment or not.

He grins. 'Thanks for dinner' is his parting remark. When he's gone, I turn back to Logan, hoping to see a

81

glimmer of a smile, or some realisation of how petulant he's being.

'I'm fed up with this place,' he sighs.

'Logan, you do have your own room. The biggest room, in fact.'

'There's not even a TV in it.'

'So what?' I counter. 'There's one in the living room that you have virtually free rein of. I hardly ever watch it.'

'You watch *Casablanca* all the time . . .'

I blink at him, trying to keep a lid on the irritation that's bubbling inside me. What is wrong with him these days? Why is he being so foul, and is it likely to stop anytime soon?

'I happen to watch it about once a year at the very most,' I inform him.

Fergus has appeared now, and is warming to the 'teasing Mum about her old movies' theme.

'There's that bit,' he says, 'when the guy says, "We'll always have Paris"—'

'And that's when you start crying,' Logan adds. With that, they both bark with laughter, and I stomp to my bedroom, reminding myself that I'm not one of those obsessives who sits glued to the same movie night after night, with a bunch of sodden tissues on her lap. Honestly – I only watch *Casablanca* about once a year, usually around Christmas time. Well, maybe twice. And, anyway, what business is it of theirs?

In the kitchen, I set to work, switching on the radio and cracking eggs until, gradually, my irritation begins to subside. At least Blake likes it here, I remind myself, so it can't be that bad. As I pipe tray after tray of rosette-shaped kisses, I decide I don't care that Tom has managed to grab himself a magazine-style life. Bet that picture was staged

anyway, and someone brought along those gnarly vegetables that Tom was clutching lovingly to his manly chest.
Anyway, it's not as if I'd be happier if he were huddled
in a miserable bedsit, warming his hands on a Pot Noodle;
it was my decision to split, which has caused me no small
amount of guilt over the years, and Patsy has been good
for Tom. Somehow, she has managed to realise his potential. It's a pretty safe bet that he no longer turns his boxer
shorts inside out so he can eke an extra day's wear out
of them.

I've just filled the oven with another batch of trays when
my phone bleeps – a text from an unknown number. *Hi
Alice*, it reads, *Giles here, I work with Viv. Hope ok to
get in touch. Wondered if you fancy a drink sometime?*

Hell, why not? Tomorrow I'll be finishing off the
meringues – at least, doing the packing and labelling –
and it's the boys' last night with me before their trip
with Tom, not that Logan will regard that as anything
significant, but still . . . I pause before replying, wondering
whether to play down my commitments, or to be honest
from the start. After all, Viv has told him I have kids.
No point in trying to pretend I'm just back from my gap
year travels . . .

Sounds good, I reply. *Maybe Wed eve as my boys are
going away with their dad . . .*

No, no, no! *So we can come back here and have
rampant sex*, it implies. Jesus. I delete it, typing instead:
Would Wed eve suit you, about 8?

Great, he replies. *Will call you Gxx.*

Two kisses? Seems rather forward, although I find
myself smiling all the same.

83

Chapter Eight

By Tuesday evening, Clemmie's meringues are ready to go. With no help from Logan, I might add – although Fergus has spent about ten minutes carefully packaging a few tiny, pastel-coloured kisses into clear cellophane bags, and boy-hero Blake has hand-written the labels in beautiful calligraphy script. It's almost eerie, a sixteen-year-old boy being able to write legibly, let alone scripting '*Handmade for the Morgan Hotel by Sugar Mummy*' on three hundred tiny buff-coloured labels. I'd be no more surprised if his next task was to perform a complex medical procedure on a human eye.

'They look great,' I enthuse as Fergus, Blake and I set about attaching the labels to the cellophane bags while Logan hovers around in a supervisory role.

'You should pay him, Mum,' Fergus suggests.

'Don't be stupid,' Blake replies, 'I like doing stuff like that', while Logan guffaws as if he's just admitted to a love of embroidery. It's gone ten p.m. when the boys help me to carry the filled boxes up the street to Clemmie's.

'These are amazing,' she exclaims. 'God – the colours. So pretty! And the dusting of glitter on the lilac ones . . .'

'Blake's been a huge help,' I tell her. 'He did the lettering for all the labels.'

'Well, he is very artistic,' she says with a trace of pride, as it strikes me that perhaps I don't boast about my own sons enough. Of course, I adore my boys; we are a gang, the three of us – yet so often I seem to fixate on small annoyances. I'd hate to think I'm turning into someone who puts down her kids, like Mum and her, 'Ooh – you'll be glad I gave you that diet' remarks.

'You will come to the party tomorrow night?' Clemmie says, handing me a glass of wine which I accept gratefully.

'You mean the Morgan do?'

'Yes, I've put your name down with a plus one . . .'

'Oh, I'm sorry – I've got something on.'

'Where are you going, Mum?' Fergus asks.

'Just out,' I say lightly, feeling my cheeks burning. I'd tell Clemmie, of course I would – she is always amused by my occasional dating forays, and I'm grateful that at least someone derives entertainment from them. But the boys are aware that I was out with Fat-Tongue Man a mere four days ago, and I don't want them to think I've become *frenzied*.

'Who with?' Fergus wants to know.

'Er, just a friend of Viv's,' I reply, relieved when the conversation swerves to the forthcoming party with its live music, vast seafood bar and savoury lollipop canapés. And by the time we're getting ready to leave, I'm in pretty high spirits.

'So you boys are off on a week's holiday tomorrow,' Clemmie says as she sees us out.

'Yeah,' Logan murmurs.

'Hmm.' She smirks. 'Off the leash, eh, Alice? God knows what kind of debauchery you'll be getting up to.' At that, everyone sniggers for slightly too long. Is it really that funny, the idea of me doing something a little bit . . . well, not debauched exactly, but just for fun?

'She'll be having the *girls* round,' Logan quips as we step out into the cool spring night.

'What'll you do really?' Fergus asks as we head home.

'Oh, just the usual. Bit of batch-cooking, catch up on a few jobs around the flat . . .'

While his brother strides ahead, Fergus ambles along at my side. 'I'll actually miss you, Mum.'

'I'll miss you too,' I reply, only just managing not to take his hand. 'It won't be the same without you.'

'Well,' he adds with a sly grin, 'you can always phone me if you get *really* lonely and depressed.'

*

School breaks up for Easter next day, meaning an early finish for me and the boys. Yet, although we're all home by three, I'm wishing now that Tom and Patsy were picking up the boys tomorrow so it wasn't so horribly rushed. As it is, Tom has already called en route to say they've passed Carlisle and should be with us by four. That gives me forty-five minutes. Christ.

To explain, I'm not usually a terribly appearance-focused person, as Botox-Anthony would testify. My hair, which is long and dark brown, is usually pulled up into a topknot affair, in the hope that its messiness will be interpreted as 'artfully undone' and not a complete state. As for daily beautification, we're generally talking a speedy lick of brown mascara and tinted lip balm. (Unless we're visiting my mother, in which case I'll do my eyes properly – old school, using all three shades of an eye shadow trio, in the hope that it'll detract from the size of my arse.) And there you have it. Except on the rare occasions when Tom and Patsy are coming, when we're talking a level of grooming generally enjoyed only by a dressage horse.

So, while the boys gather together the last of their things, I apply a full face of make-up and give my hair a quick spritz and blow-dry. I even dig out a rather glitzy top to wear with my newest jeans. Why go to such lengths? Well, there's the date with Giles, of course, but that's hours away (and, to be honest, I'd rather not dress up too much for such a young pup in case it hints at middle-aged desperation). No, I am ashamed to admit that my efforts are entirely for Tom and Patsy's benefit – to show that, even though my home is unlikely to feature in *Stylish Living* magazine, I am still capable of looking presentable.

I'm just slicking on some *extra* lipstick in the bathroom mirror when I remember my tainted cleansing cloth lying behind the loo. I pick it up delicately, by its sole clean corner; it really does look as if someone's wiped their bum on it. Why would anyone do this? Perhaps I'm more uptight than I've realised about the boys going away, because before I know it I'm marching furiously to the kitchen with the cloth dangling between thumb and forefinger. I know, too, that it's ridiculous to snatch a clear plastic freezer bag from a drawer, drop the sullied cloth into it and tie it up with a little wire bag tie, then grab a leftover blank meringue label and write in big bold capital letters: EXHIBIT A.

'Can you tell me what this is please?' I'm in the living room now, dangling the bag in front of Logan and Fergus who gaze up at it from the sofa.

Fergus frowns. 'I thought you'd bought us a goldfish for a minute.'

'No, it's not a goldfish,' I reply.

'I can see that. What is it – a dirty hankie? Why've you got it in a bag?'

Logan gives it a quick glance before flicking his eyes back to the screen where David Attenborough has encountered a baby rhino on an African plain. 'Is it an oily rag?' he murmurs.

'Why would I have an oily rag in a bag, Logan?'

He shrugs. 'Dunno. Maybe you've been fixing the washing machine or something?'

'It's neither of those things,' I start. 'It's my special cleansing cloth.'

'What?' Logan mutters, eyes fixed on the screen.

'For cleaning my face. Except now it appears to have poo on it.'

Fergus narrows his eyes and peers up at it. 'Oh yeah.'

'Yes, exactly, so could you tell me who did it?'

'Not me,' he says firmly.

Logan shakes his head. 'Nah.'

'The thing is,' I say, knowing it's the wrong time to get into this, but unable to stop myself, 'it's just not fair, boys, using my things without asking . . .'

'So if I'd *asked* if I could wipe my bum on your cloth, that would've been okay?' Logan chortles.

'Oh, so it was you!'

'No! No, I just mean . . . hypothetically.' On TV, the baby rhino is making an endearing squeaking noise.

'Can't you just get another one?' Fergus asks.

'It's not as simple as that.'

'Why not?'

'Because it came with the . . .' I tail off as David Attenborough explains, in his lovely mellow voice, that the baby rhino is blind and desperately needs a cataract operation. And here I am, banging on about a sodding scrap of muslin . . .

'What, Mum?' Fergus asks distractedly, eyes glued to the screen.

The doorbell buzzes. 'Nothing, love.' I swallow hard, blinking rapidly in the hope that that'll clear my vision, which is fuzzing rapidly as my eyes fill with tears.

Fergus turns to me with a solemn gaze. 'You've upset, Mum,' he snaps at Logan.

'No I haven't. What have I done? I'm just sitting here, watching TV!'

'*Hypothetically,*' Fergus mocks him as the doorbell buzzes again.

'That'll be Dad at the door,' Logan offers. Without further discussion, and dabbing my eyes on my sleeve, I leave the room, furious with myself at getting upset over a stupid cloth at the precise moment when my carrot-cultivating ex is standing on the pavement outside. Phone, front door – it's my duty to answer these, like a butler. Sometimes I think I should wear white gloves and carry a little silver tray. Not right now, though, as here comes Tom, all smiles and lush, wavy dark hair, still looking irritatingly youthful as if preserved in aspic; followed by Patsy, tastefully high-lighted with apparently no make-up at all, and smelling fresh, like a spring meadow. There are hugs all round, and Jessica, who's just turned four, very sweetly plants a kiss on my cheek.

'What's that?' she asks. I realise I'm still clutching Exhibit A.

'Oh, just a bit of dirty material, love.'

She fixes me with wide blue eyes. 'Why's it in a bag?'

'Um, I was just about to put it in the bin. Anyway, come on through to the kitchen, there's a fresh batch of meringues waiting for you. I'll just put the kettle on . . . Boys, are you pretty much ready to go?' There's nodding and mumbling as they drift off to fetch their rucksacks.

'You look great, Alice,' Patsy says, while Tom grabs a meringue from the towering stack on the table.

'Thanks,' I say, 'so do you. So, how are things? How's the business going?' As she fills me in on Dandelion's latest triumphs, Logan reappears, grabbing and tickling Jessica, making her squeal with delight. It warms my heart to see him making a fuss over his adorable little sister.

'We're lucky,' Patsy tells me, sipping the mint tea she requested. 'We've had lots of great publicity and Tom's brilliant on the creative side. Things are going better than we could have expected . . .'

'I saw you in *Stylish Living*,' I say with a grin.

'Oh, that,' Tom blusters, cheeks flushing instantly.

'It was through a friend of a friend,' Patsy adds. 'Just a great plug for the company. We'd never have done it otherwise . . .'

And how is *the purple sprouting broccoli?* I want to ask Tom, but manage to restrain myself.

'Well, I think you've done it all brilliantly,' I tell Patsy. It's true: in flogging pyjamas, she has somehow managed to sell the very essence of a perfect childhood. It's all about walking in the woods, and coming home rosy-cheeked to feast on buttered crumpets at the fireside. In Dandelion world, no one wipes their arse on a Liz Earle cleansing cloth.

'Honestly,' she says, casting her beloved a fond glance, 'I couldn't have done it without Tom.'

'And your house looked amazing in the magazine. I never realised . . .'

'Oh, it's a wreck really. It's incredible what they can do in photos.' Patsy emits sparkly laughter and I sense that vein again, throbbing urgently in my neck.

'I've told you loads of times how nice it is,' Fergus says.

'. . . But she wasn't listening,' Logan quips, causing everyone to laugh. 'Anyway, Jessie, are you looking forward to sleeping in the camper van?' He knows full well that Patsy prefers people not to shorten Jessica's name.

'Yeah,' she grins at him. 'I'm getting the best bed.'

'No you're not,' he teases, 'I am.' She squeals with laughter as Logan starts to chase her around the kitchen table, deftly grabbing a pink meringue from the plate as she hurtles by.

'God, these are good, Alice,' Tom says with a full mouth. 'Nice and fruity, not too sweet . . .'

'Oh, don't let Jessica have that!' Patsy blurts out, scuttling towards them.

'But they're yummy,' her daughter exclaims.

'Jessica, you've had one already . . .'

'I haven't!' she roars, still gripping the meringue as Patsy swipes it from her grasp. I glance at Tom, who is expressing rapt interest in the view from the kitchen window as if he's never been here before.

'Mummy-I-want-a-meringue . . .' Jessica's face crumples.

'I'm sorry, darling, but you can't have it.' Patsy gives me a firm smile. 'It's just, you know – the sugar.'

'Oh, I thought just one might be okay . . .'

'I'd rather not. She's very young. It's . . .' She pulls a terse little smile. 'Her teeth.'

'Of course, yes.' Sensing my cheeks burning, as if I've been caught offering her cocaine, I glance down at Jessica who is crying heartily now, despite Logan wrapping a conciliatory arm around her shoulders and Fergus trying to show her his translator.

'We've got some banana bread in the car,' Patsy offers, her face creased into a frown.

'Don't want banana bread . . .'

'Darling.' Patsy bobs down to Jessica's level. 'It's your favourite, I made it specially for you yesterday—'

'DON'T WANT BANANA BREAD!' she shrieks, mouth crumpling, fresh tears springing from her eyes.

'Jessica,' her mother snaps, 'stop this.' She stands up and turns to me. 'I'm so sorry, Alice. She doesn't normally behave like this. She's probably just tired after the drive . . .'

'It's fine,' I say, placing the offending plate of meringues on a high shelf while Patsy whisks Jessica off to the loo.

Tom clears his throat. 'Patsy's just a bit, y'know . . . careful about what Jessica eats.'

'So I see.'

'They *are* delicious, though,' he adds with an apologetic smile. 'So how's your business going?'

'Not bad. To be honest, I have as many orders as I can cope with while still having a life . . .'

'And how is, um . . . *life*?'

I shrug. 'It's fine, Tom.'

'Seeing anyone just now?' he asks lightly.

With a small laugh, I reach for a rose-flavoured meringue from the plate. 'When you say life, you mean love life, right?'

He laughs awkwardly. 'Just curious.'

'Well, there's nothing to report,' I say firmly. 'So anyway, d'you reckon you'll get to Skye tomorrow?'

'That's the plan. I hope the boys have a good time. How d'you think they'll be?'

'You mean, trapped in a camper van for a week?' I chuckle. 'I've no idea, Tom. I think Fergus will enjoy it but Logan's so hard to predict these days . . .'

'He's great with Jessica, though,' Tom murmurs, as if to reassure himself.

'I know he is. They both adore her – you know that.' I drop my voice to a murmur. 'Is Patsy okay about this trip?'

'Oh, yes, she hasn't seen much of Scotland.' That's not what I meant, and he knows it; I meant spending a week in a van with one pubescent boy and one hairy, almost fully formed adult man.

'Hon? Shall we get going soon?' Patsy has reappeared in the doorway, clutching Jessica's hand.

'Yep, s'pose we'd better,' Tom murmurs.

'Boys,' I call out, 'are you ready?'

'Yeah,' Fergus replies, and both appear with stuffed rucksacks. Jessica still looks crestfallen, and I'd love to sneak her a contraband meringue to cheer her up.

'Great to see you, Alice,' Patsy says in an overly bright voice. 'Sorry it's such a quick visit but we want to be up in Fort William before dark . . .'

It will be dark, but never mind. Perhaps suspecting that no one is paying attention, Jessica reaches up towards the meringue plate, but is tugged away by her mother as if she were about to plunge her hand into a fire. I catch Logan's eye as he picks up his rucksack; there's a glimmer of amusement in his eyes, and I smile back. Then we're all heading downstairs, laden with bags, and I should be joyous at the prospect of much tranquillity ahead, punctuated by at least one date. But I'm not. I'm hugging them all – first Logan, who goes stiff and awkward, then Fergus, who hugs me back in his gangly way, as if his arms have come loose in their sockets.

'C'mon, Jessie,' Logan says, frowning at her tear-blotched face, 'cheer up. This is gonna be fun.' She musters a stoical smile as they all clamber into the palatial camper van.

They are waving with the windows down – even Logan, who never waves at anyone. A lump forms in my throat as I stand there, feeling stranded, in our street. I know it's silly, and that my boys aren't babies any more, so I should feel *fine* about them leaving. Last week, Fergus packed up all his soft toys for charity – even beloved Rex, a small, grubby white dog with no obvious appeal (instead of being furry, in approximation of a real dog, he has the unsettling texture of 40-denier tights). But I can't help it. My vision is blurring again and I'm blinking madly, hoping that'll force the tears back in. Meanwhile Tom tries not to look petrified as he slowly manoeuvres the gigantic vehicle out of its tight parking space.

I give them a final wave and turn away, just as Patsy's voice drifts out of the passenger window: 'Alice is always so kind, Tom, but I *wish* she wouldn't try to stuff Jessica full of sugar.'

Chapter Nine

That's my role, you see – to destroy the dental enamel of every child who enters my home. In fact, Logan and Fergus have zero fillings, a fact I cling on to as evidence of my brilliant parenting when it's probably nothing to do with me. Both Tom and his father have rather large, sparkling, filling-less teeth, the kind that seem wasted not being on TV.

In order to shrug off Patsy's comment, I try to focus on the fact that I have a whole child-free week ahead of me. In sixteen years I have never had such a thing, and the prospect is at once thrilling yet faintly alarming. What the hell will I do with myself? I can see friends, of course, and bake; I can catch up on niggling jobs and, more crucially, go out with a man who just sneaks over the half-your-age-plus-seven boundary, a concept which causes my stomach to fizzle with excitement and nerves. What would Mum say about that? She'd probably remind me that twenty-something girls tend to have fabulous figures, and that perhaps I should give up on eating anything at all.

Stomach rumbling now, I make cheese on toast and a pot of tea and tuck in at the kitchen table, picturing Tom at the helm of that camper van. While he looked rather scared, he was still managing to put on a show of being a big, capable, 'taking my family away on an adventure' type-dad. When we were together, he couldn't even drive; he passed his test when Patsy was pregnant with Jessica. That's probably around the time he learnt how to grow kale when, a couple of years previously, he wouldn't have recognised it if it had bitten him on the bum. There's a definite pattern here, i.e. Tom-with-me = useless lump, often forgetting to flush the lavatory. Whereas Tom-with-Patsy = superhero dad. And while I'm not fond of women blaming themselves for men's foibles, you have to consider the facts. Patsy always seems to be *completely delighted* with Tom. I've never known any woman to be so pleased with her husband, all of the time. Was it me who somehow drained the potential out of him?

I finish my tea, feeling a little anchorless now with two hours to go before I'm due to meet Giles. My phone rings; seeing Kirsty's name displayed cheers me up instantly.

'So, have they gone?' she asks.

'Yeah.'

'A whole week to yourself. God, you're lucky. I'd *kill* for that.'

I bite my lip. 'It feels a bit weird, to be honest. I'm redundant, completely without purpose . . .' We both laugh, because I *am* joking, sort of. 'Anyway,' I add, 'what are you up to in the holidays?'

Kirsty sighs loudly. 'Business as usual around here. That's the thing with home educating – they're *here*, all the time, with me. Holidays don't actually exist for us.'

'Isn't Dan taking some time off work?'

'Says he can't. Too much on. The financial industry would crumble without him being ever-present . . .'

'Well, I think you're brilliant,' I say firmly. 'I couldn't do it. I'm in awe of you.'

She snorts. 'Well, I have no intention of doing this beyond primary, you know.'

'Really?' I'm taken aback by her frankness. 'I thought you and Dan felt really strongly—'

'*He* does,' she cuts in. 'He's the one who's adamant that the kids shouldn't go anywhere near a dastardly classroom, that it would crush their spirit and ruin their souls. D'you know he's started referring to schools as *child-prisons*?'

'Oh, for God's sake,' I splutter.

She laughs dryly. 'I know I was all for it at the start, but only because of all the bullying Hamish went through at that school of his. I was so put off by the whole system, and the teachers being unwilling to do anything about it, that I really thought it was for the best. I didn't want Alfie and Maya to go through all that.'

'Yes,' I say, 'and maybe it was the best option at that point . . .'

'But it was only meant to be temporary,' Kirsty goes on, as what sounds like a brawl kicks off in the background, 'only now, Dan's adamant that it's best for *all* of them and that's it.' She pauses. 'Alfie, put that hammer back in Daddy's tool drawer right now.'

'It's not a hammer,' he retorts. 'It's a *mallet*.'

I sip my tepid tea, wondering how best to respond. 'Maybe it's time to be firmer,' I suggest. 'It has to be mainly your decision – I mean, you're the one doing it all.'

'I've tried and he won't hear of it. He seems reluctant to even discuss it.'

'Okay, but what happens if you want to go back to work?'

'I do actually,' she retorts. 'You know, sometimes I could cry with envy when Dan sets off to the office, and when he moans about colleagues, and how tedious it all is, I could shake him and say, "Okay, shall we swap places then? I'll go out and do the paid job, surrounded by adults and with a proper lunch hour, while you try to help three children, all at different levels, with their reading, when all they want to do is run about in the garden and throw soil."' She stops, catching her breath.

'I don't blame you at all. I'd feel exactly the same.' It's frustrating, actually, seeing my friend trapped into the home educating scenario like this, and I have to bite my tongue to stop myself blurting out what I really think of Dan. Glimpsing Exhibit A sitting in its plastic bag on top of the fridge, I quickly drop it into the bin. Although it's been months since Erica's home inspection, I can't shake off the fear that she might pop around again at any time.

Kirsty sighs loudly. 'Oh, never mind all that. Has my lovely dentist called you?'

'No, not yet, but I am seeing Giles tonight – Viv's intern . . .'

'Oh, she mentioned him,' she exclaims. 'Why didn't you say? I shouldn't be wittering on. You should be getting ready . . .'

'I *am* ready,' I say with a smile, not adding that my readiness was in fact for the benefit of Tom and Patsy. 'At least, as ready as I'll ever be.'

'Not having second thoughts, are you?'

I pause. 'Not really – I mean, it's only a drink – but, you know. He's *twenty-nine*, for Christ's sake . . .'

'Come on,' she says, not unkindly. 'It'll be fun if nothing else. Off you go and tell me all about it.'

We finish the call, and I wonder if it's actually the magazine feature that's sapped my enthusiasm today – the fact that Tom and Patsy's sofa deserved two full pages in a glossy magazine, whereas ours came from one of those out-of-town stores where everything seems to be permanently fifty per cent off. It has long lost its springiness, due to years of being pummelled by the boys – a bit like my face, I decide, catching my reflection in the mirror in the hall. As I study my wrinkles, Patsy's face shimmers into my mind: rosy-cheeked, line-free, no spiky roller required there. She probably just sprinkles her complexion with morning dew.

I head for my bedroom, trying to push such dark thoughts away. For someone who spends much of her life handling vast quantities of sugar, I seem to be turning awfully bitter.

*

I leave to meet Giles a little early, just to escape from the flat. I stroll past the fancy interiors shops, and the posh French deli with its artisan breads and chocolate cubes on sticks that you dunk in hot milk – the ones Clemmie always seems to have a stock of in order to make drinks 'fun', even though Blake, her only child, is nearly seventeen years old. Before I know it I'm outside the pub where Giles suggested we meet. Still ten minutes early but never mind.

I go in, immediately cheered by the warmth and

cosiness of the place. Considering his vintage, I'd been worried that Giles would suggest a young, shouty bar where I wouldn't recognise any of the drinks. It's nearly eight and the place is pretty busy; in fact, there's only one table free. I grab it and glance around, deciding there's no one here who remotely fits Giles's description and is conspicuously alone. In fact it soon becomes apparent that I am the only alone-person here, but that's fine. It's actually incredibly pleasing not to be in the empty flat, feeling as if I should be in an egg-beating frenzy or *enjoying some me-time*, as the magazines put it. Then, just as I'm starting to think, actually, it *would* be quite nice if Giles appeared now – being nearly twenty past eight – the door opens and in comes this . . . well, the only way I can describe him is a vision of loveliness.

It's all I can do not to gasp. For a moment I sit there, thinking it can't be him. He is *far* too handsome and this will be mortifying. I glance down at my wine, hoping that, in the millisecond it takes him to realise it's me and come over, his appearance will have settled into something approaching merely *pleasant-looking*. But no. When I glance back he's just as lovely as before, reminiscent of a Gap ad, clean-cut and square-jawed, wearing a white T-shirt and jeans. His skin is olive, his eyes dark and chin faintly stubbled, his mid-brown hair mussed just so . . .

'Alice?' he says, flashing a heart-flipping smile.

'Hi Giles.' I jump up, and he goes for the single cheek-kiss, which by some miracle I manage to negotiate with aplomb.

'What can I get you?' He glances down at my glass; only a few sips left.

'A white wine would be great.'

'Large one?'

Bloody massive please as I'm freaking out over your handsomeness . . . But then, there is the real danger of turning into drunken middle-aged-berk . . .

'Er, yes please.'

He orders our drinks and brings them back to our table. 'So you and Viv are old college mates,' he says, taking the seat opposite and flashing another disarming smile.

'That's right,' I say, realising he's already said 'old', but that in this case he meant 'long-term', which is fine, isn't it? 'We met in the halls of residence,' I add, 'then got together with a couple of others and shared a house.'

Giles nods and sips his beer. 'She's great to work with. Can't believe she gave me the chance, to be honest – I mean, I know it's just an internship but there was a lot of competition for it.'

'Well, maybe she saw potential in you,' I suggest.

'Maybe.' He laughs, and his eyes seem to actually sparkle. 'Anyway, what about you? Is that a Yorkshire accent I detect?'

'Yep, I grew up near Leeds, but we moved to Scotland in my teens as my parents had both landed jobs up here.'

'And you work in a primary school, right?'

I nod. 'I'm the person who sits in the office dealing with a constant stream of parental complaints.'

He chuckles. 'That bad, huh?'

'Actually no, I do enjoy it. It's a lovely school and the kids are great . . .' *No-no-don't-talk-about-children . . .*

'So what does it involve?' he asks.

I suspect it would be futile to try to thrill this fine specimen of manhood with tales of lost permission forms and tearful, vomiting children.

'Just admin mainly,' I say quickly, 'and I run my own business, a small thing on the side, a meringue-type thing.'

'Viv mentioned that. It's a great idea, specialising in one thing you know everyone loves—'

'Not quite everyone,' I cut in, and without thinking, I'm telling him about Patsy's alarm when I offered Jessica possibly the smallest meringue ever – 'I mean, it was about the size of an olive.' Giles seems to enjoy this – at least he doesn't bolt for the door – and then, of course, I have to explain about Tom, and how we still get along reasonably well (in a purely practical way), which leads me on to our sons, specifically Logan demanding an annexe, like his best friend's, ideally with a full-sized pool table . . . 'I mean, when I was a kid I was happy with a box of Fuzzy Felts.'

Giles laughs, a little uncertainly now. I've been babbling on, I realise, due to my intensely nervous state, and I clearly lost him at Fuzzy Felts. What the hell am I rabbiting on about? He'll assume I'm not just old, but mad as well, and likely to start wittering away about my childhood Etch a Sketch and Buckaroo game. *Fuzzy Felts*. Christ.

'So, um . . . are you from Edinburgh?' I ask.

'No, I grew up in Aberdeen, went to a scarily posh school there . . .' He laughs. 'And I was – I *am* – dyslexic, but the school didn't spot it. In fact, no one did, and I struggled so much with reading and stuff that it seemed far easier to behave like a complete twat.' He shrugs. 'So they threw me out.'

'God, so no one knew there was anything wrong?'

'Not at that point, no. People didn't tend to in those days.' *In those days!* How endearing. It was virtually last week.

'So what happened then?' I prompt him.

Giles shrugs. 'A lot of drifting about. Couple more schools, hardly any qualifications to speak of – then I worked with friends on various projects, did a bit of travelling and an evening course in graphic design and here I am.' He grins, and we have another drink, by which time the wine is having the miraculous effect of making me feel far more relaxed.

Just be natural, I instruct myself silently when he goes to the loo. In fact, Giles is so obviously out of my league on the attractiveness scale that I've decided there's no point in trying to come across as a hip young thing, or pretending to be au fait with the bands in *NME*, because he cannot possibly be interested in me *in that way*. I'm no longer fretting about my hair looking flat, and whether the loose powder I swept over my face has settled into the crevices. It's like being in the presence of a fine-looking creature from a distant land, like a snow leopard. Faced with one at close quarters, you don't think, 'Do I fancy this snow leopard? Does it fancy me? Would it laugh at my old person's CDs?' You just enjoy its beauty in a slightly detached way, pretty certain that your paths are unlikely to cross again.

'Listen,' Giles is saying, 'I didn't have a chance to eat before I came out. Don't suppose you fancy going to that Italian next door, if we can get a table?'

I haven't eaten much either – just that measly slice of cheese on toast, mother-alone food – and right now, I can think of nothing more lovely than prolonging the evening.

'Sounds great,' I say, plucking my ringing phone from my bag as we leave the pub. 'Hi, Mum, everything okay?'

'Oh, just the same, rattling along. How's the diet?'

'Er, it's going really well, thanks.' I throw Giles an apologetic glance.

'Good, isn't it? Do you find you're not hungry at all?' *Actually, no – because my existence is entirely fuelled by refined sugar and carbs.* Giles and I are outside the restaurant now. I skim the menu in its glass-fronted frame, salivating at the array of pastas on offer.

'That's right,' I tell her, a little wine-giddy already. 'It's very . . . satisfying. Sorry, Mum, I'm out just now, can we chat tomorrow?'

'Are you out with that dentist?' she barks.

'Um, no . . . someone else.' *Sorry*, I mouth at Giles.

'And what does this one do?'

He's on work experience, Mother – ha, that'd put the cat among the pigeons . . . *In fact, he is younger than many of the dried goods in your pantry.*

'Um, we'll talk in the morning, okay? Bye, Mum.' I stuff my phone into my pocket as we head into the Italian with its bare wooden tables and welcoming vibe.

'That was very nice of you,' Giles murmurs.

'What was?'

'Telling your mum your date's going well. That it's *satisfying.*' He grins flirtatiously and touches my arm, causing me to flinch, as if prodded with Fergus's 'hilarious' electric-shock pen.

'Oh,' I laugh, 'it wasn't that. She was talking about a diet—'

'Not on one, are you?'

'No, but Mum thinks I should be.'

'She's insane then,' Giles declares as we're shown to a table. 'You're lovely, Alice. Viv didn't do you justice.'

I laugh awkwardly, unsure of how to handle such a comment. 'That's friends for you,' I say, holding the menu at arm's length in order to read it in the dim light. Would he be so complimentary if he knew about my old-lady vision, my occasional haemorrhoid outbreaks and ravaged pelvic floor? Or the fact that, while I was once able to guzzle as much wine as I liked, I now wake up with a mouth like the inside of a particularly unsavoury slipper after a mere four glasses? It's not that I think I'm some hideous gargoyle, not really; as far as I'm aware, none of the children at school weep and cling on to their mothers on glimpsing me in the playground. It's just . . . Giles is *insanely* attractive and, as dates go, I can't help suspect that we are being secretly filmed for some reality TV thing, and that the audience are cackling, 'Look – she really believes he fancies her.' A slender blonde waitress has already given him a quick, 'Oooh, *hello*' look, which he seemed not to notice, and an unavoidable fact keeps jabbing away at my brain: this is a little . . . *unbalanced*.

'You have amazing eyes,' Giles murmurs, fixing me with a penetrating smile.

I glance up. 'Thank you, that's a sweet thing to say.'

'No, I mean it. With those little amber flecks, they're mesmerising . . .'

I laugh, wondering if this is how young men operate these days: batting out compliments and oozing confidence. If only he knew that, in the normal scheme of things, I'd be simmering up a giant pot of chilli con carne right now, to divide into various receptacles for freezing and labelling with my special indelible pen. An older couple are locked in conversation at a nearby table, and the woman – mid-sixties at a guess, finely boned with silvery hair artfully piled up – casts us an indulgent smile.

'It's hard to decide, isn't it?' she remarks. 'Took us ages.'

'What did you have?' I ask.

'The sea bass,' the woman replies, 'and David had the lamb . . . both delicious.'

We choose from the specials on the blackboard – they're easy to read, my distance vision is *fine* – and, before they arrive, Giles's mobile rings. 'Sorry, this is terribly rude of me but I'd better take it.' He strides out to chatter away on the pavement outside, allowing me a few moments to assess the evening so far. Maybe I *am* making a big deal of our age difference. After all, it's not as if I order elasticated-waisted 'slacks' from Sunday supplements, or have bunions – yet.

I glance towards the door. Giles is raking a hand through his lush, posh-boy hair, and still gabbing away on his phone. The older woman nearby asks a waiter for their bill, and she and her husband chat companionably for a few moments.

'So nice to see, isn't it?' she tells him, giving me a quick glance. 'I wish Owen would do that with me.'

The man chuckles. 'Not many young men would go out for dinner with their mothers.'

She looks back at me, unaware of the crashing sensation in the pit of my stomach. *He complimented my eyes!* I want to tell her. *Didn't you hear?* Giles returns to our table, and the older couple leaves as our main courses arrive – risotto for me, pork cutlets for him. I sip my white wine, managing to convince myself that it's okay, we are having a lovely time and I really shouldn't care what people think. When I notice Giles's gaze skimming the restaurant, and settling upon a point in the distance, I look around, expecting him to be admiring the Bardot-esque young waitress. But it's a woman of around my age, perhaps even older, smoothing

106

back her neatly cropped auburn hair as she emerges from the loos.

'D'you know,' I tell Giles, 'the woman next to us thought I was your mum.'

'For God's sake,' he exclaims, with a hearty laugh. 'She must be half-blind.'

'I don't think she was.'

'Well, it's as ridiculous as your mum telling you to go on a diet. Are you having pudding, by the way?' We both do and, by the time we emerge from the restaurant, I'm pleasantly tiddly and full of delicious food, and happier than I should be for a woman whose sons have gone on holiday without her.

'Fancy another drink?' Giles asks. He touches my arm again, and my head whirls with possibilities: a whole child-free night ahead, and a bottle of wine in the fridge in my empty flat . . .

'No, I'd better head back,' I say firmly. But why? Viv wouldn't scurry home. She'd seize the opportunity, and the thought of this sculpted God of a man seeing her naked wouldn't trigger the fear in her. In fact, she'd have dragged him off back to her boudoir already, if she wasn't technically his boss . . .

'Are you sure?' Giles says, his smile teasing.

'Yes, it's pretty late.' *Go on, scuttle home to your crossword then, Granny* . . .

'Okay,' Giles says lightly. 'But would it be okay to call you again?' He focuses on my eyes, as if counting the flecks, then he kisses my lips – a brief, barely-there gesture, a million miles from Anthony's lizard tongue, and for a moment I lose all sense of reason. *Oh, just come home with me. I'm pretty sure I could conquer my sex-fear with you* . . .

107

'That would be great,' I manage. 'I've had a lovely evening.'

'Me too. So how will you get home?'

'I'll walk. It's literally five minutes . . .'

'Great. See you again, then.' There's a broad, melty smile, then he strides away into the crisp, cool night without looking back.

Chapter Ten

I wake up with slipper-tongue and aware of a faint odour permeating the flat. Sitting up in bed, I replay last night's events, feeling quite pleased that a) I didn't make a complete arse of myself, apart from mentioning Fuzzy Felts, and b) Giles seemed to enjoy himself too. Okay, there was the being mistaken for his mother bit – but it could have been worse, it could have been his *granny*. Perhaps he was right, and that woman had forgotten to put her contacts in. Whatever, if I'm going to get 'back out there' – and, after last night, a glimmer of optimism has awakened in me – then I need to stop worrying so much.

So everything's good – apart from the pong which definitely seems to be *in* the flat, rather than coming in from outside (there are never any bad smells in our neighbourhood – the residents' association wouldn't allow it). I climb out of bed, pad across my bedroom and into the hallway. I stand there for a moment, sniffing experimentally, and decide that the smell is most likely to be coming from Logan's bedroom. I'm not exhibiting favouritism here. I just have a hunch that, as I'm generally forbidden from entering, it's the room in which things are most likely to fester.

Right, I'm going in. I push open the door and peer around in the gloom. The room is dark, apart from a sliver of sunlight which is bravely forcing its way through the gap between the drawn curtains. As David Attenborough might observe, it's actually impressive that such inhospitable terrain can support human life. Yet, while it's clear that atmospheric conditions are different in here – there's a distinct staleness, reminiscent of old biscuits and socks – the actual *odour* doesn't seem to be any worse than it was in the hallway. I draw back the curtains, allowing a gasp of bright April sunshine to stream in.

A plate on the black shag-pile rug is daubed with mysterious splodges of red, yellow and orange which, on closer inspection, are identified as baked beans, ketchup and egg. On another plate is a small collection of crusts, and dotted around the floor are numerous crumpled sheets of paper covered with his spiky handwriting, which may or may not be crucial English essays. Being as quick and light-footed as possible, so as to cause minimal disruption to Logan's natural habitat, I round up several glasses, sticky with flat Coke and find tons of coins nestling in the rug. There's almost enough here for a week's groceries. His rumpled duvet is strewn with underwear, a ratty paperback copy of *The Shining* and several plectrums – some of which appear to have been cut out of a store charge card I thought I'd lost. It is hardly evocative of the Dandelion sleepwear catalogue. More like Tracy Emin's bed.

I click into action, clearing up the debris and opening the window; instantly, it feels less like a place where an injured animal might limp off to die. Oh, I know Logan will probably be horrified that I've 'moved' things – but I'm sorry, I'm the adult here and I must seize control. I fetch a duster, then the Hoover, and by the time I'm done the room looks heaps better – not an *annexe* exactly, but fresh and welcoming. The doorbell buzzes and I run to answer it.

'Alice? It's me.'

'Viv, come on up.' This is a surprise. It's Thursday, late morning, and I'd have assumed she'd be at the studio; she works more than anyone else I know, perhaps because she doesn't have children and therefore has no reason to feel guilty for loving her job.

'So?' she asks as I welcome her in. 'How did it go? Not interrupting anything, am I?'

'No,' I laugh, 'of course not.'

'It's just, you look a bit . . . tousled.' She raises a brow.

'I've been tackling the horror of Logan's room. Anyway, I'll make you a coffee. How come you're not at work?'

She takes a seat at the kitchen table and grins expectantly. 'I'm officially out visiting suppliers but I was so close by, I had to see you—'

'I know there's an awful smell in here,' I cut in. 'I'm trying to find out where it's coming from.'

'Um, yeah, I did notice. But anyway. Giles . . .'

With a smile, and eking out the suspense, I pour our coffees and check both the bin and fridge for ponginess; both seem fine.

'It was a nice evening,' I say lightly.

'A nice evening? What does that mean?'

I laugh, taking the seat opposite her. 'Well, it was fun. We chatted loads, had a laugh, went on for something to eat . . . has he mentioned anything today?'

111

'No, I wouldn't ask him at work . . .'

'Yes you would,' I exclaim.

'Oh, okay – I just haven't had the chance. So, are you seeing him again?'

I sip from my mug. 'Maybe.'

'What d'you mean, maybe?'

'Well, I'd like to,' I start to explain, 'and he said he'd call. But I can't get away from the fact that he's a whole decade younger and the woman at the next table thought I was his mum—'

'What?' she gasps.

'Oh, that doesn't matter. I don't really care. But, you know – the age thing is an issue. I mean, he looked completely baffled when I mentioned Fuzzy Felts . . .'

'Fuzzy Felts,' she repeats. 'Please don't tell me I set you up on a date with Giles Henderson and you talked about Fuzzy Felts.'

'I wasn't talking *about* them,' I say defensively. 'They just came up in passing.'

She fixes me with a cool stare. 'Did you mention playing hopscotch as well? And that you used to love watching *Swap Shop*?'

'Of course not. Anyway, I'm not imagining this smell, am I? My senses haven't gone all haywire?'

'No, it really *is* pongy . . .'

'Help me find out where it's coming from – that is, if you're not in a mad rush to get back.'

'No, it's fine. Could it be coming from Logan's room, d'you think?'

'Checked that already. Come on – let's try Fergus's.' Compared to Logan's quarters pre-clean, it really is a show room. All around his bed, Fergus has neatly Blu-tacked up his own hand-drawn comic strips; he's a budding

112

cartoonist, his vigorous drawings alive with bizarre humour and boyish jokes. In the corner sits the knotted carrier bag of the soft toys he rounded up for charity (Rex's grimy visage is squashed against the clear plastic). His bed has been made, and books are neatly lined up on the shelf. The floor is eerily devoid of socks, pants or empty Lynx cans. But the smell is worse than ever; pungent and sour. 'Ugh, it's horrible in here,' Viv exclaims.

'I know. It's definitely coming from something in this room.' I get down on my hands and knees and start sniffing around the rug, like a dog. It's even stinkier down here, as if the smell weighs more than normal air and is pooling invisibly at floor level. Then, under the bed, I spy a red and white striped milkshake carton bearing the Crispi Crust logo from our local pizza place. It's lying on its side, lidless, its contents apparently having sunk into the sky blue rug.

'Found it,' I groan, scrambling up to show it to Viv.

'That's disgusting.' In her aesthetically pleasing world, there's no stinky, milky seepage; in fact I doubt if she's ever had anything from Crispi Crust.

'I know. God, how will I ever get rid of this smell?'

'There must be something you can do . . .' She turns to Fergus's laptop at his desk.

'What are you doing?'

'Googling it – spilt milk on carpet.'

'How did you get in? I'm sure he has a password—'

'It was already on,' she says, tapping away. 'Ah, look. It says here that it smells because it's a breeding ground for micro-bacteria but it's okay, you can try baking powder or vinegar and if it's really bad . . .' As she rattles off various cleaning solutions, I decide that this kind of thing never happens in Tom and Patsy's house. 'Sounds like you'll need some strong detergent to tackle the rancid proteins,' she adds cheerfully.

'Right, I'll try that.' I'm back to sniffing at floor level while Viv continues to tap away at the laptop, showing no desire to resume her working day.

'D'you ever have the urge to check his browsing history?' she asks casually.

'Not really,' I say, straightening up.

'Oh, come on, you must do.'

'Viv, you're the nosiest person I've ever known. You even snuck off work to find out how it went with Giles. I don't believe you were just in the area at all . . .'

'If I were you I'd want to take a little look,' she sniggers, clearly having no understanding of how wrong that would be. Okay, I've been *tempted* to check Logan's laptop, especially as he too is lax about leaving it on, unprotected – but have always managed to wrestle myself away.

'Well, I don't,' I fib, busying myself by fetching cloths from the kitchen and blotting up what I can of the milkshake. Viv remains at Fergus's desk, where I assume she's shutting down his laptop – but no, she taps a few keys and, up it pops . . . a woman's naked bottom, with a smouldering cigarette poking out of it.

'Look at this!' she exclaims.

'Oh, God, Viv.' I stare at the image, feeling slightly nauseous and very, very sad. 'A smoking bum, Christ. What's that all about?'

'It's a cigarette butt,' she cackles, clearly unaware of what this signifies: the end of my beloved boy's innocence, basically. The corruption of a young mind which I'd naively believed was consumed with the fixing of old gadgets. 'It's pretty innocent,' she adds with a shrug.

'Innocent? Of course it's not!'

'All boys have a look,' she cuts in. 'I read something recently. It said seventy-five per cent of thirteen-year-olds access porn at least three times a week . . .'

'But this is *Fergus*.'

'Yes, but he's a boy, Alice. A growing male who'll soon be a man. It's part of life . . .'

I stare at her, wondering how to explain that I don't want it to be part of *his* life. I'm fine with sex education at school, and I've always been happy to answer any body-related questions the boys have had, but I've never felt it necessary to explain that it is in fact possible for a woman to smoke a fag out of her bottom. In fact I'd never known it was, until now.

'It's probably not even real,' Viv goes on. 'Bet it was Photoshopped on . . .'

'I hope so,' I mutter. 'Poor girl could've burnt herself.'

'Ouch,' she winces with a smile.

'Please just shut it down, Viv,' I say, landing heavily on the edge of Fergus's bed. In fact, I am crushingly upset. It feels only yesterday that he was tucked up under his Buzz Lightyear duvet, cuddling Rex.

'It's only a bare arse,' she says, perching beside me.

'I just wish I hadn't seen it.' We sit in silence for a moment in the sour-smelling room.

'Hey.' She puts an arm around my shoulders.

'Oh, I'm okay, really. Guess you'd better get back to work . . .' I glance at her pretty, unlined face.

'I should actually,' she says gently. '*Please* don't spend all day worrying about this. It's pretty quaint, when you think what he could've been looking at . . .'

I laugh dryly. 'Stamp collecting is quaint, Viv. Collecting *Famous Five* books and fantasising about running off to

Kirrin Island is quaint. Not a bare bum with a Silk Cut sticking out of it.'

We both snigger. 'He probably stumbled on it by accident,' she adds, getting up and heading through the kitchen to collect her jacket and bag.

'How would he have done that?' I follow her, still clutching the milkshake carton, and clinging on to the faint possibility that she may be right.

'Like . . .' She shrugs. 'A homework topic maybe?'

'You mean like a report on why smoking is bad for you?'

'Or something about Native Americans?' she adds, trying to cheer me up. 'They were big on smoking with their peace-pipe ceremonies and, what d'you call it . . . smudging, is it? When smoke is wafted around to ward off evil spirits?'

I can't help smiling at that. 'Obviously, that's what she was trying to do in that picture. Trying to make bad things go away.'

She laughs and we hug in the hallway. 'Not fed up, are you?'

I shrug. 'Just a bit.'

'Oh, come on, it's not a big deal. Your boys are fantastic – you know that.' She gives my arm a reassuring squeeze and trots off down the stone stairs.

In a blink, I'm back on Fergus's laptop, checking everything he's looked at during the past few days. There's a web page about the construction of the Eiffel Tower, and another on the role of the viola in an orchestra. It's all innocent, homeworky stuff. Maybe Viv is right, and it's horribly normal, and so what if he fancied a quick peek at a naked girl? Doesn't virtually every boy do that at some point? Tom once laughingly told me that finding

116

a page ripped out of a porno mag blowing along the street on his way to school was one of the most memorable events of his childhood. He'd been ten, I recall – three years younger than Fergus is now.

Minutes later I'm lifting his bed to drag out the rug from beneath it. Then I haul it downstairs and round to the back of our block where I prop it up against the wall. Feeling better already, I grab my keys and drive to Ikea to buy a new one. That way, I'll get rid of the stink *and* make Fergus's room nicer, thus (hopefully) cancelling out the guilt that's currently surging through my veins at seeing the thing in the first place. While I'm there, I also buy a chest of drawers for Logan and, back at home, set about building it.

In fact, I'm rather proud of my ability to construct flatpack without shouting or resorting to drink. It's rather like baking: methodical, slightly tedious in parts, but generally okay if you can keep your nerve. And, when it's done, it looks great. In fact both of the boys' bedrooms are vastly improved – not quite *Stylish Living* magazine standard, but it'll be a pleasant surprise when they get home.

My phone rings as I'm gathering up the cardboard packaging. 'Hi, Alice?'

'Hi, listen,' I blurt out, 'something happened today and I know what you're going to say . . .'

'Sorry?'

I blow out air. 'I know I shouldn't have looked. It was wrong of me. It just kind of happened . . .' I clear my throat anxiously.

'Er . . . Kirsty gave me your number. I'm Stephen . . .'

Oh, Christ. 'You're her dentist,' I exclaim. 'Sorry, I assumed you were someone else.'

117

'Well, er, she suggested I call you. You sound busy, hope it's not a bad time.'

'No, not at all,' I say quickly. 'I'm just clearing up after building some flatpack.'

'You can build flatpack? I'm impressed.'

Oh, for goodness' sake. I could explain that the alternative would be to have to rope in a friend every time I need something building, or paying someone to do it, which would be ridiculous.

'It's not that difficult,' I remark.

'Well, no. But a handy skill to have, I guess.' He sounds shy, and more than a little awkward. I regret sounding snappy and try to adopt a calmer tone.

'So . . . did Kirsty explain, um . . .'

'About your three dates?' He chuckles warmly. 'Yes, she did. So, would you like to meet up sometime?'

I scrunch up some clear plastic packaging. 'Sure. That would be nice.'

'Don't suppose you're free on Saturday?' he asks.

'Actually, I am.'

'Great – shall we have lunch then? Grab a pizza?' This sounds distinctly un-date-like, but that's fine.

'Sounds perfect,' I say, wandering back into Logan's room to admire my handiwork.

'How about Mario's in Leith Walk – d'you know it?'

'I don't think so, but I'll find it.'

'Great, see you at one then? I'll book.'

Hmmm. Pizza with a shy-sounding dentist – he seemed nice, but my pulse is hardly racing. *Keep an open mind*, Kirsty urged me. I vow to do just that because, if nothing else, an impending lunch date will at least take my mind off the smouldering bum.

Chapter Eleven

I spend the rest of Thursday and most of Friday up to my eyes in meringues. Clemmie reports that several of the guests at the Morgan expressed an interest in giving them out at their own events, so I've been making small batches in various flavours, as samples. Luckily, being so busy has helped to dispel the anchorless feeling which had set in when the boys left. By late Saturday morning, though, I'm a little put out that neither Logan nor Fergus has responded to any of my, 'How's it going?' texts. While I haven't been expecting hourly updates or, heaven forbid, an actual postcard penned by human hand, there has been not a peep since they left.

So I call Tom, and before I can stop myself it's all poured out about the image on Fergus's laptop.

Oh,' he says, followed by silence. 'God. Are you sure that's what it was?'

'Tom, I could hardly mistake a naked bum with a ciggie poking out of it for anything else.'

'No, I suppose you couldn't.' There are outdoorsy

sounds in the background; children playing, bursts of youthful laughter, and a dog barking in the distance.

'So what d'you think we should do?' I prompt him.

'*Whoo*, I don't know. . . .' He exhales. Then silence. What is it about the males in my life and their allergy to communication? I'm reminded of why I left Tom, why I broke up our family – for which I still have flashes of remorse, even now – because he cannot express an opinion one way or the other. *Doesn't your arse get sore*, I often wanted to ask him, *sitting on the fence the whole time?*

'Never mind,' I say firmly. 'I'll have a chat with him when he's back home. Viv reckons he might have stumbled across it by accident.'

'Er, that's possible,' Tom says vaguely.

'So, anyway, how's the trip so far?'

'Great. I think the boys are enjoying it, but it's hard to tell, isn't it? They don't give much away . . .'

Tell me about it. 'Do they want to say hi?'

'Hang on . . .' There's mumbling in the background, then, 'Oh, come on, Mum wants to talk to you, just a quick *hello* . . .' Further mutterings. 'Er,' Tom says, clearing his throat, 'they're both a bit busy right now.'

Something slumps inside me. My boys, who've been away since Wednesday, don't even want to say hi.

'Okay,' I say, adopting a perky tone, 'please don't mention the porno pic, all right?'

'Sure. I won't say anything.'

'I mean, there are worse things, aren't there? When you think of the kind of stuff he could have been looking at.'

'Yep, definitely.'

'So I'd just prefer it if we didn't blow this up into a

huge thing.' I pause. 'Mind you, I hope it doesn't give him any ideas about taking up smoking.'

We both laugh, causing the tension to ease.

'Yeah,' Tom chuckles, 'they never show *that* on the packets, do they?'

I'm still wondering how to handle all this as I set out to meet Stephen for lunch. I'm wearing smart jeans, an embroidered cream top and flat shoes; it's only lunch, after all. Plus, it's a fresh, blue-skied day and I want to walk to the restaurant – hence no heels – to shake off any lingering irritation over bum-gate.

I've never heard of Mario's, and as I walk in I realise why. It's the kind of restaurant we used to come to when the boys were little but which, like soft-play centres and 'splash time' at the swimming pool, I have since banished from my consciousness. I have nothing against such places; without them, Tom and I would never have managed to eat out with the boys. But as they grew older, I was happy to move on.

I pause just inside the entrance. The place is packed with stoical parents and their rowdy offspring, including several children who are running, unchecked, around the restaurant. One little boy is charging about with his arms out, being an aeroplane, while a waiter with a tray of drinks smiles benignly and says, 'Whoops, careful there!' And then I spot him – Stephen-the-dentist, raising a hand in greeting across the restaurant. His light-brown hair is nicely cut and a broad, open smile lights up his amiable face. Great eyes, too – greenish, sparkly, radiating good humour.

'Alice, hi, good to meet you.' He is out of his seat now, and all smiles – lovely teeth, but they'd have to be, wouldn't they? I guess they're his shop window, so to speak.

121

'Nice to meet you too,' I say, sitting down. 'Hope you haven't been waiting long.'

'No, I just came early so I'd be here before you, not that I thought it would bother you, being alone – I mean, you can handle flatpack without any problems . . . ha.' He blushes and laughs in a flustered way, and I will him to relax. Christ, he seems as tense as I was when I first clapped eyes on Giles.

'So, um . . . you come here a lot?' I eye the wipeable place mats and clusters of drinks with bendy straws at the next table. On ours, there's even a pot of pencils for colouring in the menu.

'With my daughter, yes,' Stephen explains. 'It's her favourite restaurant. They make children so welcome here.' He smiles, lips pressed together this time.

'Right . . . I can see that.'

'Which is making me wonder,' he adds, already seeming to relax a little, 'why on earth I suggested this place.'

'Oh, it's fine,' I say firmly.

'No, really. It's for *children*. What was I thinking?' He laughs. 'Sometimes I forget I'm allowed to eat in proper grown-up places.'

I smile, studying his face as he reads the menu. It's an appealing face; kind and sympathetic, the kind of man you'd be inclined to trust with complicated dental work. While I'm not fond of going to the dentist, with Stephen at the helm – or the drill, rather – I'd at least think, he'll explain things patiently and do his best not to hurt me. It feels right, I realise, being in a noisy restaurant as he politely quizzes me about school, my meringues and my family. It feels entirely fitting that we're in the kind of environment where nothing untoward could happen. Oh, I know a flying olive might have someone's eye out, or a child might start crying when his pizza arrives mistakenly dotted with capers. But nothing naughty, I mean. No drunken flirting or other wanton behaviour. It is about as sexy as a bathroom fittings shop, and that's fine. If anything, it's a relief.

'So how old is your daughter?' I ask as our enormous pizzas arrive.

'Molly's eight, nine next month.'

'And she lives with you?'

Stephen nods. I want to ask why this came about, but am not sure how to without sounding as if I'm prying.

'It's just the two of us,' he goes on, tucking into his pizza with enthusiasm, 'which is probably why I have such a limited knowledge of restaurants.'

I laugh. 'Honestly, the restaurant's great. This pizza is lovely, actually. Far nicer than the usual takeaways the boys and I have.'

'So what about you and your sons?' he asks. 'If that's not too intrusive of me . . .'

'Oh, it's fine – I split up with their dad six years ago.'

'That's about the same as me and Molly's mum . . .' Although I'm now itching to know what happened, I don't ask. 'It's funny,' he adds, sipping his wine, 'I'd expected this to feel weirder than it actually does.'

'You mean the kind of contrived, set-up-ness of it?'

'Yeah, I guess so.' He chuckles and sets down his cutlery.

'So you haven't done much of this?'

'Um, no, not really.' He *is* shy, I decide, despite the ready smiles and the fact that, clearly, his life is pretty together. Perhaps, I muse, he's perfectly happy being single.

'I'd have thought your friends would be constantly trying to set you up,' I suggest with a grin.

123

Stephen chuckles, his cheeks flushing endearingly. 'Not really. I don't think it would occur to them and, anyway, there's Molly to consider . . .'

'Yes, I know, but most people our age have kids, don't they? Not everyone of course. But it can hardly come as a huge surprise to women when they discover you're a dad.'

He shrugs. 'I guess that's true.'

'And I know it's not easy when they're little,' I continue. 'But there are babysitters, and people do go out and have social lives and meet new partners, don't they?' I mean this generally, and not in a me-and-you-hooking-up situation, and hope he realises this. I can sense Stephen's slight reserve, despite the affableness, and have already decided that Kirsty is unlikely to 'win' the challenge.

'It's just tricky,' he explains. 'I have seen a couple of people but there hasn't been anything serious . . .' He smiles his thanks as the waitress takes away our plates.

'I know what you mean,' I say. 'You don't want to get involved with just anyone.' Something about being surrounded by children yelping excitedly, and squabbling with siblings, means it feels okay to say this. I could be at parents' evening at the boys' school, chatting to an extremely pleasant English teacher, the kind the sixth-year girls all secretly fancy.

'You're right,' Stephen says. 'God, it's not easy, is it?' He turns towards the waitress who's returned to our table. 'Are you having anything else?' he asks me.

The Tuc biscuit diet flashes into my mind. 'Profiteroles please.'

'Apple pie for me,' Stephen says, which seems to fit him perfectly: reliable and comforting. He looks back at me as the waitress leaves. 'Alice, I'm not trying to be cagey. I'm sorry if it seems that way.'

'Not at all,' I insist.

'It's just . . . my situation's a bit tricky with Molly.'

I sip my wine. 'Well, mine can be too. You know what Fergus, my youngest, said to me recently? "What d'you want a boyfriend for? You're a mum."' Stephen laughs obligingly, and I add, 'Not that I'm desperate to meet anyone either. I just . . . well,' I smile broadly, 'my friends were adamant that I should *get out there*, as they put it. So I am actually here under duress.'

His green eyes crinkle with warmth. 'Perhaps I should find some friends like that, to get my life in order.'

'To bully you into being more proactive . . .'

'Yeah.' He nods. 'Exactly.'

'Well, I don't see why not,' I say, delving a spoon into my dessert. 'I mean, our kids aren't with us forever, are they? They're only on loan, as people always say. It must be tough on you, though, managing by yourself . . .'

'Yep, I'm one of those poor, hapless dads,' he teases.

'Oh, I didn't mean to sound patronising.'

'No, but it's funny – I do get that a lot. Like the casserole thing . . .' I nod, eager to hear more. 'There's a neighbour who's been coming round with a big pot of stew for years now, twice a week . . .'

'That's kind of her,' I venture.

'But I *love* to cook,' he goes on, 'and I know this sounds churlish but it's terrible stuff, tough meat in a greyish gravy . . .' He laughs. 'Molly and I call her CK – Casserole Kate.'

'You know,' I say, grinning, 'no one does that for me. I've never had a casserole showing up at my door.'

'That's because you're obviously very capable . . .'

125

'No, it's because I'm a woman.'

'Ah, yes, there is that.' We finish our desserts and, as neither of us are in a hurry to go anywhere, we linger over coffee and tiny cubes of fudge. 'Seriously, though,' I venture, 'it must be pretty full-on, running your own practice.'

'Yes, far too much. But there's a brilliant after-school club and we have a lovely childminder to help out in the holidays.'

'Does Molly spend much time at her mum's?'

'Not really. Joanne has a new husband and a baby . . . there's not much time left over, unfortunately.' Stephen shrugs.

Poor kid, I decide. Maybe that's why he's reluctant to meet someone new. 'So,' I say carefully, 'I suppose the time you're with Molly, you just want to focus completely on her.'

'Yes, I do.' As he finishes his coffee, I decide that grown-up places aren't on his radar and neither, I suspect, is a proper adult life for himself. Which is a pity, really, as I have thoroughly enjoyed our lunch. 'Well,' he says, 'I'd better pick up Molly from her friend's . . .'

'Yes, of course, I've got things to do too,' I fib.

We part outside the restaurant with a brief kiss on the cheek. 'It's been great meeting you,' he says.

I am overcome by a rush of fondness for this sweet, well-meaning man. 'You too. And you have my number if you ever fancy meeting up for coffee or lunch or something.'

'Yes, let's stay in touch,' he says, before hurrying away on this sunny spring afternoon. While I hope he meant it, I have the feeling I'll never hear from Stephen again, because his life is just a little too full to allow anyone new into it right now.

That's preferable to the strong possibility that he simply didn't fancy me.

Chapter Twelve

'You were snooping,' Logan rages. 'I can't believe you did that, Mum.'

'It wasn't like that,' I protest, catching my breath as I march home from the restaurant.

'Yeah, it was. It was totally wrong. You've *violated his human rights.*'

I splutter ineffectually, furious at Tom for mentioning the smoking bum when I'd far rather have discussed it with Fergus face-to-face.

'What else have you been doing while we've been away?' Logan wants to know.

'Nothing,' I retort. 'Well, apart from tidying your hovel of a room—'

'Tidying my *room*?' he exclaims.

'Logan, stop speaking to me like this, like I'm forever delving through your private things. I've actually bought you a new chest of drawers . . .'

'What for?'

'To look at. To amuse yourself by opening and closing the drawers. What d'you think it's for?'

'Dunno,' he says crossly.

I bite my lip, any lingering pleasure from my lunch with Stephen having ebbed away, and will myself to remain calm and not start shouting in the street.

'Could you put Fergus on the phone,' I mutter, 'seeing as it was his laptop, not yours?'

'He doesn't wanna talk to you.'

Something twists inside me. 'Why not?'

'Because,' he announces, 'he doesn't feel like it.'

This is ludicrous. Here I am, being harangued by my sixteen-year-old son who still relies on me to get him up for school on time. Does he speak to his father this way? Of course he doesn't.

'Listen,' I say firmly, 'it happened completely by accident. Viv and I were in Fergus's room, and we needed to Google something . . .'

'And it just sort of *appeared*,' he cuts in.

'Well, yes.' He emits a nasal snorty noise. 'There's obviously no point in talking about this,' I add firmly. 'In fact, it's really nothing to do with you.' After a few more terse exchanges we finish the call in a fizz of ill-humour. Christ, that boy. While Kirsty's kids are a handful, none of them are actually rude to her. And what about Clemmie? She has managed to raise a considerate son who wipes down worktops without being asked, *and* takes off his trainers in other people's houses. I often spot him trotting down the road with bags of groceries. If ever I ask Logan to nip out to the shops for me, he comes back with most items forgotten, plus Fanta, toffee popcorn and a whole host of un-asked-for delights.

Maybe it's me, and I'm just too soft on the boys – but then, is the alternative to be as frosty and distant as my own mother? Surely there's some kind of middle ground.

129

When your children are little, there's no end of advice from books, magazines and the mums you meet at toddler groups. Then they hit their teens and – wham. When you desperately need someone to say, '*This* is how you do it,' there's just a big void. Anyway, I have a good mind to *un*-build Logan's sodding chest of drawers, stuff the pieces back into their cardboard box and donate it to Blake for his annexe.

Instead, I call Ingrid, who says of course I can come over. 'I need to catch up on all this dating,' she says, making recent events sound far more gossip-worthy than they really are. So I march through the New Town towards her lovely Georgian garden flat, Logan's parting line still ringing in my ears: 'Clemmie would *never* do anything like that to Blake.'

*

Ingrid's daughter Saskia, who's nine years old and practising piano when I arrive, is a further example of impeccable parenting. Working part-time for a video production company, Ingrid manages family life in the manner of the head of a large, smooth-running corporation. She even manages to schedule twice-weekly fitness classes, hence being easily able to slip into size ten skinny jeans. Today, she and Saskia have been making juice – there's a large jug of it on the sparkling granite worktop.

'I'm really impressed that you drink that,' I tell Saskia when she takes a break.

'It's really nice,' she says pleasantly.

'Oh, I know it is – it's lovely and gingery. It's just . . . the colour, you know? That terracotta shade. Fergus and Logan wouldn't touch it.'

130

Ingrid laughs. 'It always turns out that colour, unless you throw in spinach or beetroot and that's a bridge too far, even for Saskia. Anyway,' she adds, pouring us a glass each, 'it's lovely outside, let's go and sit in the garden.'

As Saskia recommences her practice, Ingrid and I install ourselves at the wooden table on the patio overlooking her well-tended lawn. Daffodils are already in flower, and the delicious juice is helping to soothe my irritation over Logan's accusations.

'He'll have calmed down by the time they come home,' she reassures me, adding, 'So tell me how it's gone so far. With the dates, I mean.'

I fill her in on my Giles encounter, including being mistaken for his mother, and the brief kiss at the end. 'D'you want to see him again?' she asks.

'Sort of. I mean, yes, I suppose I do, although I don't expect it to go anywhere. Anyway, he might not even call again . . .'

'And what about the dentist?'

I sip my juice, sensing it counteracting my cheese-laden pizza and cream-filled profiteroles. 'We had lunch today at Mario's.'

'You mean that kiddie place? With the design-your-own pizzas?'

'Yes, but it's not compulsory, you know,' I say, laughing. 'You can just order them ready-made.'

She frowns. 'God, Alice, what were you thinking, meeting him there? It's hardly . . . *conducive*, is it?'

'It was his idea,' I say with a shrug.

'So where are you going next time, Wacky Warehouse?'

I snigger. 'I know it sounds weird but it was actually fine. More than fine, in fact. I enjoyed it. I think we might become friends, you know?'

'Never mind that,' she says briskly, 'because Charlie is dying to meet you.'

'Who's Charlie?'

She pauses, as if wondering how best to explain. 'I met him at my gym. Don't worry,' she adds quickly, 'he's not one of those obsessives – in fact, he was only there to write a feature about some killer thousand-calorie workout they've just introduced. He's a freelance journalist, had to try it out for a health mag he writes for. Poor guy looked like he was about to peg it.' Ingrid laughs, her long blonde hair gleaming in the afternoon sun. 'Anyway, we got chatting in the cafe and it turned out he's just split from his girlfriend and he seemed like a really fun, lovely guy. I know you'll like him.'

'And you mentioned me?'

'Yes, he wants to meet you. Seemed really keen. I've got his number and, God, I hope you don't mind but I gave him yours.' She grimaces. 'I was just excited, I guess . . .'

'That's okay,' I say as Saskia appears at the back door and arranges herself on the step with a book.

'Listen,' Ingrid goes on, dropping her voice to a murmur, 'I know you liked Giles, and Stephen sounds like a real sweetie but you're not exactly bowled over by either of them, are you?'

I consider this for a moment. 'Not exactly, but is that the way it happens anyway? When you're our age, I mean?'

'Thirty-nine isn't *that* old. We're not past it yet, Alice. At least, that's what Dr Neilsen says . . .' She smiles stoically, and I study her face, aware of the fact that she doesn't like to discuss IVF; after a failed attempt, she threw herself into her job, going all out to promote the company and attract new clients. *Talking about it too much feels like jinxing it,* she told me once.

'I know it's not,' I say gently as Saskia skips to the bottom of the garden where her rabbit resides in its hutch.

'Oh, I'm just nervous, I guess.' Ingrid musters a smile. 'My eggs are being harvested next week . . .'

I wrap an arm around her bronzed shoulders. 'Oh, love. I really hope it happens this time.'

She shrugs. 'At best, it's a one in four chance. So the odds—'

She breaks off as Saskia lifts the rabbit from his hutch and places him carefully on the lawn. He nibbles daintily at the clipped grass; even their pet is beautifully behaved.

'But it could work,' I say. 'You're fit and healthy, and think of how many IVF babies we know.'

She turns to me. 'Yes, but the disappointment last time . . .' Ingrid shakes her head. 'This is the last go, anyway. Sean wasn't even that keen and I can't help thinking why are we doing this when we have Saskia? I know people who've been through three, four rounds of treatment and still don't have a baby and here's me, wanting more . . .' She shakes her head. 'Just greedy, I guess.'

'Not at all,' I insist. 'Why shouldn't you try, if it's what you want?'

She sips from her glass. 'Oh, enough about that. I really think you'll like Charlie. There was something about him, you know? Something a bit naughty. Bit of a handful . . .' She sniggers, and my interest is piqued.

'In what way?'

'Hard to tell – we only talked over coffee. But I can tell you one thing,' she adds with a smirk, 'I'm pretty sure he's not the type to take you to a pizza place with coloured pencils on the table.'

Although I leave with Charlie's number in my phone, it's Ingrid who's playing on my mind. I don't think she's greedy in wanting another child. I did too, desperately, once Logan was a toddler and I'd just about got to grips with the business of looking after him. Fergus was planned; in the blink of an eye I was pregnant, this time more able to enjoy early motherhood, as by then I'd discovered that social services wouldn't whisk my baby away if he happened to be wearing a Monday bib on a Wednesday, or if said bib had a blob of pasta sauce on it. And Saskia *is* always beautifully dressed – a stained garment is quickly replaced – and plays piano, flute and guitar. Ingrid's entire focus, and Sean's too, has been poured into the care and nurturing of their talented little girl – yet I can't help feeling, or even hoping, that another child might cause them to ease off a little.

They don't even have a TV, which seems mind-boggling; would the occasional cartoon really do her any harm? If you asked Logan and Fergus, they'd probably cite *Scooby Doo* as one of the highlights of their early childhood. Perhaps I'm just a little in awe of how Ingrid and Sean manage to keep on top of music practice, alongside a whole raft of other wholesome pursuits, when both of my boys have always battled against any kind of organised activity. ('I'm just not a joiner-inner, Mum,' Logan informed me, at eight years old, tearing off his karate jacket in disgust.)

Back home, I soak in a bath, really to put off calling Fergus. In fact, maybe I should just leave it. He's not exactly forthcoming on the phone, and I'll be able to handle the whole bum-gate situation more delicately when he's home. Yet I *need* to talk to him. I can't settle to anything until I do.

'Hi, Mum,' he says warily as I pace the hallway in my dressing gown.

'Hi, love.' I clear my throat. 'Having a good time with Dad?'

'Yuh.'

Something sinks inside me. 'Look, darling, I just wanted to call about that *thing*, you know . . .'

'Oh. Yeah,' he says dully.

An awkward pause. 'Um . . . I wanted to say I'm sorry I looked at your laptop. I mean – I trust you, hon, and I wouldn't normally do it. It just kind of happened when Viv went to look something up . . .'

''S'okay,' he says quietly.

'It's just, if you're looking at stuff like that, you might start getting all kinds of horrible pop-ups on your computer. So you're best not doing it at all.'

'Yeah, I know,' he mutters. Tension simmers between us, and I wish I could spirit myself up to Skye right now and hold my boy in my arms. He sounds so young and far away. God, I *wish* I hadn't seen that picture. It would bother me slightly less if it had been Logan's laptop; he's nearly grown up, with hair sprouting all over and a deep, growly voice. He has a razor, a debit card and a national insurance number. Fergus is still a child.

'So what kind of things have you been doing?' I ask when it becomes clear that we've reached the limit of our communication on the matter.

'Uh, we've been to the beach and that.'

'Bet Jessica loved it.'

'Yeah,' he says, sounding more relaxed now, 'she's really funny, Mum. Me and Logan helped her build this massive sandcastle with a wall to try and stop the sea coming in . . .' I smile at that; lately, I haven't known how to be with the boys on beaches. Logan sulked during last year's summer holiday in Cornwall, and Fergus didn't seem to know what to do with himself. I couldn't figure out how to gee them up. Boys of their age don't want their mother splashing in the sea in her mortifying bikini, or sending them off to find razor shells.

'She loves spending time with you,' I add.

'Yeah, she does.' I can tell he's smiling now.

'I really miss you, you know.'

'Miss you too,' he says. Then, to my delight, he adds, 'Love you, Mum.'

'Love you too,' I say, filled with warmth at the sound of his voice, and understanding completely why Ingrid wants another baby more than she can even bear to admit.

Chapter Thirteen

'There are plenty of *Grazia*s left,' says Ali, the jovial man who runs our local newsagents.

'It's okay, thanks, my mum's coming today.' I smile and fish out money to pay for the *New Statesman*, *Observer* and a fat, extremely posh-looking magazine called *Intelligent Life*.

'Ah.' He grins. 'Need anything else? Prozac, Valium?'

I laugh, sticking the magazines and newspaper into my bag and wondering why, at my advanced age, I'm still all antsy at the prospect of Mum and I spending two whole days together. I'm taking her out for her birthday today, and tomorrow she's planning to meet up with a couple of old friends for lunch and to see a play – I mean, a proper grown-up play, in a theatre. Clearly, Mum's life isn't quite as dismal as she makes out. I don't think I've seen anything on stage in over a decade that hasn't had a dame in it.

On the way home, I stop off at Pascal's, the swanky French deli-cum-cafe that's frequented by smart, glossy women in Henley tops and pastel sweaters. I'm planning to drop in some meringue samples, but keep putting it off. Even their butter – genuine Breton demi-sel, in chic gingham wrapping – is intimidating.

'Can I help you?' asks the man behind the counter. I look up from the glass-topped display. He is tall and dark-haired, with a hint of grey around the temples and the lean, rangy frame of a runner. Around mid-forties at a guess, he's clearly pretty clean-living, like the rest of the staff here. They obviously have some kind of looks policy.

'I'm just looking for a few bits for lunch,' I say, glancing back down to the goodies on offer and aware of the shuffling queue which has already formed behind me. (Pascal's is incredibly popular on a weekend morning, and this being Easter Sunday, the place is milling with families poring over the chocolate display.)

'Some ham perhaps?' the man suggests in his light French accent.

'Yes – six slices of that please, and one of those loaves.' He smiles before cutting the ham, and by the time he's wrapped it I've selected various little stuffed items, which I hope will meet with Mum's approval – peppers, olives, plus marinated anchovies which he spoons into tubs.

He packs my purchases into a brown paper bag and hands it to me. 'There you go.'

'Oh, just a sec . . .' Although I've paid, and the man behind me is sighing impatiently, I have a feeling that what I've bought isn't enough. I know Mum likes to keep a keen eye on her weight, but it *is* her birthday. 'Sorry – could I add some cheese?' I ask.

'Sure, what would you like?'

I look down. So many to choose from: cow's milk, goat, ewe . . .

'That one's very good,' comes an elderly male voice behind me, 'the Abbeye de Belloc.'

'Sheep's milk,' says the man behind the counter, 'made by Trappist monks.'

Hmmm. Sounds pleasingly historic, Mum will appreciate that. 'Yes, I'll have a big wedge of that please.'

'This much?' The shop guy angles his knife.

'Bit more . . .'

He edges it round. Still looks rather mean. Can't have Mum thinking I'm fat, ill-educated *and* stingy . . .

'Just give me a huge piece please,' I say, thinking to hell with the cost: Mum and I will get through the next two evenings sipping wine and nibbling little pieces of it. Then I worry that one massive chunk might look rather lonely, so I pick a couple of others which the man weighs and wraps.

He stabs at the old-fashioned till. 'Thirty-eight pounds please.'

Bloody hell! I freeze for a moment, wondering what he'd do if I asked him to slice a bit off the monks' one and stick it back on to the enormous cheese wheel, the fromage mothership. But I can't do that. The man behind me is now gusting air at the back of my head, and a small child is whining for a foil-wrapped praline Easter egg. I poke at the buttons on the credit card machine, figuring that I could feed my family for five days for the price of this piddly cheese stash.

As I leave the shop, I'm also wondering if Tom has thought to buy Easter eggs for the boys. I know Logan won't care, but Fergus still expects one and Tom can hardly buy him one without treating his big brother too. I'm tempted to text him but know it would seem a little control freakish. Gritting my teeth, I march back with my shopping to the flat.

In the living room, I fan out the magazines and newspaper on the coffee table, then give the entire flat a speedy check for any trashy novels lying about. Mum would scorn any book with an embossed gold title, and God forbid she should spy a mag with Victoria Beckham on the cover. In Fergus's room, where Mum will be sleeping, I check the bookshelf to make sure his entire collection of Horrible Histories books are clearly visible. Selecting *The Measly Middle Ages*, I have a quick flick through so I can impress her with facts such as: those Medievals feasted on hedgehog and murdered a load of monks, probably for overcharging for cheese. Are they even referred to as Medievals, as in Victorians or Edwardians? Tucking the book back on the shelf, I carry out Fergus's laptop and stash it on top of my wardrobe. Overly cautious, I know, but Mum is pretty au fait with her own Medieval computer and I don't want to risk her having a fiddle about and being confronted by some smoking-ass-type situation. She is not exactly relaxed about bodily functions, and the only sex education I received from her was a leaflet thrust at me, detailing the numerous infections I could contract if I ever got around to doing it. No wonder I practically leapt upon Tom when I met him at nineteen years old. The first guy I'd slept with, he helped me discover that sex could actually be a lovely thing, and not just the cause of terrible diseases and a humiliating trip to a 'special' clinic.

Shaking off an unwelcome wave of nostalgia, I carry out Fergus's enormous sack of ratty old toys to my car.

I set off, trying to convince myself that it's silly to feel a wrench in my gut at bidding farewell to Rex, Panda and all the other cuddly toys – because *other children will treasure them*. Plus, they're quite smelly (the toys, not other children). I'm still trying to convince myself that I'm doing the right thing as I pull up outside the charity shop and hand over the sack. The assistant is an elderly woman with curiously mauve-tinted hair. Although she thanks me, rather curtly, her small, narrowed eyes say, 'And what do you expect us to do with *these*?'

I planned to have a quick poke around the shop for any duff old gadgets for Fergus. But it's so depressing in here – the woman having slung my sack into the back room along with the snaggy old underskirts and misshapen shoes – that I have an urge to leave immediately. *Another child will cherish Rex*, I remind myself silently as I climb into my car, crank the radio up loud and set off for the wilds of Lanarkshire.

Perhaps I'm having some kind of hormonal meltdown. Why else would it bother me so much to rid our flat of some ratty old playthings? Ingrid doesn't cling on to Saskia's discarded teddies; they are washed and passed swiftly on to friends' younger children in order to keep their place clutter-free. I picture myself aged eighty-seven, like some tragic Miss Haversham character – not clad in an ancient wedding dress but surrounded by dozens of quietly decaying soft toys.

Maybe I'm peri-menopausal, heading for irrational mood swings and night sweats, which makes the fact that I recently had dinner with a twenty-nine-year-old seem even more ridiculous. *And* he hasn't called. Does that bother me? Yes, a bit. I could call him, of course; I am an adult, after all, capable of operating a phone. However,

I suspect that any move on my part may be interpreted as distinctly cougar-like. And I'm not that type at all. Even Viv would agree with that. Cougars have glossed lips and ample cleavages, not grease-smeared cardigans and sensible M&S cotton knickers.

Also, I am mulling over my other date, with Stephen. I can't say there was any wild attraction, but perhaps it could develop over time, enriching and intensifying like a curry left overnight in the fridge. Maybe lunch with a perfectly lovely dentist is as good as it gets, and to hope for more is – to steal Ingrid's term – downright greedy.

When I arrive at Mum's, she is sitting there in readiness, with her shower-proof jacket zipped up to the neck.

'Happy birthday,' I say, hugging her bird-like body, and wondering if this is why she has me down as a size 24: compared to her, almost *everyone* is huge. All the way back to Edinburgh, she regales me with exciting developments regarding her septic tank.

'I'm sure it's backed up,' she informs me. 'Nothing's flushing away as it should and sometimes there's a sort of choking noise.'

I picture Logan and Fergus, hanging out on some beautiful Skye beach. 'If you're worried,' I remark, 'it's probably best to call someone sooner rather than later.'

She chooses to ignore this. 'If your father had maintained it properly, then I wouldn't be having these problems now.'

'Is there a reason you're not getting someone to look at it?' I ask.

She turns and squints at me. 'Plumbers are very expensive.'

'Yes, but if you think something serious is about to happen—'

'Let's just hope it doesn't,' she says bleakly. Good lord. It's almost as if she's willing the damn septic tank to explode in her face, just so she can say, 'Told you so, this is *all* your father's fault.' We fall into silence in the slow-moving Edinburgh traffic, passing through well-heeled suburbs where attractive mothers with bouncy hair and toddlers in hydraulic buggies march happily in the spring sunshine. And a small thought starts to form, one of which I'm not proud: how the hell will I get through the next two days? When he mentioned Valium, Ali-the-newsagent wasn't far wrong. I could spend the evenings mildly pissed, but suspect that it'll only loosen my tongue in a not particularly helpful way – especially if Mum launches into one of her rants about Dad, or sewage. Plus, I'll be tired and crotchety in the mornings, and she expects a full Scottish breakfast (including black pudding and potato scones – her dietary restrictions don't extend to breakfast) at a 'decent hour', i.e. eight a.m. latest. I turn into our narrow side street and pull up outside my block, still a little edgy in case I've left a well-thumbed Jilly Cooper beside the loo.

Upstairs we go, with me carrying Mum's brown carpet bag and letting us into the flat.

'Happy birthday,' I say again, handing her a card and a tissue-wrapped parcel in the kitchen.

'Oh, thank you,' she says, rather stiffly. Rather than standing there watching her open it, I busy myself by assembling our deli lunch, hoping she shows more enthusiasm for the cheeses than the present I selected after much deliberation in John Lewis last week.

'This is very nice,' Mum says, studying the cornflower-blue sweater for a microsecond before draping it over the back of a chair.

143

'I thought you'd like the colour,' I say. 'Blue really suits you.'

'It's lovely, Alice.'

Pay it some more attention then. Fondle it, like a pet. With no more feedback forthcoming, I set out plates and cutlery and pour glasses of wine. As we sit down for lunch, it starts to feel a little more companionable; at least when it's just the two of us, I don't have the added pressure of worrying about the boys being surly with Grandma.

'Viv's been commissioned to make some huge hangings for the Surgeons' Hall Museum,' I tell her. 'I thought we could drop by and see them, if you fancy it.'

'Sounds interesting,' Mum says, although I'm aware that she has never entirely approved of Viv and her free-spirited ways.

'The boys used to love it there,' I continue. 'Logan especially enjoyed all the gruesome body parts in jars. If ever we were bored, and it was raining, he'd ask to go and see the pickled warts.'

She chuckles and tucks into the cheese and olives. 'Don't you take them to museums any more?'

I can't help laughing at that. 'Mum, Logan would no more be seen walking around a museum with me than in Marks and Spencer's knicker department.'

'Why not?' She regards me with genuine bafflement.

'Because it's a *museum*, full of old things, and one of his friends might spot him going in and that would be his young life ruined.'

'Really?' she says, still failing to understand. Having polished off at least half the monks' cheese, she pulls on her birthday sweater over her green and black spotty shirt, and the mood lifts as we venture out into the bright spring day.

My entire adult life I've been wrestling the great conundrum: *How to Enjoy Spending Time With Mother*. And as our day begins to unfold, I wonder if I've had a tendency to overcomplicate things. Mum may be a world authority on Medieval literature, but she's still capable of enjoying simple things like strolling through Princes Street Gardens beneath a clear blue sky, and pausing to admire the spectacular view of the castle, even though she has seen it numerous times before. We stop for coffee at a kiosk and, by the time the Surgeons' Hall comes into view, I'm thinking, is this all there is to it? You just go out with your mum, have a bit of a chat and it ends up being a pretty nice time? It's taken me *thirty-nine years* to realise this? Mum hasn't even mentioned my weight today. Just before we go into the museum, I bend down to re-buckle my sandal (I think part of me wants to test her) which causes my embroidered top to ride up, exposing a little muffin top above my jeans. While I can sense her glancing at the offending squidge, she manages not to say anything. She even seems to have forgotten about her septic tank.

We make our way into the museum. It's a grand old building with huge, stern pillars, which feels somehow right for a Day Out With Mum. In the first hall, Viv's enormous canvasses are suspended from the ceiling; they are portraits of famous Scottish doctors, made up of tiny, sketchy machine-embroidered lines, shimmering like water.

'They're *very* good,' Mum concedes. 'I didn't realise Viv was up to that standard.'

'Well, she has been doing textiles for about twenty years,' I remind her. 'But, yes, she is brilliant.'

'Alice?' comes the male voice to my left.

I swing round. 'Stephen,' I exclaim. 'How are you?'

'Great,' he says, smiling. 'This is obviously the place to be on Easter Sunday.'

I laugh. 'Mum – this is Stephen . . . this is Eileen, my mum . . .'

He shakes her hand as I glance down at the small, pale-faced girl who's standing patiently at his side. 'This is Molly, my daughter,' he says.

'Hello, Molly,' I say. 'I'm Alice.'

She has mournful grey eyes and her long dark hair is neatly secured in a single plait that snakes down her back. 'Is Daddy your dentist?' she asks politely.

'No, I'm just, er, a friend,' I reply.

'Ah, you're the *dentist*,' Mum barks, causing him to give her a look of surprise.

'Um . . . yes,' he replies as she regards him intensely, probably sizing him up as my future husband, a clearly well-educated man to steer me away from my fluffy pursuits. Mum has been a tad uneasy since Tom and I split as if, without a husband to anchor me, I am in serious danger of screwing up my life.

Molly looks up at me with a shy smile. 'I like your top,' she says.

'Thank you, Molly,' I say, grateful for the distraction, 'it's just an old thing—'

'Alice shops in those cheap places,' Mum says, eyes twinkling mischievously. 'You know – the ones that use child labour in India . . .'

I turn to her, aghast. 'Mum, I don't. How can you *say* that?'

'You never can tell, though,' she adds sagely, addressing both Molly and Stephen, 'because the factories subcontract some of the finishing processes, so there's no way of

146

knowing exactly where it's been made. I saw it in a documentary last week.' She glares at my top, obviously having forgotten our pleasant lunch and stroll through the gardens; what I'd assumed was the start of an enjoyable mother-and-daughter day.

Molly is gazing up at her, transfixed. 'Is that true?' she asks.

'Oh, yes,' Mum says confidently. 'There are children your age, Molly, stitching on beads and doing embroidery just like that for twelve hours a day. Their little fingers are ideal for that fiddly work, you see.' Molly blinks slowly, perhaps imagining herself being whisked away from her kind father and deposited in a scary factory thousands of miles from home. I swallow hard, aware that I must remain pleasant in front of Stephen and Molly. Since when did Mum start caring about how clothes are made? She buys the cheapest things imaginable. I spotted her newest blouse in a shop the other day. It was £4.99, not even reduced – that was its *actual price*. How could its seams *not* have been gummed together by the tears of orphans? Still, at least my cheese was handcrafted, or did that somehow involve the exploitation of ewes?

I catch Stephen's eye, relieved that at least Mum has managed to resist forcing him to ask me out on another date. 'Anyway,' I say quickly, 'we should let you have a look around.'

'Why don't we all go around together?' Mum suggests. 'It's nice to have the company of a bright young person.' She turns to me, all smiles. 'Alice used to bring her boys here but she doesn't bother any more.'

*

147

Although it pains me to admit it, Mum turns out to be right. There is something especially enjoyable about looking around a museum with an enthusiastic child. Molly's delight is infectious and, as she has clearly been here many times before, she turns out to be an impeccable guide.

'. . . And that's what they used to give chloroform in,' she says, pointing at an antique inhaler-type object. 'It stopped it hurting when people had operations.'

'Right,' I say, wondering if my boys and I should have spent our visits here looking at the exhibits properly, and reading the captions instead of squealing moronically over the pickled body parts.

'They used to saw off people's legs without anaesthetic,' Molly adds cheerfully. 'There was blood everywhere and they screamed in agony.'

'Did they? Ugh.' I glance at Stephen who beckons me over.

'She loves this place,' he murmurs. 'I hope we're not ruining your day.'

'Of course not,' I reply truthfully. 'Molly's so clever, Stephen. I've never met a child quite like her. I hope she doesn't mind *us* tagging along.'

He casts her a quick glance as she and my mother move on to the next room. 'No, she's obviously warmed to you already . . .'

'Warmed to Mum, you mean,' I laugh. 'The two of them have really hit it off. You see, that's the kind of daughter she would have loved. Molly's amazing, you must be so proud.'

He smiles and stuffs his hands into the back pockets of his jeans. 'I am, of course. She's a great kid, but I don't think I've had much influence really . . .'

'You must have,' I reply, '*and* you can do girls' hair. At least, I'm assuming she didn't manage to do that plait all by herself.'

His greenish eyes crinkle. 'No, she did need a bit of help with that.'

'Well, I'm impressed.'

'And your mum . . .' He tails off, as if wondering how to put it. 'She's very, um, *forthright*, isn't she?'

'You mean the child labour thing?' I chuckle. 'That's a new one to add to her catalogue of my failings.'

'Hard going, is she?'

I pause, considering this. 'Actually, she's staying with me for a couple of days and so far it's not going too badly. She's . . . tricky, yeah. But then, Dad left her last year so she hasn't had the best time of it lately.'

'Sounds tough,' he ventures. 'For both of you, I mean.'

'Well, it knocked her for six, and I'm trying to learn not to take things personally.'

He smiles. 'That's very grown-up of you.'

I laugh, buoyed up by Stephen's presence; somehow, he is helping to dispel my annoyance over Mum implying that I'm single-handedly supporting the sweatshops of Calcutta.

'I figured it's better than being the petulant teenager. I have enough of that at home, frankly. Anyway, shall we see what they're up to?'

'Yes, we'd better,' Stephen says. We find Mum and Molly in the next room, poring over an early X-ray machine made of polished wood.

'It looks just like your trouser press, Daddy,' Molly announces, spinning around to face us.

'So it does,' he replies. A *trouser press*? I've never encountered one outside a hotel room setting, and Stephen doesn't strike me as the kind of man who'd own one. His dark jeans don't look especially well-pressed, but maybe he uses it for work clothes. Do dentists tend to dress smartly? I have to admit, I've always focused on their looming faces and poky fingers rather than their trousers. Seems odd, though. I mean, any man I have ever known has managed perfectly well with an iron.

We all make our way through to the body parts room where I find myself next to Molly. 'You obviously love coming here,' I remark.

'Yeah, it's great.' She peers intently at a human eyeball in a jar.

'What other things d'you like doing?'

She frowns, as if considering this. 'Um, I'm a pixie,' she offers.

'You mean, like a fairy?'

'No,' she says firmly, 'pixies are *different*.'

'They originate in Celtic mythology,' Mum cuts in, heading towards us.

'They're Medieval,' Molly adds.

Mum beams approvingly. 'You're right, Molly. They actually go right back to the fourteenth century . . .'

'We meet every Wednesday and make things,' Molly continues.

'What kind of things?' I ask.

She twiddles the end of her plait. 'Um . . . we did cards last week.'

'Oh, my boys used to make Mother's Day cards for me, usually out of pasta sprayed gold.' I stop, registering her unblinking gaze and small mouth set in a frown. Hell, what made me say that? Stephen mentioned that Molly's mum is preoccupied with her new family; is it even okay to mention mothers at all?

'I don't do that,' she says quietly. Oh, God. I have really upset her now. I glance towards Stephen, hoping he'll jump in to jolly her up, but he's chatting away with Mum beside a human skeleton. 'Spray paint is bad for the planet,' Molly adds gravely, 'so we use ordinary paint instead.'

She was only concerned about the casual use of aerosols. Thank Christ for that.

'D'you wanna see a book made of human skin, Eileen?' she pipes up, beckoning my mother over. 'It's the creepiest thing I ever saw!'

Mum laughs, the first proper, genuine one I've heard coming from her mouth since, well, since *forever* really. I'd be no more surprised to see a pony laughing.

'That sounds marvellous, Molly,' she enthuses. 'Lead the way.'

*

'Well, *he's* a nice man,' she declares loudly, the instant we part company from Stephen and Molly outside the museum.

'Yes, he is,' I reply.

I can sense her giving me quick glances as we make our way down towards Princes Street. 'Lovely daughter too. *Very* bright . . .'

'Yes, Mum.'

'So he's the one Kirsty introduced you to?'

I nod, a smile teasing my lips; out of my three oldest friends, Mum far prefers Kirsty, probably because she has devoted her *life* to the home educating of her children – and clearly regards her as a trustworthy assessor of men.

'So . . . are you and Stephen getting along well?' she wants to know.

'Mum, I don't really know him. I like him, yes, but I've only met him once before today, and that was for lunch.'

'But you were chatting away in the museum . . .'

I blow out air. 'Yes, he's nice but—'

'But what?' She stops outside a beleaguered dry-cleaners.

'But . . . I don't know. It's early days and, anyway, the whole point is that Ingrid, Viv and Kirsty are each setting me up on a blind date. I've also met Giles, who Viv chose . . .'

'What was he like?'

An extremely hot twenty-nine-year-old. 'He was . . . interesting.'

We start walking again, but no matter how often I try to change the subject, she keeps swerving it back to Stephen and what an almighty catch he is.

'He seemed like a very interesting man,' she offers with a sly smile.

'I know, Mum,' I reply, 'but it doesn't mean I'm going to dive on the first man who shows a glimmer of interest. Anyway, I don't even know how he feels about me. I'm sure he just wants to be friends, if that. He has a pretty full life.'

Mum frowns, causing a little furrow to appear between her faint brows. 'He said, "I'll call you" when we left the museum.'

'Yes, to be polite.'

'He didn't have to—'

'Well, he sort of did. People say it just to be nice. Saying, "Goodbye" and then marching off would seem

152

a little abrupt.' Like I know *anything* about twenty-first-century dating etiquette . . .

'Would it?' she asks, a hint of sadness creeping into her voice. 'I suppose I'm just out of touch.'

'I just mean it probably wasn't a declaration of love,' I say, trying to lighten things up as we make our way to the shops. We have a little poke around, avoiding any places in which the clothes are suspiciously cheap, but I can tell Mum's heart isn't in it. Stephen-the-dentist hangs over us like a spectre, with Mum making it clear that I'm crazy not to have grabbed him by the hair and dragged him off to the registry office.

'I think you should at least give him a chance,' she ventures as we tuck into an early supper in a tapas bar. 'Why would you let a man like that go to waste?'

'Go to waste?' I say, laughing. 'He's not a leftover egg yolk, Mum. And he's hardly short of admirers. In fact he mentioned some woman who pops around with a casserole twice a week—'

'There you go then,' she declares.

'You're suggesting *I* make him casseroles?'

Her lips purse and she throws me an exasperated look. 'I'd just like to see you happy and settled, Alice. If nothing else, he could probably do something about that overbite you have.'

Chapter Fourteen

Mum's comment is still ringing shrilly in my ears next morning. I check my alarm – 7.14 – and peer into my dressing-table mirror to see if any changes have occurred without me realising. No, my face is precisely as I expect it to be: dark eyes, pale skin, a few faint freckles scattered across my long, straight nose. Teeth a little, well, *toothy*, but not overly protruding. They're just sturdy and serviceable, all the better for nibbling on all those Tuc biscuits.

A thought hits me: I could call Stephen and ask his expert opinion. Heck, why not? It was lovely, spending yesterday afternoon examining preserved body parts together, and although he hasn't shown the slightest sign of being attracted to me, I *would* like to see him again.

'Of course you don't have an overbite,' he laughs when I phone after a full cooked breakfast with Mum. 'Is this an April fool?'

'No, not at all. I just, er, wanted to check.'

'So what on earth makes you think you do?'

'Something Mum said,' I reply, keeping my voice low,

even though she's pottering about in Fergus's room, getting ready for her grand day out. 'And I know my top teeth overlap the bottom ones a bit,' I add, now feeling faintly ridiculous: vain, shallow and appearing to be fishing for compliments, even though that wasn't my intention at all.

'I think you have very nice teeth,' Stephen adds.

'Like a show pony,' I snigger, deciding I'm definitely warming to this man. Apart from his distinct *togetherness*, there's also the plait thing, which I can't quite get over. I mean, if he can manage that, what else might he be capable of – a chignon, or a ballet-style bun? Or am I being faintly patronising here, in the way that Stephen seemed amazed by my ability to build flatpack?

'. . . With a true overbite,' he's explaining, 'the top teeth overlap the lower ones by at least three millimetres. So I can promise you, you really have nothing to worry about.'

'Great. Well, I just thought I'd consult an expert.' I laugh awkwardly, leaving a tiny pause for him to ask me out for a drink.

'Just a minute, Molly,' he says. 'I'm trying to have a phone conversation here.' I wait for him to add, *I'm talking to Alice, that nice lady from the museum who didn't know the difference between pixies and fairies*, but there's just faint cartoony music in the background.

'Um, so what are you up to this week?' I ask, wondering how I might work around to suggesting we meet up.

'Bit of a juggling act with the Easter holidays,' he says. 'How about you?'

'Well, my boys are still away with their dad . . .' I

155

clear my throat. 'Don't suppose you fancy a drink some-time?' My voice has risen a couple of tones higher than normal.

'Sure,' Stephen says brightly. 'Can I call you, though? As I said, things are a bit—'

'Daddy!' comes Molly's urgent tone. 'Kate's at the door.' A woman's voice rings out, clear and confident, in the background. '*Kate's* here,' Molly reiterates.

'Oh, sorry, Alice—'

Kate? Ah, yes – Casserole Kate, with her bubbling hotpot . . .

'Better let you go,' I say quickly.

'Yep, have a good week,' is his brisk response. I stick the landline back on its cradle as Mum appears.

'All ready then?' I ask, quickly composing myself and fixing on a wide smile.

'Yes, I think so,' she replies, clearly relishing the prospect of a day out with her old friends. Her blue birthday sweater is being treated to a second outing and, not one to wear make-up normally, today she has applied a slick of peachy lipstick.

'You look great,' I add truthfully.

'Oh, thank you.' She checks her watch. 'Well, I'd better be going . . .'

'Sure you don't want me to drive you into town?'

'No, it's a lovely morning and I'll enjoy the walk.'

'So you're off to the gallery, then lunch and the theatre this evening?'

Mum nods. 'I should be back by eleven at the latest.'

I go to give her a hug; for once, she actually returns it. 'Mum, stay out as late as you like. I never go to bed early and anyway, I've got a big meringue order to do for tomorrow . . .'

'Okay.' She smiles. 'Well, enjoy your day and . . .' she pauses, looking almost embarrassed before adding, 'and thank you, Alice. It's good to spend some time together, just the two of us. I don't think we do it often enough.'

I'm so taken aback that, after she's gone, I sit at the kitchen table with my mug of tea, just to reflect on what she said. She's right; sweatshop and overbite comments aside, we are managing to coexist without too much friction. Even so, without her the flat is pleasingly quiet and still. I have no crucial errands to run and, although I'll need to start baking at some point, I have the whole of this fine spring day to do it.

When my mobile rings, I only pick it up to see if it's Tom or one of the boys. It's not, though – it's unknown. Giles, maybe, as I haven't saved his number?

'Hello?' I say.

'Hi, is that Alice?'

'Yes?'

'Sorry to call you out of the blue like this. Hope it's not a bad time. I'm Charlie, your friend Ingrid gave me your number . . .'

'Oh, yes, she mentioned you . . .'

'We got chatting at that gym she belongs to, the one with, what d'you call it? A *hypoxic chamber* . . .' He laughs amiably, an infectious chuckle that makes me smile.

'What *is* that?' I ask.

'Something to do with reduced oxygen so you can experience the effects of high altitude.'

I snigger. 'What fun.'

'But I wasn't there for that,' Charlie goes on. 'I was writing a piece about some torturous thousand-calorie workout which nearly fucking finished me off . . .'

I can't help laughing. He talks fast, with a twangy accent – south of England, but not London, I can't quite place it. 'A thousand-calorie workout? Is that actually possible?'

'So they say. Anyway, I was chatting to Ingrid in the cafe, and we got around to talking about you and this *thing* your friends are doing – finding all these men for you to date . . .'

'Only three,' I say quickly.

'Yeah. Well. I was wondering, how are you fixed this evening?'

Hmm. Better not, in case Mum comes home earlier than expected. 'Tonight's not good,' I say.

'Could you do lunch then? My treat, got a review to knock out. You can be my companion.'

Despite his distinct pushiness, I'm intrigued. 'You mean today?'

'Yeah.'

Should I? It's short notice but why on earth not? Yes, I could start baking, but then, it would be a terrible waste of a sun-filled Easter Monday, and there's all evening for that.

'You mean you'll be reviewing the restaurant?' I ask.

'Yep, it's serious work, you know. The public needs to know where to find the best lemon sole . . .'

'So,' I say, 'when you write, "My companion had a savoury mushroom amuse-bouche", that person will be me?'

'That's it,' Charlie laughs, 'only there won't be any amuse-bouche 'cause it's not that kind of thing. It's that rooftop place opposite the castle – the Terrace – d'you know it?'

'I've heard of it, yes . . .' A sliver of sea bream costs about the same as my ewe cheese, I believe.

'Fantastic fish – meant to be the best in Edinburgh. So it's probably worth us checking it out.'

Hmm. He's so cocky, so sure I'll agree that part of me thinks, hold back a bit, tell him you're busy. But Charlie sounds fun, and the girls are always urging me to be more spontaneous.

'What sort of time?' I ask.

'Table's booked for one.'

Right. So he knew I'd say yes, or perhaps there's always a spare person knocking around who's delighted to have lunch with him at a moment's notice.

'Okay,' I say, 'I'll see you then.'

'Fantastic. I'll be the one sitting outside on the terrace, looking terrified at the prospect of your vetting.'

Well, there it is. I'm going for lunch in a beautiful rooftop restaurant overlooking the castle, which I've read about in the magazines Clemmie gives me (they employ foragers, I believe, to gather mysterious greenery). By the time I turn up at the Terrace, having jumped on a bus so as not to arrive all red-faced and sweaty – it really is unusually warm today – I'm in a state of high excitement. A little antsy too, despite this being my fourth date in less than a month . . . is there a point at which, like with public speaking, you stop feeling nervous and breeze through it? Will I become a practised dater, treating each encounter as if it's no more extraordinary than popping out to buy a newspaper?

I enter the foyer, press the lift button and wipe my slightly clammy hands on my skirt. Damn, they've left a faint mark on the fabric. The lift arrives, and I step in, taking in my reflection in its mirrored interior and hoping I've got it right this time. Charlie didn't strike me as someone who'd berate me for possibly supporting child labour, but as you can never tell, I've chosen a plain white shirt (no embellishments which might have been stitched by infant hands) plus a simple, bias-cut black linen skirt. Legs are bare – rather pallid of hue but that's preferable, I think, to hastily applied cheap fake tan and its inevitable gravy-coloured tidemarks. I look smart, I decide. Grown-up yet not stuffy . . . possibly even a little sexy, with my hair hastily blow-dried and worn loose? It's impossible to tell. Certainly, I realise as the lift doors open, several other women are all carrying off the look, as they too are wearing the white-shirt-black-skirt combo – the waitresses' uniform here. As if to confirm this, a gangly man with a sculpted, rich-person's jawline (and possibly an *underbite*?) shoots up a hand in my direction and calls out, 'Excuse me, we're just waiting for that glass of Sauvignon?'

'I, er . . . don't work here,' I reply.

'Oh, I'm *so* sorry,' the man booms as several diners swivel round to watch our exchange.

'That's okay,' I reply with a big, barky laugh. 'Happens all the time . . .' Shit, shit, shit, what made me say that? And did Charlie hear? No, he said he'd definitely be out on the terrace . . . I glance around the restaurant in all its white-tiled, glass-walled glory. One entire glass wall has been pushed back, allowing a faint breeze to drift in, and out on the actual terrace several couples and one large family group are all chattering away. Marching out, I pray that no one will try to catch my attention and ask for their bill.

I spot him immediately at a table for two, wearing a dark blue open-necked shirt and jeans, with dark curly hair flopping around his face. He has a nicely shaped mouth (looks like he smiles a lot) and cheeky brown

160

eyes behind black-framed rectangular specs. It all adds up to one of those lively, animated faces that somehow draw you in.

On seeing me, Charlie grins and springs up, knocking over a glass pepper pot – a gesture that causes my anxiety to melt away instantly.

'Alice,' he says warmly, 'how lovely to meet you.'

'And you.' He kisses my cheek, and I have a good feeling about today as we take our seats.

'I'm really glad you said yes,' he adds. 'Hope I didn't completely ruin your day.'

I laugh and glance towards the castle against the searing blue sky. 'Of course you didn't. This place is amazing.'

He grins broadly; it's a lovely smile, showing good but not-quite-perfect teeth, and causing those dark eyes to glint mischievously. 'Like being in a Visit Scotland calendar.'

'Yes, a bit. So, d'you live in Edinburgh?'

'At the moment, yes, just for a few months – my parents have a flat here that they let out for an extortionate rate during the festival. Rest of the time I'm in London, but I fancied a change – there's been stuff going on . . .'

'You're on the run?' I suggest, raising a brow.

'Oh . . .' He wafts a hand. 'Girlfriend stuff. All over now, just before Christmas . . .'

'Rotten timing.'

He shakes his head. 'Only in that I'd already bought her present, a bloody hideous red Chloé handbag with a gold-link chain strap . . . tried to palm it off on my mum but she said it wasn't her style.' He smirks. 'The only reason I'd known Matilda wanted it is because she'd

161

not only ringed it in biro in her magazine, but stuck all these hint stickers around it.'

I smile, a little taken aback by how easily he offered this information, particularly about a recent ex. But then, I'm used to the males in my life – Logan, Fergus, Tom – barely communicating at all. It is, I decide, quite refreshing.

'I've never come across hint stickers,' I tell him.

'Oh, you know – those arrow-shaped stickers with "choose me" printed on them . . .' Charlie laughs loudly, fills my glass from the bottle that's already sitting in its silvery ice bucket on the table, and takes a big swig from his own. 'They're not especially subtle,' he adds. 'Matilda had a whole sheet of those damn stickers but I can tell you're not like that.'

'What aren't I like?' I ask, wondering if he's actually *comparing* us here.

'The handbaggy sort. You know.'

'No, I'm not handbaggy . . .'

'And that's good.' Charlie meets my gaze and smiles, then turns to the waiter who's approached our table. We order, choosing simple grilled fish which feels right with sunshine beaming down on us.

'So, you've wound up in Edinburgh,' I remark.

'Yeah, I've wanted to spend some time here for ages – it's such a great city. Whereabouts are you from?'

'Yorkshire originally, but I moved to Scotland in my teens, then came to college here. I had my first son pretty young – I'd only just graduated – so Tom, my ex, and I found ourselves getting a life together in Edinburgh . . .'

'And then what happened?'

I pause, unaccustomed to such intense curiosity about my life. 'Well, we split up six years ago and I've been

162

working as a school secretary for a few years now . . .'
Charlie nods, showing no sign of itching to dive in and
talk about himself. I take a sip of wine, noting at once
how different it is to the stuff I drink at home; in compar-
ison, my usual plonk might be concocted in some gigantic
chemical plant in Wolverhampton, with not a whisper
of grape.

'Like it?' Charlie asks.

'It's delicious. It's one of the nicest wines I've ever
had.'

He grins approvingly. 'I take no credit for choosing it.
The waiter foisted it on me and I'm glad he did. Anyway,'
he goes on, 'Ingrid said you also run a successful meringue
business.'

I laugh and sip more wine. 'I'm flattered that she did
a great PR job on me, but it's pretty small-scale at the
moment.'

'Well, you're a busy woman with two boys to raise
. . .'

I meet his gaze. 'You seem to know a lot about me,
Charlie.'

He shrugs. 'You sounded interesting.'

'You and Ingrid must have had a pretty long chat at
the gym . . .'

'I'd actually, er . . . strained something during the
workout,' he says with a rueful smile. 'So I was hanging
around in the hope that it'd wear off.'

'What had you done?' I ask.

'A kind of groin thing.'

'Oh dear. How is it today?'

'Still recovering.' He laughs loudly and tops up our
glasses, even though mine is barely touched. 'But the plan
is still to anaesthetise myself today . . .'

'Isn't that unprofessional, though? I mean, I'd have thought you'd be keeping a clear head, ready to make detailed notes on the texture of the halibut . . .'

Charlie grins cheekily. 'I like the way you say "halibut" in that Yorkshire way.'

I burst out laughing. '*No one* has ever said that to me before. And I've lived in Scotland for twenty-five years – I didn't think there was any Yorkshire left in me . . .'

'There is, and it's lovely. Your voice, I mean.'

I look at him and smile, realising I've felt completely at ease since I joined him at the table. Even being mistaken for staff seems funny now, and I find myself telling Charlie about it.

'I like that look, though,' he says. 'It's very foxy.'

'Oh, come on.'

'Seriously, you look great.' By the time our lunch arrives, I'm silently thanking Ingrid for giving Charlie my number and starting to wish this was dinner, and that Mum wasn't staying over tonight, and that we had a whole, long evening ahead of us. Somehow, I've found myself telling him about Mum's visit, and her comments about overbites and child labour, at which he laughs in disbelief.

'So,' I say, conscious of prattling on about myself, 'tell me about the kind of writing you do.'

'Oh, I just trot out any old stuff – whatever comes along. Actually, I'm off to Paris on Wednesday to review a hotel.'

'So you do travel writing too?'

Charlie shrugs. 'Anything that pays, basically.'

'Sounds like fun.' I smile. 'Anyway, shouldn't you be focusing on the food here?'

'Oh, I'll bash something together later,' he says distractedly.

'Are you sure you'll remember? I mean, this green stuff—'

'Samphire, yeah . . .'

'Aren't you going to write about its silken texture? Sorry to go on, but the whole restaurant critic thing intrigues me. I mean, to go into that amount of detail about something on a plate . . .'

He pulls a mock-aghast face. 'Don't you like food?'

'Of course I do. I just mean the *pernicketiness* of restaurant reviews, you know?'

'I'm teasing you,' Charlie says with a grin. 'I know exactly what you mean. Why the fuck does anyone need to know precisely how buttery the sauce was, or how crisp the pastry on their silly little tart?' He shrugs dramatically. 'But apparently they do.'

'And who d'you write all this for?'

He pushes back his dark hair which keeps flapping into his eyes in the light breeze. 'Anyone who asks me. Guess I've been lucky. I've been freelance for ten years now and managed to ride out the recession by the skin of my teeth. But then,' he adds, 'it's just me, no kids to support . . .'

'Have you ever been married?'

'Just the once.' He smiles, studying my face as our plates are cleared away. 'An early one, far too young – don't they call them starter marriages?'

'A sort of practice run,' I suggest. 'Well, Tom and I were never married, but I suppose that's sort of what it was.'

'I assume he's still in your life,' he suggests.

'Yes, well, we have our boys so there'll always be that bond . . .' I break off and laugh. 'Which is a little scary.'

'No escape,' he agrees. 'So, can I tempt you with dessert?'

'Oh, I guess we should,' I say, 'for research purposes.'

And so we do, researching not only a beautiful lemon tart and an Eton-mess-type crushed meringue dessert (Charlie chose this, I tend to avoid meringues beyond my own kitchen), and also – just to be thorough in our investigations – a second bottle of wine. We're all giddy and giggly as he pays the bill – "Course it's on expenses,' he insists, batting me away as I pull out my purse – then totter off to the lift. I glimpse at the woman in its mirrored walls: no longer stiff and awkward with sweat marks on her skirt, but actually glowing with flushed cheeks and bright, sparkling eyes. As the lift doors open at the ground floor, a besuited businessman walks in and fixes me with an undeniably flirtatious grin. Christ, what is happening?

'Hey,' Charlie says as we step out, 'don't suppose you fancy hanging out together this afternoon? We could go places. *Do* stuff. You could show me the best bits of Edinburgh. I mean, you don't have to start meringuing right now, do you? Or rush off to tend to your mother?'

I look at him, my heart quickened by his hopeful smile. Why not? whispers the voice in my head. And that phrase from *Stylish Living* pops into my mind: *spontaneous suppers with friends*. Well, maybe it's time I spent a whole *day* being spontaneous, and seeing where it takes me.

'Oh, I'm sure they can wait,' I tell him.

'Mum or meringues?'

'Both,' I say as Charlie takes my hand in his, making my entire body tingle as we step out into the glorious afternoon.

*

166

'Say it again,' he drawls in a Humphrey Bogart voice. 'You know what I wanna hear . . .'

'You're crazy,' I laugh. 'You are *completely* insane.'

'Go on, say it again. Say, "halibut".'

We have reached the stage, after our distinctly winey lunch, of not only knowing each other's surnames and ages (Charlie is thirty-seven – yes, a little younger than me, but no Giles-sized age gap), but also having a little in-joke. The halibut thing, I mean. As we stroll down to the Botanic Gardens, we also fill each other in on our favourite music, books and films – all those things you really want to match, but which rarely do.

And, when they do, it seems too good to be true.

'I've never met any man who even likes *Casablanca*, let alone says it's their favourite film,' I tell him.

'Then you've been hanging out with the wrong men,' he retorts.

I laugh, shielding my eyes against the sun. We buy take-away coffees from the Botanic Gardens cafe; Charlie was all for grabbing another bottle of wine from an off-licence, sneaking it in and downing it surreptitiously among the exotic flora ('I mean, there must be a jungly bit we could hide in, right?'), but any more alcohol today would tip the day from being lovely into potentially messy, especially as I need to be ready with the cocoa and chit-chat when Mum returns.

'I've had an idea,' he announces, lounging on his back on the grass. 'I could come home with you and help make your meringues.'

'I don't think so, Charlie. Drunk in charge of a piping bag? You might do yourself another injury on top of the groin one.'

'You think I know nothing about baking,' he retorts

in mock-indignation. 'Know what my last commission was? Testing out bizarre kitchen contraptions from the point of view of an idiot cook.'

I laugh and sip my coffee, grateful for its sobering effect, and the fact that there are still hours to go before Mum's due back at the flat.

'What kind of contraptions?' I ask.

'Mad stuff like, um . . . a cream-horn mould. I didn't even know what a cream horn was. I mean, I thought I did. I assumed it was a sex thing . . .' I crease up with laughter. 'But turns out it's just a *cake*. Don't make those as well, do you?'

'Sorry to disappoint you, but I never have.'

He adopts a serious face. 'You're a cream-horn virgin. Well, I can't blame you actually because who wants a cake you have to *mould*? So there was that, and a plastic thing to make omelettes in the microwave . . . but the one *you* want is the Yolk Plucker.'

'The *what*?'

'Yolk Plucker. It's brilliant, can't believe you haven't got one. It looks like a miniature toilet plunger – that thing you stick down the loo to clear a blockage . . .' An unsavoury image of Mum's septic tank shimmers into my mind. '. . . And the idea is, you crack your egg into its little rubber bowl, squeeze the balloon at the end and it sucks your yolk right in – sorry if this is sounding a bit medical – leaving you with a perfectly separated white.' He grins triumphantly.

'Come on, that is *not* a real thing.'

'It is, I swear. See the top-notch commissions I get?' He laughs self-mockingly.

'So you'll pretty much do anything for money,' I suggest.

'Just about.' He shrugs. 'A man's got to earn a crust.'

I sip my coffee and lean forward. 'Really? Like . . . anything?'

Charlie sniggers and plucks at the grass. 'In my dark and murky past, I've done things that . . .' He tails off. 'Well, that I probably wouldn't do now I'm a highly mature and responsible adult.'

'What kind of things?' I ask greedily.

'Never mind that, nosy girl.'

'Oh, come on, you can't tell me half the story. You're a horrible tease.'

He gives me an impish grin. 'I might when we know each other better.'

I grin, pushing hair from my eyes and watching a squirrel scurry up a tree. The azaleas are bursting with reds and oranges, as zingy as poster paint splattered on by a child, and an entire border is filled with cheerful yellow daffodils. I glance at Charlie, figuring that, yes, I would like to get to know him better. Does this mean that Ingrid has won the Date-off? I'm not sure yet. Then Charlie lifts a hand towards my face, and for a moment I think he's just going to flick something away from my cheek – an insect or, horrors, a speck of foraged greenery from lunch – but instead he smiles tenderly and brushes back a strand of hair.

He moves closer, and I notice how lovely his mouth is close up – just full enough, made for kissing, really. Then we are kissing, in the warmth of a perfect Monday afternoon. It is *dizzying*. I am no longer a mother, thinking up ways to use up hundreds of leftover egg yolks. I am no longer trying to ignore the fact that my fortieth birthday is hurtling towards me like an out-of-control train. Right now, on this patch of neatly clipped grass,

169

I am kissing a man who tastes of wine and perhaps a hint of soft, sweet berries from his meringue dessert. My head is spinning as we finally pull apart.

'Well,' Charlie says with a lazy smile. 'What now?'

Reluctantly, I glance at my watch. 'It's nearly six. The gardens are closing any minute.'

'So where shall we go?' he asks hopefully.

I smile, brushing grass from my bare legs. 'Sorry, but I need to get back. I really do have to bake tonight . . .'

'Okay, so what are you doing on Wednesday?'

I study his eyes. They are deep brown, like the darkest chocolate, and framed by long black lashes. 'I thought you said you were going to Paris?'

'I am.' He grins, then kisses me gently again. 'So why don't you come too?'

Chapter Fifteen

I'm still dizzy from all that wine and kissing as we make our way to the main gates. What's happened to me? I've snogged a stranger and am leaving the Botanic Gardens all mussed up and covered in bits of grass, *and* I have to face Mummy Dearest in a few hours' time.

'I can't come with you, Charlie,' I say.

'Why not?' He sounds taken aback.

'Well, for one thing I've known you for, what – about six hours?'

'We'd have a great time, I know we would—'

'And you'll be working anyway.'

'Yeah, writing a pissy little hotel review that'll take me about ten minutes, that I'll do when I get back home anyway. I won't turn on my laptop, I promise. I won't even take it. C'mon, Alice. When's the last time you did something completely impulsive?' *Today*, I think, my lips twitching into a smile. 'No, not that,' he says, reading my mind. 'You know what I mean. When's your birthday, by the way?'

'In three weeks' time, why?'

'Well then. It's always on those lists, isn't it – things to do before you're forty? Never mind hang-gliding and swimming with dolphins and all that shit. There's always something on those lists about going to Paris with someone you've only just met.'

'I don't remember reading that,' I laugh. 'Anyway, I know they're made up by people like you. Everyone makes out that turning forty is this enormous event, and it's just not—'

'It's just a number,' he says, deadpan.

'It *is*, Charlie . . .' For once, I really don't care about that looming milestone, as it's always called. Not when I've just had the most amazing afternoon . . .

'Forget it then. Forget your birthday, I mean. Come just for the hell of it. I'll go home and book you a flight right now. I've got tons of air miles and the hotel's free, it won't cost you anything . . .' He takes my hand as we head back up the steep hill towards Princes Street.

'It's not about money,' I insist. 'The main thing is, my boys are coming home tomorrow. They've been away for a week with their dad and I can't just not be there.'

'Oh.' He frowns, clearly deflated. 'Couldn't they stay away a bit longer?'

'No,' I exclaim, laughing. 'What d'you think I'd say? "Um, d'you mind not coming home for a few more days because I'm off to Paris with a man who, at about a quarter to one this afternoon, I didn't actually know?" That'd go down well.'

He chuckles softly. 'Well, I think it's good for kids to see that their parents have a sense of adventure.'

'Look,' I say with a sigh, 'it's lovely of you to ask me, and maybe if things were different . . .' We've reached the top of the hill now, both of us a little breathless. 'But

172

I'm going home to get myself sorted before Mum comes home . . .'

Charlie smiles, plucking a blade of grass from my hair, a gesture which is so sweet and tender it causes my heart to perform a little flip. 'So we'll get together when I come back? I'm only away for a night . . .'

'Yes, I'd love that.'

He takes both of my hands in his and kisses me softly on the lips. I'm still glowing as I climb into a cab, and possibly even when I get out, as Clemmie, who's striding briskly towards me in a figure-hugging dress in a loud poppy print, gives me a significant stare. 'Well, *you* look like you've been out having fun!'

'Do I?' Inadvertently, I touch my lips, trying to assess whether they look freshly kissed.

'In a good way,' she adds as Stanley snuffles around my ankles. 'Been somewhere nice?'

'Just for lunch,' I say blithely, realising that it must be getting on for seven, and suspecting I reek of booze.

'Must have been a fun lunch,' she titters.

'Yes, it was. It was lovely.' I smile tightly, wondering what she's referring to. I glance down at my skirt; there are no bits of grass or azalea petals sticking to it that I can see.

'You're so funny,' she adds with a rich, throaty laugh. 'Well, it's lovely seeing you out having a good time. You *deserve* it, Alice.'

'I'd better get home,' I say quickly. 'Got a night's baking ahead . . .'

'Good luck with that,' she says with a smirk. I say goodbye, still perplexed as to why she kept looking at me in that way – faintly appalled, but also rather thrilled by my obvious wantonness. I march quickly to my front door, and hurry upstairs to my slightly stale-smelling flat (the milkshake odour still lingers, I'm sure of it) to study my reflection in the mirror in the hallway.

And there I see the worst case of beard rash I have ever seen. *Shit.* Charlie wasn't even that stubbly, at least not that I'd noticed. Sexiest man I've met since God knows when, and it turns out I'm allergic to him.

To take my mind off my disfigurement, I tear into whisking up eggs and sugar and pipe the mixture, in slightly wobbly fashion, on to the trays. They are marbled pink from the sieved raspberry I've swirled in, and flecked with chips of toasted almond. Once my first batch is in the oven, I call Ingrid and fill her in on the day's events.

'Oh, God, I'm so sorry,' she exclaims. 'Is it really bad?'

'Hopefully it'll be gone by morning,' I say, feeling calmer now. 'And there's nothing to apologise for. We had such a great afternoon.'

'And he asked you to go to Paris with him? Are you sure it wasn't an April fool?'

'Thanks,' I tease her. 'You think men only ever offer to whisk me away as some kind of seasonal prank?'

'Of course not,' Ingrid retorts. 'I'm sure loads of men would love to take you to Paris. But, you know, after *one* lunch . . .'

'Well,' I murmur, 'like I said, it was lovely. A bit reckless. Can't remember the last time I did something like that.'

She chuckles. 'So you're sure you're not going to jump on a plane with him?'

I smile, breathing in the warm, sugary aroma that's filling my kitchen. 'Of course not,' I say, omitting to add that I would actually love to, very much.

Mum rolls in just after eleven, a little tipsy and

unable to stop herself from remarking, 'You're all pink around the chin, Alice – have you had a reaction to something?'

'No, Mum,' I fib, 'my skin just flares up from time to time.'

'Why would that be?'

'I don't know. Maybe the cream I've been using . . .'

She tuts. 'You do have a lot of potions in your bathroom.' Compared to her, she means; Mum uses only Imperial Leather soap. 'Awful lot of money,' she goes on, perhaps referring to the serum I bought last week, a blowout purchase of £2.99.

'Anyway,' I say, to deflect her attention from my face, 'how was your day?'

'Lovely. Perfect, in fact.' She smiles with her lips pressed together. 'Have you heard from that dentist again?'

I smile and pour her cocoa: a dark, rich cupful instead of a mug, the way she likes it. 'We had a quick chat this morning.'

'And . . .?'

'And *nothing*, Mum. I hate to disappoint you but I think we're just going to be mates, which is fine. I haven't met a new man friend in a very long time.'

'That's nice,' she says unconvincingly. We part with a hug, and it's a relief to escape to my bed and replay the day's events.

Kissing in the Botanic Gardens, on the very patch of grass where the boys and I once ate our egg sandwiches and bags of crisps. Will he call, when he gets back from Paris? If not, I decide, I'll phone him – definitely. Then my mind races ahead, and I'm actually boarding a plane to Paris, having asked Clemmie to look after the boys overnight. What's the worst that

175

could happen? That Charlie and I discover that, fleeting attraction aside, we have little in common? Well, so what? We'd be in *Paris*. I haven't been to Paris since I was pregnant with Logan, and Tom and I wandered around holding hands, with me in gargantuan dungarees and a permanent smile on my face.

Mum pokes her head around my bedroom door, making me flinch in the glow of my bedside lamp. 'Maybe some chamomile lotion would help.'

'Sorry?'

'For your face, Alice. To take the heat out of it.'

'Er, I don't have any, Mum. Anyway, I'm sure it'll die down on its own.'

'Hmmm.' She makes no move to leave. Perhaps she feels lonely in Fergus's room. At home, she always has Brian to talk to. 'So what have you been doing today?' she asks, looking sleepy now.

'Just had lunch with a friend, then we went for a stroll around the Botanics.'

'A man friend?' she enquires.

'Yes.'

'Was it the dentist?' she asks, hovering in the doorway with a hopeful smile.

I consider lying, but realise how pointless that would be. 'No, someone else. But I did call Stephen, and he says anything less than three millimetres is absolutely fine, so both of us can sleep easily tonight.' She blinks at me, confused. 'I mean I don't have an overbite,' I add cheerfully.

'Oh,' she says, sounding a little disappointed, before disappearing off to bed. My mobile bleeps on the floor and I snatch it, greedy for further communication with Charlie – but it's Tom.

Weather still great, he writes. *Everyone seems to be enjoying Skye. Jessica loving being with her brothers. Would it mess up your plans if we stayed away longer and kept the boys until Friday?*

Chapter Sixteen

I glance out of my car window at the lambs nibbling grass through gaps in the fence at the roadside. The sun is struggling through a hazy sky, and I'm filled with the kind of smug pleasure you experience when you've leapt out of bed and cooked a full fried breakfast, all the while making the kind of pleasant conversation befitting a properly grown-up daughter. Naturally, I omitted to tell Mum that I am going to Paris with Charlie tomorrow, who she hasn't even had the opportunity to vet, and certainly wouldn't approve of. Reviewing yolk pluckers and cream-horn moulds – what kind of career is *that*? Plus, I shudder to think what she'd have made of us ignoring the beautiful architecture of the glasshouses in the hallowed Botanic Gardens in favour of kissing on the grass . . .

I'm filled with a delicious sense of anticipation as we speed over the moors towards her cottage. It's as if yesterday flicked some kind of switch, triggering a distinct recklessness to the point at which I no longer fear anything, because really, with the boys staying up in Skye, I couldn't think of a single reason not to go. Viv was right, I *do* worry too much – about Logan and Fergus, and whether we have enough batch-cooked meals in the freezer to see us through a famine, and where I put all those school trip permission forms which I filed away for 'safekeeping'. Now all that's gone. Of course I'll be Mum again in just a few days – and it'll be lovely to see the boys, as long as Logan is speaking to me – but right now, I'm going to drop off Mum and go home to get ready for Paris. Where I will drink wine, and eat delicious food, and *stay in a hotel with a man*. I could actually scream with excitement, if Mum wasn't sitting in the passenger seat beside me.

Our parting is unusually fond, perhaps because our two days have gone pretty well, considering. I drive away slowly – my usual tactic, so she doesn't think I'm eager to leave – admiring the lambs and recalling how, when the boys were little, they would nag me to stop the car at this time of year so they could watch them playing. These days, now that Logan and Fergus don't care a jot for livestock, I often experience a pang of nostalgia on seeing them playing in the fields. But today feels different. I no longer feel sad about anything. I turn the radio up loud – it's a cheesy chart song the boys would scoff at – and put my foot down, smiling at the realisation of what is happening to me.

I am going to Paris with a man I barely know, and it's fine, it's better than fine . . .

I am so excited I actually let out a yelp of delight.

*

But first, business must be attended to. Back home, I have last night's marathon bake to deliver, so I pack them in neat rows in large, flat boxes, and drive over to Betsy's.

'I wondered if you could deliver an extra batch tomorrow?' Jenny says, plucking one out of a box and biting into it. 'I was going to ask for some chocolate ones but forgot to mention it last time . . .' She pulls an apologetic face.

'Sorry, I'll be away, but I can make them over the weekend, no problem.'

Jenny smiles. 'Going somewhere nice with the boys?'

'Er – no, they're on Skye with their dad. I'm going away with a friend actually, to Paris.'

'Oh, how lovely.' Jenny gives Max a sharp nudge in the ribs. 'Are you listening to this? Other people do fun stuff. They don't just sit at home with a box set.'

'And they don't have a cafe to run,' I say, laughing, my head whirling with the rest of today's tasks: pack, unearth passport, prepare myself for spending a night in a hotel room with Charlie.

Back at the flat, I call Kirsty to fill her in on the latest development.

'Lucky you,' she exclaims, amidst what sounds like a brawl in the background.

'I thought you'd disapprove, that you'd say I'm mad to go . . .'

'God, no, not at all.'

The background noise has reached such a level that it's difficult to hear her. 'Are you okay? Sounds a bit hectic . . .'

'Hectic?' she says witheringly. 'It's full-on war here. Worst thing is, Dan finally agreed to take a couple of days holiday so you'd think it should be a *bit* easier . . .' Her voice wobbles.

'Why isn't it?' I ask.

'Because he's not actually *here*. He's spending the whole time in his sodding shed, doing God knows what, and when he's in the house he's jabbing away at his phone like a teenager . . .' She blasts this out, which has the effect of silencing her children immediately. *Why are you doing this? I want to ask her. School starts again the week after next. Can't Dan see what a fine invention it really is?*

'Couldn't he take the kids out for a few hours?' I suggest, aware of the unspoken rule that, no matter how much a friend berates her husband, you can't say what you really think because – hopefully – it'll sort itself out.

'You're right,' Kirsty says briskly. 'I just need to get Dan more involved. Anyway – you just have a great time and remember, I want to hear every detail.'

As we finish the call, I try to shake off the twinge of annoyance I have for Dan. The truth is, while I know Kirsty would hate me to feel sorry for her, I can't help it. I imagine she weeps with frustration every time she walks past the lovely primary school at the end of the road and sees all those children playing happily at break time. In some ways, I had it easier with Tom; he never expressed any preference as to how the boys spent their time, so there was no wrangling, no, '*This* is how it must be.'

'I can't believe it,' Viv shrieks when I call her. 'You never do things like this.'

'You mean I'm never spontaneous?' I say, eyeing the contents of my open suitcase.

A small pause. 'Not especially, no. That's not a criticism,' she adds quickly. 'I'm just amazed you agreed. God, Alice. You're off to *Paris* . . .'

'Well, I just thought, why not? I've only been once,

with Tom, and it was lovely but he did grumble about the admission fees—'

'Stop pretending you're going on some cultural trip,' she sniggers. 'You're making out it'll be all about the Louvre and the Pompidou Centre when, let's face it, you're actually going to be in bed the whole time with – what's his name again?'

'Charlie.'

'What about Giles?' she adds, lowering her voice to a murmur, reminding me that she's at work. 'Hasn't he called you?'

'Haven't heard a thing,' I tell her. 'Anyway, I'd better finish packing . . .'

'Oh, good luck. I'm *so* envious.' Which, coming from Viv, is quite something.

In fact, getting ready for the trip is so easy, it's almost eerie. When Tom was still here, preparing for a family jaunt was such a mammoth task, it would literally take days. 'I don't know why you make such a fuss about packing,' Tom would retort, having dropped his pants, swimming trunks and a razor into a bag the size of a pencil case (it was up to me to remember his T-shirts, shorts, etc. – i.e. proper clothing, not to mention also packing for the kids). This time, I've flung just a couple of outfits into my case, plus what Mum regards as my excessive array of skincare products (i.e. facial wash, serum). Is it really possible to travel so lightly? Doubt starts to creep in. Will a stripy Breton top look silly in Paris, as if I'm trying too hard to look Parisian? No, Breton tops are from Brittany, obviously . . . Deciding I need to reassess it later, I settle down with a coffee in the kitchen and call Logan's mobile. There's much jollity and laughter in the background. I can hear Jessica chattering excitedly, and Fergus's loud, barky laugh.

'Hi, darling,' I say.

'Hi, Mum.' He sounds perky, which I take as a good sign.

'Just wondered how things are going.'

'Yeah, good. Really good.'

I remove the Breton top from my case and add the embroidered one which I can't stop liking, despite Mum's sudden concern over its production.

'What have you been up to, love?'

'Just stuff, y'know . . .' When will it stop being so difficult to communicate with Logan? When will he start saying, 'Are there any light jobs you need doing around the flat, Mother?'

'So . . . Dad mentioned the weather's been great.'

'Yeah . . .'

'I hope you've been wearing sunscreen . . .'

'*Mum,*' he says, exasperated.

More silence. 'Could I have a quick word with Fergus, please?'

'Yeah, here he is.'

At least his brother is more talkative. 'Are you missing us, Mum?' he wants to know.

''Course I am, love. I'm missing you so much it hurts.'

He sniggers. 'What have you been doing?'

Nothing much. Baking and dating, baking and dating . . . 'Just baking, really. Grandma was here for a couple of days for her birthday. Oh, and I took that carrier bag of toys in your room to the charity shop.'

'Huh?'

'You know – your old teddies and Rex and all that.'

There's an awkward pause. Even Jessica has stopped chattering away in the background.

'Rex?' Fergus repeats. 'You took *Rex* to the charity shop?'

'Well, yes, but only because you left him all packed up and ready to go in that big plastic bag . . .' A trace of defensiveness has crept into my voice.

'You mean that bag in my room?'

'Yes . . . that *was* okay, wasn't it?'

'Mum,' he says slowly, 'I was gonna have another look through them when I got back. They weren't ready to go. They were *still being sorted* . . .' There's a distinct wobble in his voice, not unlike Kirsty's a few moments ago.

'Did you want to keep Rex?' I ask fearfully.

'Yeah, I did!'

'What is it?' Logan mutters in the background. 'What's she done with your stuff?'

'Shut up,' Fergus snaps at him.

'Has she given your stuff away? She did that with me once! Remember that Lego pirate ship—'

'He said that pirate ship could go to the school bring-and-buy,' I protest, to no avail: my sons are now discussing my habit of giving away their beloved possessions to any old passing kid in the street.

'What about your train set?' Logan reminds him.

'Yeah! I *loved* that train.' Fergus appears to have forgotten that I'm even on the phone.

'But it was broken,' I insist. 'It didn't even go, and half its track was missing . . .' I'm still gripping the phone as they detail my crimes.

'Remember when she gave away our sea monkeys?' Fergus bleats.

Sea monkeys? They were dead, for crying out loud,

because Logan had knocked over the tank and they fell on the carpet . . .

'Fergus,' I snap. 'Please stop this . . .' Christ, I'd actually called to tell them about my Paris trip. It would be better, I figured, than sneaking off and freaking out if they happened to glimpse a Ladurée carrier bag, or the packet of French cigarettes which I am now looking forward to stuffing into my mouth, all at once. A soft packet of twenty, *sans filtre*. YUM.

'Fergus!' I repeat, more loudly this time.

'Yeah?'

'Listen to me, please. Just tell me why, when you haven't played with or even looked at Rex for about twenty-five years—'

'I wasn't born then,' he says coldly. 'I wasn't even a foetus.'

'Yes, I know, love. I was exaggerating—'

'The thing is,' he cuts in, sounding desperately upset now, 'I've been drawing a lot in the evenings, making comics for Jessica . . .'

'That's lovely of you,' I murmur.

'. . . Starring *Rex*,' he shouts, 'and she really liked 'em, and I've promised she can have Rex – real Rex, I mean – when we get back.'

Silence hangs in the air, tense and sweat-making. That's the thing with charity shops, I realise now: you pick something up – a smelly old girdle, or a scuffed shoe – and you wrinkle your nose at it before dumping it back on the shelf, without realising it was someone's most precious thing.

'Fergus, I'm sorry,' I mutter.

'Mum, I *really* need him back. I promised her. She talks about him all the time.'

185

I swallow hard. 'I *did* get permission from Logan to give his pirate ship to school . . .'

'Yeah,' he whispers, 'he's just being an arse.'

I blow out a big gust of air. 'Well, maybe I could run round to the charity shop right now and see if they still have him.'

'Would you?' A trace of hope has crept into his voice.

'Yes, of course I will.' We finish the call, and I take a sip of my coffee which is now stone cold. When I glimpse myself in the hall mirror, I am pale with pinkish eyes, and prominent horizontal lines are etched across my clammy forehead. I don't have the aura of someone who's on the verge of jumping into bed with a very sexy man in Paris. I look as if I've just had a marital row. Which might explain why, as I scamper along to the end of our road, that tall, dark-eyed deli man – pusher of extortionate cheese – gives me a concerned frown as he finishes chalking the sign outside his shop.

'You okay?' he asks when I'm nearly level with him.

'Yes thanks.' I have slowed down to a more manage-able trot.

'Are you sure?' I see him glancing behind me as if expecting to see a furious husband with a meat tenderiser.

'I'm fine, thanks, just in a hurry,' I add, forcing a smile as I speed-walk by. My arrival at the charity shop is announced by a jingling of Tibetan bells above the door. I hone in on the toy section, praying for a glimpse of a sullied white dog with the texture of hosiery among the tired Barbies. It occurs to me, as I rake through a wire basket of beanie toys, that most women wouldn't be doing this the day before a trip with a prospective new lover. They would be choosing new lingerie, enjoying

186

a manicure, or even having a Brazilian. They would not be examining a sorry-looking polar bear and wondering if it might pass as a dog.

'Excuse me,' I say, now at the till, 'I brought in a bag of soft toys last week and the lady put them in the back room. I wondered if it might still be there?'

The short, stocky, blonde woman purses her scarlet lips, as if I might be planning to purloin something that was never mine in the first place.

'I'll have a look,' she says. 'Sorry, nothing there,' she announces, reappearing a moment later.

I frown. 'Are you sure? It's a big clear plastic bag of soft toys—'

'Did they have Kitemarks?'

Does she think I spend my time forensically examining teddies? 'Er . . . I have no idea.'

She shrugs. 'If they didn't, then we can't sell them. Against regulations. Sorry.'

'No, but you see, the lady who was here last week took them, she *accepted* them . . .'

She throws me a baffled glance and turns to serve the man beside me. I slope out of the shop, picturing Fergus and Jessica's doleful expressions when it's announced that my mission failed. What happens to unwanted soft toys anyway? Are they slung into some gigantic wheelie bin round the back of the shop? Or sent to a factory to be turned into the filling for cheap sofas? As I approach the deli, the French guy is still out there, drawing a fancy border around the edge of his sign.

'Did you make it?' he asks, looking up.

'Sorry?'

'You were in a hurry—'

'Oh,' I say distractedly. 'Um . . . not really. I actually

187

went back to the charity shop to try and rescue one of my son's toys.' I shrug. 'But they didn't have it.'

'Ah,' he says, straightening up, 'the one that's suddenly a favourite again.'

I smile, impressed that he grasps the urgency of the situation. 'Yes, sort of.'

'Could you buy a replacement? There's that new place along there . . .' He indicates the side street where a toyshop has opened. Being past that stage with the boys, I have barely registered its existence.

'Good idea, but I think it has to be the actual one. A substitute wouldn't be the same.'

'Ah, shame.' I thank him and decide to try the toyshop anyway. But Noah's is all handcrafted wooden arks and reproduction Victorian theatres; the only nod to a soft toy is a large brown monkey costing fifty quid. It's becoming harder to buy ordinary things around here. Where's the plain old dyed Cheddar, and the cheap synthetic cuddly toy when you need it? I'm starting to think that maybe the boys and I should trade down to a less chi-chi neighbourhood. Maybe then we'd be able to afford the East Wing that Logan so desires.

Back home, I toy with the idea of calling Logan and/or Fergus again, but at the risk of further accusations being flung at me, I decide to text instead. Cowardly, I know. Shamefully, I decide not to mention Paris.

Just been asked on a jaunt, last minute thing, back home Thursday phone me any time xxx.

I perch on the edge of my bed, next to my open suitcase, and wait for a response. There is none.

Chapter Seventeen

I think my friends would say I try to focus on the positive. For instance, when I recall our last visit to Mum's, it's not the salmonella-burgers that instantly spring to mind, but being with my boys in the steamy warmth of the chip shop. And when I sneak another look at Tom flaunting his brassicas in that darned magazine, I just think, thank Christ Patsy is in charge of him now, and that I can buy our vegetables from a shop.

And so, when I wake up not with a surge of anticipation but an attack of piles on Paris Day, I think: they're actually not *too* bad. I mean, I've known worse. In the past, they've been so vicious I've literally had to hobble around the flat, wincing and clutching at my rear, while Tom spouted a seemingly endless supply of bottom-related funnies. And at least the beard rash has died down at last.

As with most low-level irritations, I employ my usual tactic of trying to ignore the issue. It's something I've learnt to do during these past few years. When you're a single parent of adolescents, you simply can't create an enormous ding-dong over every little thing, or you'd spend your whole *life* raging and issuing threats. So I shower and dress, doing everything in a slightly stilted way, as if expecting a crucial part of my anatomy to snap.

The taxi sounds its horn in the street below. Grabbing my bag and small wheeled suitcase, I trot gingerly downstairs to where Charlie is waiting, looking rakishly handsome in jeans and a checked shirt, at the front door.

'Hey,' he says, kissing my cheek before looking me up and down. 'I love your dress, and your hair looks great up like that – shows off your lovely neck.'

'Thanks.' I smile, a little overawed by his gushing compliments. *Relax*, I instruct myself silently. *He's attracted to you, as you are to him. Giving compliments is just what nice guys do.*

'Well,' he says as we climb into the cab, 'I'm really glad you said yes to this. It was very . . . spontaneous of you.'

I laugh. 'I'm not in the habit of turning down invitations to Paris, you know.'

'I'm a lucky man then, especially as you're in the midst of your dating whirlwind—'

'Charlie,' I cut in, 'it's not a whirlwind. More like a light breeze. Anyway, that's pretty much fizzled out now. I'm just looking forward to this.'

He smiles and kisses me tenderly on the lips as the cab pulls out of my road. I glance at him, taking in the intense brown eyes and lovely, flirtatious mouth. Looks like he's freshly shaved, thank goodness. One minor medical issue is enough to deal with today without a ravaged face. That is, assuming there'll be some *ravaging*

190

going on later . . . I try to picture us in a Parisian hotel room, and my stomach flips with a combination of excitement and sheer nerves.

'So when were you last in Paris?' I ask him.

'Um . . . just before Christmas.'

'Another freebie?'

'Not exactly, no.' He clears his throat. Ah, a romantic tryst of some kind, perhaps with the Chloé handbag girl. 'How about you?'

'It's seventeen years since I was there.'

'Ah, you're long overdue then.' He smiles, taking my hand and squeezing it.

'Just a bit.' *I'm long overdue a lot of things*, I want to say.

'What's your French like?' he asks.

'I can just about muddle through as long as everyone sticks to the present tense . . .'

He grins. 'Afraid I'm hopeless. I can tell you now, I'm not going to sweep you off your feet with my linguistic skills.'

'I think I can just about forgive you for that.' *And who cares, when you have plenty of other appealing qualities?* I smile, and we fall into an easy silence for a few moments. As the driver turns on to the bypass towards the airport, I'm aware of a kernel of excitement, fizzling and growing in my stomach. I have already decided not to fret about where this thing might lead. I'm going to just go with it, and relish every moment – once I've nipped into a chemist for some pile cream, obviously, seeing as Viv swiped the last of mine to shrink her eyebags. And once that's been dealt with . . . who knows? We are speeding towards the airport now, filling each other in on the bits of our lives we had yet to share. The

191

sky is watery blue, the sun high and bright, and it feels as if anything could happen.

*

Four hours later, having dropped our bags at our hotel in a shady avenue in the Latin Quarter, we are installed in an extremely pleasing bistro for lunch. My boys have never been to France – well, Logan has, but he was in my womb at the time – but even they, if asked what a typical Parisian bistro looks like, would describe this one. It has all the essentials: crisp white tablecloths, yellowy wall lamps and not especially friendly waitresses. We order a bottle of Pinot Noir and, within minutes, Charlie has knocked back his first glass. Today, however, I am on a mission to a) Dive into a chemist without alerting Charlie as to what I need to buy, as there was no blasted ointment at Edinburgh airport and, b) Pace Myself With Booze.

'You're taking your time with that,' he says, indicating my glass as I tuck into perhaps the most heavenly steak on earth.

I laugh and take a sip, just to appease him. 'What's the rush? We've got the whole day ahead, haven't we?'

'Oh, come on,' he teases, 'you weren't hanging back like this at the Terrace . . .'

'That was different.'

'How different?'

'Well . . .' I smirk, 'we'd only just met. I was nervous. I had to bolster myself up with booze—'

'Yeah, you looked terrified,' he sniggers. 'I could tell.'

'But now I'm more relaxed,' I go on in a mock-serious tone, spearing a perfectly crisp chip with my fork, 'and,

192

seeing as I've only been to Paris twice in two decades, I want to enjoy it, you know? And not be crashed out in the hotel by teatime, dribbling on to a pillow.'

'That could be fun.' He grins mischievously.

'Anyway,' I add, 'this place is lovely, isn't it? Why isn't there anywhere like this back home? Even the French deli near my flat isn't quite the same as a proper Parisian one.'

He smiles warmly and squeezes my hand across the table. 'It's all the better for you being here.'

'So,' I say, deciding to bite the bullet, 'who were you here with last time, if you don't mind me asking?'

'Oh, that was Becky.'

I nod. Wasn't the hint-stickers girl called Matilda?

'Just a fling,' he goes on, sloshing more wine into his glass, then waggling the bottle and flashing a charming smile in the waitress's line of vision, to indicate that we'd like another. Blimey, he's knocking it back fast. 'Bit tempestuous, to be honest,' he adds. 'Wasn't my happiest experience of this city.'

'What did she do?' I ask.

'Battered my credit card,' he says with a rueful laugh.

'No, I mean job-wise.'

He shrugs. 'Bit of this, bit of that . . .' He thanks the waitress as she uncorks the wine. 'Okay – she was a model back in the day. All eyes and teeth – you know the kind.'

'Er, yes,' I say, grabbing the dessert menu and deciding to swerve away from the subject of Charlie's high maintenance exes. Why am I complicating an otherwise lovely scenario? Here we are, in the kind of restaurant I dream about – buzzing, unpretentious, filled with fabulous smells – yet some chip in my brain is compelling me to quiz him about former girlfriends.

'Anyway, that's way in the past,' he says firmly. 'I fancy one of those little chocolate sponge things with the melted inside, don't you?'

'I'm completely full,' I say truthfully.

'Oh, come on, Alice – you've gone all *moderate* on me . . .'

'It's just, I would quite like to be able to move this afternoon,' I say with a smile.

'I don't mind, you know,' he adds.

'What, if I can't move?'

'No – you being nosy, quizzing me about Becky.' He leans forward. 'You can ask me anything. There's not one thing in the world I won't tell you.' He turns to our waitress who seems impervious to his charm. 'Two of those chocolate melty things, thank you.'

'But Charlie, I don't want—'

'Go on,' he cuts in, 'ask me anything.'

I smile, draining my glass. He's right – I *am* nosy. Maybe it was no accident that I just so happened to have Viv with me as I investigated the foul smell in Fergus's room. Perhaps my subconscious had known all along that she'd have a good old pry through his browsing history, and that a murky image would lurk therein.

'Okay,' I say, grinning, 'remember at the Terrace, when you said you'd done all kinds of things for money?'

'Did I say that?' He's all wide-eyed, boyish innocence.

'Yes, you did.'

He frowns, feigning bafflement.

'Come on, Charlie,' I prompt him.

'Okay, okay,' he laughs. 'This was years ago, right? I was about twenty. I was stupid and only agreed to do it because somebody asked me and I didn't think it through.'

Now, of course, I'm *bursting* with curiosity. Our chocolate puddings arrive and, all poised and ready for gossip, I plunge in a spoon. 'Did you sleep with someone for money?'

'No! God, no. I've never done that. That would be . . .' He shudders. 'Tawdry.'

'So what was it, then?'

Charlie refills our glasses, even though I'm not sure it's quite the thing to accompany chocolate pudding with a heady red wine. 'I did a bit of modelling,' he says.

'Oh. Is that it?' Now I get it. Becky was a model, and perhaps Matilda too. His younger years were mostly spent in impossibly beautiful couple scenarios – like Kate Moss and Johnny Depp, a million light years ago. He certainly has the bone structure for it.

'Well, it was a very specific sort of modelling,' he adds.

'Catalogue?'

'No,' he chuckles.

I study his face. 'Not porn, was it?'

I can tell by his guarded expression that I'm in the right kind of area, and immediately, I know I'm *not* entirely fine about this; the fact that he's probably done it with hundreds of women, I mean.

'It was a one-off thing,' he says quickly, 'and it wasn't a movie, okay? It was for a mag. A kind of fishing mag . . .'

'Porno fishing?' I splutter. 'Is that a thing?'

'Guess it was,' he laughs, 'or *is* – I have no idea. All I know is, a friend of a friend was let down by a model and I was broke at the time, and the money was good considering that all I had to do was stand on a riverbank in a green waterproof cape and a deer-stalker-type hat,

195

holding a massive fish – not a halibut, bigger than that – what are those huge things with teeth?'

'A pike?'

He spoons in some pudding. 'Yeah, it might've been that. Scary-looking bugger.'

'But . . .' I squint across the table at him, 'I don't understand why this was such a big deal. Holding a fish, I mean, on a riverbank.'

He grins. 'Well, I wasn't wearing any trousers. *Or* pants.'

'You mean you were naked apart from the cape?'

'And the hat,' he reminds me. 'Don't forget the hat.'

By now, I'm convulsing with laughter. Christ, he's clearly quite bonkers, but charmingly so and maybe I need someone like this in my life – a man who doesn't care what anyone thinks. I can't believe I was all torn up inside when that charity shop lady sneered at my bag of soft toys. 'They didn't even cordon off that part of the river,' Charlie goes on, 'so you'd get the odd person wandering along walking their dog . . .'

I am now laughing so hard I've had to abandon my pudding. '*Charlie*. You were a flasher on a riverbank! That's so creepy.'

'Not a flasher,' he hisses. 'It was a professional job.' I'm still in hysterics as we leave the restaurant. I don't know if laughing so much has, uh, put a strain on something, but my tender bottom 'issue' seems to have worsened.

'You okay?' Charlie asks, giving me a concerned look as we stop at the street corner.

'Yes, I'm fine.'

He keeps shooting me quizzical looks as we stroll along the bustling street, filled with market stalls bearing fruit. 'Are your shoes hurting?'

'No, my shoes are fine.'

He stops and scrutinises my face. 'Alice, you keep saying you're fine, but you're obviously not. What's the matter? Are you ill or something?'

I grimace. 'Oh, I wasn't going to say anything because I didn't want to put a damper on the day and, to be honest, it's a little embarrassing, I have a small, er, medical issue,' I say, wincing.

He blinks at me. 'You're actually a man.'

'Haha – no. No. Jesus.'

He grabs at my hand. 'I'm kidding. So what's up? Nothing serious, I hope?'

'It's um . . . something I've had on and off since I had Logan . . .'

'A kind of lady trouble?' He raises a brow.

I burst out laughing. 'I've got piles, Charlie, and I need to buy some cream.'

'Is that all?' His eyebrows shoot up. 'Right – let's get you sorted, then.' While I have a distinctly sparkly edge afforded by several glasses of wine over lunch, Charlie is clearly tipsy as he takes my hand. His eyes are unfocused, his voice growing louder as he keeps reassuring me that we'll find just the thing and I'm not to worry *at all*. Of course, this being France, there are numerous places to buy pharmaceutical supplies; the one we wander into is more medical emporium than plain old chemist. The women at the till are all cool blondes of a certain age in pristine white tunics.

Leaving Charlie loitering by the men's fragrances, I peruse the shelves. There's an entire wall of posh skincare which everyone seems to be able to afford here. Perhaps that's why the women look so radiant and fresh. Despite our exquisite surroundings, I do not feel fresh. I'd like to find the right medication and a public loo where I can bung it on and be done with it.

I sidle over to Charlie. 'Can't find anything.'

'Why don't you ask at the counter?'

'Um . . . I'm not sure how to.'

'Go on.' He smiles encouragingly. 'You said you're great at French, that you're a language person . . .'

'No I didn't,' I exclaim. 'I said I can just about get by in the present tense.'

'This *is* the present tense. It's, "I need some pile cream," not, "I needed pile cream yesterday." How hard can that be?' God, does he have to talk so loudly? I glance around the shop, cursing myself for caring, yet again, what people might think.

'Charlie,' I whisper, 'I meant I can order an omelette or ask for directions to the post office, okay? Schoolgirl stuff. We never got around to describing embarrassing bum problems.'

He laughs raucously. 'You should've, it would have been a lot more useful . . .'

'What'll I *do*?'

'I'm sure you'll manage,' he says levelly. 'They look perfectly friendly in here.'

I glance towards the counter, and decide they do not; the women are gliding back and forth with neutral expressions, like incredibly lifelike robots designed to dispense medication more efficiently than any human ever could. I look back at Charlie, wondering if he might possibly be what's often termed as 'a bit of a handful', what with the nudie fisherman stuff, and now this – goading me in front of the haughty pharmacy ladies. In fact, I've always favoured an adventurous man over the kind of safe, secure type who has all his pensions in order and takes

198

time to thoroughly prepare a surface before slapping on paint (in the early days with Tom, I actually regarded his fondness for staying up all night drinking, then lying in bed all day sweating and bleating for cups of tea, as a desirable attribute). But I'm no longer nineteen. I'm nearly forty, for God's sake, and Charlie's drunk, smirking face is starting to irk a bit.

'Hang on,' I mutter, pulling my phone from my pocket.

'Who are you calling?' he asks. 'Arse-busters?'

'I'm texting Fergus,' I say huffily, typing, *Hi love, got your translator with you? If so could you ask it the French for ointment?*

He pings back a reply – *pomade* – with a smiley emoticon. Hmm.

'Sounds like a hair product,' I murmur, making my way to the till. I'm feeling bolder now, determined to show Charlie what I'm made of. But as soon as I'm face to face with one of the assistants, who's a dead ringer for how I imagine Gwyneth Paltrow will look in her sixties, my glimmer of courage melts away. I clear my throat. *'Je voudrais du pomade . . .'*

The woman frowns at me.

'De la pomade,' I continue, *'pour ma,* uh . . .' I glance at a silently hysterical Charlie, then back at mature-Gwynnie with her peachy lips and perfectly arched brows. She is still studying me with mild interest, as if I might possibly produce a live rabbit from my bag. *'J'ai une probleme,'* I hiss, *'dans ma . . .'* I grimace and point to my rear end, aware of Charlie convulsing by the hair conditioners.

The woman frowns and says something that I don't understand.

'Er . . . *les piles. J'ai les piles dans ma derrière . . .'*

I'm not sure whether I'm failing to communicate properly, or if the woman knows perfectly well what I need but is feigning ignorance so as to maximise my humiliation. I'm sweating now, my underarms prickling, no doubt staining the pale blue spotty dress I chose so carefully for this trip. A small queue has formed, and the woman beside me is clearing her throat. I look around in desperation, and all I can think of is to snatch two nail polishes from the little wicker basket on the counter – one pink, the other pale mint, which are going to be a *fat* lot of use in soothing my tender backside. As I hand over ten euros, Charlie appears at my side, having blithely jumped the queue to point at a shelf behind the counter.

'*Preparation-ash, s'il vous plaît,*' he says, his accent perfect.

I blink at him. *Preparation-ash?* And it dawns on me that he knew all along that the French use exactly the same stuff as we do – Preparation H – and that all the silent sniggering was actually his idea of a bloody *joke*.

'*C'est tout?*' the woman asks pleasantly, extracting the box from the shelf and ringing it through the till.

'*Oui, merci,*' Charlie says.

Bastard.

'Here you go,' he says with a grin as we leave the shop.

I take the paper bag from him. 'I can't believe you did that.'

He widens his eyes, all innocence. 'Did what?'

'Stood there watching while I made a complete fool of myself buying nail polishes!'

'But I thought you spoke French—'

'Like I said, I don't really, and even if I did . . .' I tail off, frowning. 'Oh, never mind.' We are marching briskly past a row of smart boutiques. 'It's just, you knew what to ask for all along.'

'Well, yeah.' He grins ruefully, causing my irritation to subside a little.

'How did you know?'

'Um, Becky had the same problem . . .' Ah, how heartening to discover that I have something in common with one of those all-eyes-and-teeth models. 'Also,' he adds, 'piles actually means batteries in French. So when you said, "*J'ai les piles dans ma derrière*", you were actually telling that woman you have batteries up your arse.'

'Oh, for God's sake!' I stop abruptly. 'Is that why she was looking at me that way?'

Charlie smirks, his brown eyes gleaming playfully. 'Yeah, I'd imagine it was.'

I gawp at him, lost for words for a moment. And for the first time, a rogue thought darts into my mind: *What on earth are you doing here, Alice Sweet?*

Chapter Eighteen

By the time we're back at the hotel – to check in properly, and so I can attend to *Prep-Ash* duties – I'm starting to think I overreacted a little there. I'm just not used to being around someone like Charlie, who's clearly up for mischief. It's not that I'm some buttoned-up trout who's incapable of having fun; just that it's been so long since I could entirely please myself that I've almost forgotten how.

'D'you forgive me?' Charlie asks, pulling me in for a hug as we set down our bags in our room.

'Yes, of course I do.'

'I promise, if there are any more medical emergencies, I'll be a gallant gentleman and handle it all.'

'Sure, I know I'm completely safe in your hands,' I say with a dry laugh.

'But you are! Truly. You're a gorgeous woman, you know that? And I'm sorry I poked fun at you . . .' I grin as I untangle myself from his arms and pull out my phone from my bag.

How's it going? reads Ingrid's text.

Funny, sort of, I reply.

Eh? Good or bad funny? she responds in a blink. I'm about to reply *Good, don't worry* when Charlie's arms are around me again, and we're kissing and kissing, standing up at first, then somehow tumbling on to the enormous bed. I pull back and smile, studying his flushed face.

'What's wrong?' he asks, frowning.

'Let's go out. We're only here for one day. Let's do some exploring . . .'

'Mmm, later,' he says, gathering me into his arms again and going in for a wine-scented kiss.

'And remember you're meant to be reviewing this hotel . . .'

'Yeah, yeah.' He sniggers. 'I picked up a leaflet about it at reception.'

'That's the sum total of your research?' I tease him, at which he shrugs. 'Oh, come on, Charlie. It's a beautiful day, I really don't want to miss it.' He pulls away this time, lying on his side of the bed and regarding me with mild amusement. He looks lovely; relaxed and handsome, his dark eyes sparkling and hair saucily mussed from our cavortings. It's not that I don't want to go to bed with him; I really do. But I sort of want to save it till later because – I know Viv would despair of me here – I really would like to explore Paris.

'You want to go up the sodding Eiffel Tower,' he says with a wry smile.

'No, not that. I'd just like to . . .' I jump off the bed and smooth down my rumpled hair and dress in preparation for leaving.

'Visit the Sacré-Coeur?'

'Yes!' I say, grabbing his hand. 'Come on – I know you're all blasé about travel but I'm not.'

203

'Okay, okay,' he says, laughing as he gathers himself up. 'I can see you've got a whole itinerary worked out.'

'Not quite, but there are places I'm dying to see. Let's start with the Musée d'Orsay, then head over to Montmartre . . .'

As it turns out, Charlie responds well to a little gentle encouragement. He is hugely enthusiastic as we make our way through the gallery, partly, I suspect, due to the wine he knocked back at lunch, but also because he appears to be having a great time. Now and again, he grabs my hand or snakes an arm around my waist; it's extremely giddying.

We head onwards to Sacré-Coeur, where he bounds up the seemingly never-ending steps (impressive, considering that he claims to be a stranger to exercise). Up there, the view over the city is breathtaking. For a brief moment, I almost wish Logan and Fergus were here so I could grab them and say, 'Look – isn't it amazing?' But of course, they'd be all huffy from hiking up those steps and being made to look at a boring old church.

By now we're all hungry again, so we drift towards the Marais, my attention momentarily diverted by the cluttered window of a toyshop. 'Look,' I yelp, indicating a cheap-looking soft toy.

'What is it?' Charlie asks.

'It's the same one! It's Rex – my son's dog that I took to the charity shop and need to replace. Come on.' Grabbing his hand, I pull him into the shop, every inch of which is crammed with a crazy jumble of toys. Unlike Noah's back in Edinburgh, this one has been filled with everything from the tackiest teddy to precious items costing hundreds of euros. There's a hand-carved rocking horse with a real hair mane, and a family of fifty Russian dolls, all intricately painted in reds and golds.

'This place is amazing,' I breathe, unhooking a dangling Rex from the ceiling and making my way to the counter, while Charlie amuses himself by grabbing an old-fashioned jack-in-a-box – of a similar vintage to my Fuzzy Felts, I'd guess – and setting it off in my face.

'You're such a child,' I laugh.

'So are you,' he shoots back. 'Why are you buying that horrible dog? It's ugly, Alice. Surely you can find him a nicer souvenir.'

'It's not a souvenir,' I explain. 'You see, I'm going to try and pass this off as the one he loved when he was little.'

Charlie looks baffled. 'You're gonna *lie* to him?'

'Well, sort of, but sometimes it's the best way.' I smile at him. 'D'you know much about kids?'

'Hell, no. They're confusing and unpredictable, like small, drunk people.' He pauses, then adds, 'I'll be nice with yours, though. I won't scare them.'

I grin as he takes my hand, and as we leave the shop I start thinking, could I introduce Charlie to Logan and Fergus? They'd like him, I think, and anyway, they'll have to accept that I'll meet someone one day. I can't live my weird baking nun's life forever.

Starving by now, we find a beautiful little Turkish restaurant where we feast on delicious charred lamb and even more wine. At least, I have two glasses and Charlie has more than I can keep track of, and when we leave the place he is *reeling*.

It's nearly midnight by the time we've pottered back to the hotel. It was my idea to walk, in the hope that it would give him a chance to sober up a little. I have nothing against a drunk man, and he's still excellent company, regaling me with tales of crazy commissions and his louche London life. But still, having hauled him out to do the whole touristy thing, I'm now rather eager to get him back to our room.

A shiver of excitement runs through me as we step into the hotel lift. As soon as its metal gate closes, we are kissing again. We tumble out at the third floor and into our room. Charlie totters off to the bathroom, giving me a few moments to gather myself; it's been so long since I found myself in a situation like this – an about-to-go-to-bed situation, I mean. And I literally have forgotten what the etiquette is. Undress and leap into bed? That seems a little . . . hasty. What, then? Should I put the kettle on and make us a pot of tea, or would he think I'm a tragic old square?

The shower is on; he must have had a drunken urge to cleanse himself. Well, at least he'll be lovely and fresh.

'Alice,' he shouts through the closed bathroom door, 'come in with me.'

What – in the shower? Christ. I'm not entirely sure I could carry it off – the whole sex in the shower thing, I mean, with the potential for skidding and cracking my head on the tiles. The thought of normal, uncomplicated bed-sex is nerve-racking enough without the introduction of water and slippery porcelain surfaces.

'Alice?' he yells again.

'Just getting a breath of air,' I call back, like an old lady who's become overheated at a wedding reception. I push open the tall glass doors which lead on to our balcony, and step out. We are on the top floor of this grand old building, and the sky is inky blue. It's still bustling in the street below and, ridiculously, I find myself wishing the boys were with me again. It's wrong, surely, to keep thinking about my kids when I should be plotting all kinds of things to get up to with Charlie.

I inhale deeply, smiling as I replay our day in my mind. The pile incident I could have done without, but that aside, I can't remember having so much fun. I glance back into our room where Charlie has emerged from the bathroom. Without staring directly, I see him whip off his hotel gown with a flourish, throw it over the phone on the desk and tumble on to the bed. God, he's pissed. While I'm not against a fun drunken encounter, it doesn't seem quite as appealing when there's a huge imbalance in inebriation levels – as there is right now. It strikes me as bizarre how *brilliant* sex can be when you're both sloshed, and how uninviting it seems when you're the relatively sober one. Winey breath, drunken fumblings . . . it's not quite how I imagined ending my eighteen months of celibacy.

'Alice, you coming to bed?' Charlie drawls. Out of the corner of my eye, I see him pat the pillow hopefully.

'Yep, in a minute.'

'What are you doing out there?'

'Just taking some photos,' I fib. I swallow hard, looking down to the street where a couple are striding along the pavement. He has choppy dark hair and is wearing a long black coat over a crew-necked sweater and jeans, and she is in a little figure-hugging red dress, with a black cardi thrown over her shoulders. She looks stunning. They both do. They are holding hands and laughing, and the sight of them makes me think, *Get a grip, Alice: there's a lovely, sexy man waiting for you in that bed, so why are you hiding out here on the balcony?* I look back down at the couple. They seem so very Parisian, as if they've stepped out of that black-and-white Robert

Doisneau photo, the one called The Kiss, where it looks as if he's just grabbed her in the middle of a busy street. Right on cue, he *does* kiss her. I turn away and step back into our room where Charlie is lying in bed, head propped up on one hand, and covered from the waist down with the cream sheet.

'Hey,' he says with an unsteady smile.

'Lovely night out there,' I say.

'Must be,' he teases, 'you've been ages. How many pictures did you take?'

'Hundreds,' I reply.

'Are you happy?' he asks squiffily.

'Of course I am. It's been a lovely day. Amazing food and wine, *and* a fake-Rex . . .'

'What more could a girl ask for?' he asks. I study him for a moment: this funny, sexy man who I can imagine shaking me out of my domestic doldrums. He is fun and attentive, and undeniably handsome – even more so lying there in bed, his lightly tanned body displayed to fine effect against the sheets. His shoulders are nicely shaped, his whole upper body muscled in a way that would appear to be his natural physique. He is, I notice, slowly tugging down the upper sheet with his foot, an impressively dexterous move considering how drunk he is.

Down and down the sheet goes, his gaze remaining fixed on mine. I watch it with interest, wondering if this is some kind of party trick. Maybe, when it gets to a certain crucial point, something will pop out – like that jack-in-a-box in the toyshop. I glimpse Fake-Rex parked there on the dressing table and am seized by an urge to shield him from this naked man.

For now he has disposed of the sheet with one final,

dramatic flick of his foot, and is lying there, dead still, as if in a gallery.

A smile teases his lips. I try to smile back, in a way that shows I am appreciating the vision of beauty before me. But I can't because my lips are starting to quiver with mirth, so I have to clamp them together instead.

'C'mon, Alice,' Charlie murmurs.

It's no good. Hysterical laughter is bubbling up inside me, about to burst out.

'Just a minute,' I say, diving into the bathroom and shutting the door behind me. *Breathe*, I command myself. *Breathe, think of serious things. Like, er, library fines and stern letters from the Inland Revenue . . .* But my shoulders are bobbing with mirth and, try as I might, I can't shift the image of that slowly descending sheet from my mind – a sort of horizontal striptease, involving bed linen. Oh, God. I am now laughing so hard, tears have sprung into my eyes, and when I glimpse my reflection there are patches of wet mascara beneath my eyes.

I sit on the loo, trying to steady my breathing. *Think of sad things*, I command myself silently. I picture the inside of Mum's fridge, and the time she gathered up Dad's ratty old jumpers and made a fire of them in her back garden. I imagine Tom and Patsy smugly gathering kale in their cottage garden – Tom even has a trug, I saw it in that magazine – but even that doesn't work, because it doesn't make me feel sad at all. It just makes me laugh even harder.

I pour myself a glass of water at the wash basin and gulp it down. Ripping off a square of loo roll, I blot my eyes, then pull off my clothes and drape them over the side of the bath. There. I am naked, ready for anything. I glance down at my pubes and think, maybe I should have

209

had a Brazilian to haul me into the modern age, but too late now. Maybe he'll find me pleasingly retro. I try to remember the last time I had sex, and the unsettling vision of a long-ago one-night stand shimmers into my mind – of a sweaty policeman I met at Kirsty's sister's wedding, and slept with when Logan and Fergus were staying at Tom's. And it was hideous: loud nasal breathing and clammy hands, if I recall. Hairy back and fungal toenails which he proudly informed me he hoped to cure with some kind of light therapy. And of course, tonight will be *nothing* like that. Charlie has been incredibly sweet – apart from the pharmacy incident, but I've forgiven him for that – and the sex will be amazing.

I take a huge deep breath, mustering every ounce of courage, and stride naked out of the bathroom. Soft snores are coming from our queen-sized bed, and on my pillow lies a tiny puddle of drool.

Chapter Nineteen

'*Uuuuurrrrrrggghh . . .*' Charlie emits a groan as he flips over on to his back in bed. I am up already, wrapped up in a hotel robe that's so soft, I can barely feel it against my skin. I have opened the shutters, and the door which leads onto the balcony. Pale, milky light is streaming in, giving our beautiful room a dreamy quality. 'Alice?' Charlie croaks, managing to separate upper and lower eyelids with some difficulty.

'*Morn*-ing,' I sing-song (hugely irritating, I know, to display one's lack of hangover, but I can't resist).

'Urrr . . . what time is it?' He rubs at an eye with a fist.

'Almost eight.'

'Jesus – I thought it must be much later. Why have you opened that door?'

'To let the day in,' I laugh. *And your booze breath out . . .*

He pats the vacant side of bed. 'Come back in. It's far too early to be bounding about.'

'I'm not bounding,' I point out.

'Yes you are. You're being all energetic like . . . like a little foal. A very cute one, by the way. You look very *pure* in that gown. What happened last night anyway?' He is sitting up now, squinting at me as if having difficulty bringing me into focus. 'Oh God, I didn't fall asleep, did I?'

I nod. 'Out like a light.'

He rubs his face with his hands. 'Fuck, I'm *so* sorry. Jesus.'

'It's okay,' I say lightly. 'You were very sweet, all tucked up like a baby.'

'Stop it.' He laughs throatily, which morphs into an urgent cough. 'God, you look far fresher than I feel. How have you managed that?'

'Well, I didn't drink quite as much as you yesterday . . .'

He grins rakishly. 'Nah, it's that cream, isn't it? That bum lotion. It's giving you an all-over glow.'

'I really think your vision's gone funny,' I tease him.

'No – you do. You look so . . . lovely.' Once again, he pats the space beside him. I grit my teeth, concerned that he's planning to try the moving-sheet trick again. But no; it remains pulled up to his chest. 'Come back to bed,' he murmurs with a dozy smile.

'Let's get some breakfast, Charlie.'

'Uhhh, no, I can't eat anything yet.' He checks the watch which he omitted to take off last night.

'I think they stop serving at half-eight,' I fib.

'No, it'll be ten at the latest. Come on – we've got loads of time.' He makes a beckoning motion and I pull my bathrobe cord a little tighter.

'I'm really hungry,' I add, 'and if we leave it much longer all the best stuff'll be gone.'

He emits a raspy laugh. 'For God's sake, Alice – it's a

hotel, not a jumble sale. Hotels never run out of breakfast.'

'I know but . . .' I tail off, wondering how to explain that I'm just eager to get out of this room, lovely though it is, and on with the day. After all, we have only a few hours left in Paris.

'You're all antsy,' he observes.

'It's just, I've been awake for ages . . .'

'Since when?' he frowns.

'About half-six.'

'Half-six?' Charlie exclaims. 'Who wakes up at half-six in a hotel?'

'Well, I did.'

He shakes his head in wonderment. 'I wasn't snoring, was I?'

'No . . . I just woke up.' I don't add that it felt so weird, sharing a bed with a man, that I barely slept a wink all night. Will I ever be capable of sleeping with anyone ever again?

He is out of bed now, naked and rubbing his eyes with one hand, while clutching the bedside table for support with the other. *Very* nice body; long legs, finely-shaped butt, not a hint of chubbiness around the stomach.

'Oh, you're probably right,' he concedes. 'Maybe I could do with something to eat. S'pose you've had a shower already?'

'Yes.'

''Course you have,' he says with a fond laugh. 'You've probably been out for a bloody five-mile jog as well.' He grabs the other bathrobe from the hook on the door and shrugs it on.

'No, I was waiting for you so we can do that together.

213

I thought we could go back to the Sacré-Coeur and run up all those steps.'

'Fuck off,' he chuckles, taking my hands in his and kissing me lightly on the lips. 'Are you pissed off with me? Sorry if I behaved like a drunken arse last night . . .'

'You didn't,' I say firmly. 'I told you – it was a wonderful day. I'm just hungry, okay?' I shrug off the robe and quickly pull on my skirt and top, aware of him watching me intently. While he showers, I wait on the balcony, and this time I do take photos: the whole of Paris shimmers before me on this crisp, cool morning.

He emerges from the bathroom, dressed in a crumpled cream linen shirt and yesterday's jeans. 'Are you sure everything's all right?' he asks, rubbing at his hair with a towel.

Ah, a touch of hangover fear. 'Yes, of course it is.'

'It's just . . .' He fixes me with a quizzical look. 'You've changed.'

'Well, I did bring two outfits with me . . .' I look down. 'I thought this would be best for sightseeing, as it's not so warm today.'

'*More* sightseeing?' Charlie scowls. 'Didn't we do enough of that yesterday?' I prickle slightly, his petulance reminding me of Tom, whenever I'd gently suggest that he might consider applying for jobs instead of lying about the flat all day.

'Our flight's not until three,' I say with a smile, 'so we have all morning.'

He sighs. 'Okay. Let's have a think over breakfast – that is, if there's any left.' He pulls on his jacket as we leave the room.

'Will you need that?' I ask.

'Need what?'

I laugh. 'Your jacket. It's just, we're only going down for breakfast . . .' I stop abruptly under his bemused gaze. 'God, take no notice of me. I'm so used to trying to cajole my boys into wearing the right kind of clothes—'

'I *am* thirty-seven years old, Alice,' he says hotly. 'I'm capable of dressing appropriately.'

'Yes, of course you are.' I grit my teeth. This time, we don't kiss in the lift. It's filled with his breath, sour from yesterday's wine, and we ride to the ground floor in silence. In the hotel's dining room, which overlooks a leafy courtyard, breakfast is laid out buffet-style. The room is half-filled with middle-aged couples and a couple of lone businessmen installed behind newspapers, and the atmosphere is muted as we peruse the goodies on offer. *Why did you mention his jacket?* I ask myself, cheeks blazing as I pour myself a glass of orange juice. *You're not his mother. You're a fully fledged adult woman in Paris and you're one small step away from screwing this up.*

I blink at the enormous selection of pastries on offer: dainty tarts decorated with fresh berries, and every kind of croissant imaginable. There are oozing pains aux chocolat, and tiny pastry twists dusted with cinnamon and sugar. I select a couple of mini croissants, plus some fruit, and glance over at Charlie just in time to see him drop two pains aux raisins into his jacket pocket.

No, I must have imagined that.

A man with a neatly clipped silvery moustache peers over his newspaper and narrows his eyes at him. Charlie's hand hovers over the chilled buffet selection. Calmly, and making no attempt to conceal his actions, he drops two yoghurts, plus a handful of individual

215

cheeses, into his other pocket. He then glances around, frowning slightly, and stuffs in a handful of croissants too.

Horrified, I step away, wishing to distance myself from his antics. I've always considered myself a tolerant person; fisherman porn I could handle, that didn't faze me at all. If anything, it boosted his appeal – interesting past, up for anything. I like that in a man. But not this. Not breakfast thievery. I can't bear it. He's over at the fresh fruit now, nicking a banana and two apples and stuffing them into what I now suspect are special thieving pockets, leading to pillowcase-sized pouches stitched to the inside of his jacket. He scans the room before plucking a bunch of dried flowers from a vase, and slips the now-empty vessel into his pocket. It's a small white porcelain vase with fluted edges. What the hell does he want that for? There's more food, too: several packets of muesli, plus a small bunch of grapes, which are bound to get squashed in his pocket. Or maybe that's his intention and he's hoping they'll turn into wine? What is he *thinking*? Just as well it's not a cooked breakfast buffet or he'd be shoving sausages and handfuls of scrambled egg in there as well.

I have stomped back to our table where a bored young waiter pours our coffees from a silver pot. 'Thank you,' I mutter.

He gives me a sly smile, then turns to look pointedly over at Charlie who's still prowling around the buffet like a child at a pick 'n' mix counter. The waiter clears his throat ostentatiously. I force a big, bright smile which I hope conveys the message: *Yes, I am fully aware of what my companion is doing. But let me also make it clear that it is nothing to do with me.*

'That's all you're having?' Charlie is back at our table now, setting down his own generously loaded plate.

'Yes,' I say curtly.

He frowns. 'Thought you said you were starving.' He takes a big swig of coffee and chomps into a pastry.

'Why were you filling your pockets, Charlie?' I hiss.

'Huh?'

'You were nicking food, *and* a vase, I saw you . . .'

'Oh, everyone does that.' He pats a bulging pocket and grins.

'*That's* why you put your jacket on.' Charlie nods and tops up his mug from the coffee pot. 'But . . . why d'you do it?'

'For lunch,' he says simply.

'What about the vase?'

He shrugs. 'It's got the hotel emblem on.'

'So what? You travel all the time, surely you don't feel the need to steal souvenirs . . .'

He tries to reach for my hand across the table but I snatch mine away. 'Don't you ever take the mini shampoos and stuff?' he asks. 'Or the shower cap or the little shoe shining thing?'

'Yes, sometimes, but that's different . . .'

'No, it's not,' he cuts in. 'Sounds like you've got a packed itinerary worked out for us today so we'll need some sustenance.'

'But we could go to a cafe,' I insist, aware of the moustache man casting amused glances in our direction. 'We could stop off for coffee and a baguette. Isn't that what Paris is all about?'

He chuckles softly. 'As far as you're concerned it's all about galleries and churches . . .'

'That was Sacré-Coeur! Not just a *church*. God, Charlie. You sound like my sixteen-year-old son . . .'

'Hey . . .' He smiles and tries again to reach for my hand.

'I just don't feel comfortable about stealing from a hotel buffet,' I growl.

'I told you, everyone does it.'

'No, they don't. I never met anyone who does.'

'Oh, come on,' he goads me, 'you must've been tempted . . .'

'No!' It comes out far louder than I intended.

Charlie shoots me a bemused grin. 'Goody-two-shoes.'

I glare at him. 'Because I haven't crammed my pockets with pastries? Because I haven't grabbed the coffee pot and stuffed it down my knickers?'

'Don't do that, you could scorch yourself . . .'

'God, Charlie.' I exhale loudly. 'I just think it's so *cheap*, and anyway, do you really want to be sitting on a park bench eating a flattened croissant five hours from now?'

He looks at me for a moment, and then he does it – he *rolls his eyes*, in precisely the way Logan does. What remained of my wilting libido has now shrivelled up into the tiniest ball, and is about to disappear forever.

'I might,' he says grumpily, 'if I fancy a snack.'

'Or tipping a yoghurt straight from the jar into your mouth because you forgot to steal a spoon?'

Charlie shrugs. 'That would be all right.'

'All right for you, maybe.'

He turns and stares pointedly through the glass doors towards the courtyard. 'I don't mean I expect another posh lunch,' I start to explain, 'and I know you're not mean, Charlie. You've been incredibly generous since we

218

left Edinburgh. You keep saying it's all on expenses but they're still *your* expenses, not mine, and I appreciate that . . .'

Charlie yawns without covering his mouth. 'It only goes to waste, you know.'

'What does? A *vase*?'

'No,' he huffs, wafting a hand in the direction of the depleted buffet, 'all that.'

We slump into ill-humoured silence, and I'm sure the moustache man is laughing at us now; he keeps leaning across the table towards his wife, and the two of them are chortling away. I sip my cool coffee, wondering if this is to be a feature in my life: the business of food becoming a thing not of pleasure, but of disappointment and stress. Like the amuse-bouche with Botox-Anthony, and Mum's stinky burgers, and now this: breakfasty things, re-presented hours later, because you never know when you'll be hit by the urge for a sweaty cheese portion plucked from your pocket.

We start to make polite chit-chat, but it's no use – everything has changed. Even as we head out to explore the Jardin des Tuileries, the mood fails to lift. While I buy a crêpe from the kiosk, Charlie says he has 'plenty here, thank you', having parked himself on a bench in order to pick at his spoils from the buffet. 'Like one?' He waggles a squashed pain au raisin at me.

'It looks delicious, Charlie, but no thanks.' In a fit of petulance, he rips it to bits and throws it down for the pigeons.

By the time we're heading out by taxi to the airport, we have used up our final dregs of conversation, and when our plane touches down at Edinburgh airport Charlie has descended into barely speaking mode.

Sulking, I suspect, because the only action he's had is a measly snog.

'Well, thanks again,' I say, pecking his cheek as the taxi pulls up outside my flat.

'It's been fun,' he says unconvincingly.

'Yes, it has.'

'Er . . . got much on this week?' That's all he can muster, conversation-wise.

'Well, my boys are back tomorrow.'

'Oh.' He glazes over. 'That'll be nice for you. Hope Felix likes his dog.'

'Fergus,' I say. 'He's called Fergus.'

'Oh yeah. So, uh . . .' He bends to unzip the bag at his feet and pulls out the small white vase. 'I nicked it for you, you know.'

'No thanks,' I say, conscious now of disappointment pooling in my stomach.

'Suit yourself,' he says, stuffing it back in. 'Bye then. I'll call you.' We both know he won't, and I don't want him to either. I meant it when I said he's clearly not tight, in that he invited me on the trip, and has lavished me with fabulous food and wine. Yet part of him *must* be, in that small, mean-spirited way. And somehow, petty meanness seems worse than stinginess on a grander scale, like my mother refusing to heat her house properly, or to have the septic tank seen to. It's penny-pinching, and it sucks all the joy out of life.

Oh, I know I should focus on all the fun we've had these past twenty-four hours: the screaming with laughter over his riverbank shoot, and giggling like kids in the toyshop. Being far away from my shrunken little world has been lovely. But I also know I could never love a man who takes his good fortune for granted, not pausing for a moment to reflect on how lucky he is.

I climb out of the taxi, glancing back to wave goodbye. Charlie is staring gloomily ahead and, as the car pulls away, he extracts a mini cheese from his pocket and devours it in one bite.

Chapter Twenty

The boys are dropped off at lunchtime on Friday. The handover is brief and a little awkward; Tom seems distracted, and in a terrible hurry to 'get on the road', while Patsy and Jessica don't even get out of the camper van. 'Is everything all right?' I ask in a general, addressing-everyone sort of way.

'Yeah, it was great,' Fergus says with genuine enthusiasm, while Logan zooms straight for the living room.

'What's wrong with him?' I hiss at Tom as Fergus wanders off to join his brother.

He shrugs. 'He's fine, I think. Maybe just tired after the drive.'

'He doesn't seem in a particularly good mood . . .' I glance in the direction of the living room where the TV is already blaring at old person's volume.

Tom blows out air. 'He's been fine, they both have. Anyway, I'd really better be off. Bye, boys,' he calls through.

'Bye, Dad,' they both reply.

'Boys,' I call out, 'come through and say goodbye to

Dad properly.' They appear in the hallway, each bestowing their father with a brief hug before hurtling back to the TV.

'I'll be off then,' Tom says briskly, bounding downstairs as if he's just delivered a fridge.

That was weird. While Fergus seems fine, and appears to be the picture of health – face flushed and hair lightened by days spent outdoors – Logan appears anxious and even paler than usual. He has barely looked at me since they came home. I consider trying to quiz him further, but that's always impossible when the TV is on. I could turn the telly off, but that sends out the signal that this is a Massive Deal requiring *everyone's full attention*, and I don't have the heart for that when they've barely been home ten minutes. No, I'll leave them be and hopefully, if anything is wrong, I'll be able to coax it out of Logan when he's in the mood to talk.

Having gathered that the boys have eaten nothing since breakfast, I set about rustling up a favourite lunch of stir-fried prawns and noodles. Lured by the aroma of garlic and soy, Fergus appears in the kitchen. 'Mmm, that smells great, Mum.'

'I thought you'd like it.'

'And I see you got Rex back from the charity shop.' I smile stiffly, waiting for him to add, *but he looks and smells different*, despite the fact that the first thing I did when I got back from Paris last night was to grubby him up and attack him with a nail brush – thus achieving an authentic 'worn' effect – then put him through a hot wash cycle.

'Er, yes,' I say.

'You put him on my bed.' He chuckles. 'That was nice of you. I'm not going to sleep with him, though—'

223

'No, I know, darling. It was just a joke.'

He grins and slides an arm around my shoulders. 'I know it seemed a bit stupid but Jessica wants him. In fact, maybe I'll keep him. She's probably forgotten anyway. Remember that holiday with Dad, where was it again . . .'

'Devon?' I suggest, trying to squash a flurry of guilt.

'Yeah, that was it. And we did that mad thing of putting Rex in every single photo, remember? Like, he was at the table in that pizza place and sunbathing on a flannel on the beach, and . . .' He stops, trying to think of further examples.

'And you tied him to the bow of the boat when we went on that mackerel fishing trip—'

'Yeah, that was great. He was our figurehead!' Fergus laughs and rakes back his growing-out hair.

'I'm amazed you can remember so much,' I tell him. 'You were only seven, you know.'

He taps the side of his head. 'I've got a good brain. Grandma's brain.' Fortunately, he hasn't recalled – or perhaps he's chosen not to mention – that that was our last holiday as a family of four; one I embarked on filled with hope that two weeks together, in new surroundings, would help to fix things between Tom and me. However, despite wonderful highlights – building a fire on the beach, and feasting on paper cups of cockles as the sun slipped down – by the end of the trip, my reserves of patience had run out.

I clear my throat. 'Could you fetch me three big bowls please?'

Fergus obliges, adding, 'The great thing about stir-fry is it's so fast.'

'Yep, it's one of the handiest things ever. You've probably had it at least once a week your whole life.'

He watches as I throw fat prawns into the wok. 'D'you remember we were saying, instead of meringues, you should start making something that's quicker?' I frown, uncomprehending. 'You know,' he adds, 'that doesn't need the oven on for hours and hours?'

'Oh, that.' I chuckle. 'The thing is, Ferg, stir-fry has to be served straight away, and the only way I'd be able to do that is to set up a cafe or a little kiosk or something.'

'Well, you could . . .'

'No thanks,' I say briskly, whirling everything around in the wok and dolloping it into three bowls.

'Why not?'

'Because I already have a job, remember, and I enjoy it and have no plans to give it up. Whereas meringues can be fitted around work and done at night, or whenever I have a bit of spare time . . . they're *flexible*.'

'Actually,' he says, grinning, 'they're crumbly and stiff. They're about the *least* flexible thing there is.'

I laugh and call his brother. 'Logan! Lunch is ready . . .' He lumbers in and we all take our seats at the table, with Fergus making it clear that he's not letting me off the hook just yet.

'I just think we should be more green,' he murmurs, spearing a prawn with his fork.

'Hon, there's nothing I can do about the oven thing, okay? We need the meringue money. I mean, I'd sit for hours, breathing warm air on them if I thought they'd cook that way, but I don't think the kitchen inspector lady would approve of that.'

'Dad and Patsy are really green,' he adds slyly, at which Logan shoots him a warning look.

'Yes, I'd imagine they are.'

'Yeah,' Fergus continues, 'they're getting this thing where they'll collect rainwater in tubs and it'll be piped into the house.'

'That sounds good.' I try, with difficulty, to swallow a noodle.

'That eco-house on TV had a special toilet,' Logan reminds me, 'where all the stuff – the sewage – gets turned into—'

'Odourless bricks that can be burnt as fuel,' I cut. 'Yes, I saw it too, but I'm afraid we're not getting one of those.'

'Why not?' asks Fergus, looking crestfallen.

'Because the residents' association wouldn't like it. Anyway, maybe the two of you could think about being green in other ways.'

'Like what?' Logan growls.

I set down my fork. 'Like walking more and not using your Xbox so much.'

He looks aghast. 'What would I do instead?'

'I'm sure you could think of other, non-fuel-burning ways to amuse yourself,' I tease him.

'Like *reading*,' Logan groans.

'Yes. Or drawing beards on the ladies in the Boden catalogue.' I grin as the two of them stare at me, then get up and wash out my bowl at the sink. When I glance back at Logan, his face is set in a frown. 'I'm joking,' I tell him. 'I don't even get the Boden catalogue.'

'Hmmm,' he mumbles. Shaking my head, I clear up the veg remains from the worktop; clearly, he's in no mood for fun so I'm better leaving him to it. The two of them are bickering at the table now, about something I can't quite catch, with Logan calling his brother a *swotty arse* and adding, 'It's none of your fucking business.'

'Logan!' I snap, swinging round from the worktop. 'That's enough.'

'I only said—'

'I heard what you said.'

'*You* swear.' He juts out his chin.

'Yes, understandably, I'd say. Anyway, can I just point out that neither of you have thanked me for sprucing up your bedrooms while you were away?'

'Oh yeah,' Logan says, 'I meant to ask, why did you move all my stuff?'

I blink at him. 'I haven't moved things. I just took a few things away.'

'What's the difference?' Logan asks.

'One means shifting things from one position to another and the other is subtraction, like maths.'

Fergus sniggers. '*What* did you subtract?' Logan demands.

I'm trying so hard not to lose it. Christ, I deserve a medal for exercising such self-control. 'Just some old socks, a few toast crusts and a plate with dried-up egg on it. I hope they weren't precious to you, love.'

'I s'pose that's okay,' he says reluctantly.

'Are you sure, or did you want to hang on to the plate to see how long it'd take for it be completely covered in fur?'

'It takes at least a month for something like egg yolk to putrefy,' Fergus remarks, dumping his fork into his empty bowl. The boys leave the kitchen and, although I try not to follow Logan to his room, my willpower falters. I knock and peer in to see him lying on his bed and stabbing at his phone.

'So, how was the holiday really?' I ask.

'It was all right.'

'It's just, you've obviously come back in a pretty foul mood and I wondered what was wrong.'

'It was fine,' he says, pursing his mouth, the face he pulls when he hands me a school report which he knows isn't brilliant. I sense him trying to mentally shoo me out of his room: *Be gone, tedious mother, with your incessant questioning* . . .

'Were Dad and Patsy getting on all right?'

'Yeah, they were *fine*.'

I study Logan's face, which still looks winter pale; I do hope they fed him properly. I know how keen Patsy is to festoon Jessica with quinoa salads, and I hope she realised that most teenage boys aren't crazy for that sort of thing.

'So,' I continue, 'did you visit many places? Castles, that kind of thing?'

'Yeah, we went to a castle,' he replies.

'What was that like?'

He shrugs. 'Big. Old. There was a falconry display . . .'

'Oh, what was that like?'

'Mum,' he exclaims, swivelling towards me, 'it was a falconry display. There were big birds flying about, all right?'

'Were they kestrels or hawks or—'

'They were falcons, hence *falconry display*. What is this, a what-I-did-on-my-holidays thing?' He emits a loud, bitter laugh. 'Should I have kept a diary so you'd give me a sticker at the end of it?'

'Of course not,' I retort, marching away while muttering, 'They do use other birds too, you know.' In fact, I'm so agitated by his attitude that I switch on my laptop and Google 'falconry display birds', and it turns out there are *loads* of different types – buzzards, kestrels and no less than five different species of owl. It's so tempting to yell for Logan and make him come and see but instead, I shut down my laptop at the kitchen table. Great: he's been back for less than an hour and already there's that perpetual exasperation that seems to foul up the air between us. Shamefully, I start to picture life *after* children, when they're set up with jobs and wives and I am an old lady. Whenever I try to envisage my future self, it's usually one of two versions. In the first, I am fat and unkempt with wiry hairs poking out of my chin, dragging a wheeled shopping basket around Poundland. In the other version, I am lying beside a beautiful palm-fringed pool, and bear a striking resemblance to Helen Mirren. I'm multitasking, too, being able to sip a gin and tonic, pick at a dish of olives *and* have oil rubbed into my back by some man with large, firm hands, all at once. However, right now I am unable to shift the trolley/Poundland version from my mind. No matter how hard I try to visualise Helen Mirren gliding along at the poolside, with her sarong flapping in the light breeze, it's my mother I see – or, rather, someone who looks a bit like Mum, but is about five stones heavier and nibbling morosely on a tinned hot dog (NO BREAD).

Dammit all. I need to talk to someone, someone who actually likes me and doesn't pull a pained expression whenever I walk into the room. I need the girls (yes, I *know* we have a combined age of one hundred and fifty-six) and, besides, despite her reluctance to 'make a big deal of it', I suspect that Ingrid might appreciate a get-together seeing as she's due to have her eggs collected any day now.

As luck would have it, Viv 'can't be bothered' to go out tonight, and would far rather get together over a bottle of wine in my kitchen if it means hearing every detail about Paris. And Ingrid and Kirsty sound delighted too.

'Want me to bring anything?' Ingrid asks.

'No, I'll rustle something up, no problem.' It's only later, when I've battled my way through Logan and Fergus's holiday laundry mountain, that I stop to peruse the fridge and cupboards and realise there's hardly anything to snack on. As I can't face baking, I decide to nip into Pascal's, the French deli, instead.

Feeling emboldened, I also package up and label some leftover meringue kisses from my last order (despite Fergus's moans about meringues' *colossal* carbon footprint, they do have a pleasingly lengthy shelf-life if kept in a tin). With any luck, the deli will agree to stock a trial run.

'Just popping to the shops,' I call out to the boys, to deafening silence.

As it turns out, Pascal's is pleasingly quiet when I go in. There's just one other customer – an elderly lady perusing the flavoured oils – and the French man who served me last time, tending his cooked meats behind the counter. I fill a wicker basket with olives, pâté and crackers, and choose several *modest* slivers of cheese.

'Anything else?' he asks. Pleasant, but no flicker of recognition, even though he pointed me in the direction of the toyshop when I was searching for a substitute Rex.

'Erm, I actually wondered if you might be interested in stocking my meringues,' I say, taking the packets from my bag and placing them on the counter. 'They're all natural ingredients – even the flavourings. If you like them, I can deliver on a weekly or twice-weekly basis, or even more often – whatever suits you best.'

He picks up a packet and studies it. 'You make these in your home kitchen?'

'Yes.'

'That's very . . . industrious of you,' he says, and it strikes me how very attractive his accent is.

'Well, it's a sort of sideline,' I explain, 'and actually, I love it. It's pretty therapeutic.' I laugh awkwardly.

He nods. 'I can imagine. And I know they're very difficult to get right.'

The elderly woman is standing next to me now, clutching a bottle of garlic oil. 'Meringues must never be chalky,' she observes.

'No, absolutely not.' I smile at her.

'They should be slightly gooey in the centre,' the man adds approvingly.

'Like the perfect man,' the woman adds, giving my arm a playful nudge.

I laugh. 'That's so strange. It's what I always think – that the ideal qualities are pretty much right there, in a meringue.'

The man is laughing too and, as I pick up my brown paper bag of goodies, I wonder why on earth I found this place intimidating.

'I'll get back to you about the samples,' he says with a warm smile.

'Thanks – would you mind mentioning to the owner that I've dropped them off?'

'I am the owner,' he replies.

'You're Pascal?'

'That's right.' He turns over a brown paper label attached to one of the packets. 'And you're Sugar Mummy.'

'Yes.' I smile. 'But my real name's Alice. Anyway, I'll pop back soon.'

Then, just as I'm leaving, he calls out, 'Did your mother enjoy the cheeses?'

'She did, especially the monks' one . . .'

He smiles a lovely warm, open smile that seems to light up his eyes, and causes dimples to appear on his cheeks. 'There are a couple of new ones coming in next week that she might like to try. Not that I'm suggesting you spend all your time sitting around eating cheese with your mother . . .' He laughs. Is he flirting, or just being friendly-shopkeeper-man? It's impossible to tell.

'Not if I can help it,' I say with a grin, feeling as light as a cloud as I hurry back to the flat.

*

Ingrid arrives early, clearly desperate to hear about my Paris trip. Within minutes, Kirsty and Viv have shown up, and all three bombard me with questions.

'You didn't sleep with him?' Viv says this in the manner of an incredulous hairdresser. ('You want to look like Scarlett Johansson? Are you out of your *mind*?').

'No, I didn't.' I look around the table at my friends' expectant faces. 'Well, yes, I *slept*, but—'

'You went to a hotel in Paris with a man you fancy – otherwise you wouldn't have gone, right – and didn't do it?' Viv blinks at me. 'So what *did* you do?'

'I told you – we went to the Sacré-Coeur, we ate loads, we had a brilliant time considering we'd only known each other for about five minutes before the trip . . .'

'But what happened in the *room*?' Ingrid asks, sipping her tea while Kirsty throws me a knowing look, understanding at once that my jaunt wasn't wholly successful.

'In the room?' I tease them. 'Well, I made tea . . .'

'You cooked?' Viv barks, pouring glasses of wine for all of us, including Ingrid, who's already reminded her that she's not drinking right now.

'No, I mean a *pot* of tea.'

'Jesus Christ,' Viv mutters.

'Leave her alone,' Kirsty sniggers. 'I love a cup of tea and biscuit in a hotel room.'

'. . . And I took tons of pictures from the balcony, which had an amazing view,' I go on. 'Honestly, I'd forgotten how beautiful the city is . . .'

Viv shakes her head in despair. 'What a wasted opportunity.'

'Oh, there was plenty of kissing,' I say as she lights a cigarette, 'which was lovely – but then, the pile thing put a bit of a dampener on things—'

'What pile thing?' Ingrid asks.

'You had *piles*?' Kirsty radiates sympathy which morphs into hysterical laughter as I regale them with the Preparation-Ash incident, when Charlie had refused to help me out.

'Haemorrhoids in Paris,' Ingrid says sadly. 'It's hardly a Woody Allen film, is it?' She sighs. 'It just seems so wrong.'

'I know.' I sip my wine, noticing that Viv's glass is empty already; Christ, she's hoovering it down these days. Maybe she'd have been a better match for Charlie. I try to picture them together, and decide she'd have found the breakfast-thievery thing a big hoot; perhaps I've just become a judgemental old spoilsport.

'So what else happened?' Kirsty prompts me, breaking off a corner of Pascal's monk cheese.

I go on to describe how Charlie became progressively more pissed as the day wore on. 'Which was *fine*,' I say firmly, in case my friends are under the impression that I'm considering heading up the temperance movement, 'but, you know, something was making me hold back . . .'

'Probably your little medical problem,' Kirsty remarks sagely.

'Yeah. Anyway, we got back to the hotel, which was lovely – you know those tall, elegant windows that seem so Parisian, with the shutters? Ours were a kind of washed-out, greeny-blue—'

'Never mind the architectural details,' Viv sniggers, flicking her still-burning cigarette butt out of the open window.

'And the spiral staircase, in a sort of central well, was amazing—'

Viv sniggers. 'Just get on with it.'

I grin and sip more wine. 'Okay, so he was smashed by this point, and he'd tottered off for a shower so I stood there on the balcony, just looking out over the city at night . . .' I glance around at the three rapt faces, realising, not for the first time, how very lucky I am that we're all still here, living just a few miles apart and, more importantly, still relish each other's company (although Ingrid winces as Viv lights up another Marlboro). 'But what I was *really* doing,' I continue, 'was playing for time.'

'What d'you mean?' Ingrid asks.

'Well, you know how, in football, when a team has enough goals to get their point or whatever, and they just want to hog the ball till the final whistle goes?'

'You mean you didn't want to have sex with him,' she observes, shuffling her chair away from Viv.

I nod. 'That's about it.'

Viv frowns. 'But why? You said he's lovely, that you'd had such a great day . . .'

There's an explosion of laughter from the living room. Both Logan and Fergus have friends over tonight (I'm not allowed to use the term 'sleepover' any more – the boys merely *crash out*) and everyone is hanging out with a movie and the obligatory pizzas.

'When it came down to it,' I try to explain, 'I suppose I didn't want it enough.'

'You don't have to want it *loads*,' Viv says bossily, wafting her cigarette in Ingrid's face.

'You think I should've slept with him just because he'd taken me to Paris?'

'No! No, God, of course not. What I mean is, if you're with a guy who's attractive and fun, and the possibility of sex comes up . . .' She pauses, glancing around for affirmation from the others. 'Well, even if he's not going to be the love of your live or even some amazing, passionate affair, then at least it'll kick-start things, get you all revved up again . . .'

'Like a rusty old engine,' I snigger.

'You know what I mean.'

'Maybe I need a good squirt of WD-40.'

Viv gives my arm a squeeze. Although the gesture is well-meant, it comes across as faintly patronising, the kind of thing you'd to do a frail relative you were visiting in hospital.

'Anyway,' I add, 'as it turns out, I'm glad we didn't do it,' and proceed to fill them in on Charlie's antics at breakfast.

'Ugh, I'd rather go without lunch than eat stale baked things out of someone's pocket,' Ingrid declares.

'I couldn't put up with that,' Kirsty agrees. 'Maya once

stuck a Babybel cheese in her pocket in a hotel in Windermere, but Dan made her put it back and gave her a lecture about stealing.' Hmm. A different kind of meanness, I'd say.

'Anyway,' Ingrid cuts in, 'what about Stephen? D'you reckon you'll see him again?'

'Well, my mother would like me to.' I glance at the column of ash that's hanging precariously from Viv's cigarette, and get up to find a saucer for her to use as an ashtray.

'It's getting really smoky in here,' Ingrid points out, throwing Viv a pained look.

'The window's open,' she points out.

'It's still blowing right in my face, Viv, and it makes me feel a bit sick—'

'So-*rree*,' she says, rolling her eyes and adding, incredibly, 'God knows what you'll be like when you're pregnant, Ing—' We all stare at Viv who, realising her *faux pas*, grabs Ingrid's hand. 'Oh, I'm sorry. I know there's big stuff coming up – the treatment and all that . . .'

'Yes, anyway,' Ingrid says, her cheeks flushing hot, 'we were talking about Stephen . . .'

'I still think you should give Giles a chance,' Viv adds, her lipstick a little askew.

'She probably put him off by discussing Fuzzy Felts,' Kirsty chuckles, clearly trying to lighten the tense atmosphere.

'Maybe he thought it was code for pubic hair,' Ingrid observes.

'Yeah,' Viv sniggers, 'you do realise most men under thirty have never seen any? It's like they've forgotten it's actually a natural thing and, when they're finally confronted with it, they're completely freaked out and assume it's some kind of weird phenomenon, like those bearded ladies in fairgrounds in Victorian times.'

I laugh, my annoyance at her insensitivity ebbing away. Maybe if I was child-free and single like Viv, I'd be drinking the way she does, and smoking tons of fags – and perhaps that's why Ingrid, Kirsty and I find her a bit much occasionally. Maybe she reminds us of our younger selves, and although I have no desire to swap lives with her – truly – occasionally, I can't help thinking: God, that looks like a whole load of fun.

'D'you have it all waxed off, Viv?' asks Kirsty.

'I do now, yeah.'

'Doesn't anyone like it left natural these days?' I ask, frowning. 'I'd have thought it might have some retro seventies appeal, like flares or ponchos—'

'Or Annie Hall,' Kirsty chips in. 'I love that look . . .'

'Bet she had the full fuzz,' Ingrid offers. 'Diane Keaton, I mean.'

'Everyone did,' Viv declares, 'but not any more. It's viewed as unhygienic.'

We all fall silent for a moment. '*What's* unhygienic?' Fergus asks, sauntering into the kitchen to extract a bottle of Coke from the fridge.

'Dipping your fingers in the meringue mixture bowl,' I shoot back, adding as soon as he's left the room, 'God, if that's what younger men expect, I'm finding myself some doddery old guy who can hardly *see*.'

Everyone laughs, and I refill Ingrid's mug with raspberry leaf tea. 'I think you're too picky,' Viv drawls.

'Maybe you're right,' I say with a shrug. 'I mean, I'm not prepared to get involved with a man just to, you know . . . *be* with someone.'

'Don't you ever fancy anyone?' Viv enquires.

'No. Well, yes. There is someone – he owns that lovely deli up the road, you know Pascal's? I dropped off some meringue samples today and we were chatting . . .'

'There you go then,' Viv says, as if that's all there is to it.

'He's probably married or gay, though.' I look around at my friends, relieved that the tension has eased between Ingrid and Viv. 'Anyway, I'm thinking about forgetting this whole dating thing. I know you were all trying to help, but I'm just not sure it's working out for me.'

'Let me find someone else,' Ingrid cuts in. 'Charlie doesn't count because I didn't actually know him. I must've had a rush of blood to the head after my fab-abs class. He was just *there*.'

Viv swings round to face her. 'You can't have another go. That's unfair . . .'

'It's fine,' I cut in quickly, 'I don't want to be set up with anyone else. I've had a great time – I've been to Paris, for God's sake – and it's coincided with the boys being away so it's stopped me mooching about, feeling sorry for myself. But that's the end of it.'

'So you're not seeing any of them again?' Kirsty asks, sounding deflated.

I pop a morsel of delicious nutty cheese into my mouth. 'I don't think so. Have you tried this cheese? It's French, made by monks.'

Ingrid pops a sliver into her mouth. 'Oh, I know this. It's one of my favourites. Why d'you think so many monks make cheese?'

'I suppose,' Viv suggests, fixing me with a squiffy grin, 'when you take a vow of celibacy, you've got to find *something* to do.'

Chapter Twenty-One

Saturday morning consists of a whirl of pancake-making for the horde of boys who stayed over last night. There's much chatter and jollity around the table as I make a big pot of hot chocolate to serve French-breakfast style – which reminds me, I haven't deliberately omitted to mention my jaunt to Paris. However, Logan clearly wasn't in the sunniest mood when they came home yesterday, and I want to pick my moment.

With my mammoth frying session finished, and the boys and their friends having drifted back to Logan and Fergus's rooms, I nip out for the paper and sneak back to bed to read it. When my phone bleeps, I assume it's one of my friends texting further thoughts on how we might resurrect our 'project' – but, in fact, it's the baby-faced intern.

Sorry haven't been in touch, he writes. *Crazy busy. Fancy a drink soon? Giles x.*

Hmmm. I'm really not sure, especially after Viv's 'bearded lady' theory. We could just be friends, but really, what would be the point? I have plenty of friends: as well as the inner circle, there's Clemmie and a bunch of mums I met during the toddler group years, plus Jacqui, the classroom assistant at school, and a couple of teachers I go for drinks with occasionally. And, despite his obvious qualities, I just can't imagine Giles and I simply hanging out together.

As soon as the last visitor has drifted off home, I wander casually into the living room where the boys are flopped out on the sofa; scoffing pancakes is clearly exhausting work.

'I thought I should let you know,' I begin, 'that I was in Paris when you were away with Dad.'

'Were you?' Fergus stares at me, wide-eyed.

'Why didn't you say?' Logan asks.

'Erm, I'm telling you now, love. Anyway, I just went for one night and it was great, but I have to say, I kept thinking about you two and wishing you were there.'

'Will you take us some time?' Fergus asks brightly.

'Yes, of course I will.'

'When?'

I laugh. 'One day, sweetheart.'

'She always says that.' Logan peers at me suspiciously. 'So who did you go with?'

I start to gather up the few remaining drinks cans from their boys' night in. 'Just-a-friend. No one you know.'

'Like a man?' Logan wants to know.

'Yes, it was a man,' I say firmly, 'but it's no big deal, it was just a little trip.'

My sons' eyes are fixed upon me, dark, intense, probing. 'Was it Fat-Tongue Man?' Fergus asks with a grin.

'No,' I splutter, 'I won't be seeing *him* again.'

'Who was it then?'

'Just someone Ingrid met, and he was writing a thing about Paris and asked if I'd like to go.' I smile tightly.

Fergus frowns. 'Are you going out with him?'

'No,' I exclaim, 'and I'm pretty sure I'll never see him again either . . .'

'You keep saying that,' Logan asks, a hint of amusement now playing on his lips. 'How come you keep going out with *all* these men, then never seeing them again?'

I open my mouth, trying in vain to concoct some kind of feasible explanation.

'I have absolutely no idea,' is the best I can do.

*

Next morning, unable to face the boys flopping about the flat all day, I make an executive decision.

'We're going to the beach,' I announce, having lured them from their beds with a prospect of a cooked breakfast.

'Nah, it's all right, thanks,' Logan says, which I pretend not to hear.

'Which beach?' Fergus asks.

'North Berwick,' I say, in my best *wouldn't-that-be-a-treat?* voice. It was a big favourite of ours when they were younger, with its gorgeous sweep of sand and craggy rocks to climb on.

'All right,' Fergus says noncommittally.

'No thanks,' Logan says, cramming his mouth with bacon.

'Come on, darling. We're all back at school tomorrow and I've hardly seen you over the holidays. Kirsty's coming too – she's bringing the kids and I said we'd meet her there.'

241

I get up to make more toast, wondering how far to push this. Whereas I really want Logan to come, I can hardly expect a sixteen-year-old to be overjoyed at the prospect of spending a day on a windswept beach with his mother. Then, to my delight, his mood changes. 'Oh, all right, I'll come.'

'Great. Kirsty's bringing a picnic . . .'

'Uhhh, not one of Kirsty's picnics,' he groans.

'Please, Mum,' Fergus whines, 'she never brings anything we like.'

'Yes,' I snigger, 'because Kirsty is a fantastic cook and cares what her kids eat—'

'Whereas we've been stuffed with sugar and additives,' Logan snorts.

'It's a wonder we've got any teeth left,' Fergus chips in, clearly enjoying the game as I start to rustle up a picnic of our own. And so, an hour later and armed with provisions, we set off.

The sky is a brilliant blue, with wisps of gauzy white cloud and, by the time we arrive, Kirsty has already set up camp in our favourite sheltered spot close to the rocks. Hamish and Alfie demand piggybacks from Logan while Maya, who's just turned seven, tries to clamber on too.

'You're so honoured,' I laugh. 'I can't imagine Logan doing that for anyone else.'

Kirsty smiles, accepting a handful of shells that Maya has collected for her from the flat, wet sand. 'They'd actually like to adopt him as a big brother, wouldn't you, Hamish?'

'Yeah,' he exclaims, all wide, toothy grin and a mass of chaotic blonde curls. All three of Kirsty's kids are incredibly photogenic.

242

'I'm actually surprised he agreed to come,' I add, sprawling on the checked blanket beside her as all five of our offspring head off to explore the rocks.

'Maybe he missed you more than he's letting on,' she suggests.

I shrug. 'I very much doubt that. But, yes – he's been slightly odd since he came back. A bit tetchy yesterday, then surprisingly agreeable today. Very up and down mood-wise.'

She shrugs. 'I guess that's teenagers for you.'

I nod, glancing over to where my boys are helping Kirsty's children to climb to the upper reaches of the rocks.

'Yes,' I say. 'I know it's full-on when the children are little, but in some ways it's simpler. I mean, it might not feel like it now, but you can control so much – what they eat, who they play with, how they spend their days.'

'Guess you can,' she says with a laugh, 'in theory, at least.'

'There were no nasty surprises on laptops back then,' I add, 'and remember how I used to fiddle the clocks on really desperate days and pretend it was night time at six o'clock? Then they grow into big, hairy teenagers and you can't control anything at all.'

'I still fiddle the clock,' she sniggers as I set out our contribution to the picnic. Compared to Kirsty's offerings of Thai noodle salads, savoury tarts and an array of exotic dips, ours are terribly workaday: hastily made sandwiches and crisps. 'You don't miss the old days, do you?' she adds. 'Remember how tough it was when you first split with Tom . . .'

I turn this over in my mind. 'I don't really. I mean, I'm not one of those mums who wants to keep her

243

children little and playing with Duplo forever. It's just confusing, you know? One minute Fergus is gawping at a smoking bum on his laptop and the next he's devastated because I took his soft toys to the charity shop.'

Kirsty laughs, glancing towards the children in the distance. 'It's just lovely seeing them all hanging out together.'

'It really is. Being with younger ones seems to bring out the best in Logan, especially. He's great with his little sister.'

'You're lucky, you know. They're both lovely boys.'

I smile. 'I think sometimes I can forget that. They *are* great, and we muddle along somehow, and maybe that's why I'm kind of happy on my own.'

'Because you're *not* on your own,' she suggests.

'That's right. I mean, yes, it'd be lovely to have someone to grow older with, because we all know our children won't be around forever—' I stop abruptly as Kirsty's expression changes. 'Is something wrong?' I ask.

Kirsty pauses and pokes a finger into the pale sand. 'This will be their last term at home with me,' she says firmly. 'I'm done with it, Alice. I told Dan they're all starting school after the summer holidays.'

'Really?' I exclaim, impressed by the determination in her voice.

'Yes – spending all day with me just isn't enough for them any more.'

'Well, they're sociable,' I remark, 'and they'll love being with other children—'

'Dan doesn't see it that way,' she cuts in. 'He's absolutely livid. Says we agreed we'd home educate all the way through—'

'What, even when they're sixteen, seventeen..?'

244

'Yes!' she exclaims, cheeks flushing an angry shade of pink. 'How crazy is that? How the hell am I supposed to cover every subject to that level?'

'I've no idea. Christ, I know I couldn't . . .'

'He says I can buy coursebooks and work through them but—' She breaks off and turns to me, fury burning in her eyes.

'God, Kirsty.' I put my arm around her slender shoulders.

'The thing is,' she hisses, 'I know it's about more than the children and what's best for them. It's like he wants to keep me trapped in a little box, at home . . .' She breaks off, brushing back her windblown hair distractedly.

'Will you go back to work?' I venture.

'That's the plan – at least, it's *my* plan. I want to get back into nursing as soon as I can. I need my life back, Alice, and I want to earn my own money instead of having to ask Dan for every penny, and then have him quizzing me about whether I really need a dress *and* shoes, or if I could make do with my knackered Birkenstocks . . .' She glares down at her feet in their battered old sandals. Then, as the children surge back towards us, driven by hunger, she somehow manages to switch back into the sunny earth-mummy persona she carries off so well, even when Logan and Fergus pointedly avoid her fabulous picnic offerings, 'aubergine dip' ranking as the devil's work in their opinion.

With her children within earshot for the rest of the day, we can't discuss what might possibly be going on in Dan's mind. She seems cheerier, though, directing the kids to gather driftwood so we can build a fire and cook sausages for our second feast of the day. Logan appears to relish his role as chief sausage fryer, and it warms my heart to see him happy, involved and not gripping a remote control like some kind of crucial lifesupport system.

Finally, as our shadows lengthen, we haul everything back to our cars. 'I want to go in Logan's car,' Hamish announces.

'Me too,' says Alfie. 'Can we, Mum?'

Kirsty laughs, opening the back door for Maya to hop in. 'Sure, if it's okay with Alice.'

'Of course it is,' I say.

'Looks like it's just you and me then, Maya,' she says. We set off, with Fergus beside me and Logan squished on the back seat in between Kirsty's boys, our car filled with laughter and excitable chatter, the way it used to be.

'Mum,' Logan says as we head out to open countryside, 'Hamish says he feels a bit sick.'

'Okay, I'll stop as soon as I can. Could you open the window for him?'

He does as I ask, and there's some muttering I can't catch, then Logan blurts out, 'Mum, you need to stop *now*!'

'Honey, I can't, someone's driving right up my backside . . .'

'MUM!'

'Lean over to the back, there should be some empty bags there, give him one of those . . . Hamish, are you okay, darling?'

'I'm going to puke,' he wails, and there's a rustling of carrier bag followed by a violent splattering noise.

'Mum! He's puked!' Logan shouts.

'Oh, God. Are you okay, Hamish? I promise I'll stop as soon as I can . . .'

'I feel a bit better now,' he whimpers.

246

'Good,' I mutter, frantically looking for somewhere to pull over.

'. . . But this bag's got holes in it . . .'

'It's leaking out all over Hamish's trousers,' Logan announces. 'Ugh, I think I'm gonna puke too . . .'

'Take it off him, open the window and hold it out—'

'Stop the car, Mum!' Fergus demands.

'No, darling, it's not safe, the road's too twisty—'

'It really stinks,' Alfie announces. I glance back and can't help twitching with mirth at the sight of Logan holding the dripping bag at arm's length out of the open window.

'Christ, Mum.' He, too, is laughing now. 'Funny that no one's driving up your backside any more.'

'This is the stinkiest car in the world,' Alfie announces. 'I hate it!'

'So do I,' Hamish declares.

'You can't moan about it,' Alfie counters, 'when it came out of *your* mouth.'

'Just throw the bag out, Logan,' Fergus instructs.

'No, don't do that,' Hamish exclaims. 'That would be *litter*.'

'Yeah, it takes a carrier bag two hundred years to break down,' Alfie adds gravely.

'He's right, Fergus,' I say. 'You were saying we should be greener . . .'

Although the car does smell disgusting – worse, even, than the rancid milkshake carton – I can't help sniggering every time I glimpse Logan in the rear-view mirror with his arm outstretched, still gamely gripping on to the dribbling carrier bag.

'You're a hero, Logan,' I say, finally indicating to pull into a lay-by where, miraculously, there happens to be a picnic table and a bin.

'You owe me one, Mum,' he says gruffly, flinging the bag into it.

Later still, after we've dropped off Hamish and Alfie at their place and arrived home beach-tired, I land beside Logan on the sofa and hug him. Incredibly, he doesn't shrug me off.

'Thanks so much for today,' I say.

He gives me a baffled look. 'What for?'

'For coming when you didn't really want to, and for being so lovely with Kirsty's kids.'

'That's okay.' He smiles awkwardly.

'And for holding that sick bag out of the window,' I add. 'You were a real trouper, love.' We fall into silence for a moment, broken only by the tinny murmur of music from Fergus's room.

'Didn't have much choice, did I?' he says.

'Well, you did actually. You could have just chucked it out into the road.' I look at him, trying to make eye contact, but he's focused on his lap and twisting his fingers together awkwardly. 'Are you okay, darling?' I ask.

He presses his lips together and nods.

'Tired?'

'No, not really.'

I frown, wondering why his mood has changed yet again when he turns to face me, his eyes large and fearful, his face chalk-white. 'Mum . . . I need to talk to you about something.'

My heart lurches. 'What is it?'

'Um . . . when I was away with Dad and Patsy . . .' He tails off and clears his throat. 'They said I could live at their place,' he adds. 'Mum . . . I really want to live with Dad.'

Chapter Twenty-Two

At first I think it's some kind of joke. Or he's only saying this because he's still annoyed about something – Logan can't half harbour a grudge – like me *accidentally* checking his brother's browsing history, or our snappy exchange about falcons. Or is it my cooking? Is he sick of my tedious batch-cooked offerings, and all the omelettes and frittatas we have to force down in order to use up copious amounts of egg yolks after every meringue bake?

'Logan,' I say carefully, 'you can't live with Dad. That just wouldn't work.'

'Why not?'

Because you're my boy, and I'm not ready to let you go. 'It's a crazy idea. You haven't thought it through properly . . .'

Now he's blurted it out, his gaze is unwavering. 'Yeah, I have. We talked about it when we were away.'

It feels as if something cold and heavy is pressing down on to my chest. 'But why would you want to?'

'Because of space.'

249

'What? You have your own bedroom here, what more d'you need? And I've just spruced it up and been to Ikea—' I stop abruptly. How pathetic does that sound, expecting him to be excited by a new chest of drawers?

Logan frowns. 'Yeah, I know. But, y'see, Dad and Patsy have the barn and they're gonna do it up for me. So it'd be like my own place. It'll be amazing.'

'You want to live in a *barn*?'

'Yeah, but it won't be, like, *barn-ish*. It'll be all done out like a kind of open-plan apartment. We planned it all on holiday.'

I blink at him, momentarily lost for words. This is my boy, who can barely make toast without incinerating it, and still fears crusts. 'I . . . I still can't understand why on earth you think this is a good idea.'

'Oh, it'll be great,' he exclaims, brightening. 'I mean, it's a bit of a state, Dad says, and there's a horse in it at the moment—'

'They don't have a horse!'

'It's Patsy's friend's but it'll be gone by the time I move in.'

'Well, that's good to know,' I snap, sensing my cheeks blazing. 'At least you won't be bedding down on hay with Dobbin, I suppose we should be thankful for *that*—'

'Jeez, Mum.' He tuts loudly, clearly amazed that I'm not wholly supportive of this startling development.

'And you'd do your own cooking, would you?' My voice is shrill but I can't help it. 'I mean, what would be the set-up in this *barn*?'

Logan shrugs, clearly not having considered this. 'S'pose I could do my own thing when I wanted to and have dinner with them when I couldn't be bothered.'

'I'm sure that'd go down well,' I snap. 'Anyway, never

250

mind that. I can't believe Dad didn't mention this when he brought you home. Why hasn't he spoken to me about it? Doesn't he think I should know what's being planned here? It seems crazy, Logan, that he's going to be solely responsible for you when he could barely get it together to go to a bloody parents' evening, and even then it'd be all about being charming and matey with the teachers instead of actually finding out how you were getting on with—'

'Why are you so mad at Dad?' he blasts out.

'I'm not! Well, yes, I am, Logan, because of this. A plan concocted without anyone thinking I might possibly need to know about it.' My heart is pounding, my chest juddering visibly with every beat.

'He knew you'd be mad,' Logan murmurs. 'That's why he didn't say anything.'

'Mad? Of course I'm mad! I'm your mum, Logan. For Christ's sake – you can't just casually say you're moving out on a whim . . .' To my horror, my voice is wobbling and my eyes are filling with tears.

'It's not a whim,' he says firmly.

'So, you're prepared to move hundreds of miles away and leave Blake and all your friends and your school for, for . . .'

'Dad can enrol me in Thornbank High.'

'Where the hell's that?'

'Near them, just down the road. It's a really good school – I've checked.'

I wipe my eyes with my sleeve. 'You mean you've studied the Ofsted reports?'

'Um, no, but I'm sure it's fine.'

'Your father will have, obviously.'

He shoots me a look of disdain. '*Stop* getting on at Dad.'

251

'I'm not,' I say firmly. 'What I'm saying is, you deciding it's fine isn't the same as finding out if it's any good or not. Anyway, it's completely the wrong time to change schools. It's a different system from the Scottish one – you do know that? And you're just about to sit your exams. It'd be far too disruptive to move now.' I reach for his hand but he pulls it away. 'I know I'm a pain sometimes,' I rant on, 'but everyone gets sick of their parents, especially at your age when you're desperate to get out in the world . . .'

'I just want to live with Dad,' he mutters.

'But *why*?'

Logan shrugs, remaining silent.

'I know you've just been away with him,' I go on, 'whereas with me, it's just the tedious day-to-day stuff – but we can go away too. I've got a bit of money saved, and I'll go all out to promote the meringues more, and any spare cash can be put aside for a summer holiday.' No, no, don't try to bribe him . . .

'I've made up my mind,' he says quietly. Pink patches have sprung up on his cheeks, and I so want to wrap my arms around him and say, *What's got into you? What is this all about really?* But he'd hate that, and anyway, I know what it's about: quite simply, Logan adores his dad. 'I'll go after my exams,' he adds, 'so I can get settled in at my new school before the summer holidays. Dad says he can have the barn ready for me by then.'

'You're seriously going to live in a horse house?'

'I told you – the pony's moving out . . .'

'Right. So what are we talking – the end of May?' A tear rolls down my cheek, and I swipe at it with the back of my hand.

'Yeah,' he murmurs.

'Are you sure Patsy's okay about this?'

Logan nods. 'Yeah, it's cool.'

Fine! Go then, go and live with a woman who freaks out if her own child ingests so much as a *crumb* of meringue . . .

'Dad says I can help with the business,' he adds, 'packing stuff up. Orders and all that. So that could be my summer job.'

'But they already have people to do that. It's not just Patsy and Dad putting pyjamas in boxes, you know. They have a warehouse, they employ people, it's a major operation these days . . .'

'Well, I'm sure I'll be able to do *something*.'

'Right,' I say, and we fall into silence as Fergus wanders in, clutching an ancient Game Boy he picked up at a charity shop in the Highlands.

He glances at both of us sitting hunched and sullen on the sofa. 'What's up?'

I look up at him. 'Logan says he wants to go and live with Dad,' I say flatly.

'Oh. Yeah. I kinda heard them talking about that.'

I meet his gaze, incredibly stung that this secret has hung in the air between them. Fergus perches on the sofa arm, and the three of us sit there for a few moments with the TV on mute. From outside comes the distant hum of traffic, and someone laughs in the street below.

'How would you feel about Logan moving out?' I ask tentatively.

Fergus pauses for a moment, as if he hasn't really considered this. Then his face brightens as he says, 'It'd be fine, Mum, 'cause then I'd get the biggest room.'

*

I spend the rest of the evening attempting to contact Tom, to no avail. My voicemail messages to his mobile and landline are at first restrained – 'Could you call me, please?' then virtually spat out: 'Tom, I really need to talk to you NOW.' He doesn't phone back. He's either torturing me deliberately, or dead.

Next morning – Monday, first day of the new term – I somehow manage to get through the whole breakfast-and-getting-ready routine without mentioning the move at all. I know it would only result in Logan and I stomping off to our respective schools in filthy moods. Instead, I try to affect a calm manner, pleased with myself for having bought mini variety boxes of cereals, as if that might possibly persuade him that it's not so terrible here after all. Bet Patsy doesn't have those, all coated in sugar and honey to attack tooth enamel. At her place it'll be gravelly muesli all the way, or a dense lump of pumpernickel bread if he's lucky.

'Have a nice day, boys,' I say lightly as they gather up their bags to leave. 'D'you both have your lunch money?'

They nod. 'Take a bit extra from the jar for a snack on your way home.' I realise I'm trying to bribe Logan again, *paying* him to stay. As if a quid for a Kit Kat will swing it. More sugar, too. Is that why he wants to break up our little gang of three – as a last-ditch attempt to hang on to his own teeth?

Once they're gone, I take a moment to sip the remains of my coffee before grabbing my handbag and checking my reflection in the mirror in the hall. God, I look old. Two grey hairs have appeared at the front – in fact, not so much hairs but *wires*. I yank them out and, with my scalp still smarting, try to maintain my calm demeanour as I hurry off to school.

In the office, it's tempting to blurt it all out to Jacqui, the classroom assistant with whom I get on especially well. But she has a headstrong sixteen-year-old of her own – a stunning, red-haired daughter called Kayla – and I know she'd be so sympathetic and understanding, I'd end up weeping all over the boxes of newly delivered school photography. And one thing you can't do at school is cry – at least, not when you're a grown-up. It's a sign of weakness and children never forget that. A bunch of them once spotted Jacqui having a sly ciggie on her way home, and it's still mentioned three years on: 'That Time We Saw Mrs Harrington Smoking Outside the Co-Op.' You'd think it had been a spliff. Anyway, Tom is the person I need to speak to, damn him. How dare he avoid my texts and calls when he must know precisely why I need to talk to him? The spineless arse, hatching plans with Logan – then being too cowardly to discuss them with me.

'His mobile must be broken,' Viv suggests as I march home, phone clamped to my ear. 'There's got to be some explanation.'

'Yes,' I say, 'maybe it fell out of his pocket when he was furrowing the land.'

She sniggers dryly. 'I can't actually believe Logan would rather live with them than you. Patsy sounds like such a *priss*.'

'She's okay. She's just, you know – everything has to be right. She's very particular.'

'You've called their landline, obviously?' Viv says.

'Yes, but I'll try again.'

'It'll just be a whim,' Viv says. 'He'll soon change his mind.'

'That's what I said – what I'm *hoping* – but it doesn't

sound like it. I mean, I know he can be fickle, but he has always loved being with Tom because he's fun and spontaneous and not an uptight old fart . . .' My voice splinters.

'Alice, you're so not,' Viv declares. 'You're a brilliant mum. God, I don't know how you manage sometimes . . .'

'. . . But he's never mentioned living with Tom before,' I cut in. 'I think maybe it all spiralled from Blake getting his own annexe . . .'

'His *what*?'

'Oh, Clemmie had the whole top floor converted for his sole use and now Logan feels horribly hard done by.'

'Is that what teenagers expect these days?' she gasps, and I can sense her thanking her lucky stars that she's never produced a child of her own.

'Seems to be,' I say gruffly.

Viv sighs. 'Cheer yourself up,' she says in a softer tone. 'Give Giles a call, I know he'd love to hear from you . . .'

'He texted actually,' I say dully, 'but I haven't got around to replying.'

'You will do, though, yeah?'

'I might,' I mutter, not certain that going out drinking with a twenty-nine-year-old will help matters right now.

By the time I turn into our street, both Kirsty and Ingrid have both expressed horror at Logan's plans. (I knew Kirsty would be especially aghast – all three of her kids were virtually strapped to her body for their first two years of life; back then, she was a firm believer in '*wearing your children*'.) I let myself into our block, realising with shame that I didn't ask Ingrid what's happening about her eggs being harvested this week, and decide I'm a pretty cruddy friend, too.

I dump my bag in our hallway, relieved that I'm home

before Logan and Fergus, and call Tom's landline for the umpteenth time.

'Patsy?' I say when she picks up. 'It's me, Alice. I've been trying to get hold of Tom. Is everything all right?'

'Erm, it's fine,' she says, in the kind of brittle tone that says things are patently *not* fine, then she adds, 'Sorry, Alice, bit caught up at the moment. I'll ask Tom to ring you, okay?' And she clonks the phone down. While I don't want to read too much into our brief exchange, it sounds as if they were possibly in the middle of a row. Wasn't that the main reason I split from Tom – so the boys wouldn't grow up in an atmosphere of seething resentment? I knew it would be tough, and they'd miss out on dad-type stuff – but then I figured that we could possibly survive without his day-to-day input. This, of course, was long before his reincarnation as Monty Don.

The boys arrive home tired and faintly grumpy, and although I try to give Logan some space, I can't help prowling around him, like a cat.

'I just need to understand why you've come to this decision,' I blurt out as we clear the table after dinner.

'I don't want to talk about it now.'

'It's just, you do know their house is in a tiny village—'

'Yeah, I've been loads of times, haven't I?'

'And you don't even like the countryside. You think it's boring. You said you *couldn't see the point of it*, remember?'

'Yeah, that was different. That was near Grandma's.'

'It's still countryside, isn't it?'

He eyes me disdainfully as if I am an irritating child, then shuts the dishwasher with a bang and disappears to his bedroom. *If you're so fond of the country*, I want to shout after him, *how about living at Grandma's for a while with the malfunctioning septic tank and her delicious lunches – see how you get along there? There'd be no pancakes or takeaway pizzas, no Xbox to boggle your brain for hours at a time* . . . I don't, of course. I just stomp off and do lots of silent swearing in the bathroom, marvelling at – on top of the grey hairs this morning – the new facial crevices which seem to have appeared since Logan's announcement. Perhaps I should get back in touch with Anthony, see if he'd do me some fillers in exchange for a smack on the arse with my spatula. I look exhausted, frankly, like a particularly tragic 'before' picture in a makeover, under which the caption would read, 'Alice had *completely* let herself go . . .' Is it really only five days since I was giggling tipsily in the Marais and snogging Charlie in the street?

The next evening, mainly by keeping my mouth clamped tightly shut, I manage to not mention Tom's glorious outhouse at all, even to suggest that, post-renovations, it'll probably still stink of horse shit. Right now, the best tactic seems to be to carry on normally as if nothing untoward is happening at all. Logan heads out to his usual Tuesday guitar lesson down the road, and when he comes back, he actually invites Fergus into his private lair to play on the Xbox. There's the sound of rapid gunfire and many explosions, and part of me wishes that my kids had grown up like Kirsty's wholesome trio, or Ingrid's daughter Saskia, happy to while away the hours making flapjacks and little clay owls and tinkle away on the piano. But at least they're hanging out together. That's a good sign, surely. Maybe Logan is softening, and all that living-with-Dad stuff was just a whim after all. I

258

spend the evening trying to build on this glimmer of hope.

First, I try to woo him by baking one of his favourite treats – not my tedious meringues, but apple crumble. While the crumble is great, the custard is less successful, but at least the vigorous beating required helps to dispel any lingering tension in my brain. I even transport bowls of pudding to the boys in Logan's room, gliding back and forth with a beatific smile on my face, like a stoned waitress.

'Thanks,' they mutter, eyes glued to the screen. Then, instead of throwing Logan's laundry from the dryer into a basket, I actually fold each item – even his pants, like he'll really appreciate that. I'm about to return his fragrant clothes to his room when I catch a snippet of conversation from behind the closed door: 'She tries to be nice and everything but she's such a *Nazi*.' That's Fergus speaking. Fergus, who I actually thought still liked me, perhaps because I managed to 'rescue' Rex, ahem.

'Yeah, she is a bit,' Logan replies.

'She's like one of them top Nazis, the ones in the long coats and the caps with the shiny peaks . . .'

'Haha,' Logan guffaws as my blood starts to curdle, not unlike the custard I just made.

'What d'you call the top Nazi?' Fergus asks.

'Commandant?'

'Nah, something else . . .' The rim of the heavily laden plastic laundry basket digs into my fingers as I stand, motionless, outside Logan's room. How dare they? Do they have no idea of how incredibly *un*-fascist I am? They have friends around constantly, watch virtually anything they want to on TV, *and* there's no consequence to speak of when someone sullies my cleansing cloth in the most degrading manner imaginable.

'*Obergruppenführer*!' Fergus exclaims.

'Yeah, that's it.' There are peals of raucous laughter as I back away with my basket, heart pounding, face burning hot. At least they're having a bloody fine time, insulting me, after I made a crumble *and* folded twelve pairs of Topman boxer shorts – who needs so many pants anyway?

'Spoilt, spoilt, spoilt,' I mutter, storming back to the kitchen, dumping the basket on the floor and grabbing my jacket from a chair.

'I'm going out,' I bark, back in the hall now.

'Where're you going?' Fergus yells.

'Out.'

Logan's bedroom door opens and Fergus's head appears around it. 'Are you going to the shops?'

'Yes.' I soften momentarily at the sight of his perky face. 'D'you want something?'

'Could you get those chocolate sticks, the ones you dunk in hot milk?'

'They only do those in Pascal's. I wasn't planning on going there.'

He frowns. 'Why not?'

Because everything costs eight thousand pounds . . ..
'It'll be shut,' I reply, heading for the door and clattering downstairs, realising I don't have the faintest idea of where I plan to go.

Chapter Twenty-Three

I don't have my purse with me either, but never mind that. I march down our street, grateful for lungfuls of cool evening air after all the cooking and pant-folding and being likened to a senior-ranking Nazi. While the high street is usually bustling – there's a decent selection of pubs and restaurants as well as our collection of rinky-dinky shops – our residential road tends to be quiet. There are tenement flats on either side, and three large, creamy-stone detached houses at the high street end; Clemmie's is the biggest and finest, the one with the walled garden and the annexe on top. I could pop in and have a good old grumble, but wonder if being in her gleaming kitchen with its island the size of Fiji and special fridge *just for wine* will actually make me feel any better about my own life.

I could, of course, just keep walking with no destination in mind. Doesn't every parent fantasise about doing that occasionally? I could walk and walk until Edinburgh peters out into open countryside, the kind of featureless terrain that Logan 'doesn't see the point of'. And I'd be fine, even without money. I could feast on wild berries – does anything edible grow in April? I could ask horticultural expert Tom, but he seems to be avoiding me at present. Anyway, if things became desperate I could barbecue some roadkill, and when I was sick of *that*, I could service a passing trucker in order to buy myself a loaf of bread. Do roadside hookers exist in rural places? I'd be a novelty if I was the only one. God, I could probably make more in one swift transaction than I do from a whole night's baking. Would the boys even notice I'd gone? Probably not. They could go feral, feasting on dry cereal scooped straight from those mini variety boxes they so love. They could throw wild parties where people are sick in the bath, and break the world record for Time Spent on the Xbox, handsets welded to their sweaty paws. Occasionally, Fergus might say, 'Wonder when Mum's coming back with our hot chocolate sticks?' Then his attention will be caught by a massive explosion on screen and he'll forget all about me.

I turn the corner and head along the high street, trying to wrestle my thoughts back into some semblance of order. Somehow, I'm going to have to get through the next seven weeks leading up to Logan's departure without being in a simmering bad mood all the time. It can't be good for my health, or my business; how can I possibly bake shop-worthy meringues when my head is swirling with angry thoughts? They require patience, and a light touch – qualities that don't come easily when I'm under duress. If I carry on like this, they'll end up like bitter, joyless grenades. And I must remember that Logan is sixteen, i.e. old enough to know his own mind. Who am I to decide he should live with me?

On a more positive note, the small lump I've just

noticed in the hip pocket of my jeans turns out to be a scrunched up ten pound note. Perhaps, if I'm careful, I can put off being a prostitute until the weekend, when people might be more inclined to treat themselves.

My phone rings, and I snatch it from my back pocket, expecting it to be Logan or Fergus remembering something else they want me to fetch them from the shops. Which I will dutifully buy them, because I am the sort of fascist dictator who dutifully scurries along the biscuit aisle to grab the Caramel Logs they so enjoy.

But it's not them – it's Giles. 'Hi, Alice?'

'Hi, Giles,' I say distractedly.

'How've you been?'

I try to steady my breathing. 'Fine. Good, actually. I've been to Paris . . .'

'That sounds fun . . .'

'Oh, it was.'

A small pause. 'Did you get my text?'

'Yes, sorry, I meant to reply—'

'That's okay,' he says brightly. 'Just wondered if you'd like to get together later this week?' I'm still walking briskly, and as I approach the top of the hill I can see that there's some kind of event happening in Pascal's.

'I'm not sure. It's just . . . life's a bit hectic at the moment.' *And, apart from that one brief text, you haven't exactly been in a tearing hurry to contact me.* Then again, maybe that's the way it works these days. Dating etiquette is, I realise, as baffling to me as Medieval literature.

'Friend's having a private view,' Giles is saying, 'at Space, that gallery just down the hill from Harvey Nicks . . . d'you know it?'

'Er, yes.' *Why* do I pretend to know places I've never heard of? To sound less geriatric?

263

'Thursday evening, starts at seven, just a few drinks . . . you'll love his stuff.' I can't help smirking at that; for all Giles knows, my idea of great art might be a crying Pierrot print. 'Fancy coming along?' he prompts me.

'Can I let you know?' I've arrived at Pascal's now, the lovely aromas of baked goods and cheeses forcing me to a halt. On the pavement a chalked blackboard announces, in ever-so-pretty French handwriting: *Tuesday April 9 * tasting evening * open till late * drop in and try our delicious new ranges.*

'Sure,' Giles says as I step into the busting deli. 'Anyway, sorry, I didn't realise you were out—'

'That's okay.'

'Sounds busy for a Tuesday night . . .'

'It is a bit.'

'Where are you?' Ah, now his interest is piqued. I am a woman about town who goes to lively places – on a school night too. And I'm not going to spoil the illusion by saying, 'I'm actually in a shop.'

'Just a little place near my flat. Better go.'

'Sure. Have a fun night and let me know about Thursday . . . I'd really like to see you again.'

My mouth curls into a smile as we finish the call. Slipping my phone back into my pocket, I glance around, not quite sure why I've ended up in the deli. Staff are milling around with trays bearing all kinds of delights – tiny samples of cheeses and pâtés on crostini, plus miniature raspberry and apple tarts. A wine tasting session is happening at one end of the shop; spotting Jacqui from school, chatting animatedly with Moira, our deputy head, I zoom over and am offered a glass containing a tasting measure by a caramel-limbed girl who flashes me a broad smile.

'It's our new Burgundy, just in,' she explains.

I take a sip. 'Mmm, it's lovely.'

'Amazing, isn't it?' agrees Jacqui. 'I'm going to buy a couple of bottles.'

'We're going for a drink afterwards,' Moira says, 'if you fancy joining us.'

'It's okay, thanks. I was just, er, on my way to pick up some shopping and noticed this was happening . . .'

'You were lured in,' Moira laughs. 'I know the feeling. I love this place, can't walk past without popping in for a little something . . .'

'That reminds me,' I say, placing my empty glass on a passing tray, 'the boys asked me to pick up some of those hot chocolate stick things.'

'They're in a basket in the corner,' offers a tiny blonde girl with another tray.

'Great, I'll grab some before I forget.' I squeeze my way through the chattering groups, but by the time I reach the chocolate sticks, and realise I'd only get three for my tenner, I am overwhelmingly distracted by the display of Burgundy on the neighbouring shelf. I know it's bad, and that I'm putting my own fierce desire for booze before the whims of my sons, but hell – that's probably what Hitler would do too. Only he didn't have children. But if he *had*, I doubt if he'd have experienced a second's remorse in brushing off a casual request for what amounts to a gimmicky way of making a very ordinary hot chocolate.

My arm shoots out like a robot's as I grab a bottle by its neck.

'Ooh, looks like *you* fancy a drink tonight, darling!'

I spring round, bristling defensively until I realise it's Clemmie. 'Don't ask,' I say, laughing. 'Anyway, looks like everyone's here tonight.'

'Are you surprised?' She grins, indicating Pascal as he chats charmingly to some elderly customers from behind the counter. 'Isn't he gorgeous? That sexy voice! Must be good for business . . .'

'You know it's his place?'

'Really? I did wonder . . .' She drops her voice to a whisper. 'You should get in there, Alice. A thriving business *and* drop-dead handsome in that sexy Gallic way. I imagine he's just your type.'

I burst out laughing again. 'You *are* joking. I don't even know if he's single—'

'Find out then! Do some research. If you don't, *I* will . . .' She turns and beckons over two tall, pink-cheeked blondes who are dressed in coordinated shades of red and grey. 'Rachel, Olivia, come and meet my friend Alice . . .'

'*You're* the one who made the amazing meringues for the Morgan party,' Rachel exclaims. 'God, they were good.'

'Glad you liked them.'

'The three of us worked on the event together,' Clemmie adds.

'With Clemmie at the helm,' Olivia explains. 'She's amazing, a *powerhouse*. The most dynamic person I've ever met . . .'

Clemmie tosses back her freshly blow-dried mane. 'Well, it is my job. Oh, Alice, I wish you'd let me pull something together for your fortieth . . .'

'Is that coming up?' Olivia asks.

'Yes, but I'm sort of hoping it slips by unnoticed.' I smile tightly and take another glass of wine from a passing tray.

'Why?' she frowns. 'Come on, it's meant to be a real

biggie, an excuse to throw the kind of party you've always wanted.'

'Or have a trip,' Rachel cuts in. 'One of those holidays-of-a-lifetime . . .' An image flashes into my mind: of me and Fergus on a beautiful beach, and Logan a speck in the distance, parked on a towel which he's carefully positioned half a mile away so as to minimise contact.

Clemmie clutches at my wrist as if taking my pulse. 'It's not fair to pressurise you, sweetie. I know you don't like being the centre of attention and if you're not in the mood, well . . .' She shrugs and gives me a pitiful look.

'I honestly don't think I could face a big do,' I admit.

Rachel nods sympathetically. 'I'm not sure what I'm going to do for mine.'

'But I remember yours,' Clemmie says. 'It was years ago.'

'No,' she titters, 'I mean my fiftieth . . .'

'You're nearly *fifty*?' I bark, far too loudly.

'Yes.' She laughs ruefully. 'But don't shout about it.'

'But . . . you look amazing.' It's true: her skin is flawless, glowing, as if illuminated from the inside. I'd have put her at late thirties at the very most.

Rachel winks and sidles closer. 'I'll let you into a little secret. I see a great guy about three times a year and he's made all the difference.'

'You mean you've had stuff done?' I bite into a herb-flecked crostini.

'Just a bit.'

'Go on,' Clemmie cajoles her with a chuckle, 'tell Alice your entire treatment history.'

'Oh, I couldn't possibly,' she giggles. 'But he's amazing. If you're interested, his name's Anthony Lane and his clinic's—'

'In the New Town,' I cut in. 'Yes, I know him actually.'

'Oh.' I can sense Rachel scrutinising my face.

'I don't mean I've been to him,' I add hurriedly. 'I mean, er, I had dinner with him once.'

'God, did you? You mean a date?' She looks hugely impressed.

'Sort of. Well, yes.'

Rachel glances round at the others, eyes wide. 'I've told you about Anthony. He's absolutely gorgeous. Mid-forties but looks so much younger, really takes care of himself *and* very sexy.' She grins at me. 'God, you lucky thing.'

'Er . . . he wasn't really my type,' I say with a smile.

'Really?' She blinks at me.

'We just didn't click,' I say, trying to shoo away the memory of his jabby tongue.

'But think of all the free treatments you could have had,' Olivia teases with a gravelly laugh. For a moment, I prickle at the suggestion that I might have considered sleeping with him in return for a little light Botox around the crow's feet. Then I remember that, just twenty minutes ago, I was considering servicing truckers out on the moors, so perhaps I am being a little oversensitive.

'I'm not sure it's the right way to go,' Clemmie adds. 'You do look great, Rachel, but didn't you say you couldn't raise your eyebrows after that last shot?'

'Eyebrows aren't that important,' she retorts, 'in the grand scheme of things.'

We all laugh, and Clemmie nudges me and adds, 'I think you should grab another glass of that wine while we think of something you *can* do to mark your birthday.'

I smile, flattered that she cares so much. 'I'd love to

stay a while but the boys will be wondering where I am. Um . . . I'd actually stomped out in a bit of a huff.'

'Oh, nothing serious I hope,' Clemmie says.

'No, just a silly little thing.'

'Alice,' she adds grandly, 'is an *amazing* mum to two lovely boys.' I grin awkwardly, not knowing how to respond to that, then say my goodbyes. As I make my way through the crowd, clutching the paper bag containing my wine, I'm already vowing to be all smiley and non Führer-like when I get home. Damn, maybe I should have bought them a treat after all.

I'm almost at the door, about to leave, when one of the serving girls appears at my side, bearing a tray of tiny raspberry tarts. 'You must try one of these.' She smiles, flicking her ash-blonde fringe from her eyes.

'Go on then.' I pick one up and bite into it; she's right, it's delicious.

'Amazing,' I tell her. 'My God, that is the best.'

'Have another if you like.'

I laugh, wondering how it's possible to make pastry so light and melty, to perfectly hold its filling of crème pâtissière and plump, sweet raspberries.

'Well, if you insist.' I take a second tart and devour it virtually in one. 'D'you think I could buy a couple of these to take home to my sons?' I ask. 'They'd love them.' And it would make up for me blowing my money on wine . . . oh, hell. I have precisely £3.01 left in my pocket . . .

'Just take them,' the girl murmurs. 'Grab one of those paper bags from the shelf and I'll pop them in for you.' She grins conspiratorially. 'Pascal will never know.'

'Thanks,' I say warmly, glancing back to see him through the crowds, being jovial and attentive with everyone, and wondering what he made of my meringues. I feel foolish now, expecting him to stock them; how can I compete with these heavenly tarts? He catches my eye and makes some kind of gesture, and a brief smile lights up his face. I smile back, then realise how awkward it'll be if he comes over – how he'll feel obliged to say something about my meringues, while I act all blasé and say it's fine, I didn't think they'd be his kind of thing . . .

I hurry out of the shop, clutching the tart bag in one hand and the wine to my chest as if someone might try to wrestle it from my grasp.

Chapter Twenty-Four

I spend Wednesday morning desperately trying – and failing – to keep my mind on work. Where the hell is Tom, and why won't he speak to me? Didn't Patsy ask him to call me back? It doesn't help that it's a hassly morning with a plumbing emergency in the boys' loos, caused by some bright spark using about five thousand sheets of loo paper, plus a clog-up of parents in the office all firing questions and requesting various forms, none of which I can locate at the moment.

I know it's my job, and most of the parents are lovely; however, there is a small core who regard school not as excellent free childcare with some learning thrown in, but as something to wage war against. Why was Irn-Bru offered at the school car boot sale before the Easter holidays? someone wants to know. Why aren't there CDs available of the choir's last performance, and when will Sophie McLelland be given a solo spot? (I politely point out that my responsibilities do not extend to the choosing of soloists.) And now Belinda Troop has barged into the small, cramped office and thrust a stapled wad of A4 at me, covered in signatures.

'Here's a petition,' she barks, flaring her nostrils like a vexed pony.

'What about?' I frown at her, conscious of the *bzzz-bzzz* of my mobile as it vibrates somewhere on my desk.

'Teachers having the car wash man round after school.'

I blink at her. 'But it's only once a month and it's always long after the children have gone home. It doesn't actually affect anyone . . .'

I'm desperate to grab my phone and see who's just called in case it's Tom. But Belinda is glaring at me across the cluttered desk, brandishing the petition. I take it from her and try to regard it with interest.

'I didn't realise this was an issue,' I remark.

'Well, it is when it's happening in our children's playground.' *Yes, but we're talking about washing cars, not nude mud wrestling . . .*

'It's just, some of the teachers find it really useful,' I go on as the lunch bell rings, long and shrill, and not before time either.

'The thing is,' she says, towering over me in her spotted shirt and candy-pink pencil skirt, 'things get washed *off* cars and on to the ground. It's a hazard and every parent here –' she jabs at the petition – 'wants it to stop.'

Christ-on-a-bike. 'What kind of things get washed off?' I ask as my phone starts vibrating again. I grab it; it *is* Tom. So he's alive, at least. No fatal injury with a trowel.

'Oil,' she announces.

'I'm sorry, I don't—'

'Oil can be washed off the cars and sit there on the tarmac.'

272

I am starting to feel as old and gnarled as that human skin book in the Surgeons' Museum. 'I'll pass on your concerns,' I say, willing her to leave the office so I can call Tom back.

'They're not *my* concerns, they're the concerns of all—'

'The people who've signed this,' I say, 'about the oil. Yes.'

'I have noticed a few spots of it,' she adds darkly. *Bzzz-bzzz*. There goes my phone again, third time now.

'Sorry, I really have to take this,' I say firmly as I answer the call. 'Tom? I've been trying to get hold of you for days.'

'Um, yeah, Patsy said you'd called . . .'

Belinda is still standing there, arms firmly folded. What is she waiting for – the Pearl & Dean jingle, or a hot dog?

'Well, we need to talk about Logan, don't we?' I say in a tight voice.

'Guess we do,' Tom replies with a sigh.

'Hang on . . .' I hiss, blinking at Belinda. 'Thanks for bringing in the petition. I'll call you as soon as there's any feedback, okay?'

She nods.

That means *please go away now.*

Mercifully, she turns and leaves the office as I mouth *BYE-BYE* at the back of her shiny blonde head.

'Tom, where the hell have you been?' I hiss.

'I've just been busy, I've had stuff on—'

'You didn't think I'd want to speak to you about Logan moving into your stable?'

'Yes, but—'

'He's our son, not the baby Jesus,' I snap.

'It's a *barn*,' Tom corrects me as I get up, shrug on my jacket and grab my bag, then make my way out of the office.

'The thing is,' I continue through gritted teeth, 'you discussed this with Logan without even mentioning it to me. What the hell were you thinking?' I push the main door open and march outside.

'Yeah, sorry, it just kind of came out.'

I'm crossing the playground now, which appears to be oil-free, despite Belinda reporting a spillage disaster on an Exxon scale. 'What d'you mean, it just came out?'

'We were just chatting one night over a few beers—'

'You gave Logan beer?' Sue, our head teacher, gives me a look of surprise as we pass at the ornate iron gates.

'He *is* sixteen,' Tom reminds me.

'You tipped alcohol down his throat!'

'Christ, you make it sound like I forced it on him. He was actually quite keen to try it—'

'Of course he was! What d'you expect him to say – "No thank you, Dad, I'd rather have a lemonade"?' I clamp my mouth. Standing just outside school is not the place to be shouty. 'Okay,' I mutter, 'so you gave him alcohol . . .'

'It was beer, not absinthe,' he snaps.

'. . . And then you announced that he could live with you . . .'

'We were just having a chat,' Tom says coolly.

'. . . Without even clearing it with me . . .'

'How could I clear it with you? What was I supposed to say – "Stop talking, Logan. We must speak of this no more, at least not until I've okayed it with Mum . . ."?'

'Don't be facetious,' I growl.

'*Well.*'

274

We fall into a huffy silence as I march along, past shops selling scented candles and antique mirrors and hand-painted tiles, things people can't get enough of around here.

'Listen,' Tom says finally, 'I didn't plan it. Like I said, it just came up, and I was surprised at how keen he was.'

Great. Just bloody great.

'But it wasn't a this-is-definitely-going-to-happen kind of thing.'

'Well, Logan thinks it is,' I point out.

'Um, well, that's . . . fine.'

'What does Patsy make of all this?'

'She'll be *fine*,' Tom says, sounding less confident now. Alarmingly, my eyes are filling with tears, to be noted and commented upon when I return to school after lunch. *Have you been crying, Miss Sweet? No, just some kind of allergic reaction . . . to MY SON LEAVING HOME.*

I clear my throat. 'It sounds like she's not remotely fine about it,' I venture. 'I mean, I know you have Jessica, and Patsy's a great mum – but a teenage boy is a very different proposition.'

'Not really,' Tom says in the kind of weedy voice that makes me want to shake him. 'She'll be okay, honestly.'

'You mean you haven't actually mentioned it?'

'Look, she was in the camper van with Fergus and Jessica—'

'Tom, I can't believe you haven't even discussed this with Patsy!'

'I *will,* and she'll be fine . . .'

'You keep saying that,' I cut in, 'as if you've, I don't know, ordered a new stair carpet without checking with

275

her first. But you're foisting a sixteen-year-old boy on your wife, Tom—'

'He's my son,' Tom snaps.

'I know that.' A weird gulping sound pops out of my throat, like something a toad might make. 'It's just, I'm so upset I can't tell you . . .'

'I . . . I'm sorry, Alice,' Tom murmurs. And that's where our conversation ends, because if we carry on in this vein, my pink, puffy face will scare the kids so much, Belinda Troop will probably organise a petition about it.

*

I scramble through the afternoon, mainly by keeping my head down and dealing with gargantuan amounts of filing, and arrive home just before the boys. While Fergus lopes in in his usual *feed-me-now* sort of way, Logan is eerily jovial.

'Good day, Mum?' he asks.

'Er, yes, fine thanks, love.' *Apart from discussing your looming departure with your father and blubbing in the street, it was bloody fantastic.*

'Great.' Awkward grin. 'Right, then. There's stuff I need to do in my room and I might be quite a while.'

As I start to prepare dinner, aware of loud knocking and banging coming from his room, I figure that the kind of 'stuff' he's talking about isn't chemistry revision. I'm itching to investigate, but am holding out for as long as possible, to prove that I do possess some willpower after all.

Four minutes later I'm rapping sharply on his bedroom door. 'Can I come in, hon?'

'Uh, yeah. I'm warning you, though, it's a bit of a mess.'

I push open the door and survey the scene. Logan is sprawled on the floor on his belly, unscrewing something and surrounded by numerous sections of MDF.

'What are you doing?' I ask, frowning.

'Taking my chest of drawer to bits.'

'You mean your new one? The one I built for you?'

He looks up, and his smile – just like his little boy's smile – twists my heart. 'Yeah. I wanna take it to Dad's so I thought I'd get it ready.'

'By turning it back into flatpack?'

'Yeah.' He nods. 'I'm *deconstructing* it.' For a moment, I don't know how to respond. It's his keenness that gets me; the fact that, even with seven weeks and a whole pile of exams to get through, he's so thrilled to be leaving that he's getting ready now. Like when he was seven years old, and we'd booked a family holiday to Majorca, and I discovered his Finding Nemo rucksack all packed in his bedroom a full three weeks before our flight.

'You could probably take it without deconstructing it,' I say dryly. 'Is Dad planning to hire a van to move your stuff?'

'Dunno.'

I fall silent and retreat from his room, trying to come to terms with the fact that this is how the next few weeks will be. It will involve Logan taking stuff to bits, and packing his books, CDs, games and guitar, and being all jovial and smiley like the sunny little boy he used to be. I know I should be relieved that at least he's cheerful for once. But I'm also aware that he's only happy because he's off to a place where there's no *Obergruppenführer*, where he will be allowed to drink beer.

277

It's okay, I tell myself as I start to get ready for my date with Giles. *In fact, we might get along better when there's some distance between us.* However, as I carefully apply eyeliner and lipstick, I suspect that no amount of Revlon's finest will make me appear full of *joie de vivre* tonight.

Chapter Twenty-Five

Although I'd pretended to know the gallery, I've actually had to Google its address. The truth is, I don't tend to frequent places where the cheapest artwork is around nine hundred pounds.

'You won't be expected to buy anything,' Viv points out when she calls. 'It's a private view, not a Jamie Oliver cookware party.'

'I know but . . .' I pause, reminding myself that I turn forty in just over a week's time; I should know how to look appreciatively at art. And it's all right for Viv, who buys proper paintings – not even prints – as casually as M&S knickers. Her living room is dominated by a huge canvas depicting a chaotic dinner party, which I love and always make a big show of pretending to steal whenever I'm round there.

'Just go and have a glass of wine and admire the pictures,' she instructs.

'Right.'

'And, Alice, give him a chance, would you? Giles is a lovely guy.'

She's right, I decide, having seen the boys off to Clemmie's where they've been invited to a sci-fi screening up in the annexe, as Blake now has a projector (amazingly, it would appear that even the prospect of having virtually unlimited access to such a facility isn't enough to persuade Logan to stay). As it's still too early to set off, I also Google the most recent Ofsted report for Thornbank High, the school Logan assumes he'll go to, hoping it says: *School completely out of control. Teachers lying about drunk. Massive penis 'drawn' on the sports field with weedkiller* . . .

The report is headed: 'This is an outstanding school' and goes on: 'Exceptionally strong in English, mathematics and science . . . teachers are highly committed, devoting much of their spare time to offering extra support . . .' Ah. I decide to phone Tom to ask if he's actually enrolled Logan at this establishment of academic excellence. 'I'll give them a call later this week,' he says vaguely. I want to point out that it's probably a little more taxing than that – i.e. he might have to actually fill in a form, with a *pen* – but can't face another terse exchange right now, not just before my date. I've noticed that more and more situations are making me blotchy of face these days, and if I'm not careful I'll start looking that way all the time.

I set off, trying to feel full of hope, and wondering how this evening will turn out. Giles is extremely good-looking, it has to be said – and it's flattering to be invited to such an event. I mean, we'll be *visible* at the exhibition. This suggests that he doesn't just want to shag an old lady to see what it's like.

As it turns out, I spot him milling about with a glass of red wine as soon as I step into the brightly lit gallery.

He is wearing skinny jeans and a fine-knit sweater with two curious details: a breast pocket embroidered with a flamboyant gold skull, and a little knitted belt.

'Hey,' he says, smiling broadly and kissing my cheek, 'great to see you. What would you like? Red, white, champagne?'

'Champagne would be lovely, thank you.' Hell, why not?

He goes to fetch me a glass, giving me the chance to check out the art, which he reckoned I'd love. And I really *want* to love it. This will be so much easier if I can be genuinely enthusiastic; in fact, that's the only way it'll be bearable because, I realise now, everyone is around Giles's age, or even younger. In fact, most of them look as if they are barely out of college. There are bursts of youthful laughter and all the men appear to have either three-day stubble or decorative facial hair – and all their own head hair too.

'So what d'you think?' Giles asks, handing me a glass and surveying a row of evenly spaced artworks. They're not paintings, but collages, using maps as their base and adorned with what I can only describe as various splatterings. I'm reminded of Hamish being carsick on the way home from North Berwick.

'They're interesting,' I say. 'I've never seen anything quite like them before.' That's true, at least.

'Maurice is really innovative,' Giles offers.

'I can see that,' I say, flinching as he snakes an arm around my waist. It feels too much, too soon in the evening.

'Excuse me a sec,' I say, beetling off to examine an enormous map with bits of paper napkin and sugar wrappers stuck all over it, with the words, *Why are we here?* painted across them in gold ink. Does the artist mean here – i.e. alive, on earth – or somewhere more specific, like . . . I peer closely at the map for a place name . . . Milton Keynes? I glance back at Giles who flashes me an undeniably saucy grin. Is he drunk, I wonder, or feeling especially up for it tonight? Perhaps he's still at the mercy of rampaging adolescent hormones? God, this is weird. He'd been mildly flirty that night at the Italian restaurant, but this is different: the way he's looking at me with a sly, slow grin, doing that checking-out-your-boobs thing which men seem to think women don't notice. In fact, so intently is he gazing at my tits, I glance down to check that a bra underwire isn't poking out through my top.

Someone wanders over to talk to him, and they embark on what seems like a pretty intense, muttered exchange. The other young man has a shock of startling auburn hair, like a fox.

'Alice,' Giles calls over, flapping his hand, 'come and meet the artist, a great friend of mine.' Gripping my glass, I make my way across the room, quickly formulating positive things to say about his work.

'I'm Maurice,' he says, extending a hand.

'Hi Maurice. I'm Alice. Your work's really, uh, interesting.'

'Thanks,' he says, a smirk playing on his lips as he glances at Giles; what's so funny?

'These are great, Maurice,' Giles says quickly. 'The whole exhibition hangs together so coherently, you know?'

'Well, I hope so,' Maurice says, still giving Giles odd looks, as if trying to communicate something – but what? Perhaps, *Why are you with this woman when*

282

this room is filled with gorgeous girls with an average age of twenty-five . . .?

I take a fortifying sip of champagne. 'So, what's the idea behind the maps?' I ask.

'Uh, it's about man's futile attempts to formalise his environment,' Maurice replies, bringing to mind Logan's bedroom and my futile attempts to formalise that. 'And how nature wreaks havoc with the topography of our minds,' he goes on, still smirking infuriatingly as if possibly taking the piss, while I wonder if what he's actually done is make pictures from the debris he found lying about on the floor of his car.

'That's fascinating,' I say, struggling now.

'So, um, where did you two meet?' Maurice asks, arching a brow.

'I work with a friend of Alice's,' Giles explains, flushing a little.

'And how *is* the internship going?' Maurice wants to know.

'It's fine,' Giles says, a trace of irritation in his voice, which I take as my cue to turn away and study a collage consisting of leaves and ripped-up doilies, reminding me of the one Fergus made at nursery, which is still proudly displayed on our fridge. Now Giles and Maurice are muttering again, until Giles snaps, 'Yeah, all *right*.' I glance around the gallery, trying to plot my escape. My glass is empty but I don't want another as that would mean staying for longer; that's how bad it is, that I'm passing up free champagne. The door opens and a woman who's easily six foot tall has swept in. And I mean *literally* swept, in a long, swishy black coat, her pale blonde hair piled up artfully to expose a long, elegant neck. She spies Giles and Maurice and strides over.

'Hi, how lovely this is,' she drawls, planting a kiss on each of their cheeks.

'Hello Eleanor,' Giles says, forcing a smile.

'Lovely work,' she says, turning her attention to Maurice.

'Really glad you could come,' he says, sounding rather less than sincere.

'Wouldn't have missed it for the world, darling.' Giles thrusts his hands into his pockets, looking horribly flustered. At once, I know he's slept with her. I can understand why; she is stunning close up, all savage cheekbones and sparkly blue eyes. She is also aged around fifty. Giles's cheeks flush even pinker as he introduces us, and sweat has sprung from his upper lip. After a moment's polite chit-chat, she too glides away, and I'm compelled to follow her and try to figure out what's going on.

I find her admiring a collection of ceramic bowls in aqua tones, arranged on white cubes of varying sizes. 'These are lovely, aren't they?' I remark. It's true: they gleam beautifully, like the pearlised interiors of shells.

'Better than those godawful collages,' she whispers with an earthy cackle.

I snigger. 'I'm not too keen either but I didn't like to say.'

She grins and touches my arm. 'They remind me of interminable car journeys when my children were little . . .'

'My thoughts exactly,' I reply, beginning to relax for the first time this evening.

'Ugh,' she shudders, 'all those emergency stops in lay-bys . . . mind you, map-reading always made me feel a little queasy. I'm sure that's why my ex insisted on me doing it, while he drove.'

'Oh, mine too,' I say, conscious of Giles shooting us alarmed looks across the gallery.

Without asking if I'd like one, Eleanor hands me a glass of champagne from the nearby table, taking one for herself. 'So you were relegated to the role of navigator too?' she asks with an engaging smile.

'Yes, I was. At least, as soon as he'd passed his test, despite the fact that I'd been driving for years. And on the rare occasions when I had to drive – when he'd had a drink, usually – he'd sit there terrified in the passenger seat, gripping the door handle for support, as if that would save him.'

Eleanor laughs even louder this time. 'What is it with men who can't bear to inhabit a car with a woman at the wheel?'

'I have no idea, but it seems to be horribly common.' I sip my drink, no longer seized by an urge to escape.

'It's so nice to meet you, Alice,' Eleanor adds. 'These events can be terribly dull.'

'What made you come?' I ask. 'Are you a friend of Maurice's?'

She laughs. 'I'm his step-mum. His dad's away on business in the States so I had to show support really.' She leans closer, adding, 'You're not a step-mum, are you?'

'No, just a mum.'

'Ah. I was hoping you could offer me some tips.'

'Afraid not. So, is it quite a new marriage then?'

Eleanor nods. 'Nearly six months, and we'd only been together for another eight months before that.' She rolls her eyes and laughs. 'Fools rush in.'

'And . . .' I pause, wondering how to put this. 'I hope you don't mind me asking, but you and Giles . . .'

'Oh, God, that was nothing.' She shivers and touches my arm. 'It's best forgotten.'

As I'm digesting this, she murmurs, 'He's very sweet, as I'm sure you know – but you do realise how he operates?'

'Operates?' I repeat, frowning.

Eleanor scans the room as if checking for eavesdroppers and murmurs, 'Are you familiar with a club called Honey?' I shake my head. 'Of course you're not,' she adds with a grin. 'Sleazy little place. Pretends to be ever-so upmarket but everyone knows it's a grab-a-granny joint—'

'D'you mean,' I cut in, 'where younger guys go on the prowl for older women?'

'Exactly.' Eleanor flicks her gaze towards Giles, who is standing alone, looking a little stranded now, and gives him a little wave. 'Not my usual haunt,' she adds, 'but a friend dragged me there and that's where I met Giles . . .'

'So,' I whisper as things begin to fall into place, 'is that a regular hang-out of his?'

'Absolutely. He seemed to know just about everyone there and he's obviously *extremely* popular . . .' She emits another gravelly laugh and finishes her drink. 'But then, it's understandable, isn't it? He's very . . . easy on the eye.'

'Oh, yes.'

'Anyway,' she goes on, 'we had a little fling, but I can't be doing with someone who can literally spend all his time shopping, or playing tennis, and meeting friends for lunch. It's too tedious for words . . .'

'But he works,' I point out. 'I mean, he has that internship—'

'Only because I made such fun of him being a trust-fund boy,' she declares.

'Really?'

Eleanor nods. 'His father owns several Hebridean islands, darling. Let's just say Giles could get away with never doing a day's work in his life.'

I sneak another glance at him, picture him charming the female clientele of a dimly lit club; what's the attraction, I wonder? Does he find women our age genuinely alluring, or simply easier to pull?

'Anyway,' Eleanor continues, 'it wasn't a complete waste of time, as I ended up meeting my husband through him . . .'

'Really? How did that happen?'

'Well . . .' She drops her voice. 'Maurice is one of his oldest friends, and there was some big family birthday do that Giles took me too, and Maurice's father was there . . .'

'Wow,' I murmur, a little disappointed when I see Giles making his way towards us.

'Erm, I was thinking we could go somewhere else,' he announces, placing a hand on my arm and checking his watch ostentatiously.

'I'm fine here,' I say. 'Eleanor and I were just having a chat—'

'It's just, we could go to a bar, or a club, if you fancy it.'

'Like Honey?' I suggest with a grin.

'Er, no, I was thinking of—'

'Excuse me, I'd better go and make more fuss of the artist,' Eleanor says with a tinkly laugh, leaving me and Giles stranded by the ceramics. There's an awkward pause as if we are two complete strangers who've been forced together at a wedding.

'Eleanor seems lovely,' I venture.

Giles shrugs. 'She's a bit bonkers really.'

'I hear she's married to Maurice's dad?'

He frowns. 'Er, yeah.'

'And that you had a bit of a fling with her . . .'

'It was all a bit weird,' he mutters.

'Why?' I ask, unable to resist teasing him. 'Because she found someone her own age?'

'It wasn't like that,' he blusters. 'It was just, just a *thing* with us. Can't believe she told you actually.'

I smile, placing my empty glass on the table and checking my own watch. 'She mentioned that she's the one who persuaded you to apply for that internship . . .'

'Um, sort of,' he mutters hotly.

It's so tempting to tease him some more, but I manage to resist. Anyway, there's nothing *wrong* with preferring older women; I'm just intrigued as to what his motives might be. Maurice obviously finds it highly amusing and keeps smirking at him across the room.

'Sure you don't want to go on somewhere else?' Giles asks, raking back his dark hair.

'Just a quick one, then,' I say, overcome by curiosity as I wave goodbye to Eleanor across the room. Now there's a fine example of a woman growing older beautifully, with her naughty sense of humour intact; clearly not Botoxed, and she doesn't need it either with that fabulous bone structure. And what a filthy laugh! Makes me feel a whole lot better about my impending birthday . . .

'I'll get these,' I say quickly as we wander into the Cross Keys over the road. It's a cosy, cluttered old Edinburgh pub, a pleasing contrast to the starkness of the gallery.

'So,' Giles says, as I hand him a beer and take the seat opposite him, 'you were having quite a chat, the two of you . . .' He smiles resignedly.

'She was fun. I liked her.'

He fixes me with those dark eyes, but they have no loin-stirring effect this time. 'What did she tell you about Honey?'

I shrug. 'Just that it's a grab-a-granny kind of place . . .'

'That's so insulting,' he declares.

'To who? The older women or the younger guys?'

He looks irritated now. 'It's not like that, Alice.'

'It doesn't really matter if it is,' I say truthfully, because clearly nothing's going to happen between Giles and me. If he finds it remarkably easy to meet intelligent, consenting women like Eleanor this way, then why not? It's more the fact that he wouldn't get my life at all; what on earth would we do, apart from have sex?

'I do like older women,' he murmurs, brushing my hand with his fingers.

'Why is that?' I ask.

'It's just . . . girls my age can be so spoilt, you know?'

'The ones you meet, maybe.'

'But they *are*, Alice, and they're so demanding . . .'

'Whereas we older birds are grateful for anything we can get,' I tease him.

He looks aghast. 'I don't mean that.'

'It's okay,' I laugh, 'I'm not offended, but you know, it's funny – a few weeks ago, a man told me he reckons older women know their onions . . .'

'What did he mean by that?'

'That . . .' I laugh and sip my drink. 'That we're experienced, I guess – only in my case, I was with the same guy from the age of nineteen to thirty-four—'

'What an arse,' Giles mutters.

'You mean my ex?'

'No, the onion man . . .'

289

'And the worst thing was,' I add, 'he was actually *older* than me.' We're both sniggering away now. Although it might be mildly amusing to while away the rest of the evening with Giles, the thought of heading home is, in fact, more enticing, especially as I notice him darting a quick glance towards the barmaid, who's quite the fox in her tight black dress, and is old enough to be his mother.

'I'm going to head off, Giles,' I tell him, getting up and planting a speedy kiss on his cheek. 'Thanks for this evening. It's been . . . interesting.'

'Not offended, are you?' He fixes me with a hopeful smile.

'No, not a bit. Your older woman thing – it's fine, it really is. I guess . . .' I pause '. . . I'd just feel a bit weird about being part of a running theme.'

Giles shrugs, in a can't-help-myself way. 'Think I'll stay for another drink.'

'Bye then,' I say. I'm not even out of the door before he's up at the bar, his posh accent radiating unshakeable confidence as he tells the barmaid, 'I'm sure I've seen you somewhere before.'

Chapter Twenty-Six

Over the next few days I'm too busy with orders to quiz Logan any more about moving, which is perhaps for the best. Every evening sees me either baking or packaging, and the boys – with Logan protesting at first – are drafted in to help. I do notice him paying particular attention to the mixing part, though, quizzing me on ingredients and quantities and what kind of flavours I'm partial to these days.

'The nutty varieties still seem to go pretty well,' I tell him as we tie up cellophane bags of pistachio kisses with pale green ribbon. 'And anything not too sweet, like bitter chocolate, or salted caramel – it's that contrast with the sweetness that really seems to work.'

'Cool,' he murmurs.

'You're actually doing a great job with these bags,' I add.

'Thanks.'

'I really appreciate you helping me.' Fergus, who grew bored and snuck off ages ago, is playing music in his room. 'I mean,' I add, 'some people are really cack-handed doing things like this, but you're not at all.'

When he looks up at me, the flecks in his dark brown

eyes picked out by the sunshine streaming in, I realise how much I'll miss him. Although I know it's rather cowardly, I have decided not to communicate with Tom about that wretched barn for the time being. But I'd bet my life on the fact that he hasn't got around to enrolling Logan at the school there. And so, rather belligerently, I have decided to 'forget' to tell his school here in Edinburgh that he'll be leaving after the exams. For the time being, at least. I suppose it could also be interpreted as clinging on to a shred of hope.

'I know what you're going to say, Mum,' Logan murmurs.

'What?' I ask.

'I just know! You're so transparent. You're going to say, "Why don't you *not* go to Dad's, and spend all summer working here with me, tying up little bags with ribbons? Wouldn't that be fun?"'

'I wasn't going to suggest that,' I say gruffly.

'Don't lie. You've gone red. Your cheeks are on fire, Mum.' He splutters with laughter and it's contagious, and now both of us are sniggering away. 'That was your plan all along, wasn't it?' he crows.

'Oh, stop it,' I say in mock-exasperation. 'Go on then, go to Dad's. Live in your posh barn and eat fresh herbs and make loads of money putting pyjamas in boxes, because that'll be far more rewarding than this.'

'Okay, I will,' he retorts, then he's out of his chair and beside me, giving me the tightest, most heartfelt hug I can remember. And I know he means it kindly, and it's a really sweet thing for a sixteen-year-old boy to do, but it nearly breaks my heart.

*

By the time Friday rolls around, all I'm good for is a movie night in with Ingrid. She arrives with the news that egg collection has taken place, and that, if everything continues to happen as it should, the embryos will be implanted in a few days' time.

'In a couple of weeks I could have a positive pregnancy test,' she tells me, as if daring to allow herself to feel excited at last.

'I so hope it works this time,' I tell her.

'Weirdly enough, Saskia's started nagging like mad about wanting a little sister. Like I need the pressure . . .' She breaks off and laughs. 'She says if she can't have that, then it's got to be a puppy.' I smile, remembering Fergus's incessant nagging for a dog when he was little, and explaining over and over that it wouldn't be fair to have one in a flat. He has taken himself off for one of his long, languorous baths – it tickles me that, for the first eleven years of his life, I virtually had to tie him down in order to chip the dirt off him – while Logan is over at Blake's. I'm making tea for Ingrid when my landline rings.

'Hello, Alice?' says the unfamiliar male voice.

'Yes?'

'It's Pascal, from the deli. Sorry to call you so late on a Friday evening—'

'That's fine, it's only eight . . .' Ingrid widens her eyes and mouths *Stephen*? I shake my head.

'I thought you might've come to the second tasting evening on Tuesday,' he goes on.

'Oh, I didn't realise it was a regular thing.' So he looked out for me, and noticed I wasn't there? I glance at Ingrid, unable to keep down a smile.

'Just something I want to try out,' Pascal explains, 'as

a kind of social event. It's a way of getting to know our customers . . .'

'It's a great idea,' I say. 'And I have to say, those raspberry tarts you had at the first one were amazing. Put my baking to shame actually.' I laugh a little too loudly, aware of Ingrid trying to make eye contact, desperate to know who's on the phone. On the back of an envelope that's lying on the table, I write *PASCAL THE DELI MAN!!!* Then, just for a laugh, I draw a big heart around it, with sparks shooting off.

'We didn't get the chance to talk the other evening,' he adds.

'You looked really busy,' I say quickly.

'Well, one of your friends was in the shop today – Clemmie, I think it is? Large, loud, lots of lipstick?'

'Yes, that's Clemmie,' I say with a smile.

'Thought so. I'd seen you chatting that first tasting night, so I got your number from her. Sorry – I forgot to hang on to one of those labels with your contact details . . .'

'Oh, that's all right.' I glance at Ingrid who is grinning, eyes sparkling. 'What did you think of them anyway?'

'They were delicious. I'd like to stock them if you still have the time . . .'

'Yes, of course I do. D'you have any flavours in mind? I can do any of the ones I left with you, or make up something specially . . .'

Ingrid waggles her brows so suggestively, I have to turn away to keep a straight face.

'D'you think something with pecans would work?' he asks.

'Um . . . I'm sure it would.'

'And, er . . . I was thinking of a sort of, um, bitter

294

orange variety? What d'you think?' From the bathroom comes the whoosh of water as Fergus engages in his daily quest to use all the hot water in the tank.

'Well, that's a new one for me but I'll try it. How many would you like? A tray is usually twenty-four or, if you'd like them packaged, it's usually six minis in a cellophane bag . . .'

'The bags you dropped off would be good for us . . . Shall we say ten to start with, as a trial run?'

'Great, so I'll do five pecan and five bitter orange . . . I can drop them off on Monday if that's okay.'

'Perfect,' Pascal says. We finish the call and I turn to Ingrid.

'My God,' I exclaim. 'That *voice*.'

She laughs as we take our drinks through to the living room and flop on to the sofa. 'Sexy French?' she suggests.

'Very. I mean, I know it's silly and that every French person who speaks English has an accent a bit like that . . .'

'You sounded very businesslike,' she remarks.

'Well, it *was* business. You heard.'

'Don't you think, though,' she muses, 'if he'd wanted to get in touch purely about meringues, he wouldn't have called you on a Friday night?'

I shrug. 'There was no hint of anything else.'

'Yes, because you didn't put out signals . . .'

'That's what Viv's always saying.'

'Oh, never mind all that,' she says, pulling off her shoes and tucking her feet up under her bottom. 'Would you hate it if I asked you to put *Casablanca* on?'

''Course not.' I jump up and pull it from the shelf, and we both settle down with our mugs of tea and a plate of misshapen violet-tinted meringues to watch the

295

greatest film ever made. Only one thought is niggling, and that's how on earth will I come up with a bitter orange flavour that actually works? Because, for some reason I can't quite put my finger on, it seems terribly important to get it right.

Chapter Twenty-Seven

I don't expect handmade birthday cards or a wonky breakfast in bed. I don't even expect anyone to be up and about at eight fifteen on a Saturday morning, so I'm startled by a rare sighting of Logan, not only out of bed but also dressed, in proper day clothes, not his beleaguered South Park dressing gown.

'You're up early,' I remark, dropping toast into the toaster.

'Yeah.' He grins at me, and I wonder for a moment if he's remembered.

'Any plans for today?' I ask pleasantly.

'Nah, not really.' He takes juice from the fridge and grabs the last variety box of cereal from the cupboard.

Hmm, no mention of my birthday then. I'm miffed, but determined not to show it. There's such a fuss made over decade birthdays; last week, Jacqui at work showed me one of those 'things you must do' lists in a magazine. I expected it to be all about hang-gliding and swimming with dolphins. But it wasn't like that. It was all, 'Book an eye exam now so you can start monitoring for glaucoma' and 'Wipe out your credit card debts before you're hit with the huge expense of seeing your children through college.' Christ's sake. I thanked Jacqui, handed back the magazine and vowed to make as *little* of a deal of my birthday as humanly possible.

Anyway, last night was lovely with Ingrid, and tonight the four of us are having cocktails in the bar in the refurbished Morgan, the hotel I made the meringues for.

Logan disappears from the kitchen, and Fergus must be up now as there's some muffled chat going on in the hallway. They both reappear in the kitchen, brandishing a large Quality Street tin with a dented lid and chiming, 'Happy birthday!' the way they used to when they were little.

'Thank you,' I say, quite overcome. 'You got me Quality Street? You know I love those, especially the green triangles—'

'It's not Quality Street,' Logan retorts. 'This is just the old tin from Christmas.'

'Oh.' I smile, taking it from him.

'Logan made you something,' Fergus adds, glancing at his brother.

'Really?' I am astounded. 'You haven't done that for years.'

'It's okay,' he says bashfully, 'it's not one of those cards made from pasta . . .'

'We forgot to get you cards,' Fergus adds.

'That doesn't matter.' I glance down at the tin, impressed that, without a father around to chivvy them into making an effort – which seems to be the way it generally happens – they've actually got *something* together.

'It's nothing much,' Logan adds.

'Open it,' Fergus commands.

I grin, set the tin on the table and take off the lid. 'Oh my God,' I exclaim. 'This is *amazing*.'

'Logan made it,' Fergus repeats.

'I . . . I can sort of tell. In a good way, I mean.' I stare at the extravagant construction: a sort of outsized meringue nest, filled with strawberries and passionfruit and further embellished with squirty cream, chocolate curls and silver glitter. It is *eye-popping*. 'I need to take a photo,' I exclaim, grabbing my phone and framing it in all its fruity, chocolatey glory.

'Hope you're not sick of meringues,' Logan murmurs.

'Of course I'm not. I'll *never* be . . . honestly, I can't believe you actually made this. Did you do the meringue from scratch?'

'Yeah, of course,' he says airily, as if this were a regular occurrence. 'We thought of doing a proper cake, but we weren't sure we'd get it right. And I've seen you making meringues so often I knew exactly what to do.'

'So you made this together?' I ask, glancing from Logan to Fergus.

'Nah, it was me and Blake last night at his place.'

'Wow.' So Logan and his best mate had been hanging out together and chosen to *bake*. Next time I hear someone complaining that teenage boys are perpetually stoned, or getting girls pregnant behind hedges, I'll show them the picture on my phone. 'Well,' I say, 'I can't tell you how impressed I am. Let's have some now.' I fetch plates from the cupboard, dish up three helpings and we all tuck in.

'The meringue's perfect,' I murmur. 'Lovely light texture. . . .'

'This is great,' Fergus agrees, spooning in a huge mouthful.

'It's better than *my* meringues,' I say truthfully.

Logan snorts. 'It can't be, Mum. It was my first try.'

'It really is,' I say. 'Or maybe it's that thing when you eat something you haven't made yourself. For some reason it always tastes so much nicer.'

'In that case,' Fergus sniggers, 'all the dinners you make us should taste great.'

I laugh, spooning in more cream and meringue. 'Maybe you could start doing something like this, Mum,' Fergus adds. 'I mean, meringue nests with fruit in.'

'The thing is,' I say, 'it really has to be eaten pretty much as soon as it's been assembled or everything goes soggy . . .' I turn to Logan. 'So when did you actually build this?'

'This morning, before you got up.'

'Really?' I blink at him.

He shrugs. 'It *is* your fortieth, Mum.' Then he smiles, and both of my sons envelop me in the best birthday hug of my life.

'Oh, Mum, I got you something too,' Fergus blurts out, scampering off to his room and returning with a small present wrapped in creased tissue paper.

'What's this?' It's small and squashy, like a hankie.

'Open it,' he prompts me.

I do, and it's a little muslin square – not just any muslin square, but a precise replica for my old one. 'A cleansing cloth,' I exclaim. 'Where did you get it?'

'I bought it, of course.'

'But . . . how did you know what to buy?'

Both boys are laughing heartily now. 'I researched it on that thing we call the internet,' Fergus says in a put-on boffin voice. 'And I discovered that John Lewis sell these special cloths for ladies' faces.'

'Yeah,' Logan sniggers, bottom lip smeared with fresh cream, 'he felt bad about using your old one to scrub some shit off his trainers.'

'Sorry about that, Mum,' he mutters.

'It's okay, darling. I don't care. This is the most wonderful day.' So my birthday starts brilliantly, and we spend the day just hanging out in the flat. I have no baking to do, and no crucial chores to tackle. We watch TV together and, for once, Logan does not seem appalled by having to share the sofa with me. We have a picky lunch of cold bits and bobs from the fridge, and chat about Logan's looming exams, which he seems eerily calm about. 'D'you want me to test you on anything?' I ask.

'No,' he guffaws. 'I'm fine, Mum, thanks.'

I cut myself a slice of cheddar, wishing we could afford French monks' cheese every day. 'I could help you,' I add.

'I don't think so,' he chuckles.

'Okay,' I say breezily, 'I know I'm ancient, and back in my day we used slates and chalk and the teachers thrashed the living daylights out of us, but I do *know* things, love.'

'What about *Beowulf*?' Logan teases. 'Tell us about that, Mum. We're all ears.'

'No,' I say, ignoring the sniggering from both ends of the table, 'I mean in organising your time effectively. I could draw up some revision timetables on the computer.' Logan turns to gawp at me, as if I'd added, 'While sitting naked in the middle of Princes Street.'

'Stop trying to micromanage me,' he says, not unkindly.

'Am I?' I blow out air. 'I do trust you to work hard, you know. It's just . . .'

301

'You worry too much,' he adds, patting my arm.

I smile, knowing he's right as we clear up after lunch. This is probably the crux of why he wants to live with Tom; I do, admittedly, have control-freakish tendencies, probably due to being on my own all these years, and being conscious that I needed to keep a tight rein on the minutiae of our lives, otherwise everything would spiral out of control. Later, Logan and Fergus head off to the shops and return with a large bar of very posh French chocolate, from Pascal's.

'Thought it seemed a bit mean, just giving you a piece of material,' Fergus says, handing it to me.

'It wasn't mean at all,' I reply. 'It was really thoughtful. But thanks anyway, darling. You've both been lovely today.'

And later still, as I pin up my hair in the hall mirror, Logan hovers around me. 'So what are you doing tonight?' he asks.

'I'm meeting the girls in the Morgan for cocktails at seven, and Ingrid said she'd book some new sushi place for a bite to eat. I won't be late, though.'

He follows me through to the living room where Fergus is flicking through a gadget magazine. 'Is that *all* you're doing?' Logan wants to know.

'Yes, hon. Unless we suddenly have a mad urge to go clubbing . . .'

'*What?*'

'I'm joking. God. Imagine.' In fact, cocktails and sushi with my best friends feels just right; the four of us, having some time together out of the flat for once. 'Sure you both want to hang out here and not stay over at Blake's?' I ask.

'Yeah, I just fancy a quiet night in,' Logan replies.

'Okay, old man,' I snigger, checking my make-up in the hall mirror and wondering if I should trowel on a bit more. I'm actually of the opinion that, at my age, overloading the slap seems to *add* years. So I've kept it light, while hoping that my simple jade shift dress doesn't look too 'cheap piece of cloth', and that the highest sandals I own – in scrappy black suede – don't tear my feet to pieces.

'You look nice, Mum,' Fergus concedes from the sofa, takeaway pizza menu in his hand.

'Thanks, honey. Now, you're absolutely sure you want to stay here? I could still call Clemmie—'

'Stop going on, Mum,' Logan retorts.

'Nah, we're fine,' Fergus says quickly, arousing a smidge of suspicion in me.

I pause in the living room doorway. 'You're not *planning* anything, are you?'

'Like what?' Logan snorts.

'Like . . . I don't know. Jacqui at work told me that Kayla had a party when she left her at home overnight. She'd even photographed the furniture and knick-knacks so she could put everything back in exactly the right position. Jacqui only found out because a curtain pole had come down . . .'

'But you're only going out for a few hours,' Fergus reminds me.

'And we couldn't have a party here,' Logan adds. 'There's not enough space.'

'Oh, you'd be surprised how little you need—'

'I think that's clever,' Fergus adds, looking impressed. 'The photography part, I mean. I'd never have thought of that.'

'Well, don't be getting any ideas,' I say, grinning,

realising how idiotic I'm being. The boys have never given me any reason to distrust them.

'Shouldn't you be going now, Mum?' Fergus asks.

'You're desperate to get rid of me,' I say, planting a kiss on the top of each of their heads before heading for the door.

'Yeah, because it's your birthday,' Logan calls after me. 'Now go *out*.'

*

I flag down a cab into town and climb out in front of the Morgan Hotel. Some refurb it's had. Its foyer is all smart and modern in black, white and red, with enormous chandeliers constructed from clusters of clear glass globes, like bunches of grapes. My heart quickens with anticipation as I follow the red-carpeted spiral staircase down to the cocktail bar in the basement.

'Whoa, look at you,' Viv cries, leaping up.

'Hi,' I say, hugging everyone in turn, and beaming with pleasure at being out, at night-time, with all three of my closest friends. And they all look gorgeous: Kirsty all springlike in a sweet blue and white cotton dress, Ingrid in an elegant white shift which would make me look like a medical person, and Viv in a clingy black top, displaying her pert cleavage to great effect, and a hip-hugging red skirt.

'What are you having?' Ingrid thrusts me a menu.

'Oh, God.' I focus on the tiny print. 'I forgot my reading glasses . . .'

'What?' Viv guffaws. 'You never told us—'

'I'm joking,' I snigger, then read aloud, 'Tanqueray gin, triple sec, orange bitters . . . God, that reminds me, the

304

French guy called. Pascal, remember, from the deli? He wants to stock my meringues, asked for a pecan variety which is fine, but also bitter orange . . .'

'Not sure about that.' Viv wrinkles her tiny nose.

'No, me neither.'

'Weird request,' Ingrid agrees as a waiter comes over, so generically handsome in a modelly way that it's almost comical, and takes our orders. The place is buzzing with chatter and laughter, with all the tables taken; the waiter returns with our drinks, plus a fine selection of snacks in glass bowls.

'Ooh, thank you,' says Kirsty. She's always the most delighted among us to be let off the leash.

'Lovely nibbles,' Ingrid says as the waiter departs. 'Are we allowed to call them nibbles these days?'

'Don't ask me,' Kirsty retorts. 'I haven't been out at night since 1987.'

'Me neither.' I sip my cocktail and pick at the toasted pistachios.

Ingrid chuckles. 'You're *always* out these days.'

'That's not true!'

'Yes you are. Since you started dating—'

'My God,' I hiss. 'Talking of which – don't all stare . . .'

Everyone follows my gaze to the far end of the bar. 'Who is it?' Viv hisses.

'It's Charlie.'

'So it is,' Ingrid exclaims.

'You mean Paris-Charlie?' Kirsty asks.

'The very same,' I say, fortifying myself with a gulp of orangey gin as we all try to be discreet in our peerings. He is perched on a high stool next to another man with ill-advised long hair, floating weedily down his back like a black net curtain. They are chatting animatedly and there are frequent bursts of loud, blokeish laughter.

'Aren't you going to say hi?' Viv asks, eyes wide.

'Er, not sure, Viv. It all ended a bit coolly when he dropped me off . . .'

'But you'll *always* have Paris,' Ingrid sniggers into my ear.

'He's cute though,' Viv observes, 'in that louche, rather knackered kind of way. Like, if he could get it together to do it, the sex would actually be great.'

'Isn't he a bit old for you, though, Viv?' Ingrid teases.

'He's seen us,' Viv hisses, arranging her face into a broad smile as he grins and waves, then hops off his stool and murmurs something to his companion, before making his way over.

'He looks a bit pissed,' Ingrid observes.

'Hang onto your nibbles,' Kirsty whispers, shoulders bobbing with mirth, 'before he tries to stuff them in his pocket.'

Ingrid hoots with laughter and places her hands over the bowls with fingers outstretched, as if guarding them.

'*What's* in my pocket?' Charlie is right up at our table now, grinning squiffily and more than a little sweaty around the gills.

'Just a joke,' Ingrid says quickly.

He peers at her, then turns to me. 'This is Charlie,' I say, trying to keep a straight face. 'Charlie, this is Viv and Kirsty, and you've already met Ingrid . . .'

'Hi,' everyone says as he wobbles in front of us.

'We had fun in Paris, didn't we, Alice?' he drawls.

'Er, yes,' I say with a smile.

He smirks. 'I think I maybe drank a bit too much . . .'

'It's okay,' I say truthfully, 'it was still great.'

'We could go again,' he blurts out, looking around as if for a vacant chair to drag to our table.

'Um . . . probably not,' I say pleasantly, 'but thanks anyway, Charlie.'

His bleary gaze sweeps over the four of us. 'So, just a few drinks tonight, is it?' I swear he glances covetously at our bowl of rice crackers, and nearly splutter with laughter.

'It's Alice's fortieth,' Ingrid explains.

'Oh, you mentioned that was coming up.' He bobs down to plant a wet-lipped kiss on my cheek. 'Happy birthday! Let me get you another cocktail. I'll get you *all* one. What are you all having?'

'It's fine,' I say quickly, knowing with absolute certainty that I don't want Charlie, or his curtain-haired friend – who is making his way over to join us – tagging on to our night.

'Go on, I wanna buy all you lovely girls a drink – Andy, find out what they want . . .'

His friend grins, and it feels so awkward with them towering over us, with nowhere to sit, that I'm relieved when Ingrid cuts in, 'It's lovely of you to offer but we're actually going on somewhere else.'

'Are we?' Viv asks, frowning. 'Already?'

'Yes,' Ingrid says, giving her a significant look. 'It's *time*.'

'Time?' I repeat, laughing. 'Time for what?'

'What's it time for?' Charlie slurs.

'Nothing,' Kirsty says quickly.

'Time for another drink!' Charlie bellows. I smile tightly and glance around at my friends, all of whom are up on their feet now.

'We'll have your table then,' he announces.

'Well, nice to see you again,' I say.

He beams unsteadily. 'You too. And have a lovely rest-of-birthday.'

'Thanks,' I say brightly as Viv grabs my arm and virtually manhandles me out of the bar.

This is *very* weird. The mood has changed to one of urgency as everyone hurries upstairs.

'Where are we going?' I ask Ingrid, who is trotting ahead and seems to be in charge of the proceedings.

'You'll see,' she calls back.

'Let's go to a pub,' I suggest. 'That cocktail's whooshed straight to my head and it was really hot down there. I fancy a nice cold beer before our sushi.'

'I know a place we can go,' she says, stopping as we reach the hotel foyer.

'Where?' I ask.

Ingrid grins, and I detect her exchanging a confusing array of glances and eyebrow raises with Kirsty and Viv. 'Let's see what's going on through here,' she says, setting off at a trot with the rest of us scurrying behind her. We are heading not to the exit but in the opposite direction, along a corridor illuminated with mini versions of the bunches-of-grapes chandeliers.

'Where are we going?' I ask. 'To a *room*?'

'Not quite,' Ingrid says with a throaty laugh.

'Well, sort of,' Kirsty adds.

'A *sort-of* room?' I'm starting to feel unsure about this. Since the boys were so sweet this morning, I'd like to spend a bit of time with them before they go to bed. They'll still be up, hopefully, if I'm home by eleven. While I don't want to be a killjoy, it's occurred to me that Logan and I have very little time left.

'Here we are,' Ingrid announces as we stop at a

polished wooden door. On the door is a brass sign which reads FLEMING SUITE, and I can hear a babble of voices behind it.

'What's this?' I stare at Ingrid.

She grins and pushes the door open. And – oh, my lord. It's a room, yes – but one full of people. As my mouth falls open, and my eyes scan the sea of faces all turned towards me, it dawns on me what tonight is really all about.

Chapter Twenty-Eight

The first person I see is Jacqui and a whole bunch of teachers from school. They all hug me, and when I come up for air I see all my old friends from toddler group, who I rarely have a chance to hook up with these days.

'How did you all know?' I exclaim. 'Who tracked you all down?'

'Clemmie,' announces the voice behind me, and I spin round to see Logan, Fergus and Blake all sniggering away.

'But I left you at home! You were going to order pizzas . . . what are you all *doing* here?'

'I heard the food here was a better standard,' Logan says with a smirk.

Laughing now, I look around at all the people in this beautiful room. 'I can hardly believe this. I didn't even *suspect*.' Red and silver helium-filled balloons hover at the ceiling, and there's an enormous hand-painted banner which says HAPPY 40TH ALICE pinned along a wall. The boys have, very sweetly, all made an effort – Logan is wearing his favourite top and skinny jeans, while Fergus is modelling Topman's finest, and they're liberally doused in Tommy Hilfiger and Joop!. Clemmie is here, grabbing me for a bone-crushing hug, and without warning my eyes fill with tears.

'Did you really organise all this?' I ask, wiping my eyes with a hand.

She nods, grinning. 'Guilty as charged – but Ingrid, Viv and Kirsty put their oar in too.'

'But how did you manage to contact everyone?'

'Well, the boys helped, of course . . . it just took a bit of detection work.'

'Wow.' I grin at her. 'You *are* an organisational genius.'

'It is my job, sweetheart. Anyway, I know you wanted to keep it low-key, so I hope you're not horrified.'

'Of course I'm not,' I say as someone presses a glass of champagne into my hands, and I'm festooned with cards and presents and more hugs.

And it's a fantastic party. I really *hadn't* wanted one; the thought of organising anything had been over-whelming and, as Logan would testify, our flat isn't really the place for a party. I'd also wondered whether my various groups of friends would get along, or if they'd curdle, like my custard. Which, of course, they haven't. Clemmie and Kirsty are locked in conversation with Jacqui, whose goddess-like teenage daughter Kayla has just turned up, and the teachers are laughing raucously with my toddler-group friends. I glance around for a moment, drinking it all in; the music and laughter and everyone dressed up to the nines. Kirsty's husband Dan has arrived, and I go over to say hello.

'You look fantastic,' he says.

I glance down at my dress, which now feels a little plain, considering the setting. 'Thanks, but if I'd known it was going to be this sort of night, I'd have made more of an effort.' While he's a handsome man with striking blue eyes, there's something rather brittle about him, as if, wherever he might find himself, he would prefer to be somewhere else. His detached gaze skims the dance floor, and he doesn't even acknowledge Kirsty as she joins us. 'I'm glad you could come, Dan,' I add. 'Haven't seen you in ages.'

'That's because Kirsty won't ever get a babysitter,' he remarks.

She frowns at him, then rearranges her features into a determined smile. 'Of course I will, Dan. It's just, they can be quite a handful, you know . . .'

'Oh, I'm aware of that,' he says with a bitter laugh, as if it's all her fault.

Her jaw tightens. 'And we've got one tonight, haven't we?' she goes on. 'I mean, we're *out*, in case you hadn't noticed. And you're being such fun, charming company that we must make the effort to do it more often . . .' Clearly taken aback by her sarcasm, Dan glowers at his wife, then mutters something about being hungry – an impressive buffet has been set out – and marches off. 'Sorry about him,' Kirsty whispers.

'You don't have to apologise. Is everything all right, though? He seems so . . . so *angry* about something.'

She grimaces. 'Yeah – about *life*.'

'I take it he's not happy about the kids starting at school?'

She takes a huge swig of wine. 'You could say that. Anyway, never mind him. Hasn't Clemmie done a brilliant job? And your boys, keeping it secret . . .'

'I can't tell you how pleased I am.' I glance over at Ingrid, whose husband Sean has also appeared and is chatting easily to everyone. Looking incredibly smart in a charcoal suit, he makes his way over and kisses my cheek.

'Some party,' he says, grinning. 'Never realised you were so popular, Alice.'

'The thing is,' I laugh, 'I have no idea who half these people are.'

'Gatecrashers,' he says darkly. 'Like them – those young people lurking over there. Who the hell are they?' The music is being cranked up; Logan and Blake appear to be in charge, and are thankfully catering for grown-up tastes, and not just those born in the late nineties.

'No idea,' I reply. 'They look dodgy, though.'

'Better keep an eye out in case they get out of order . . . anyway, ready for another drink?'

'Not yet, trying to pace myself.' He laughs and drifts off to where a bar has been set up, while I hone in on the food. That's another thing about turning forty: you absolutely have to eat. There is a dazzling array of dainty canapés, plus – oddly – tiny meringue kisses dotted between the plates.

'Gorgeous, isn't it?' Clemmie says, appearing at my side.

'It really is. And those meringues . . .'

'The hotel didn't do those. Blake and Logan made them – I think they had some leftover mixture from making your cake, or whatever you'd call that amazing construction . . .'

'They made these?' I marvel. 'God. It's almost too much, you know? Like the old Logan has been whisked away and replaced with an incredibly domesticated alien . . .'

'An alien with a whisk,' she giggles. 'I know. Aren't they great boys? Mind you, Blake *is* incredibly good around the house . . .'

I'm about to agree when someone catches my eye – a tall, handsome Frenchman, with neatly cropped hair, wearing a pale linen shirt and dark jeans, a hint of stubble adding to his attractiveness.

'Look who's here,' Clemmie hisses, almost choking on a filo parcel.

'Pascal,' I murmur. 'What's *he* doing here?'

She shrugs, eyes wide and glinting mischievously. 'No idea.'

'Did he do the food?'

'No, the hotel took care of all that.'

'You invited him, though,' I say, grinning. 'Clemmie, you're *so* naughty. I've had Kirsty, Ingrid and Viv all trying to set me up with men, and now you're at it too—'

'I didn't! I swear, it was nothing to do with me.' I grin, trying to read her expression, quickly brushing a hand over my mouth to check for canapé crumbs. 'He looks a little lost, though,' she adds. 'Over you go to say hi.'

Emboldened now, I make my way towards him, my heart quickening as his face breaks into a grin.

'Alice, hi. Happy birthday.' He kisses both cheeks, and everything goes a little swimmy, and not solely due to the orangey cocktail and a couple of glasses of champagne.

'How did you know?' I ask.

He laughs and taps the side of his nose. 'I know what goes on.'

I smile, silently thanking Clemmie for her meddling. 'Well, I'm delighted you're here. Let me get you a drink—'

'No, I'll get you one, what would you like?'

'Wine please . . .' He heads for the bar, reappearing at my side moments later. I don't know if it's the setting, and the fact that we're not in his shop, but I can sense

314

something different between us. A sort of . . . *charge* of some kind. My heart is racing as we fall into conversation – about how he landed in Scotland ten years ago, and how his girlfriend and their daughter couldn't settle here and went back to France.

'I'd opened a shop,' he says. 'Not the one I have now but smaller, not very successful – but I had high hopes for it. But it wasn't what Madeleine wanted . . .' He shrugs. 'We sort of drifted. We're still friends, though. It's okay.'

I keep glancing at him, drawn to his face. Slightly feline dark eyes, strong brows and very kissable lips. While I could appreciate his attractiveness in the shop, when he was all busy and brisk, it's only now that I'm fully appreciating his finer qualities . . . maybe I'm a little drunker than I realise. 'So how old's your daughter?' I ask.

'Almost sixteen,' he says as Kayla drifts past – she has her mother Jacqui's fine, rangy build, and a mane of tumbling red curls. Pascal nods towards her. 'Your daughter?'

'No – I just have two boys, Logan and Fergus.' I nod towards them, noting with interest that Logan and Kayla are now deep in conversation.

'Oh, yes, I've met them. Is that your son's girlfriend?' He glances towards Logan and Kayla.

'Wrong again,' I say, laughing. 'They've actually never met before. For all his bluster, Logan's pretty shy around girls. I mean, there are girl mates from school, but you know . . .'

'He's still young.'

I smile as our eyes meet. 'Yeah.'

'And you're forty today . . .'

315

I nod, catching a raised-eyebrow glance from Viv as she sashays by. 'Yep, and you know, it doesn't feel like such a big deal.'

'Well, you don't look anything like it . . .'

I chuckle, knowing he can't possibly mean it. 'Oh, come on.'

'It's true,' Viv declares, having been unable to resist coming back to check out Pascal at close quarters. 'Look at her – she has the face of a baby!'

We all laugh, and she turns to Pascal, her eyes beautifully made up with perfect flicks of liner, and slightly fuzzed with booze. 'So where has Alice been hiding you?' she asks.

He blinks at her, looking rather taken aback. 'I haven't been hiding anywhere.'

'How old are you, Pascal?' she goes on. 'Had your big four-o yet?'

'Um, no – that's next year . . .'

'Oh, a proper grown-up,' she declares, tottering slightly on her patent heels. 'Why do I go for younger men, Alice? *Tell* me. It's got to stop. The thing is, when you go out with younger guys, you're always the grown-up and it's bloody boring!' She hiccups loudly and giggles.

'Viv, hon, no one thinks you're boring.' I wrap an arm around her shoulders. 'You're the most *un*-boring person I know.'

'Yes, they do! They think I'm their *mum*. Remember Jake, that last guy I was seeing? Couldn't even book a restaurant table . . .'

'Just as well he had you to do it for him then,' I remark.

'He didn't even own a proper Hoover,' she exclaims.

'Just one of those little mini Vax things that are meant for the car . . .'

Pascal has started to look a little uncomfortable, so I grab Viv's arm and lead her away. 'Let's go and get something to eat. You must try the food . . .'

'God, yes, I'd better eat. Ooh, I feel pissed, Alice. Didn't have any lunch either.' Now we're in motion, I realise she is even more drunk than first appeared. We arrive at the table where she grabs a chair and flops on to it gratefully, while I fetch her a plate of the more carb-laden of the canapés.

'Viv's plastered,' Ingrid sniggers, appearing at my side.

'Yeah, I know. Would you keep an eye on her for a bit?'

'Sure.' She grins, clutching her sparkling water, her eyes glinting. 'I see your sexy Frenchman's turned up.'

I nod. 'I still haven't figured out how, or why – but I'm pretty sure Clemmie invited him.'

'Nice and local,' she says, grinning mischievously. 'You're lucky having a man like that virtually on your doorstep . . .'

'Handy for wine, cheese and chocolate,' I add, and we both laugh.

'Seriously – would you get free stuff, d'you think? Bet you would. He'd be forever popping round with little delicacies . . .' We're giggling away now, and I glance over to where Pascal and Clemmie are chatting while her husband Richard hovers nearby, looking a little left out. He's not usually shy, but I sense he's a little put out by the attention Clemmie is bestowing on Pascal.

More people are dancing now, and Viv has leapt up, abandoning her canapés and throwing herself about the floor with great enthusiasm. Some of her more flamboyant moves cause her top to ride up, exposing an enviably toned stomach, and I catch Pascal murmuring something to Clemmie and both of them throwing her a bemused look. From the far end of the room comes a burst of rowdy laughter from the boys.

'What's so funny?' I ask, sidling over.

'Nothing,' Fergus says, his cheeks burning hot.

'Tell her,' Blake commands.

'No, it's nothing—'

Oh, I know what it is. To a teenage boy, few sights are more hilarious than an adult throwing herself around on a dance floor. 'Is it Viv?' I ask, intrigued now, as Logan is still cracking up.

'We were talking about Patsy the Nazi,' Logan starts.

'Shut up!' Fergus shouts. 'Mum doesn't know . . .'

'Patsy the what?' I ask.

'Just a stupid thing we came up with on holiday,' Logan mutters.

'Patsy the Nazi?' I repeat.

'Yeah,' Fergus says, and even in this darkened room I can tell he's blushing furiously.

I frown at him. 'Why d'you call her that?'

'Oh, it's just the food thing, Mum. You know what's she's like . . .'

'You mean freaking out about Jessica having a meringue?'

'God, that was nothing,' Logan exclaims. 'Every time we went to a cafe on holiday it was, like, a *nightmare*, the fuss she made—'

'One time she made a waitress get a bag of frozen fish-cakes out of the freezer so she could check the ingredients,' Fergus adds, grinning now.

'She was the food Gestapo,' Logan declares, setting everyone off again.

'Well,' I say, 'maybe she has a reason to be like that, if Jessica has allergies . . .'

'There's nothing wrong with her, Mum,' Logan exclaims.

'When Patsy went off for a run on the beach,' Fergus adds slyly, 'Dad gave her a massive bag of Haribos—'

'And nothing terrible happened to her,' Logan cuts in

I shouldn't laugh, but I can't help myself. 'So,' I say carefully, 'the other night, when I heard the two of you talking about *Obergruppenführer* . . .'

Both boys look blank. 'Eh?' Logan mutters.

'You weren't talking about me?' I say with a grin.

They stare at me as if I have really lost it this time. 'You thought we meant you?' Logan asks, eyes wide. 'God, no, Mum. You're not like that at all. You let us eat whatever we want.'

'Yeah,' Blake cuts in, 'why d'you think I like it so much at your house? My mum's a *nightmare*.' While I'm not sure that's ideal either, it's heartening to discover I'm *not* regarded as a senior member of the Third Reich. In fact, I want to grab Logan and say, then why are you insistent on moving to Dad's? I can't go there tonight, though; it would bring down the mood. Instead, I take the glass of wine being offered by Pascal, determined to push the whole horse barn scenario out of my mind.

Falling back into conversation with him certainly helps. Although he's extremely sociable with my friends, we seem to keep meeting at the bar, or by the food, and catching up where we left off. I learn that his daughter is crazy about horses, and lives with her mother in Châteauroux a couple of hours south of Paris.

'So, d'you live on your own?' I ask boldly.

'My brother was staying with me for a few months,'

he replies, 'but he's gone home again so, basically, yes.' Just as I'm wondering how best to follow this up, he says, 'Alice, would you like to go out to dinner some time?'

The smile bursts across my face. *Thank you, Clemmie. I know you denied it but I also know you set this up, you clever thing.*

'That would be lovely,' I reply.

'Shall we do something next weekend? Can I call you?'

'Yes, of course you can. You've got my number, haven't you?'

Pascal nods and sips his beer. 'And of course, you're going to do those meringues for me.'

'I am, and I'm sorry I haven't yet. It's just been a bit hectic.'

'Hey,' he says, the smile lighting up his face, 'no rush at all. I know you have a busy life.'

'Well, it's not *that* busy,' I say quickly, meaning, not too busy to listen to that accent of yours, which is having an incredibly libido-stirring effect. That lovely, caramelly, sexy French voice – I could literally listen to it all night. I could lie back and close my eyes while he read out the ingredients in a packet of salt and vinegar crisps. I realise he's stopped talking. There's a small silence, and I find myself scanning the room with a detached smile on my face, like a teacher observing the young people having fun at a school disco. 'I'll just check how the boys are doing,' I say unnecessarily, because of course they're fine; Fergus is chatting to Kirsty – kids are drawn to her, as she always seems genuinely interested in their lives – and Logan, Blake and Kayla are all huddled in a corner in hysterics.

I know I shouldn't invade their space, but I can't help myself. 'Everyone okay?' I ask.

'Yeah, it's nothing,' Logan says, creasing up again.

'We're fine,' Kayla says, trying in vain to keep a straight face, an *honestly-I-haven't-been-drinking* face if ever I've seen one.

I peer at Blake, who has a similarly glassy look. 'Are you all right, Blake? Feeling okay?'

'Yeah, I'm good,' he says a shade too loudly. I'm not sure how to handle this. I know they're all sixteen, and that Tom let Logan drink beer on holiday – and, to be honest, I'm okay with that, one or two beers max. But these three don't look like they've had a beer or two. I'm no expert, and I haven't had a joint for decades, but they all seem pretty out of it.

'Have you been drinking?' I ask Logan, trying to avoid an accusatory tone.

'Nah.' He gives me a blank look.

'It's just, it's a hotel, you know, you're all under age . . .' I glance at Kayla who has turned a peaky shade of green.

'We haven't drunk anything,' Blake asserts.

'Only Coke,' Logan says firmly.

'Okay.' Maybe I'm mistaken, I decide. Maybe I'm just out of touch, a withered old lady who's forgotten what teenagers look like when they're having a great time. And if they have filched a drink or two from the tables, then so what? Getting a bit tiddly is a rite of passage. I look around for Jacqui, wanting to alert her that Kayla looks rather peaky, but she's nowhere to be seen. Instead, I zoom over to Clemmie.

'Having a good time, birthday girl?' she asks, cerise lipstick still immaculate at ten thirty p.m.

'Fantastic,' I tell her. 'But, listen – d'you think our darling sons might have nicked some booze?'

321

She glances towards them and frowns. 'No, they'd never do that. I know Blake wouldn't.'

'Oh, come on, Clemmie. They're *sixteen*. Didn't you have the odd sneaky rummage through your parents' drinks cabinet?'

An emphatic shake of the head. 'There was no need. They let me drink when I was old enough – a small glass of wine at dinner, that sort of thing. But Blake's just not interested in alcohol . . .'

'Well, Logan has never seemed interested either,' I cut in, 'but look at them, Clemmie. They're all over the place . . .'

She squints in their direction and adjusts the neckline on her plunging polka-dot dress. 'They're just being sociable, darling. Come on – d'you want a drink?'

'I'm fine, thanks,' I say, glimpsing Viv still dancing her heart out, and Ingrid and Sean having a little smooch in a corner, which appears to have sent Logan, Blake and Kayla into hysterics again, while Fergus attacks the buffet with gusto. Pascal catches my eye and smiles, and I make my way over to him. 'Bit worried about the teenagers,' I say.

'They look fine,' he remarks with a disarming smile.

'D'you think so?'

'Yes, and anyway, it's your birthday. You shouldn't be worrying about your kids.' He touches my arm. 'Look at her. She's the one you should be keeping an eye on . . .'

'Oh,' I say, 'Viv loves a party . . .'

'She's hugging everyone!' he observes as she flings her arms around Dan, who quickly disentangles himself, then Sean, who laughs and gently guides her back towards the dance floor.

'She's just affectionate,' I add, figuring that perhaps a

Frenchwoman would never behave in that way; and yes, she's looking decidedly unsteady now, but then, why shouldn't she when she has virtually zero responsibilities, and can do whatever the heck she likes?

'Pascal!' she cries. 'Come and dance with me.'

'No thank you.' He turns to me with a look of mild alarm.

'Don't be a spoilsport,' she bellows. 'It's a party, you can't just stand there . . .' Hell, now he's scanning the room, as if plotting a speedy escape, just as I did at the gallery.

'I don't really dance,' he says firmly.

'Oh, isn't he lovely,' Viv exclaims, eyeliner smudged now and lipstick long gone. She grabs Pascal's hand, and he quickly shakes her off, a gesture which causes her expression to change from excited to distraught.

'Viv,' I say, trying to be at once kind but firm, as if dealing with a child, 'I don't think he wants to—'

'What's *wrong* with me?' she cries as, to my horror, tears spring into her eyes.

'Nothing's wrong with you,' I insist. 'Maybe you just need to slow down a bit. Come on, come and sit with me—'

'I'm not an old lady,' she slurs. 'Do you think I'm an old lady, Pascal?' He mutters something unintelligible and escapes to the bar. I'm trying to figure out how to handle this – how to guide her away to a seat and calm her down – when my attention is diverted by Logan, who's looking even more wobbly than Viv at the far end of the room. He pulls out a chair from under a nearby table and flops on to it, somehow tipping it over and crashing to the floor himself, the glass he was holding smashing with such force, it sounds like a mini explosion.

323

'My God,' I cry, forgetting about Viv as I run towards him.

'Are you all right, Logan?' Blake yells, while a distraught Kayla is scanning the room for her mother, and shouting, 'Mum – Mum! Logan's collapsed . . .'

They both crouch down at his side, and I push my way between them as he slowly picks himself up. 'Logan, what happened?' I exclaim, holding him close, then pulling back to inspect his face. 'Oh, darling, your *mouth*.' Blood is pouring from a cut on his lip, and one of his top front teeth has snapped off, leaving just a tiny jagged shard.

'I fell, Mum,' he says as his tears start to fall. 'I'm *really* sorry to spoil your party.'

Chapter Twenty-Nine

I don't know what happens to everyone else. I assume the party disperses pretty quickly; at least, Clemmie says she'll take Fergus back to her place, and I'm too concerned with Logan to register anything else. I'm not sure if she and Jacqui realise that Blake and Kayla are pretty wasted too. But there's no time to deal with anything apart from getting Logan into a taxi outside the hotel. Kirsty climbs in with us, handing Logan a fresh wad of tissues to hold up at his mouth.

'Honestly, you don't need to come,' I say, putting an arm around Logan.

'You're not going on your own,' she says firmly. 'You could be waiting for hours.'

'But what about your kids?'

'The babysitter wasn't expecting us back till midnight and, anyway, Dan can take care of all that.'

I smile gratefully. 'The lengths you go to to prolong a night out, Kirsty Greenwood.'

She squeezes my hand and turns to Logan. 'You'll be all right, sweetheart. The cut doesn't look too bad. Lips tend to bleed a hell of a lot so it probably seems worse than it is.'

I'm relieved, actually, that she's here; being a trained nurse, Kirsty is unfazed by the amount of blood gushing from his lip.

'D'you feel sick or dizzy, love?' I ask.

'Yeah, a bit,' Logan murmurs. I also want to ask what he and the others were up to tonight, but sense that now isn't the time. All that matters is getting the cut cleaned up and possibly stitched, and to find out what'll happen about his tooth.

'I'll have to get him to an emergency dentist,' I say.

'Why don't you call Stephen for some advice?' Kirsty suggests.

'Good idea.'

'Who?' Logan asks, his voice muffled through the blood-stained tissue as we all climb out outside the hospital.

'Kirsty's dentist,' I explain as I pay the driver. We make our way into the hospital and are booked in by an older lady who tips her head to one side and tuts sympathetically, like a kind granny.

'You shouldn't have to wait too long,' she says as we take our seats in the waiting area.

Logan mutters something to the ground. 'What's that, hon?' I ask.

He takes the tissue away, exposing a livid cut, blotched with semi-dried blood. 'I said I'm sorry for what we did.'

I frown at him, still not wanting to get into a discussion about what was drunk or smoked tonight. There's a woman holding a wailing baby a few seats away, and several liberally tattooed men sporting various facial wounds. A boy of around ten has clearly done something serious to his ankle, and is being comforted by a kind-looking biker dad in a full ensemble of black leathers.

'It doesn't matter now,' I tell Logan. 'We can talk about it later.'

'But Mum—' he starts.

'I'm just going outside to phone the dentist,' I tell him, jumping up from my seat and making my way outside. He answers immediately. 'Stephen?' I say. 'It's Alice, Kirsty's friend.'

'Of course I know who you are,' he says warmly, his voice at once comforting and reassuring. 'How are you?'

'Not so great, actually. It's not me – it's Logan, my eldest son. I had a party this evening, and he – well, I don't quite know what went on but he fell off a chair, smashed his face, and a tooth's gone from the front.'

'Oh, the poor boy . . .'

It's a cool, damp evening and I shiver in my thin dress. 'I . . . I just don't know what to do next. We're at A&E right now and I imagine they'll stitch his lip, but his tooth . . .'

'Bring him to my clinic first thing tomorrow. It's in Dundas Street, number eighty-five—'

'But it's Sunday tomorrow,' I remind him.

'It's fine. Bring him at nine and we'll get him sorted, and please don't worry, okay? They'll make sure it's all cleaned up and he'll be fine overnight. Just make sure he gets a good night's sleep.'

'Thank you so much,' I exclaim. 'I feel terrible, calling you on a Saturday night—'

'Alice, it's not a problem, truly. Where are you now?'

'Right outside the hospital.'

'Get back in then,' he says kindly, 'and look after your boy. I'll see you tomorrow.' We finish the call and I pause for a moment, thinking, Now *that's* what I call a proper grown-up man.

Back inside, Logan is called in quickly and attended to by a whippet-thin chap who carefully cleans the wound and secures it with sticky strips. 'Not much left of this tooth,' he observes sympathetically.

Logan nods, still deathly pale. 'We're seeing a dentist first thing tomorrow,' I tell him.

'You mean at the dental hospital?' the doctor asks.

'No, a private dentist near us.'

'What, on a Sunday?'

'He's a friend,' I reply, at which Logan throws me a confused look.

'Well, you're lucky,' the doctor adds, pulling back to study Logan's face. 'So, now you're all fixed and ready to go, want to tell me what you took tonight?'

A livid flush rouges his cheeks.

'Logan?' I say gently.

He looks down at the shiny rubberised floor. 'It was, er . . . meringues.'

'Meringues?' the doctor repeats with a bemused smile. 'What kind were they, then? Because I've never known them to have this kind of effect.'

'Hash ones,' Logan murmurs, twisting his fingers together and looking up at me, wide-eyed. 'I'm really sorry, Mum. We made hash meringues at Blake's.'

*

It turns out Logan and Blake cooked them up in the annexe. I'm not sure this is what Clemmie had in mind when she designed his very own mini kitchen.

'Who got the hash?' I ask, perching on the edge of

328

Logan's bed at two a.m. He's tucked up in it, his lip swollen and livid pink, held together by neat adhesive strips. The rest of his face is chalk white, his eyes dull, with faint shadows underneath.

'Blake got it,' he mutters.

'And who did Blake get it from?'

'Mum, everyone has it,' he growls; then, as if realising his attitude isn't entirely justified, he adds, 'He bought it off someone in sixth year.'

'And those weren't the meringues at the party, were they?' I ask. 'I mean, everyone was eating them . . .'

Logan shakes his head. 'They were just normal. No one else had the, er, special ones. Just me and Blake and Kayla.'

'Well, I'd better call Clemmie and Jacqui to let them know.'

He looks at me, aghast. 'You mean Kayla's mum?'

'Yes, of course,' I reply. 'She needs to know, Logan. We can't just pretend this hasn't happened.' He groans, as if I've just ruined his young life. 'Are you *sure* no one else had any?'

'Honestly, it was just us.'

'Are there any left?'

He nods miserably and his eyes flick towards his wardrobe. 'There's a few in a tin in there. An old coffee tin.' I open the wardrobe, hit by a fug of worn T-shirts and pants, and rummage among the scrunched-up tops and stray socks until I find a small cylindrical coffee tin stashed in a trainer. There are three meringue kisses inside, of a dingy grey hue, like concrete; I can't imagine them exactly flying off the shelves in Pascal's, unless word got out about their secret ingredient. I check Logan's face again, then click off the light and take the tin to the kitchen.

329

It's so tempting to cram the remaining three into my mouth and get off my face, frankly. It *is* my birthday after all. But instead I tip the meringues into the sink, then turn on the hot tap and watch them slowly dissolve, until there's nothing left at all.

Chapter Thirty

You can tell a lot about a dental practice by the magazines in the waiting room. Whereas our usual place has a few crumpled *Take a Break*s, here at Dundas Street Dental it's all *Vogue*, *GQ* and *Harper's Bazaar*. So while Logan is having his front tooth rebuilt, I try to read about some art collector woman who has seven houses dotted around the world. In truth, though, it's impossible to focus on anything with the sound of drilling going on. It's to be a filling for now, Stephen explained, which will be replaced by a crown when Logan is older, so I'm not expecting perfection. I'm still hugely grateful, though. Stephen even called in his dental nurse to help out today. He's opened the place, on a Sunday, just for us. I don't care what it costs. I have plenty of meringue orders to get through over the coming week; it's almost funny that my confections, which are virtually one hundred per cent sugar, will be paying for Logan's new tooth.

He emerges with Stephen at his side and smiles with his mouth shut. The cut on his lip still looks sore, but the swelling has subsided a little already.

331

'All done,' Stephen says. He looks at Logan. 'Show your mum, then. See if she approves.'

Logan stretches his mouth wide. 'It's perfect,' I exclaim. 'It's exactly like his original tooth. That's amazing. Thank you, Stephen. I don't know what we would have done without you.'

'It's no problem at all,' he says, going to the reception desk while I fish my purse out of my bag.

'So how much do we owe you?'

He shakes his head. 'Nothing.'

'No, I *must* pay you. You've done a brilliant job. Please—'

He laughs softly and hands me a card with contact details for the clinic. 'Let me know if there are any problems. But it should be fine.' He turns back to Logan. 'No apples for at least a month, okay? Just to make sure it's all settled.'

'That's all right,' says Logan, who fears them anyway, with their impenetrable skins.

'I can't thank you enough,' I say, studying Logan's mouth again, which he opens obligingly.

'Well,' Stephen says, 'I'm glad you're happy.' There's a pause, and I'm overcome by an urge to ask if he'd like to meet up again, maybe with Molly, in one of the other museums some time. He has a lovely face, I decide, and those sparkly green eyes really are something else. The dental nurse, a fresh-faced girl with honeyed skin, emerges from surgery.

'We're really grateful to you for coming in today,' I say. 'I hope we haven't ruined your Sunday.'

She smiles and casts Logan a fond glance, despite looking no more than five years older than him. 'No problem. Just glad Logan's okay.' Then she turns to

Stephen and adds, 'Lucky it didn't happen next Sunday, huh?'

'Oh yeah,' he says with a crooked grin.

'Why, are you away then?' I ask.

He shakes his head. 'No, it's Molly's birthday party. The pressure's on, you know, when you're a lone dad.'

'People assume you can't cope,' I suggest.

'That's it exactly,' he chuckles.

'And this time she's invited the whole class,' the dental nurse adds, 'so that's – how many kids are coming, Stephen?'

He rakes back his hair. 'Err . . . about twenty-six, I think. My fault really. She *says* she asked, and that I said yes . . .' He laughs and tails off. 'I probably wasn't listening.'

'I'm sure it'll be okay,' I say, remembering Kirsty enthusing about how brilliant he'd been at another child's party, supervising the toasting of marshmallows and being Mr Wolf . . . Yet, despite his light, cheery manner, he looks more than a little worried.

'Well,' he says, 'it'll just have to be.'

'Don't other parents stay to help?' I turn to Logan. 'They used to, didn't they, when we had parties?'

He frowns, as if he hasn't the faintest idea of what I'm talking about. 'These days they kind of drop and run,' Stephen remarks.

'I'll help you then,' I hear myself blurting out. 'When is it again – next Sunday?'

'Yes, but I'm sure you'll have better things to do.' He looks a little startled.

'Honestly, I don't. You've really put yourselves out for us today, when you could have been lying around reading the Sunday papers' – Stephen emits a wry snort at this – 'and it's the least I can do. Honestly, I'd love to help. It's been years since we had a proper children's party and I quite miss them.'

'Well . . . yes, okay,' Stephen says, his eyes crinkling fetchingly. 'I'd appreciate that. You'll have done far more of these things than I have . . .'

'Let's speak during the week,' I say as we make our way out, 'and you can tell me if you need help with getting stuff ready.'

'There is one thing,' he adds hesitantly. 'This might sound a bit weird, but remember how enthusiastic Molly was at the museum?'

I sense Logan glancing at me, clearly thinking, *You went to a museum together?*

'Yes, I do,' I say.

'Well, she's had an idea for a theme. It's a Medieval party so any ideas you have . . .' He breaks off and laughs. 'It's not really my area of expertise, you see.'

Logan still seems baffled as we drive home. 'What did you offer to do that for?' he asks. 'It was really *pushy*, Mum.'

'No, it wasn't. He seemed like he needs some help, didn't you see?'

He shrugs and stares out of the passenger window. 'He seemed nice,' he adds grudgingly.

'Yes, he is.'

'So . . .' I can sense him studying me, trying to figure things out. 'You've met him before then?'

'Yep, we had lunch once, and then I ran into him at the Surgeons' Museum when I was out with Grandma . . .'

'God, the Surgeons' Museum,' he groans, as if it's as thrilling as a kitchen showroom, but at least his tone is warmer.

334

'You used to love it actually. Remember that horrible book made of human skin?'

'Oh yeah.' He lapses into silence again, and I hope he's reflecting upon the fact that I haven't given him much grief over the hash meringues. Clearly, we have to talk about it, but it felt more important to have his lip and tooth sorted first. Maybe an incident like this is more effective than any amount of drugs talks he's had at school. Or maybe not. 'Did you really enjoy our birthday parties?' he asks with a sly grin.

'Yes, I really did. They were mad, of course, but at least there were always plenty of friends around to help.' Mum, I recall, was surprisingly adept at keeping order, the more bookish of the children liking her teacherly demeanour, the way Molly did at the museum.

'Were they easier when Dad was still here?' Logan asks.

'Er . . . sort of,' I say diplomatically.

I'm startled by what he does next, actually reaching out and patting my leg while we're sitting at a red light, as if I'm a pet.

'You *are* great, Mum,' he says, so quietly I can barely make out the words.

I laugh involuntarily. 'That's a nice thing to say.'

'No, really, you are. I remember some of those parties. That time we had the insect-themed one and you made me this massive papier mâché costume with long hairy legs . . .'

'And a spider cake,' I add, 'which freaked out some of the kids because that was hairy as well—'

'How did you do that? How did you make a hairy cake?'

'I can't divulge that, Logan. That's classified information.'

335

'C'mon, Mum, what did you do?'

I smirk as we turn into our road. 'It's a special icing nozzle with lots of little holes so it comes out like fur . . .'

'It was *amazing*.'

Pulling up outside our block, I turn to look at him, relieved that we are still capable of chatting like this. Reminiscing feels nice, reassuring me that my loveable boy is still there, despite the moods and the experimental baking. 'Anyway,' I add, 'I meant to say, it looked like you and Kayla were getting along well last night.'

He blushes and blows out air. 'Er, yeah, she's all right.'

'Think you'll see her again?'

'Uh, maybe.' He pulls a face that says: subject closed. So we wander up the street to Clemmie's, where Logan's new tooth is admired in the manner of a curious artefact, while Blake skulks about like a scolded dog.

'Thanks for having Fergus to stay over,' I say, giving Clemmie a hug. 'And thanks for the party, too. It was brilliant – the best one I've ever had.'

She pulls back and glares at Blake. 'Just a shame it ended like that. I can't tell you how furious I am with him for getting off his face like that.'

'*Viv* was drunk,' he growls. 'Loads of people were. All we had was a few meringues—'

'Yes, and Viv's an adult,' Clemmie snaps back.

'So that's all right then. It's okay to dance like a loony with your arms in the air and run around telling everyone you love them when you're *forty* . . .'

'Blake!' Her lips turn pale and a vein juts from her neck. 'Don't you dare speak to me like that. You can forget your clothing allowance—'

'It was both of them, Clemmie,' I say quickly. 'Logan's to blame as well.' I glance at him; he is picking at his fingers, clearly wishing he could spirit himself far away.

Clemmie sighs, then takes me by the arm and guides me into the conservatory. 'You don't think it was that Kayla girl who put them up to it?' she whispers. 'It just seems so out of character for Blake.'

'Of course not,' I say firmly. 'She doesn't even go to their school. They'd never met her before last night.'

'It's just, I'm so, so *disappointed*, Alice,' she declares, her face flushing pink. 'Richard and I are still figuring out what sort of consequence there should be. I mean, imagine doing that, in our house! Cooking up drugs . . .'

'You make it sound like crystal meth,' I say, trying to calm her down.

'Well, who's to say that won't be next? After all the expense in having the conversion done . . .' Maybe he didn't really need the cooker, I think darkly.

'Come on,' I say, 'I can't imagine they'll be doing it again. They both seem pretty shell-shocked and I can tell Logan is mortified as he's actually been quite civil today.'

She smiles wryly. 'Well, that's one good thing.'

'I'll get Fergus,' I say, stepping back into the hallway and calling him down from upstairs.

'Cool,' he says, checking out his brother's tooth. Then he frowns and shudders dramatically. 'Your lip's still horrible and crusty though. What'll Kayla think of *that*?'

*

Back home, I reiterate to Logan that his little meringue enterprise wasn't at all smart and must never be repeated.

'If you're smoking grass,' I say firmly, 'I want to know about it.'

337

'I'm not, Mum, honestly.'

'You had some, though – it was a completely stupid thing to do, Logan. If you weren't moving to Dad's, you'd be grounded, you know? And you can forget about me giving you any money over the next few weeks.'

'All right,' he murmurs, not flying on the defensive for once. Perhaps he's grateful for the swift dental repairs, or feels guilty for being jointly responsibly for the premature end to my party. 'Clemmie's really mad at Blake,' he adds.

'Yes, and no wonder.'

'But it was his idea—'

'I don't care whose idea it was,' I snap, anger bubbling inside me now. 'You're sixteen, Logan – you can't just say, he made me do it. Take some responsibility. It could have been far, far worse. You think you know everything but you had no idea how strong those meringues would be or what the hell you were doing . . .'

'I know it was stupid,' he says, eyes filling with tears now as he indicates his lip. 'Look at the state of me, Mum.'

'Okay.' I exhale slowly. 'We'll leave it at that. But I hope you're going to be helpful from now on, and not roll your eyes every time I ask you to do something.'

He nods, and we start to tackle the flat together, with him wielding the Hoover and lugging an enormous pile of newspapers down to the recycling bin. He even washes the kitchen floor and sorts out a mountain of laundry.

Jobs done, he slopes off to his room. I'm filled with a burning urge to follow him and talk to him about moving to his dad's. For one thing, does he definitely have a place at that school? And is this likely to be a short-term thing, or is this *it*, until he goes to college? I knock on his bedroom door.

338

'Huh?'

'I just wanted to chat about something.' I push open the door and walk in.

Logan swivels round from his desk. 'I'm revising,' he offers with a meek smile.

'It won't take a minute. We need to talk about your move to Dad's, okay?'

He winces and passes his phone to me. 'Yeah. You should probably see this, Mum.'

I take it and peer at the image on the screen. It's a photo of what looks like the inside of a farm building. 'What's this?'

'The barn.' He pulls a wry smile.

'You mean the one at Dad's?'

He nods, lips twitching as he holds in a laugh.

'It's not exactly *Grand Designs*, love.'

'Yeah, I know. He only sent it 'cause I'd been on at him, wanting to see how it was coming along.'

I squint hard at the picture. 'It's hard to make it out properly but I'd say there's a way to go before the cushion-choosing stage.'

'Yeah,' he snorts. 'Just a bit.'

'And what's that big dark shape at the far end?'

'That's the horse.'

I splutter. 'You mean it's still there? Is Dad getting the place ready or not?'

Logan shrugs and gets up from his chair. 'He's promised he will and there's still a few weeks to go.'

'That's a hell of a lot of work though,' I remark. 'I mean, he hasn't even started.'

Logan nods. 'Yeah, I know.' His hopeful expression is heartbreaking to witness.

'Think he'll manage it?'

'Well,' he says, 'he *did* promise, didn't he?' As I can't find the words to respond to that, I leave him fishing out his chemistry textbooks from his bag.

While I prepare our stir-fry in the kitchen, I try to figure out why Logan is so trusting of Tom. If ever I suggest a trip out – to the cinema or the coast – it's all, 'What for? What are we going to *do* there?', as if I have some ulterior motive and am actually planning to take him to the BHS lighting department. Yet his father promises him his own self-contained home and, even when there's no evidence of him making that happen, Logan is confident that it'll all come right in the end. I'm so riled by Tom's ineptitude, yet can't face calling him and being subjected to feeble excuses as to why our firstborn's future home still appears to be filled with hay.

Over dinner, the conversation switches back to the party last night.

'What I think's funny,' Fergus announces, 'is you believed we were staying in and ordering pizza.' He grins at how easy I am to fool.

'Well, you were very convincing,' I say.

'Yeah, we even had the menus out . . .'

'It was incredibly well done,' I agree. 'I had no idea.'

'*And* Pascal came,' Logan adds, shooting his brother a sly glance.

I munch a forkful of vegetables. 'Yes, I couldn't quite figure that out at first, but you know Clemmie – likes to be in the thick of things, organising everyone . . .' Logan and Fergus are sniggering now, sharing a secret joke. 'What *is* it?' I ask.

'Nothing,' Fergus says with a snort.

'Boys . . .' I set down my fork. 'What's so funny about Pascal?'

'Nothing!' Fergus repeats.

'I mean, he's just the guy from the deli . . .'

'Yeah,' Logan chuckles. 'That's right, Mum.'

'The guy from the deli whose name you wrote on a big piece of paper with a heart around it,' Fergus announces.

'*What?*'

'That thing you wrote . . .'

'I don't know what you mean—' I stop, realising what he's talking about: when Ingrid was here on Friday night, and I scribbled down his name to communicate my excitement over his call. *PASCAL THE DELI MAN!!!* in massive letters, with a cluster of exclamation marks, enclosed in a pulsating heart. Jesus, I am *forty years old.* 'That was just a joke with Ingrid . . .' I mutter, cheeks burning.

Logan arches a brow. 'Have you written his name on your pencil case too?'

'Oh, stop it!'

'Mum, you are *so* red.' Fergus is laughing so much, a noodle shoots out of his mouth.

'I'm not. It's just hot in here with all the cooking—'

'Anyway,' Logan goes on, 'were you pleased when *Pascal*' – he loads the word with significance – 'came to your party?'

'Um, yes, I suppose I was.' I get up and dispense Fairy Liquid into the sink with a loud squirt.

'That sounded like a fart,' Fergus points out helpfully.

'Thank you, Fergus.' I exhale loudly. 'So what happened exactly? Is this going to be mortifying for me? I'm meant to be supplying meringues to the deli, you know. We'll be having a *business arrangement* . . .'

341

'We just asked him,' Fergus explains, 'when we went to buy you that chocolate yesterday.'

'What did you say? You didn't . . .' I'm starting to sweat now. 'You didn't tell him about that bit of paper, did you?'

'Yeah,' Logan gloats.

'You didn't!' I shriek.

'We said you *luuurve* him,' Fergus cackles.

'Oh my God.' I lean back against the sink, heart banging against my ribs.

'Nah,' Logan says, rolling his eyes as if I am an errant child, 'we just asked him to the party and said you'd love it if he could come.'

'Oh.' I stand there, wondering if my heartbeat will ever return to its normal speed.

'And he said great, he'd be there,' Logan adds.

I nod, taking this in, pretending to clear up the worktop but just repositioning things really; the kettle, some spice jars, a pot of sesame seeds from the Chinese supermarket. I clear my throat and turn back to the boys.

'So what was your plan there? Were you trying to set us up?' They both shrug. 'Ferg,' I say with a smile, 'didn't you once say you couldn't understand why I even wanted a boyfriend? "You're a mum", I think were your exact words.'

'A French one'd be good though,' Logan smirks.

'Yeah, we could go to France all the time,' Fergus chips in. 'Maybe this summer for a holiday.'

'I think that's jumping the gun a bit,' I say, laughing now.

'Well, at least we'd get loads of free stuff from his shop,' he adds. 'Like those hot chocolate sticks you never got us last time.'

There's more sniggering, and Logan adds, 'Anyway, Mum, we didn't mean to embarrass you or anything. We've talked about it and we just decided you really should get out more.'

Chapter Thirty-One

Wednesday evening, and Fergus and I are over at Kirsty's for tea. Logan didn't want to come; said he had 'stuff to do', which I hope means a bout of intense revision, as exams start on Monday, but fear may be code for 'packing my things for moving to Dad's'. And I'd rather not be around to witness that.

So here we are, in Kirsty's garden, which is just the right shade of wild with many child-pleasing accoutrements of the natural variety: a small wooden treehouse and a temporary teepee fashioned from branches and twigs. Her children are being chased around by Fergus, who's being an especially good sport today. We've already eaten homemade burgers made to Kirsty's impeccably high standards, and are now installed on an ornate wrought iron bench at the back door.

'I feel horribly out of practice with children's parties,' I admit.

'I'm sure it'll be fine,' she says, pushing back flyaway hair. 'Just make yourself incredibly useful by handing out drinks and snacks.' She grins. 'Of course, you'll gain extra points by taking charge of a couple of games as well. What's the theme again?'

'It's a Medieval party.' I pull a mock-horrified face.

'God. What does that entail, d'you think?'

'No idea.' I chuckle and sip her homemade lemonade. 'Maybe I should ask Mum. She'd enjoy that – being consulted . . .'

'And, obviously, you and Stephen are getting on really well.'

'He's lovely, but . . .' I shrug. 'I really don't know.'

'*What* don't you know?' she laughs. 'He invited you to his daughter's party, didn't he?'

'No, I invited myself.'

'Yes, but he was pleased you did,' she insists.

I watch the children running around, all clustering around Fergus as he pulls something from his pocket. Its tinny squawk triggers gales of laughter from the children. 'Make it say something else,' Hamish demands.

'What's that?' Kirsty asks.

'That's his translator, one of his charity shop finds . . .'

'Make it say sperm,' Alfie demands, at which Kirsty leaps up and yells, 'That's enough, Alf!'

Fergus looks over and smirks. 'Don't worry, Kirsty, it doesn't have that in its vocabulary.'

She sits down again, shaking her head. 'Anyway, Stephen . . .'

'You know he has a trouser press?' I say, grinning.

'Really?'

I nod. 'Don't you think it's weird? Sort of precise and a bit anal?'

She throws me a bemused look. 'You know what Viv would say, don't you?'

'That I'm far too fussy.'

'Yeah, because you allow yourself to be put off by one little thing—'

'Like Charlie stuffing a hotel vase into his pocket,' I add, 'and Giles prowling for grannies . . .'

'And a trouser press could be quite practical,' she points out.

'If your oven was broken,' I suggest, 'and you needed to heat up a pizza . . .' I look at her, expecting her to laugh, but her eyes have clouded and something serious is obviously weighing on her mind.

'Kirsty, is something wrong?' I murmur.

She nods, her pale grey eyes filling up now. 'I can't talk about it in front of the kids. Come inside and I'll tell you.'

Leaving the children all congregated in the treehouse, we decamp to her kitchen where the tears start to flow. 'Dan says it's my fault,' she blurts out as I hold her in my arms.

'*What* is? What's happened?'

'He says I've always put the kids first, and he's felt pushed out, and that's why he did it—' She breaks off, her face streaked with tears.

'Has he been seeing someone else?' She nods, grabbing a tea towel to blot her face. 'He must be insane,' I exclaim. 'Who is it?'

'*Was*,' Kirsty declares. 'He says it's definitely over. It was some consultant woman who's left the company now – I only found out because I'd started to read his texts. I mean, how pathetic is that?'

'You were obviously justified,' I say firmly, 'in the circumstances.'

She sniffs loudly, brushing back a strand of hair from her wet cheek. 'It said, "Missing you so much". I'd started to suspect something was going on, and in some ways he's right – I *have* been completely engulfed in the children for years . . .'

'But it's Dan who insisted they shouldn't go to school!' I exclaim. 'What did he expect?'

Kirsty laughs bitterly. 'I know. Ironic, isn't it, that that's what drove him into the arms of someone else—'

'He wasn't *driven*,' I cut in. 'He's an adult man. Dan made that decision himself and it's totally unfair to blame you . . .'

We sit down at the table, the children's excitable chatter drifting in through the open window. 'You're right. I think even he knows that.'

'What are you going to do?' I ask gently.

Before she can answer, Maya is up at the kitchen window, shouting, 'When can we have our fire, Mummy?'

Kirsty smooths down her hair and goes to the back door. 'Soon, sweetheart, when it's a bit darker.' With a flicker of a smile, she waits until Maya has scampered away and adds, 'They're so excited about our new fire bowl. I was so pissed off with Dan that I ordered it from the Toast catalogue just to spite him.' Then the door flies open, and all the children surge in, with Alfie shouting, 'C'mon, Mummy, *now* can we light the fire?'

Of course, it's impossible to talk about Dan any more, or what Kirsty plans to do. She is heroic in her ability to put on a brave face, and as we head outside to where the fire has been built – I *do* hope that huge metal bowl cost an arm and a leg – she seems genuinely thrilled as it splutters into life. Although we have eaten, sausages are fetched and set over a wire grill, and as dusk starts to fall I keep glancing at Kirsty, who appears determined to throw herself into the proceedings. Finally, as the fire dies down, she ushers her children, all filthy and reeking of woodsmoke, into the house. 'Call me later, when you get a chance,' I say, hugging Kirsty goodbye.

'I will.' She, too, is speckled with flecks of ash from the fire. 'I'll be all right,' she adds, her voice determined.

'Yes, I know . . .' Then her attention is diverted by Maya squabbling with Alfie, and we leave as she ushers them upstairs for a bath.

'It's so cool there,' Fergus muses as I drive us home. 'I love Kirsty's place.'

'Me too. She always makes it such fun.'

I sense him glancing at me, then he adds, 'I'm really glad you don't make us stay home with you all day, Mum. I mean, I *like* you but . . .'

'I like you too,' I say with a smile, thinking of Kirsty again, and how she's been utterly tied to that beautiful, sprawling house for years, and wondering what on earth will happen now.

Back home, there is evidence of *lots* of revision having taken place, resulting in chemistry past papers strewn all over the kitchen table and dog-eared history textbooks dumped on the living room floor. It feels rather haphazard but, summoning my every ounce of willpower, I manage not to comment. Anyway, it's too late now to muscle in with my timetable suggestions and offers of 'help'.

'Everything okay?' I ask, finding Logan in his bedroom.

'Yeah.' He turns around from his desk and flashes a quick smile.

'Did you heat up that bolognaise I left you?'

'Yeah but I'm hungry again now.'

'So am I,' Fergus announces behind me.

I turn around and laugh. 'But you had Kirsty's burgers and sausages—'

'The portions aren't massive there, Mum,' he points out.

'Yes, because her kids are little and not the swarm of locusts that you two are. Give me a minute, okay? I'll do you some cheese on toast.'

As I head to the kitchen I hear Fergus sniggering, 'Logan – Mum thinks two locusts is a *swarm*.'

Supper is dispatched, and as soon as the boys have drifted back to their rooms I call Tom. It's almost ten, and I can hear Jessica bellowing furiously in the background.

'Just wondered how the barn's coming along,' I say lightly.

'It, um . . . still needs a bit of TLC . . .'

'Tom, have you actually started work on it at all?'

He clears his throat. 'Jessica, stop that! *Stop* throwing your jigsaw around. Sorry, Alice. Things are a bit mad around here. We've had a rush of orders and Patsy's away, sourcing new fabrics, and I haven't had a chance . . .'

'But . . .' I frown, lowering myself on to a kitchen chair. 'Logan's supposed to be moving straight after his exams. D'you realise how soon that is? I know he's not expecting luxury but that picture I saw on his phone, it looked as if it was about to fall down and that horse was still lurking in the corner . . .' There's a deafening howl in the background.

'Jessie, stop that! Christ, it's all over the coffee table . . . sorry, Alice, she's sloshed her Ribena everywhere . . .' Hmm, Patsy strongly disapproves of branded drinks. 'Sorry,' he says again.

'Erm, the horse,' I prompt him.

'Oh, Pebbles went yesterday. It was only temporary. We were looking after him for a friend of Patsy's.'

'Yes, but what about the building? Will it actually be fit to live in when the exams are finished?'

349

'Er . . .' I wait for what feels like an age. 'Probably not.'

'So when will it be ready?'

He murmurs something conciliatory to Jessica, who's obviously up well past her bedtime. 'Once I get started it won't take long.'

'Tom,' I cut in, 'd'you realise how excited Logan is about this? You have enrolled him at the school, haven't you? I mean, you're not just floating about, assuming it'll all be okay when he arrives—'

'I don't *float about*,' he snaps. 'And of course I've enrolled him. It's all sorted, there's no problem with that.'

A lump forms in my throat. Damn, I was hoping he hadn't got around to that either. I still haven't told his school here that he's leaving. 'So he'll be sleeping in a horse's house,' I mutter.

'I told you, the horse has gone.'

'Okay, but I bet there are still piles of plop in there—'

'Plop?' Tom exclaims. 'God, Alice, how old are you? Of course there's no *plop* in there. It's all cleaned out, at least it *will* be. But yes, you're probably right – he'll be better sleeping in the main house for the time being . . .'

'And what will Patsy make of that?'

'Please let's not go through all that again.'

'What?' I counter. 'The fact that your wife doesn't actually want him living with you?'

'She'll be fine,' he barks, then abruptly finishes the call.

And that's when I turn around and see Logan standing right behind me.

I open my mouth to speak but he has flounced back to his room. Shit. It feels like my fault, although it isn't really. The flat is eerily quiet; Fergus has sloped off for an early night, and there's no sound from Logan's room either. I perch on the edge of our saggy sofa, heart thumping against my ribs. Damn Tom and his grandiose plans. Our lives were blighted by them when we were together: *Of course I'll get a job! I've met this guy and we're going to sell this thing that purifies water without filters, it's just a little thing you stick on your tap . . . who wouldn't want that? Water that's as pure as a mountain spring?* The only catch was, Tom would have to buy a 'starter kit' at an astronomical cost, and badger friends to do likewise, which sounded suspiciously like pyramid selling to me. Then the 'friend' disappeared, the company went under and Tom was once again free to ponder what he might want to do with his life.

I see it at school, too. There's a little girl called Lucie who likes to pop into the office, usually with a flimsy question like, 'Alice, I just wanted to know if it's all right to bring my packed lunch in a carrier bag to Deep Sea World? Or does it have to be a lunchbox?' Really, she just wants an excuse to chat. She's nine years old and often tells me, 'We're going to Egypt for our holidays! Mum said we're gonna see the actual pyramids . . .' The trip never happens, but that's okay – next thing it's, 'Mum says we're moving to her new boyfriend's massive house near London with a swimming pool.' Lucie could be making all this up, but I suspect it's more to do with promises that can't be kept. Yet she still keeps trusting and believing and it's quite heartbreaking. Oh, I know that at sixteen years old, Logan's day isn't made or broken by anything Tom or I say. But still, it seems grossly unfair.

I flinch, startled by a movement at the living room door.

'Hi, love,' I say as he ambles in, looking almost too big for the room now. All arms, legs and long bare feet.

'Hi.' He flops down beside me. It's only ten thirty but he looks tired and pale. There's a hint of dark fluff above the outer corners of his mouth.

'Sorry you heard that,' I murmur. 'I was just a bit annoyed with Dad.'

A fleeting smile. ''S'all right. I kind of believed him when we were away in the camper van but then I realised he had no intention of actually doing anything about it.'

I put an arm around his shoulders and he snuggles closer. 'I'm sure he wants you to live with him. I know he misses you.'

'Yeah.' He looks at me, his dark eyes intense. 'The whole thing was a stupid idea anyway.'

I frown, not quite grasping what he means. 'You still want to go, though?'

'What, with Patsy not wanting me there?' He makes a *pff* noise. 'No thanks.'

'Logan, she likes you, I know she's very fond of you—'

He silences me with a fierce shake of the head. 'I'm not moving, Mum.'

'Why, because of Patsy-the—'

'Nah,' he sniggers, 'it's not that. If I really wanted to I would. It's that place, the barn – I mean, Dad's done nothing. Look . . .'

'I've seen the picture with the horse in it, love.'

'No, there's another one.' He pulls his phone from his jeans pocket and holds it so close to my face, I have to shrink back to bring the picture into focus. It's the barn again, gloomy and filled with bits of wood and old buckets.

I peer at it, deciding that, at forty, I really need to

book an eye test. This holding phones and menus at arm's length is beyond a joke. 'What's that pile of stuff in the middle of the floor?' I ask.

'It's crap,' Logan says.

'No, I know it's not exactly luxury accommodation. I mean what's that—'

'Mum, I mean it's actual crap. Or plop, as you so maturely called it.' He barks with laughter.

I gawp at him. 'But why is it there?'

'Well, I imagine it fell out of Dobbin's arse.'

We both splutter with laughter. 'It's Pebbles, actually. But d'you mean Dad actually sent you a new picture with the poo still there? He didn't even shovel it up?'

'Looks like it,' he snorts, adding, 'I want to stay here, Mum, with you.'

'Really?' My eyes fuzz with tears and I quickly blink them away.

'Yeah. It's not so bad here,' he murmurs as Fergus wanders in, bleary-eyed, pyjama top askew.

'What were you laughing at?' he asks. We show him the barn picture, and he's chuckling too – but also, I notice, looking relieved. Like he's delighted not to be left alone, with me, despite no longer getting the biggest room.

'Are you horribly disappointed?' I ask Logan once Fergus has shuffled off back to bed.

'No, not really.'

I try to read his expression. 'I know you were looking forward to it, and I can see why it was appealing, having your own place like Blake does.'

'Oh, he's getting evicted,' Logan says with a shrug.

'Evicted? What d'you mean?'

He bunches a hand up at his face. 'You know, because of the meringues.'

'You mean they're throwing him out? They can't do that—'

'Nah, not out of the house, I mean the *annexe*. He's moving back into his old, poky room, packing up his stuff today. Clemmie's gonna give up her office and use the top floor as her new work place.'

'Oh.' I take a moment to digest this. 'That seems pretty harsh, doesn't it?'

'Yeah.' He exhales through his nose. 'Thank God you're not like that.'

'Well,' I say briskly, 'maybe that's one benefit of me not having the money or space to give you a whole floor of your own.' I flick a stray Pringle from the sofa.

'You'd never do that anyway,' he says.

'You're saying I'm a soft touch?'

'Er, not exactly . . .' He smiles crookedly, and there's a flash of that boy, the one who watched *Peter Pan* daily for about two years straight. 'You're all right,' he adds.

'Thank you, sweetheart. You are too.'

'Er . . .' He fiddles with the back of his hair. 'The other thing is, I'm kind of going out with Kayla.'

'Are you? Oh, I'm really pleased for you. She seems like a lovely girl.' He shrugs, cheeks flushing pink. 'Does her mum know?'

'Yeah, I think so.'

We sit in silence for a moment. 'The thing is, Logan,' I say eventually, 'there's one condition, if you're definitely going to stay.'

He frowns. 'Mum, I'm never gonna make hash meringues again, I told you that already. Please don't go on about it any more . . .'

'No, I mean your chest of drawers. You know how you deconstructed it ready for moving to Dad's?'

'Er . . . yeah.' He looks a little sheepish.

'It'll need putting back together again tomorrow, okay?'

He moves closer again, dropping his head on to my shoulder, the way he used to when he was tired and wanted a story. 'Oh, Mum,' he says, 'could you do it please? You're far better at that kind of thing than I am.'

'Nope,' I say, laughing, 'it'll be good for you to learn, darling. There's a screwdriver in the bottom kitchen drawer.'

Chapter Thirty-Two

On Thursday evening, Stephen calls in a panic. 'It's getting out of hand,' he says. 'Molly's adamant that she wants a storytelling session in the garden.'

'I'm sure you can manage that,' I say. 'Come on, how many bedtime stories have you read in her lifetime?'

'Yes, but she doesn't want stories read from a book. She wants them told the way a storyteller did last time we went to the Museum of Scotland. They had professional actors in costume and she thought it was great.' The poor man sounds exhausted.

'Come on,' I say, 'she won't mind when all her friends are there and the party's actually happening.'

'You think so?'

'Yes, of course. I'll have a think about it, though – I'm sure we'll be able to come up with something.' He sounds reassured as we finish the call, but later a text comes: *Now she's specifying a medieval cake! Any ideas?* With no expertise on such matters, I call Mum.

'You mean that lovely, bright girl from the museum?' she says. 'Oh, what a wonderful idea! You always bought the boys' cakes, didn't you? I always think they have that rather sad, factory-made look . . .'

'What about that spider cake I made?' I cut in. 'It took me *hours* to make, Mum.'

'Oh, I'd forgotten about that.' She pauses. 'Anyway, for Molly's party I think the best option would be a village scene . . .'

'That sounds a bit complicated.' While Stephen is impressive on many levels – the fixing of teeth, the plaiting of his daughter's hair – I suspect that this may stress him unnecessarily.

'It's only *houses*, Alice . . .'

'Yes, but what were they like?' I ask, deciding now that I'll offer to make the cake.

She sighs, as if to say, *Have you learnt nothing in all these years*? 'If you mean peasants' dwellings, they'd be made from a wooden structural support filled in with wattle and daub.' I daren't ask her to remind me what that is. Clearly, that particular info should be neatly filed within the historical facts department of my brain.

'That's great, Mum,' I say, feigning confidence. 'I should be able to get that together by Sunday. Oh, and Stephen's also hoping for a storytelling session . . .'

'How lovely! Isn't he a thoughtful parent?'

'He is,' I say, smiling, 'and I really want to help out. He's been brilliant with Logan – there was, er, an accident the other day. He fell and smashed out his front tooth . . .'

'For goodness' sake,' she barks, implying gross negligence on my part. 'Is he all right now?'

'Thanks to Stephen, yes, he is.'

A small pause. 'Tell you what, Alice, *I'll* come to the party. I can take care of the stories, okay? Sunday, did you say it was?'

'Er, yes. It starts at one.'

'Well, I have nothing else on and Molly's a delightful girl. Pick me up early, about tenish?'

Jesus, Mum let loose at a children's party. I'm thinking either stroke of genius, or one of those terrible occasions that'll haunt me for the rest of my life.

Fortunately, Stephen is resoundingly positive.

'Molly thought your mum was great,' he enthuses. 'She's even asked if *that lady* will be at the museum next time we go.'

'You're absolutely sure we're not muscling in?' I know Logan, who's currently installed in front of a movie in the living room – a 'revision break', I believe it's called – will think it's a bonkers idea.

'No, not at all. Molly will be so pleased.'

'Okay, and I'll do the cake, if you're okay with that . . .'

'Really? It seems like so much work for you.'

'It'll be easy,' I fib, 'and anyway, I'll enjoy it.'

Stephen pauses, his relief palpable. 'Alice,' he adds warmly, 'I think you really have saved my life.'

*

Kirsty has been in practical mode all week, politely declining offers of visits from Ingrid, Viv and me.

'We're working things out,' she told me last time I called. 'He's, er . . . *having to go away on business*.' The children were clearly in the vicinity and she sounded determined. However, we do hook up in the park round the corner from her house on Saturday afternoon. While her children scale the climbing frame, she explains, 'You know what the really galling thing is? He says he's sorry, and that he despises himself for what he's done to our family. But he still couldn't resist adding that motherhood has made me lose my *sparkle*.'

'He's insane, Kirsty.' I look at my beautiful friend with her tumble of wavy, light-brown hair, fresh-faced and gorgeous without a scrap of make-up. How can he not love her?

'So what's going to happen now?' I ask.

She smiles, her pale eyes shining. 'Well, I've applied for a nursing refresher course and so, in a bizarre way, it's quite exciting.'

'You're incredible,' I murmur. 'Most people would fall to pieces.'

She shrugs, indicating the children who are now spinning at an impressive speed on the roundabout. 'What choice do I have? I can't crumble. It's just not an option. Anyway, Dan's staying with a friend from work, a *male* friend . . .' She stops and gnaws at a fingernail. Although there's so much I want to say, I am also aware of the unspoken rule of never slagging off a friend's husband, cheating bastard or not.

'Will you let him come back eventually?' I ask.

'Oh, sure, when I think he's suffered enough.' She laughs dryly. 'But we'll be doing it on my terms, which means school for the kids, back to work for me, and couples counselling for the two of us.'

'Sounds like a good plan,' I say as the children charge towards us. 'But what if . . .'

'If we *don't* make it,' she whispers into my ear, 'then I might take a leaf out of your book and get out there and start dating again.'

My head is full of Kirsty's predicament as I drive home; I can't imagine her putting on heels and lipstick in order

359

to get 'back in the saddle' (ugh – that terrible phrase). But maybe, I decide, there comes a point when it's actually a good idea to at least give it a try. And I've had fun: I've been out with an older-woman-fancier and *almost* had sex in a Parisian hotel. And I've met a lovely, kind, devoted dad, which reminds me that the cake isn't going to decorate itself. I haven't made the meringues for Pascal either, or heard from him about going out to dinner. But there are more important matters to think about right now. I park my car and scamper upstairs to our empty flat; both boys have been asked over to friends' houses today. It's just gone six and, without stopping to eat, I lift the enormous, square cake I baked last night from its tin.

Wattle and daub consisted mainly of mud, horsehair and dung, according to Fergus's *Horrible Histories* book. Hmmm. Would it be kind of hairy, like Logan's spider cake, or smooth, or somewhere in between? As I can't face calling Mum again, I gather together every decorating implement and edible embellishment I own, and set to work.

Five hours later, at just gone eleven p.m., my work is done.

Chapter Thirty-Three

'This is the best cake I've ever seen in my whole life.' Molly looks up at me, eyes shining, a vision of beauty in her medieval sackcloth tunic.

'I'm so glad you like it.' I sense myself flushing with pleasure.

'It must have taken all night,' Stephen says. 'It's incredible, Alice. So detailed! All the little houses—'

'They're exactly the right colour,' Molly agrees as her friends all clamour around it.

'It's not bad at all,' my mother concedes.

'It's perfect,' Molly corrects her, frowning as if to say, *Can't you see?* The party has gone incredibly well so far, thanks in no small part to Mum, whose storytelling session was quite captivating. I'd almost forgotten the stories she'd read to me as a child, one aspect of parenting she excelled at.

Stephen, too, is doing a sterling job of keeping order while retaining a sense of fun. As I ferry out plates of sandwiches and cookies to join the cake on the garden table, I glimpse him being 'the donkey' on which the tail must be stuck – a game which isn't quite in keeping with the party's theme, but is clearly a favourite of Molly's.

'Hide-and-seek now,' she announces when it's finished. 'Let's hide in the house!' She turns to my mother who is 'resting' on a garden chair with a large glass of wine. 'You be the seeker, Eileen,' Molly commands.

'Not now, darling. It's not really my thing. We can do more stories later, though, if you like.'

Molly turns to me. 'Will you be seeker?'

'Sure.' I turn to Stephen. 'Is it okay for them to play inside?' However, his attention has been diverted by a statuesque woman with curiously set auburn hair, in white jeans and a navy blue lacy top, sunglasses perched on top of her head.

'Molly, darling,' she announces, 'Daddy didn't tell me it was your birthday!'

I take a moment to assess the scene. This newcomer has brought a large, burnished orange Le Creuset pot. So this is Casserole Kate, who's clearly a little put out not to have been involved in the birthday proceedings.

'I know how busy you are,' Stephen says, raking back his hair.

'Oh, you are silly. I'd love to have helped. You know you only have to ask . . .' Her eyes light upon the cake on the table. 'What on earth is that?' she asks with a sparkly laugh.

'It's Molly's birthday cake,' my mother says tersely.

'How unusual! What are all those funny little houses? Is it a farm?'

'It's a Medieval village,' Molly announces, as her father remembers that Kate and I haven't actually met.

'Alice, um, this is Kate . . .'

'Hello, Alice.' She smiles tightly, her gaze skimming

362

the cluster of children all waiting expectantly at the back door to the house. 'So which one's yours?'

'Oh, mine aren't here,' I explain. 'I'm just here to, er, lend a hand.'

'And this is Eileen, Alice's mum,' Stephen adds, looking stressed now, for the first time since the party started.

'Lovely to meet you,' Kate says, her gaze falling back upon the as yet untouched cake. 'That's quite something, Stephen. I'd no idea you were so creative.'

'Actually, Alice made it.'

'Really? Gosh.'

'Kate, I'm sorry,' Stephen blusters, 'I haven't even offered you a drink.'

'I'd love a glass of wine, darling.' She flashes a big smile, showing top and bottom teeth, and parks herself at the garden table next to Mum. I watch as he scurries away to fetch her a drink, returning with a glass of chilled white.

He looks especially handsome today in jeans and a plain navy T-shirt; definitely school-gate totty. Making no attempt to engage my mother in conversation, Kate keeps her gaze fixed firmly upon him, as if she doesn't quite trust him to behave.

And all at once, despite the success of the cake and the games and my own mother being here, I suddenly feel like an outsider.

'Sit here, Stephen,' Kate commands, patting the vacant seat beside her. 'You must be exhausted from running about all afternoon.'

'I'm fine, thanks, Kate,' he says firmly, making no move to join her.

'We want to play hide-and-seek,' Molly prompts me. 'Start counting, Alice!' Spotting Kate getting up and

363

placing a hand territorially on Stephen's arm, I quickly cover my eyes with my fingers and start counting aloud. 'Coming!' I shout, catching Mum's expression – it's as brittle as my little icing houses – before turning and running into the house.

Immediately, it's apparent that this is a welcoming family home. In the large, airy kitchen, the fridge is plastered with photos of Molly in various settings – sitting astride a decorated pony on a carousel, and blowing out the candles on a previous birthday cake. From the kitchen I make my way to the living room, where newspapers are scattered across the table. Light streams in through the tall Georgian windows and, with its well-worn leather sofa, the room feels laid-back and extremely comfortable. I check behind the sofa and several stuffed bookshelves, then peer into the tiny downstairs bathroom. Not a child in sight.

'Coming!' I call out, stepping lightly up the wooden stairs.

The first bedroom I check is clearly Stephen's. It's more orderly than what I've seen of the house so far. The bed is neatly made up with a snowy white duvet, and beside the pale oak wardrobe is the famous appliance. I blink at it, this slab of mock-mahogany for the flattening of trousers. Of course it's *fine* to own one. Very practical, I'd imagine, if supreme neatness is required.

There are muffled giggles from another upstairs room.

'I'm coming,' I call again, but remain motionless, wondering if, just before he goes to bed with a woman, Stephen removes his trousers and carefully places them in the press. Or maybe he's been single for so long, the issue of trouser pressing in a pre-romantic scenario hasn't occurred? From the window I watch Stephen and Mum, now chatting at the garden table. They both look round as Kate reappears from the house, marching across the lawn with a large jug of water.

I leave the room, figuring that it's none of my business whether he's seeing her or not. While he laughs at the way she foists casseroles on him, perhaps he secretly enjoys it? After all, who doesn't relish being made a fuss of now and again? Shaking off a sense of disappointment, and deciding that perhaps Mum and I should leave pretty soon, I peer into the next bedroom which is obviously Molly's. Stifled laughter is coming from several hiding places.

'Found you!' I cry, discovering a little red-haired boy in fits of giggles under the bed, and Molly, plus three others, in a hysterical heap beneath the duvet. Everyone except Molly charges downstairs and back out into the garden.

'I like you,' she says. 'No one ever made me a cake like that.'

'Thanks, Molly,' I say. 'You know, I loved doing it.'

'Daddy can't do icing.' Her voice has dropped to a whisper.

'No, but think of all the things he *can* do . . .' I stop as she tears out of the room, following her friends to the garden.

'Whoa!' Kate exclaims, shrinking back in her seat from the clamouring children. I loiter at the back door, wondering what to do now.

'Cut the cake, Daddy,' Molly demands.

'Give me a minute,' he laughs, 'I'll just grab a knife . . .' However, his words fall on deaf ears as, the moment he leaves, the children snatch at the houses and peel sugar-paste from the top.

'Steady on,' Kate says, looking tense around the eye region now. 'You're making a terrible mess—'

'It's okay,' I say, making my way towards her, 'it's meant to be eaten—'

'Now look what you've done!' she shrieks, staring down at her left thigh in horror.

'Sorry,' Molly cries, her eyes filling up as she surveys the huge, purple patch on Kate's white jeans.

'What is it?' she demands. 'Ribena?'

Molly nods, distraught. 'I'm sorry . . .'

Kate is up on her feet now as Stephen reappears with a knife to cut the cake. 'I've got to go,' she announces. 'Look what's happened . . .'

'It *is* a children's party,' Mum observes. 'There are bound to be spillages.'

'Yes, I know,' Kate snaps, 'but these are DKNY.'

'Oh, you shouldn't have worn those,' she says tersely, turning to me. 'You'd never wear white trousers to something like this, would you, Alice?'

'Well,' Kate announces, before I can answer, 'if there's any hope of getting this stain out, they'll have to be washed right away. Stephen, would you drop off my casserole when you've finished with it?'

'Of course,' he says quickly, 'and thank you, Kate. I'm really sorry about your jeans.'

'White jeans at a children's party,' Mum mutters as soon as she's gone.

'I don't think she knew the party was happening,' I venture as the children cluster around her for another story. While she regales them with tales of Beowulf, Stephen and I find ourselves sitting together on the back step of the house.

'So, that was Kate,' he says with a grin.

366

'She's obvious very keen on you,' I remark, at which he splutters. 'Come on, Stephen. She could hardly make it more obvious.'

'You think so?' He looks genuinely baffled.

'Yes. God, you mean you haven't picked up on her signals?'

He smiles. 'I've never been very good at that.'

'They're pretty obvious, you know. Like, in a sort of flashing neon sign sort of way . . .'

'Oh, God,' he says, shuddering. 'She's bloody terrifying.'

'She's just a woman who knows what she wants,' I say, and we fall into companionable silence, watching the children listening with rapt attention to Mum.

'You've been great today,' he adds. 'But I guess you're an old hand at all this, aren't you?'

'Our parties weren't quite like this,' I say. 'However organised I tried to be, they'd always descend into sheer chaos.'

He chuckles. 'Your boys must be much easier now.'

I consider this and, without thinking, find myself telling him that teenagers are challenging in a different way, such as announcing that they don't want to live with you any more, or accessing a smoking bum picture on their laptop.

'A smoking bum?' he repeats. 'Seriously?'

I nod. 'Yep.'

'God.' He blows out air. 'That sounds . . . *ill-advised* . . .'

'One of those don't-try-this-at-home moments,' I add with a smirk. 'You know, sometimes I think my life's full of bum . . .'

He looks at me incredulously. 'Like, there are other things?'

367

'Um, yeah.' And because I feel so relaxed here, all worn out in that pleasant, post-party way, I tell him about my ravaged hot cleansing cloth, and how I'd managed to inform the pert French pharmacy lady that I had batteries up my bottom.

Stephen is convulsing with laughter. 'Anything else?'

'Er, that's all I can think of at the moment.'

'So,' he says, shuddering with mirth, 'you think your life is too bottom-focused.'

'Yes, I really do.'

He wipes his eyes and smiles fondly at me. 'But not today, I hope. I really hope it hasn't been a bunch of arse for you.'

I shake my head and glance across the sun-dappled garden, overcome by an unexpected surge of fondness for Mum. Who else could captivate all these children like this?

'Not at all,' I say, turning back to him. 'It's actually been a wonderful day.'

Chapter Thirty-Four

I'm not stupid enough to think that all Frenchmen have that look, that Robert Doisneau Kiss thing going on – the mop of dark hair, the sharp cheekbones and chiselled jaw as featured on millions of posters. Yet that's precisely what springs to mind, when I glimpse Pascal sitting in the corner in one of Edinburgh's most beautiful Victorian pubs. He is the grown-up version of that boy I saw with his girlfriend from the hotel balcony in Paris. He hasn't seen me yet, and I'm stealing a look before he does. A week has flown by since Molly's party, and I'd almost forgotten about Pascal's promise to call. Logan is now in the throes of exams – it has been a little tense, to say the least. Then Pascal finally called, throwing me into a frenzy of pecan and orange meringue production, the results of which I have with me in a small paper carrier bag.

'Hey, how are you?' He is out of his seat now, kissing me Frenchly – not *French* kissing, obviously, but a peck on each cheek.

'I'm good, thanks.' I glance at the bar. 'What would you like?'

'No, I'll go,' he says quickly. 'Glass of wine? They have a nice Burgundy here.'

'Oh, yes please.' He returns with a glass and sits back in the seat opposite me. 'So how was your son after the party? It looked pretty bad.'

'He's okay now. I took him to A&E for his lip and a friend, a dentist, fixed his tooth the next day. His mouth's still pretty sore but it's healing well, and you'd never know anything had happened to his tooth.'

Pascal shakes his head and lifts his tall glass of beer. 'Some end to your party.'

'I know, but I loved it anyway.'

He smiles. 'It was kind of your sons to invite me. Hope you didn't mind?' A distinctly flirtatious tone has crept into his voice.

'No, of course not. I was delighted you came.'

'D'you think they were trying to set us up?' he adds, dark eyes glinting.

My entire head is now a perfect orb of hotness, and I keep glimpsing the glowing oval reflected in the huge copper pan hanging on the wall behind him. I try to cool down with a sip of wine.

'Probably,' I say. 'But I'm not sure – you know how hard teenagers are to fathom.'

'Um, not really. I don't see much of my daughter these days.'

'That's a pity . . .'

'I suppose so,' comes his perplexing reply. 'It's just the way things are.' Pascal shrugs. 'My life is here now.'

But what about your daughter? I want to ask. *Doesn't a teenage girl need her dad too?* And another father creeps into my mind: Stephen, being a brilliant sport last

370

Sunday when, clearly, the prospect of Molly's party had been causing him no small amount of anxiety.

'I nearly forgot,' I say quickly, placing the paper bag on the table between us. 'I made these for you.'

'What's this?' He raises a brow in surprise.

'Those meringues you asked for. Pecan and bitter orange.'

'Wow.' He opens the bag and takes out one of each flavour: small, perfectly formed kisses, if I say so myself. I put untold effort into these samples. 'Unusual flavours,' he adds, nibbling the orange one. 'Mmm, this is lovely.'

'The pecan ones were easy,' I explain. 'Crushed pieces with a little honey and the tiniest amount of ginger. The orange one was harder. That was quite a challenge you set me.' I smile, watching as he finishes the meringue in a second bite.

'Is that what I asked for?' He chuckles. 'I'd forgotten. I just said the first flavours that came into my head. Didn't want to seem, uh, unimaginative . . .'

'So you didn't really want bitter orange?' I ask, replaying my endeavours in the kitchen two days ago: first with finely chopped fresh orange (big fail), then, more successfully with a bitter orange peel meant for cake decorations, which had taken me an entire lunch break to track down.

'Well, I thought it would be fun to see what you could come up with,' he says, popping one into his mouth. 'And I was right, wasn't I? These really are delicious.' I prickle with annoyance, realising I could have knocked up a tried-and-tested flavour and saved myself from ruining a batch.

I clear my throat. 'You know, that's why Logan and his

friends were so out of it at the party. Meringues, I mean. They'd cooked up some hash ones, would you believe?'

'Now *they* sound interesting,' Pascal laughs. 'Had your friend had some too?'

I frown. 'Which friend?'

'The woman in the tight red skirt . . .'

'Oh, you mean Viv. No, we'd had some pretty potent cocktails, then she'd tanked into the wine.' I laugh. 'Just a little overexcited, I guess.'

He shakes his head. 'Not a good look in a woman that age.'

'Sorry?'

'You know – a middle-aged woman making a fool of herself like that. Dancing, throwing herself around, trying to kiss everyone . . .'

I frown and shift in my seat. 'She's just affectionate—'

'Is that what you call it?' He emits a scathing laugh. 'And wasn't she crying at the end?'

'Pascal,' I cut in, 'Viv's one of my closest friends. I've known her since college. I know she goes overboard sometimes, but it *was* a party, and virtually everyone was there as a couple. I think she just finds that a bit difficult sometimes.'

'But you're single,' he points out.

'I know,' I say, trying to shake off my annoyance. 'And I'm fine with that. But occasionally, I get the feeling that Viv isn't . . .'

He meets my gaze, and although his eyes are stunning – deep chocolate brown, fringed by long, outrageously curly black lashes – they are ceasing to have any effect on me at all. 'It just looks a bit . . .' He pauses to find the right word. 'Desperate.'

As we sit in silence for a moment, I try to work out why this irks me so much. I doubt if he'd be so aghast about a man being that drunk; it would be regarded as acceptable party behaviour and probably not even commented upon at all. In the cocktail bar at the Morgan, no one else seemed to register the fact that Charlie was out of his mind. Certainly, I'm not sure anyone would have labelled him as 'desperate'.

Having finished his drink, Pascal gets up from his seat. 'Same again? Another glass of wine?'

I look up at him, figuring that I could stay for another, and that it might help me to shake off the waves of irritation which are coming thick and fast. We might even have a fun evening. But, I realise, I want more than that. Now, more than anything, I want to be with the man who has lifted my heart, and who I can't get out of my mind.

'I think I might call it a night actually,' I say firmly.

'You don't want to find somewhere for dinner?'

'No thanks.'

He looks mildly nonplussed, then kisses my cheeks again, simultaneously checking his watch. 'Well, I'm going to stay for a while. Some friends of mine usually come here on a Saturday night.'

'Enjoy the rest of your evening then,' I say, mustering a broad smile. 'And I'm glad you enjoyed the meringues.'

'The bitter orange,' he calls after me as I make my way to the door, 'is sensational.'

Out in the street, I wonder what to do next. The sensible thing would be to head home, and start baking – although I suspect that Logan and Fergus are having an enjoyable boys' night in, and appreciating some time on their own. They've grown closer lately, spending more time hanging out together, with Logan no longer regarding his younger brother with disdain – at least, not *all* of the time. Besides, I don't really want to go home quite yet. Still smarting a little over Pascal's comments about Viv, I pull out my phone from my bag. It's Logan who picks up.

'Everything okay?' I ask.

'Yeah,' he says. There's muffled sniggering in the background.

'Are you sure?'

'*Yes*, Mum.' His voice shakes with mirth.

'So what are you laughing at? What are you up to?'

'*Nothing*. Blake's here. Is that all right?'

'Of course it is,' I say firmly, 'as long as there's no baking going on . . .'

'Mum says no baking,' he guffaws, and there's an explosion of laughter in the background.

'Logan, you're *not*, are you?'

'No,' he says emphatically. 'Hang on a minute.' I wait, hearing the background voices recede as he takes the phone to another room. 'Mum . . . d'you remember that . . . that *thing* on Fergus's laptop?'

'In graphic detail,' I say dryly.

'It was Blake who told Fergus to do it. He said, "Google hot chicks" and that's what came up . . .'

'God, did he?'

'Uh-huh.'

'Hot chicks?' I repeat.

'Yeah, that's why it had a ciggie in it, 'cause she was hot . . .' He starts laughing again. 'And he's telling him to do it again, right? But we won't let him . . .'

'He'd better not, okay? Turn the laptop *off*.'

'It is off,' he protests. 'Honestly – d'you think he'd do that again, after what happened last time?'

I pause, sensing that I really should head home to see what's going on. Will I *ever* manage to have a proper grown-up life of my own?

'Logan,' I say firmly, 'I was calling to say I'll be out for a little while longer. Until ten or so – not too late. But now I feel completely uncomfortable with the idea of leaving you boys alone in the flat. I thought I could trust you . . .'

'You can,' he declares. 'I promise, Mum. You were brilliant about the party thing. Still can't believe how Clemmie reacted . . .'

'Okay,' I say, a little taken aback by his outburst.

'You *can* trust us,' he repeats emphatically.

'Well, I hope so.' I smile, thinking what a gang we are, the three of us – we don't manage too badly, considering. I hear our door buzzer in the background, some high-pitched yapping and then a woman's voice. 'Who's that?' I ask.

'Clemmie's just arrived,' he hisses. 'She says she's just popped in to drop off some magazines for you but now she's here, she might as well stay for a bit.'

My mouth quivers with mirth. 'She's babysitting you, Logan. She's making sure you don't get up to any mischief.'

'For God's sake,' he exclaims. 'We're sixteen! We could get married, join the army—'

'Buy a lottery ticket,' I add. 'Never mind, darling. Say hi for me and tell her I won't be out too late.'

We finish the call, faint drizzle starting to fall as I head away from the pub. Edinburgh is bustling tonight. There are smart couples, gaggles of students and the odd hen and stag party group. The streets are filled with wafts of perfume and laughter. Still clutching my phone, I call another number.

'Stephen? Hi, it's Alice.'

'Oh, I was hoping you'd call.' He sounds genuinely pleased.

'Um . . .' I bite my lip, waiting until a particularly boisterous group of boys has meandered by. 'I'm just up the road from you. I know it's Saturday night and you're probably busy—'

'Actually,' he says, 'I've got eight friends round for dinner and I'm just about to dish up dessert . . .'

'Oh, I'm sorry—'

'Alice,' Stephen says laughing. 'Of course I'm not doing anything. Or, rather, I am, but it's not absolutely crucial that I sort out Molly's sock pile right now.'

I smile at that. 'You're pairing up socks?'

'Yes, you know how Molly is.'

'Very precise.'

'Yep.' He chuckles. 'She's still talking about that cake, by the way. You saved my life at the party, truly.'

'Well, Mum stole the show,' I say with a laugh.

'Your mum's great too.'

'She thinks you're fantastic,' I add, teasing him now and yearning to add, *And so do I.*

'It comes to something,' he goes on, 'when you realise you mainly appeal to the over-sixties.'

'Oh, not just them.' There – I've said it. For the second time tonight, I blush.

There's a pause, and then he says, 'So, if you're coming over I'll just go and pop a bottle of wine in the fridge.'

'Sounds like an excellent idea.' I walk to Stephen's, only just managing to stop myself from breaking into a trot. That would be *undignified*, right? I replay Pascal's words, and his scathing appraisal of Viv's 'behaviour',

376

realising that, yet again, I have allowed a small detail to completely put me off a man. Is that so bad, though? Surely these little things tell us a lot? My heart is in my mouth as I arrive at Stephen's, and I knock softly on the door so as not to wake Molly.

'Hey.' He opens the door and beckons me in. 'This is such a lovely surprise.'

'I really hope I'm not disturbing you . . .'

'Not at all.' He grins, indicating the pile of balled-up socks on the sofa. 'Like I said, I was having a scintillating night in. Molly's at her mother's tonight and it's good, you know . . .' He tails off. 'I mean, it's good to have a night off being Dad. But then I find myself thinking, So what shall I do now?'

I look at him and smile. 'I know that feeling so well. Time off is pretty overrated.'

'Anyway, let me get you a drink . . .' Stephen doesn't head for the fridge, though. In fact, he doesn't go anywhere at all. He just stands there, looking at me, as if wanting to say something else, but is unsure of how to put it.

'I don't think I want one, actually,' I murmur.

A flicker of a smile. 'Me neither.' What happens next makes my entire body tingle. He takes my hand, then gently touches the side of my face. Then we're kissing, and I'm not worried about anything – not the boys, or whether I have an overbite or should be on a Tuc biscuit diet – because it feels wonderful.

We pull apart, and the way he looks at me makes my head spin. Then wordlessly, he takes my hand and we go upstairs. I'm not worried or nervous, despite this not having happened for a very long time, because I know it'll be lovely.

In his bedroom, he kisses me again. As we part, I notice the empty space beside his wardrobe.

'Stephen, the trouser press has gone,' I say with a smile.

'Oh, you saw that?' He laughs.

'Yes, during hide-and-seek at the party.'

He flushes slightly. 'It *has* gone, thank Christ. Managed to palm it off on a friend's dad.'

'Er . . . why?'

He smiles. 'What kind of person uses one outside a Holiday Inn? This is a little embarrassing, but my mother is convinced I'd get my life together if only my trousers were a little less rumpled.' He looks down. 'Actually, she reckons I'm a scruffy sod. So she bought it for my fortieth . . .'

'Wow. Was it gift-wrapped?'

'Not quite.' He pushes back his light-brown hair, green eyes twinkling with amusement. 'She lives in Germany – ordered it from there. It's actually a German model. You know what they call them?'

'No . . .'

'A Hosenbugler.' We both burst out laughing.

'I can't believe your mum thinks you don't have your life together,' I add.

'I can't believe yours thinks you have an overbite,' he adds with a smile. 'She might be incredibly bright, but she's absolutely a hundred per cent wrong about that.'

I laugh again, lost for words.

'In fact, you're perfect, Alice,' he says. Then I'm in his arms again in this cool, calm room. My friends often say I overcomplicate things, and I realise now that simple is often best. Take egg white and sugar, fluffed up with tons

378

of air, which turns into something magical. Then I'm forgetting all about meringues because we are kissing, sending my head into a delicious spin, and nothing could be lovelier than that.

Chapter Thirty-Five

Seven months later: Inspection day

'Why's that woman coming again?' Fergus asks, helping me to lug bags of shopping home. With two weeks to go until Christmas, Logan and Fergus's school has been damaged by a recent storm, resulting in several bonus days off.

'She's inspecting our kitchen,' I reply.

'But didn't she do that last year?'

'Yes,' I tell him, 'that was before I could start trading. And she's coming back to make sure standards haven't slipped.'

'So you're not gonna banish us to our rooms this time?' he sniggers.

'I didn't banish you, Fergus.'

'You did! You said we weren't to come out. You were *ashamed* of us,' he adds gravely.

'That was because you were ill,' I remind him. 'I didn't want you breathing germs, infecting everything—'

'Oh, Mum, look at that.' He's pointing at Pascal's Christmas window with its display of cellophane-wrapped nougat in the window – dozens of packets piled up in a giant cone, festooned with sequins and curls of silvery ribbon. Strings of twinkling fairy lights have been hung up outside, and the blackboard reads, *Come in for a delicious cinnamon hot chocolate*, which Clemmie has become especially partial to. They stock my meringues, too – although the bitter orange variety turned out to be a little odd for most people's tastes. Pascal, who remains cordial, although a little distant, says pistachio and dark chocolate always fly off the shelves.

'That looks gorgeous,' I agree. 'He always has such great window displays.'

'D'you think *you* could start making nougat?' he asks.

I raise a brow. 'Are you saying you're getting tired of meringues?'

Fergus shrugs as we walk on. 'Um . . . a bit.'

'Hard lines, love. D'you know they paid for our summer holiday this year? Without them, we wouldn't have gone anywhere.'

'Oh, I know, Mum.' He grins, affecting a mock-patronising tone. 'You work very hard and I'm proud of you.' We continue in this teasing, good-natured vein, pausing outside the charity shop. 'Mum, look.' Fergus nudges me, indicating a rather dishevelled nativity scene in the window. It is a cast of soft toys – sheep, donkeys, dogs and, inexplicably, a parrot, all clustered around a knitted Mary, Joseph and baby Jesus tucked up in a little wicker basket.

'Sweet,' I say distractedly. 'C'mon, let's go – the inspector's due at half-four and I want to give the place another quick check.'

'Look properly,' he insists, jabbing a finger towards the glass. 'Doesn't that look like Rex?'

I follow his gaze and frown at the slightly grubby synthetic white dog. 'Yes, it really does.'

'Can't be, though, can it? 'Cause you got Rex back . . .'

'Er, yes,' I reply with a nervous laugh.

He turns to me. 'Shall we buy him for Ingrid's baby?'

'*Babies*,' I remind him. 'There are two, don't forget, and she still has a few weeks to go yet—'

'We could get a couple of toys then.'

I smile, wondering how to put it diplomatically. 'You know how precise Ingrid is about everything? To be honest, I'm not sure she'd approve of charity shop toys.'

'Yeah, you're probably right. You know, Mum, I can't believe I made such a fuss about Rex.' He rolls his eyes and grins. 'I was *so* immature.'

'Well,' I remark as we make our way down the hill towards our street, 'these things matter a lot, I guess.' I glance at my boy, the smattering of freckles across his nose fading now, his wavy hair worn longer and shaggier these days, curling down the back of his neck. Logan, too, has grown even taller. He has size eleven feet, and a pretty serious girlfriend – still Kayla, I'm delighted to see. He never mentions Tom's barn and, as far as I can gather, it has yet to be turned into a luxury self-contained home.

Back at the flat, Fergus retires to his room, and Kayla soon shows up, still in her school uniform. She and Logan amble into the kitchen for snacks. 'D'you want us to go out when the inspector comes?' he asks.

'No, you're fine. I think I'm just about ready for her anyway.' I smile, glimpsing Kayla wiping away crumbs once bagels have been toasted.

'Are you baking today, Alice?' she asks hopefully, her slender frame at odds with her fiercely sweet tooth.

'That's my plan, unless Erica decides the place is a health hazard and shuts me down.'

She laughs, leaning against the worktop as she sips her tea. I like Kayla a lot. She is extremely bright, having beaten Logan on the exam results front, although only just.

'When's she coming?' she asks.

'In about twenty minutes.'

'Good luck.' She grins, and follows Logan through to the living room while I check everything again, obsessively: fridge, oven, sinks and floor. At four-thirty on the dot Erica arrives, wearing a navy jersey dress which drapes artfully over her considerable bump.

'Congratulations,' I say.

'Thanks.' She smiles. 'Have to say it's been slightly different this time. It's a boy . . .'

'Oh,' I say, recalling her horror at the thought of raising young males.

'It's been brilliant actually,' she adds, pulling out her clipboard from her smart leather briefcase. 'No nausea, no exhaustion – nothing. It's been a breeze so far.' She opens the oven and peers in, then closes it and gives the fridge a perfunctory check. Not quite so thorough this time, I notice.

'You're lucky,' I say.

'God, yes.' She smiles warmly. 'To be honest, we had a little scare early on and we weren't sure this baby would make it.' I'm startled as her eyes fill with tears.

'Are you okay?' I exclaim. 'Sit down, can I get you something?'

Erica shakes her head, inhaling deeply as she gathers herself. 'I'm sorry. It's just my age, you know – I'm forty-three, and it hit me that this would probably be our last chance and . . .' She breaks off and musters a grin. 'I'm just delighted everything's okay, really. I'd wanted a girl

383

at first, you know. But then, after all that worry, it suddenly seemed incredibly churlish to be remotely fussy about the baby's sex.' She resumes businesslike mode, checking several boxes on her form. Kayla appears, asking if it's okay to grab a satsuma from the bowl on the table, before scampering off again. 'I thought you had two boys,' Erica remarks.

'Yes, that's right – Kayla is my eldest son's girlfriend.'

'Ah.' She grins, slipping her clipboard into her briefcase in readiness for leaving. 'I've got all that to look forward to. So, I assume Sugar Mummy's going well? I can't imagine how you keep on top of it all . . .'

'It's busy,' I say, 'but the boys help a lot, and I guess I'm more efficient these days.'

'Would you ever give up your day job and do this full time?'

'No,' I say firmly, 'I still love my job at school.'

'Don't blame you,' Erica says with a laugh. 'I mean, who wants to sweat over a hot oven all day long?'

So, my premises have passed, Erica's visit having been concluded in a brisk twenty-five minutes. It's a crisp, cold day, and I'm due to meet Stephen and Molly in Princes Street Gardens where he's taking her to the Christmas funfair after school. I pull on a sweater over my top, then a jacket, scarf and gloves, and say goodbye to the three teenagers who are installed in the living room.

'You'll remember to heat up that chilli for dinner, won't you, Logan?' I prompt him.

'Yeah, Mum.'

'Heat it properly, all the way through.'

'*Yes.*' He looks at Kayla and they both laugh. Then he turns back to me. 'You worry too much, Mum.' I smile, leaving them to it and thinking, I don't really, not any more. In fact, as I speed-walk into town, I feel as light as a perfect meringue.

The smile is still playing on my lips as I spot him among the crowds at the fairground, my lovely boyfriend with his little girl, waiting for me by the carousel. His face lights up as he sees me. I quicken my pace, throwing my arms around him as he pulls me close and kisses my lips.

'Coming on the big wheel with me, Alice?' Molly asks with a grin.

'I might just do that,' I reply. The three of us make our way towards it, and Stephen takes my gloved hand in his, making my heart soar as the first flakes of snow start to fall.

A Grown-up's guide to dating

Dating can be a minefield as my main character, Alice, discovers – especially if you haven't been 'out there' for a while. As I've been with Jimmy, my husband, for twenty years, I'm hardly au fait with modern-day etiquette. So I've asked an expert, plus my dating friends, for tips on making the whole process as far from excruciating as possible . . .

- **For a first date, coffee is fine.** It doesn't have to be the whole dinner caboodle which can be impossible to escape from if it's not going well. 'Never waste a Saturday night on a stranger,' agrees Sarah Beeny, founder of online dating site mysinglefriend.com. 'Coffee on, say, a Saturday afternoon, is ideal. A twenty-minute chat is usually enough to figure out the cut of his jib. Make sure you have somewhere to go on to afterwards so there's an excuse to leave if you want to.' Back in my dating days, I once blurted out that I had to rush home as I'd left a pan of milk simmering on the hob . . .

- **Be yourself.** It's one of the great things about growing older. 'I no longer pretend to love bands who actually make my ears bleed,' says my friend Jo. 'When I meet a man, it's like, "This is who I am – a 40 year-old woman with two young sons." Why pretend to be anything else?'

- **Scale down your expectations.** It helps to take the pressure off and calms nerves. 'If a man's not bowled over by me,' Jo says, 'it's no huge let-down as I haven't invested my hopes in him being "the one". I just enjoy meeting interesting men, and dating gees up my social life.'

- **Remember that not every man you encounter will meet all your criteria.** I couldn't help laughing when a friend declared, 'I won't waste my time on ordinary men.' So what was she looking for? 'A pilot's license,' she replied.

  'I know lots of dull pilots,' warns Sarah Beeny, 'so it's best to be open-minded in who you choose to meet. Take height, for instance. Lots of our members stipulate that he must be over six feet – when, actually, five foot eleven is perfectly fine.' She also warns that photos can be misleading, 'as charisma doesn't always shine through.'

- **Pick a neutral meeting point.** 'If it's a blind date, or we've only chatted online, I don't like to meet too close to my flat,' says my friend Kerry. 'I prefer a cafe that none of my friends are likely to go to – first dates are nervy enough without the fear of running into someone you know.' Kerry also recommends establishing beforehand whether you'll eat or not. 'I prefer not to,' she says, 'as nerves kill my appetite and I'd rather avoid the bill-splitting conundrum.'

- **Avoid clothes which start riding up and slipping down of their own accord.** Last thing you want to be fretting about is whether you're flashing acres of cleavage or thigh. This doesn't mean dressing like a buttoned-up head teacher from the 1970s.

- **For example, hold-up stockings . . .** I actually wore these on a first date many moons ago. All evening, they kept slipping down – while my skirt, which had seemed perfectly demure at home, seemed to become shorter and shorter in the pub. I spent the entire evening in a terrible sweat, trying to clamp my stocking tops to my thighs.

- **Pre-date nerves? Phone a friend.** 'Tell her how jittery you're feeling and have a laugh,' Sarah suggests. 'The secret is to not make a date feel more significant than it really is.'

- **Keep conversation light.** 'I went on a dreadful date with a man who seemed hell-bent on psychoanalysing me,' says Ruth, a former colleague of mine. 'Generally, I try to keep conversation in the small talk region. Personal problems are a no-no. One guy I went out with told me all about his dead mother. I felt sorry for him, but it didn't feel right to be discussing it on a date.'

    Other single friends rattle off more first-date taboos: 'money grumbles', 'the awful ex', 'builder problems' and 'anything medical.' And avoid the trigger question, 'So how come you're single?' which can prompt a torrent of love woes.

- **Yes, you *can* mention your kids.** It's foolhardy to pretend they don't exist. However, try to resist boasting about their amazing Lego-building skills or exam results.

- **Relax.** Yes, truly. 'A great benefit of being in our thirties and beyond is that we tend to be more relaxed in our expectations,' says Sarah. 'If a date doesn't work out, shrug it off and set up the next one. Dating is like trying to find someone you like in a whole arena of men. To be in with a chance, you've got to be in the arena to start with.'

mum
on the
run

She's on the loose...

'Laugh-out-loud funny'
News of the World

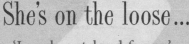

Fiona
GIBSON

The dreaded mums' race at school sports day
– every mother's worst nightmare.

'Warm, funny and poignant.' *Daily Mail*

the great escape

Sometimes you just have to get away...

MUMS ON BOARD

GIRLS 1

Fiona GIBSON

Hannah's got serious pre-wedding jitters . . .

pedigree mum

It's show time!

Fiona GIBSON

A stray husband. A town of posh pooches.
Can a crazy rescue dog mend a broken heart?